STALKED BY SHADOWS

A SIMPLY CRAFTY PARANORMAL MYSTERY

LISSA KASEY

Stalked By Shadows

1st Edition

Copyright © 2019 Lissa Kasey

Cover Art by Garrett Leigh

Edited by Christy Duke

Published by Lissa Kasey

http://www.lissakasey.com

Please Be Advised

Warning

PROLOGUE

He had no face. Or at least that's what my brain told me. Rationally there were reasons. It was too dark out in the deserts of Afghanistan in the middle of the night. He was too far away. I was too tired to see properly, maybe I *was* dehydrated and delusional.

Except alarm bells went off in my brain. The hair on the back of my neck stood up. Something wasn't right. Again, the rational part of my brain tried to parse facts. The cut of his fatigues was familiar. Maybe he was out for a late-night dump, outside base, in the middle of nowhere, without a weapon, or backup.

I squinted through the night vision goggles, pushed them up, rubbed my eyes and then put them back down. The blur of his form didn't change, just got closer as he headed my way. I radioed to the team, "Alpha Team, possible friendly outside base, Roger?"

The radio crackled back, "Location, over."

I was on post, stationed behind a dune, flat on my stomach, about two dozen yards outside the base. A glance back through the darkness and I could see the vague outline of vehicles, no

1

movement or heat signatures as those things would give the base away.

"North face," I replied. "Friendly not accounted for? Over." I asked. I'd been part of the team long enough to know everyone's name and face, but in the gear, out here with nothing but sand and wind, everyone looked the same in the dark. Size and shape could sometimes help, but even that was pretty universal with soldiers used to long hikes with hundred-pound packs on their backs.

"No friendlies unaccounted for, over," the voice crackled back.

But those were our fatigues. I squinted at him some more, trying to make out the face beneath the hat. He got closer, probably four dozen yards or so. The shadows seemed to distort his face, making it look ghoulish in the night vision lens, like it shifted, contorting, but that had to be the play of shadows. Real people didn't look like that.

"Maybe another base? Any other channel chatter? Over."

"None," the radio spat back. "Nothing in our area. Nearest friendly twelve kilometers away. Over."

What the fuck?

He was really close now, the face still distorted and shifting, a void with slits of contorting darkness where features should be. I'd never seen shadows do that to anyone.

It wasn't a local, not in fatigues like that. "Advise. Unknown approaching. Not local. Not friendly. Over." Fear intensified in my gut. I'd shoot if I had to, wouldn't even be the first time, but he was close and each step made my heart pound faster with a feeling I couldn't quite place. Dread?

"Drone shows no heat signatures, over."

I hadn't even heard the machine when my on-alert senses usually could pick up the heartbeat of the guy standing next to me, but it made sense that they would deploy one at the first hint of something unusual. My night vision gave me a vague heat signal, not unusual in the roasting evening temps, movement and shape, even if it did waver. Fuck.

The day before when we'd stopped in a small village, I'd overheard talk of something in Pashto, which for me wasn't as fluent as Dari or as it was known internationally as Farsi. A story about *jin*, mythical spirits who tricked men into following them into the desert, only to kill them, or something along those lines.

My gut rolled over. It was legend. Talk. Probably to scare us. They had no idea any of us spoke the language. Most of the team spoke a few words in Farsi, none as fluently as I did. And none that I knew of could tell the difference between Dari and Pashto. I tended to pick up languages quickly, which is why I was always on point for communications despite being a weapons expert.

"Advise, over." I aimed for his head, hands tightening around the barrel, of my gun, holding on for dear life while alarm bells screamed in my head.

"Backup headed your way, ETA minus one, over."

Would he be on me before then? He was still coming. Shouldn't he have reached me already? I could hear the approach of my team behind me, stealthy, moving quickly, but while the sand hid a lot of footsteps and the rustle of clothing, their whispers tended to echo off the small surfaces of the vehicles and tents when in an enclosed area. The sandstorm earlier in the day had forced the team to base early and in tight formation, which meant keeping a close watch on all sides until morning and we could move again now that the storm was over.

Two team members crawled up beside me, slow enough to not startle me, though I clung to the trigger and the image of whatever the fuck it was headed our way. Both stared out into the darkness, nothing but our night vision to give us clarity.

"Friendly?" I inquired of them.

Neither spoke for a minute.

"Unknown," the one on the left said.

I glanced toward the guy on the right and through the night vision I could see him frowning as he stared out into the sand. Both men beside me had faces, defined and full of shadows but nothing like what was coming our way. I glanced back. The guy —or thing, whatever he was—wavered again, face distorting almost like he yawned, but opened his mouth too wide. It was something out of a horror movie, the unhinged jaw of a skeleton or some creepy cryptid, gaping into a void, which filled my stomach with rocks and terror.

I heard the two men beside me gasp. The one on the right scrambled back, tugging on my jacket as he went. "Pull back," he said.

"Advise?" I inquired, confused.

The other scrambled away as well, dragging me back with them.

"Pull back to base," the one from the right said again. Johnson. I recognized his voice. He tapped his radio. "Team regroup, over," he said as he dragged me back toward the circle of vehicles. The man, or thing, or whatever the fuck it was, was still coming, filling me with a sense of doom.

CHAPTER 1

I awoke with a strangled scream, gasping and flailing like I was still being dragged by my teammates back to the base. But when I opened my eyes it was to my brother's tiny apartment ceiling and realization that I'd fallen asleep on his couch while waiting for him to get home from work.

Fuck.

I sat up and rubbed my face. It was after two in the afternoon. My hip ached from sleeping at a contorted angle and likely from the nightmare. Nap dreams were the worst. Though that particular memory popped up a lot. I'd stopped mentioning it to my therapist months ago. Survivor's guilt, they told me. Our base had been lost the next day, only three of the nearly two dozen making it out at all. The two men, who had seen what I'd seen, killed as well. The military said I misremembered things. There had been no man in the dark, no omen of doom, it was all in my head.

Yeah, the memories were always in my fucking head. It was easier to discredit a man by calling him crazy than explain whatever the fuck had decimated our base.

The door opened, Lukas stepped inside and closed it behind

him. He set a messenger bag on the table and went to wash his hands in the kitchen sink. It was a ritual for him. Bag down, hands clean, then usually off to change clothes. All things to leave the work day behind.

The apartment was one big space for the kitchen, living room, and dining room, and a small bedroom and bathroom. Not really enough room for two people at a little over 700 square feet, but he hadn't bought it with the idea that I'd be crashing on his couch, semi-permanently. He'd moved to NOLA while I was enlisted, leaving behind Charlotte, North Carolina and a lot of asshole cops who treated him like they'd rather hang him than work with him.

The sleeves of Lukas' white dress shirt were rolled up, the shirt tucked into fitted tan pants. He looked like a businessman instead of a police detective, but I knew it was part of being professional for him. And since he was one of the highest-ranking homicide detectives in the New Orleans Police Department, I figured his professionalism didn't hurt anything. He handled sensitive subject matter carefully and always seemed to take care of the families of the victims. He also showed up in a lot of news reports as his good looks and charming personality made great press for the police department.

His hair was cropped short, leaving a hint of blond curls to decorate the crown of his head, and a tiny sweep to soften his forehead, sides cut too close to allow for any shape. Mine was a shoulder-length mass of curls that frizzed in the humid NOLA air, the only proof in our shared brown eyes, blond hair, and bronze skins, of our African-American father. Anyone would look at Lukas and think attractive, put-together, and dateable. I was none of those things.

"You okay, little brother?" Lukas asked. Little brother because he was thirty minutes older. Identical twins, Lukas and

I, but unalike in so many ways. I must have been quiet too long because he said, "Alex?"

"I had a nightmare. Sorry."

Lukas glanced around the apartment, seeming to take in that nothing was broken. It had been known to happen. PTSD they told me. Sometimes I woke up and reality was hard to parse from fiction. I was getting better at sorting it out... most of the time.

He dried his hands and turned to lean against the counter, looking thoughtful and worried all at once. "You okay to start work today?"

"Yes, though I'm still not sure a retail job is the best idea for me." In truth, I was out of options. Not many jobs for an ex-Army Ranger weapons specialist with severe PTSD issues. My social services coordinator had given me the grim fact that over 70% of ex-Rangers were unemployed. So much for the Army's promise of great things after the horrors. Three long tours and all I got was a bum hip, added cynicism, and nightmares. I'd have preferred a T-shirt.

"It won't be all retail. Micah needs help with stock, shipping and receiving, which is a lot of his business now that he's gone online, and I already told you about the tours."

In the French Quarter of New Orleans, ghost and vampire tours were a big thing. Apparently Micah, whom I had yet to meet but was a friend of my brother's, owned a little wicca shop that also scheduled and hosted walking tours of the Quarter and the Garden District. Sometimes he even hosted ghost hunting on particular haunted properties. I'd read the brochures and studied his website.

"I don't think I know enough about New Orleans to give tours."

"You're muscle," Lukas reminded me. "He's licensed as a tour guide by the city. One of the few who is actually officially licensed." He shrugged. "Micah is small and sometimes that makes people think he's an easy target. There has been a handful of drunk frat boys who have interrupted his tours and you'll be there to send them on their way if it happens again. It will save the NOPD time."

"Ghost tours," I grumbled, running my hands through my hair. I'd have to shower and work some gel into it before going out, otherwise I'd probably scare the guy. "No such thing as ghosts. It's all in our fucking messed up heads." Mine more than most, or so my therapist told me. Simply because I saw things others didn't, didn't mean those things were real. "Does he know how crazy I am?"

"You're not crazy."

I was. Certifiable. If not for Lukas I'd still be in a psych ward somewhere, likely a ward of the state. It was how they kept me quiet until I learned it was better to not tell anyone what I had seen. Shadow men. Monsters in the dark. Omens of doom. An entire troop lost to some sort of invisible sand monster. Yeah, I was nuts, but I said nothing to Lukas because he still took care of me no matter how crazy I was. It was the only thing keeping me here.

Lukas was all I had. Without him, I'd have been homeless, probably dead from starvation or suicide. Serving had changed me. And I wasn't sure if it had changed Lukas too, or my perception of him. Had he always been so stern and silent? Or was that how he dealt with me? Was it my months in rehab and then later in the psych ward that made him so careful? Was it the burden of supporting a worthless twin brother that made the laugh lines that were beginning to appear around his eyes turn to frown lines? Thirty-two was young to have frown lines, but my own face was marred with them as well.

"You don't believe in that stuff," I said. "Supernatural bullshit."

"No," Lukas agreed. He folded his arms across his chest and looked at me. "But I believe in you."

Well didn't that take all the steam out of my self-pity. I sighed.

Lukas stood there another few seconds studying me. "You should know a few things about Micah," he finally said.

"Like?" I looked his way trying to discern the expression on his face.

"You might recognize him."

"Okay," I said.

"He's your type." He paused for a minute. "I guess both our type."

"Are you into him?" Lukas didn't have a preferred gender. Well, so long as he got sex—he was a bit of a whore—it didn't matter the gender. I was wholeheartedly gay despite having a particular kink. Lukas liked pretty. Pretty anything, boy, girl, a mix of the two, just pretty. He never dated, but maybe Micah was an ex or a weird hanger-on.

"He used to work in porn."

That wasn't something I expected.

"If I recall, you were a fan."

I tried to think back to my time between tours. It felt like a long time ago. Another lifetime even. Before endless doctors, waiting rooms, and psych wards. Before some sort of monster killed my team. "Okay?"

"Went by Cosplay Boy or something."

The vivid memory of clear blue eyes staring through the computer screen with an intensity that made me come more than once flashed through my head. I felt heat flush my face and my dick gave a little twitch. Wow, I hadn't even thought that fucker worked anymore; my dick hadn't stirred since before the attack. It wasn't at full mast, but more of a 'hey, hello, I'm awake.'

"Or maybe it was Fem Boy. I know you sent me a link once. Blue eyes, black mask, usually pink hair."

Oh fuck, yeah, him I remembered. Cute and small, with kohl rimmed blue eyes to die for. Nose and mouth always covered in a black mask while he wore little school girl outfits and cosplay bright-colored wigs when getting fucked by some guy with a big dick. Yeah, I still had those saved somewhere. "His face was always covered, not sure how'd I'd recognize him anyway."

"I recognized him," Lukas pointed out. "From the one video I saw. It's the eyes. Unmistakable. Haunting. Like they could look right through you."

Yeah, those eyes had been something. He'd been really good about eye contact in the videos. I cleared my throat. "He doesn't do that anymore?" Obviously. Not that I'd searched out his videos since I'd been back in the sane world. But if he owned a shop and did tours, did he have time for porn?

"No. Had an incident two years ago that set him on the path he's on now. I didn't want it to get weird if you met him and recognized him right away. You're not exactly subtle."

Subtle was not the army way. "You weren't in the videos with him or anything were you?" 'Cause not only would that be awkward but also kind of gross since I'd gotten off to them.

"No. Micah and I have never been anything but friends."

I breathed a sigh of relief. "So the drunk frat boys, do they hit on him because they recognize him?"

Lukas shrugged. "Maybe? All I know is that it happens a lot. I'd rather he not do the tours at all. He's one of the few guides who have access to some of the most dangerous areas of the city, like the graveyards. We don't have enough cops to be trailing him every night, and he's making enough now to pay for help. I thought maybe you could put your hero complex to work."

"Asshole," I said without heat. "I don't have a hero complex. I think you're confusing me and you."

He snorted and made his way to his bedroom, unbuttoning his shirt. "Right. Get cleaned up. I'll walk you over and introduce you before your first shift."

He vanished into his bedroom and the confines of his closet. I followed at a slower pace, making my way to the bathroom to shower, trim up the beard on my face, and make some sense of the rat's nest on my head. I'd be meeting my number one favorite porn star of all time. Only he was no longer a porn star. How did one bring that up in a conversation? Or did I avoid the topic? Fuck, I was so bad at being human anymore.

I sighed and hoped that whatever happened, at least the job would work out. I needed something. Not for money, but to keep my mind from wandering to dark places that didn't always want to let me go.

CHAPTER 2

By the time I emerged, clean and dressed in the nicest pair of jeans I owned and one of Lukas's button-ups, I felt halfway awake and was sweating like a pig. "I'm going to melt," I grumbled. "Dressing like this."

"A manbun? Really, Alex?" Lukas asked when he saw me.

I felt my cheeks heat. "I need to cut it. And I'm already sweating without having a ponytail touching my neck." At least the bun kept the ponytail from becoming a giant frizzy poof like a poodle's tail. I'd been tempted to shave clean too, but then Lukas and I really looked alike, which was weird in a city that knew him well enough for shop owners to greet him by first name.

Lukas shook his head, stepped into his closet and then back out a minute later with a T-shirt in hand. "Wear this." The shirt read: Witch Companion, and was in bright sky blue with a black cat on it. "I realize it's not black and depressing, but it's cooler, and since it's from Micah's shop, he won't mind."

I took the top, instantly liking the soft cotton feel of it. I stripped off the dress shirt, and undershirt, and slipped into the tee.

"Tuck it in," Lukas instructed, looking me over.

I sighed and did as he said. "Better? I'd hate to look like a worthless slob or something." He didn't even acknowledge my sarcasm. Lukas had changed into a pair of jeans himself, and a pale purple button-up top. He wasn't afraid of color. I'd spent years trying to blend in and avoiding color, so it was only natural that I gravitated toward the neutrals of the color spectrum.

"It's good. You ready?"

Was I? Not really, but I had to go anyway, right? "Sure."

He headed for the door with me following at a more subdued pace. He let me out and then locked the door behind us. At least it would be close enough to walk to. I thought the entire way, contemplating the cobblestone streets and narrow alleyways we passed, about what to say to a man I'd never met but often fantasized about. Funny the turns fate throws our way.

The shop was about two blocks from the apartment. A hole in the wall really, as it was attached to a row of shops and up the stairs into a narrow space. The sign "Simply Crafty" would have been invisible dangling from the overhang if not for the large chalkboard sign on the walk which read: "Tarot Readings" and pointed upward. In smaller print was written: "Schedule a ghost or graveyard tour."

"He reads cards too?" I asked as we headed up the weirdly narrow, short stairs, which led to a large set of double doors and a smaller inner door.

"Skylar does, and she's in today. Sky rents a little space from him on hot days so she doesn't have to do it in Jackson Square," Lukas replied. The shop was half a block from Jackson Square and the Cathedral, which I found an interesting location for a wicca shop. Maybe the witches liked the challenge of having the Catholics so close. Or maybe it was a 'keep your enemies closer than your friends' sort of thing with the church. "She often closes the shop on nights Micah is running tours."

The air conditioning was a blessing when we entered the second door into the small retail space. It smelled like incense, fabric, and old books. I had a moment of feeling nostalgic for the library I'd grown up hiding in as a kid. Of the two of us, I'd always been the bookworm, spending hours sitting on a beanbag in the corner reading Dune or something else with elves and fairy tales. It was an oddly sweet memory I would have completely forgotten if not for the smell.

A pretty girl stepped out of a side room when we entered the shop, her smile wide. Her brunette hair was styled up, looking silky and shiny, more like a hair model than I'd ever seen a girl's hair look in real life. Her makeup was heavy, but not off putting, and the summer dress clinging to her hips and small chest showed enough of her body without flaunting anything.

"Skylar," Lukas greeted. It wasn't until my brother leaned over to kiss her cheek and she arched up to meet his lips that I noticed the slight Adam's apple in her throat. Interesting. At least I didn't have to ask about pronouns since apparently my brother knew her pretty well. "This is my brother Alexis," Lukas said after he stepped away.

"Call me Alex," I told her.

"I expected the two of you to look more alike." She was a tiny thing, maybe five-feet, five-inches in heels. I felt like a giant next to her at six-foot, two-inches. "The beard is nice though." Skylar rewarded my brother with another wide smile. "Nice to know what you'd look like with a bit of facial hair. Not bad."

"Too much work for me."

"Bet it feels nice on the skin..."

"Behave, imp," Lukas said as he squeezed her hand. "Alex makes the beard work. Sort of like not-quite-homeless chic. I need to get him scheduled with my barber before he starts scaring the masses."

She laughed lightly. "Hush. He looks fine." She looked at me. "You're adorable, honey. Don't let Mr. Metrosexual tell you how to be no mans."

"I'm a strong independent psychopath," I promised her. "No mans required."

Lukas interrupted. "We're here to see Micah. Is he here or did he step out for a minute?"

Skylar waved her hand, dismissing his serious tone. "Oh, I know all about that. How about a reading?" She asked when she turned to me. "On the house."

"No," Lukas affirmed.

"I wasn't offering a reading to you," she protested. "I want to look into his cards."

"No," Lukas said again. "He doesn't need that in his head."

"I won't tell him anything bad."

"You don't need to tell anyone anything bad, Sky. It's always all over your face. You'd be the world's worst poker player," Lukas informed her.

"Thank you, miss," I told her, stopping Lukas before he could really hurt her feelings. "Maybe another time. I sort of need this job, and my brother has been nice enough to help me find it. He doesn't want me distracted when I'm supposed to be helping Micah."

"So respectful," Skylar t'sked at me. "Let me grab Micah. He was dragging up an order of boxes." She vanished through a doorway before I could protest.

I glanced back at Lukas, his expression something I don't think I'd ever seen on my brother's face. Longing. "You into her? 'Cause you know I've got no problem with that."

Lukas sighed. "You might not, but the department would,

and that's a hurdle I don't need right now. How about you work on settling into this job and let me worry about me?"

I put my hands up to ward him off. "I'm here, aren't I?"

"You are," a voice said from the doorway. "Is this where you are meant to be?"

I turned back that way and was surprised by the young man standing there. The eyes I knew instantly. Even without the kohl and stylized wigs of fluorescent pink. The rest of him wasn't really what I expected. He was still on the smaller side, maybe five-foot, six-or-seven inches. Lithe but toned in a pair of skinny jeans and a fitted T-shirt, that read 'Simply Crafty Witch.' His hair was a pale, chestnut brown with gold high-lights, long enough to pull back in a small ponytail, and his face freckled, a dash of them across his nose and cheeks—I'd never seen an Asian with freckles before and found it compelling. He was more pretty than handsome, and very Japanese despite the crystal-clear blue eyes. High cheek bones, a small heart-shaped mouth, and a delicate nose in a longer face, balancing the slanted eyes encased in dark lashes and porcelain skin.

Memorable, I thought. Not only the eyes. My dick did a whole stand-up routine that left me grateful that I'd worn jeans snug enough that nothing showed.

"Is that an existential question?" I asked him. "To be or not to be? Lukas is the smart one," I said before realizing it was probably a stupid thing to say to someone who was offering me a job, to call myself not smart. "I mean, book smart. Philosophy and all that. I read a lot, but mostly fantasy and sci-fi..."

Lukas snorted. "Open mouth, insert foot."

"Jerk," I grumbled at him. He *knew* I didn't people well.

"Somewhat of an existential question," Micah said. "More a question to the universe than for you directly. You probably don't know yet. We all get set in directions that curve and twist only to either find ourselves back where we started or in a place we never intended but fits us well." He closed the door he'd come through and held out a hand for me to shake. "Micah Richards," he said.

"Alexis Caine," I replied back. "Just call me Alex. Nice to meet you. Thank you for the opportunity." His grip was warm and firm, but didn't last long. Practiced, I realized. Something I didn't have enough of anymore. "I don't know if you want to actually do an interview or anything before putting me to work."

"Lukas vouched for you," Micah assured me.

"Sometimes Lukas is too nice," I said bluntly. Micah should know about the PTSD. If I had an attack and he didn't know how to respond, I could be a danger to him.

"He is," Micah agreed, "and very straightforward."

"Yeah?" I asked. "You know about the whole me being crazy thing?"

Micah smiled. "Aren't we all? Yes. I know about your PTSD."

"He's had department training," Lukas piped up. "It's part of his certification right along with his first aid training. We have a lot of vets in this city."

That shouldn't have shocked me, not with Lukas having as much influence over the city as he did. People liked him, he spoke well, and could convince a nun to sell her soul if that was what was needed. But that he'd gotten the entire police department to even have training for mental health emergencies was a miracle.

"It's not mandatory for officers," Lukas said. "But it is for the tour guides. Too much noise, movement, and opportunities for being startled at night. I convinced the mayor it was a better way to weed out the trash too. Keep the best guides certified and alert, and the city's reputation skyrockets, tourism increases, revenue increases. I'm still working on getting the department to put all officers in the training."

"Happy politicians," I said.

"Of course. Money makes all those shady bastards more agreeable."

"You two are very alike," Micah said looking between the two of us.

"We're not," Lukas and I said at the same time.

Micah laughed. "Okay."

Lukas sighed. "You good? You have my number," Lukas asked me. He looked at Micah. "If he needs to step away, is that okay? He's working on grounding if something comes up."

"He's fine," Micah assured my brother. "Five senses. I know about grounding. It's a slow day. Some stock to put away and tours later, but otherwise not much going on. I'll keep it low stress." Micah turned his gaze back my way. "You'll be okay for the cemetery tours later? They usually last about an hour. It's a two-mile walk. We have two tonight. Usually I take a dinner break in between."

"I'm good," I assured him, then looked at Lukas and repeated, "I'm good."

Lukas put a hand on my shoulder, nodded once to me, then to Micah and left the shop. I breathed a sigh of relief, feeling some of the tension leave the room with him.

"He's worried about you," Micah said. "That's why he's so intense. Does the same thing around Sky. Gets all puffed up and papa bear like. It's cute." Micah headed to the area where the cash register sat. It was one of those new set-ups with an iPad instead of a computer. "Time card tracking is here. So when you come in," he tapped the screen a few times then turned it my way. "Click on your name, enter the last four of your social, and it will clock you in. Same way to clock out. I have the same stuff on my phone so when we're out on tour we have access."

I followed his instructions and watched my name pop up on

a preformed time sheet. He navigated away from the time application and clicked another icon that put it back to the register. "There is less than $100 in cash in the register. Most people pay with cards anyway. I've never had a robbery, but if someone demands cash, give it to them. Usually the cops come through before Mardi Gras to give everyone the safety spiel, but they have so many feet on the ground that I've never had trouble. I'll show you how the register works later. If you don't mind helping me carry up a few boxes of stock first?"

"I'm all yours," I told him.

He stared at me a moment, his cheeks a little pink. Adorable. Close enough that I could study the freckles decorating his cheeks and nose. I had the feeling if I stared long enough, I could count them all.

I sighed, feeling like I really did need to lay it all out there else it would eat at me. "So I don't want it to be weird..."

"Okay?" He tilted his head to study me, waiting for my question.

"I used to watch you. I'm not sure if Lukas told you or not, but I was a fan. Well... would still be if you were, but you're not, so anyway. Fuck..."

"Oh. Okay. Thank you. For being a fan, I mean. It was the money I earned making those videos that paid for this shop." He didn't look at all ashamed or worried that I knew he was an ex-porn star.

"So you're okay with me knowing? It's not weird?"

Micah looked thoughtful and even that was cute. Fuck. "No. I did a handful of conventions while I was still doing videos. Online people are pretty creepy because they have anonymity. They say stupid shit. In person they are super respectful. I think when people met me in person, they realized I was a real person and not simply a fantasy." He looked me over. "Is it weird for you?"

19

"A little?" I admitted. "I don't want to say the wrong thing and offend you by accident. You're beautiful."

"Thank you."

"I'm glad my brother told me because I'd have known the second I saw your eyes. But it is a little weird to know that you now know that I used to get off on your videos. I mean you're still super-hot and I'd totally do you..." Well fuck my life. "I tend to put shit out there..." I sighed, thinking I probably shouldn't be swearing and saying all this stuff to my new boss at my new job. "My filter is broken."

"Thank you," Micah said and patted me on the arm. "It's okay. Lukas did warn me that you say what's on your mind. But it's okay. I work with shelter kids with the same issue. They spent time on the streets and it's a lot like a war zone. Survival of the fittest. They don't know how to interact at first, but they learn. Lukas said you've been here a couple weeks?"

Out of the psych ward a little over a month. "Yeah."

"So give it time. I'm not worried. You have no expectations of me, correct?"

"Correct." I agreed. Just because I was attracted to him didn't mean I was even on his radar. "I'm not one of those giant douchebags who think you being a porn star, ex or otherwise, means you fuck everyone you meet."

"Then we're fine."

I narrowed my eyes at him. "What if I say something stupid to a customer?"

"What if you do? They say stupid stuff to us all the time." He pointed to a sign behind the register that read:

Just because this is a wicca shop, does not mean I can
magically make an item you saw on the internet appear.
Try Amazon.

I gaped at the sign. In truth, there was a lot of little snarky things about the store from small signs that said "I'm a paranormal investigator. If you see me running, you better run too," and T-shirts with cute pictures of rabbits with vampire fangs on them. I realized in that moment that Simply Crafty wasn't all serious metaphysical witch shit, it was cute, fun, and a little snarky.

"I think I might like working here."

"Good. Now can you help me with those boxes?"

"Sure."

Sky reappeared from the doorway that must have led to a stock area or something. "Aw, did Lukas leave? Sad."

Micah turned away from me and headed for the door. "Ask him out already."

"He's out of my league," Sky said with a dreamy sigh. "And the cards say it's not time yet." I felt her eyes on me. "I'd still like to do a reading on you."

"No," Micah said. I wondered why he didn't want me to have a reading with his friend. It was all random card draws, wasn't it? Contrived meaning? I knew Lukas hadn't wanted it because he discouraged me from doing anything the world would consider supernatural, which was funny since he'd gotten me this job. But it had been advice from my therapist, so I guess I didn't have to understand all the mechanisms of my brother's brain. Though knowing now that the shop wasn't one of those crazy serious wicca shops and more fun tourist trap, might have been the reason he didn't hesitate to throw me into the job.

Micah must have noticed the expression on my face because he said, "You're not a believer, and that's okay, but Sky's predictions tend to be accurate. Whether that's due to influencing the believer to make those things happen, or because they simply happen, who knows."

"We tend to make our expectations reality," I agreed. "Even if that isn't a good thing."

Micah nodded.

"Then maybe another time." For now I need to focus on being normal, even if that was a day to day struggle. "You said something about boxes?" I reminded him.

"Right. Sky, look after the store for a few minutes, please?"

"Of course," she said and stepped up to the register like she was ready for a line that hadn't appeared. I followed Micah through the doorway. There was a small storeroom, a bathroom, and a little side room with a table dressed up in scarves and pagan symbols, then there was a door and stairway leading down. Micah took the stairs, and I followed. We came out at a mudroom sort of area, boxes stacked near the door. There were only six, but they were fairly large.

"I need these put in the storeroom so I can start sorting," Micah said, shifting through the boxes. "It's one of the downsides of having an upstairs shop. I'm always hauling boxes."

"I've got this," I assured him and picked up the first box, heading up the stairs with it. Of course my bravado didn't last long as the boxes were pretty heavy and by the fourth trip my hip ached. When I brought the last box up I was a little sweaty and thankful to be back in the air-conditioned shop. Micah was already opening boxes and sorting things into stacks. I could hear voices coming from the shop area and glanced out to find a handful of customers at the register all talking excitedly about a tour.

"St. Louis Number One tour," Micah said. "I only do them once a week as it's a drive to that location, but they are always packed since I'm only one of four tour guides allowed in the cemetery. Everyone meets at the church nearby. There's one early evening, and usually a smaller one after dark. Thursdays are my night in the cemetery. It's one of the busiest since people always seem to make weekend dinner or club plans."

"Okay," I acknowledged, remembering reading about them. "Will I need to find a ride to get there?"

"I usually take an Uber, which we can share if you're okay with that."

"Sure. Why is the after dark one less people?"

"For safety, mostly. The graveyard is very old and has a lot of uneven surfaces and jagged corners. There's a checkpoint in and out which does a headcount. As the tour guide, I'm responsible for all my clients. So if someone vandalizes something, even by accident, like tripping over something and breaking it, that's a ding against me. It's why the day group is limited to twelve and the evening to six. Some of the other cemeteries have had issues with people being shot or mugged, but security is pretty tight at St. Louis Cemetery Number One. There's only one way in and one way out, and a checkpoint with guards. It's also still an active cemetery with bodies being added as a lot of the plots are family owned. I think there was a ceremony yesterday. People like doing the night one because the atmosphere is different, psychological mostly." Micah glanced up at me from his box sorting. "You ever been?"

"No, but I'm pretty new to town."

"That's right, Lukas said you guys are from North Carolina. I bet it's an adjustment."

"Humidity is the same. Culture is a little different here, almost European?" I couldn't think of a better word for New Orleans. "Adjusting to civilian life has been the harder part," I said. "Relearning how the world works in some ways. Almost twelve years is a long time out of the real world."

Micah studied me for a minute. "I think having people shooting guns at you is pretty real."

"It is, but the military is about taking orders, looking at

everyone with suspicion, and praying you survive each day. The outside world is a little less intense. More talking and less gunfire."

"Sometimes," Micah said. "I think it depends on what part of society you're in." He picked up a stack of books and began to sort them.

I opened another box and it took me a few seconds to make sense of the contents. Dildos? Sex toys? Glass sculpture-like sex toys? Alien impregnator kit?

"Um?"

"Oh! I was waiting for that," Micah said. He put down his stack of books and stepped to my side to dig through the box, pulling out not one but three big boxes that were the "Alien Impregnator Kits" of various sizes.

"What the fuck?"

Micah laughed. "It's a thing. Someone asked me about them, if I could get them and would stock them. I have a whole section of adult stuff. Regulars shop it mostly; the rest don't notice."

"I didn't notice it. And who wants to be impregnated by an alien?" There were jelly sort of eggs that went inside some sort of phallic device which then was inserted and... "Is that even safe?"

"The eggs dissolve," Micah said examining the box. "I've heard some great reviews, especially from gay men. My ex's new boyfriend is the one who wants to try it. I thought I'd ask him after they have a go."

"You're friends with your ex's boyfriend?"

Micah shrugged. "Our break up was sort of a play of life events. We didn't fit anymore. He still makes videos with his new boyfriend. Timothy has a great cock, and people love watching him. Can't fault him for that."

I gaped at him. Maybe my filter wasn't so broken. Maybe I

was around the wrong people. "Great cock..." Though I did remember him from the videos with Micah.

"It was actually one of his best features," Micah grinned.

I frowned at him, comparing myself. Was I even on the radar?

"If you're into toys, I can give you some recommendations," Micah said as he picked up the box and entered the shop, which was blissfully empty. I hadn't noticed a sort of floating bookshelf in the back before, with a curtain behind it, enclosing a narrow doorway. Micah walked through it into a small lighted area. There was a glass case filled with elaborate cocks of all shapes, colors, sizes, and materials, from glass to steel. Was that even safe?

The walls were filled with pegs of hanging toys, plugs, vibrators, beads, lots of leather gags and jock straps, and dildos of a thousand sizes. The room was the size of a large walk-in closet, and held more sin than I thought a southern boy like me could handle. And I was so turned on at that moment. "Holy fuck."

"We have that too," Micah pointed to a dildo which looked like it had a cross on the end. "Exorcism style."

"Do I have to... would people ask me... I don't even know..."

Micah put his hand on my elbow and squeezed. "Only regulars come here for toys, or people who Google our shop looking for them specifically. Anyone comes in asking, direct them to me. I know a lot about this stuff."

That comment had me thinking of him in a lot of compromising ways with some of the more interesting toys including now an Alien Impregnator Kit. "Um..."

Micah blasted through the box fairly quickly, even finding a place for the two new glass dildos that looked more like art than sex toys. He noticed my gaze fixed on the case and said, "Those are one of a kind. I actually have two that I love. They're safe, easy to clean and warm to your body temperature fairly quickly."

"I've never..."

"Played with adult toys?"

My face felt like it was on fire. I was a gay man dammit. Had more than my share of one-night stands both fucking others and being fucked. It shouldn't send me in a twist to see some toys. "No."

"Not even a fleshlight?" He pointed toward the display on one wall. There were at least ten different kinds. I'd watched a handful of videos of him play with those.

"No."

"A prostate stimulator?" He asked hopefully as he pointed out a few curved metal rods and some odd shaped clips.

"No." I wasn't even sure I'd ever had my prostate stimulated, but my cock was rock hard. Not thinking about what those toys could make me feel, but what they could do to him while I played with him. Fuck.

Micah sighed. "Gay men are so sexually repressed." He glanced at me. "Oh, sorry. I guess you could be bi or pan. I didn't ask. Some guys who watched me claimed to be straight, *pretending* I was a girl while they jacked off. Splitting hairs if you ask me."

"I'm gay," I said, mouth dry, watching him bend over to adjust a display on the wall. "One hundred percent gay."

"Well if you decide you want to try something let me know. Employees get a thirty percent discount on regular merchandise, but a forty percent on adult stuff. Sky buys a ton, but I'm not sure she's ever used any of it. She's more of a collector. My ex still gets the discount even though he only works a few nights a month."

I was still stuck on his first sentence: *if you decide you want to try something let me know.* I wanted to try a lot of things, on him. Fuck. Was my face on fire? It felt bright red, and my cock throbbed. Would it be odd to rub one off in the bathroom? Probably. Funny how I'd worried for months that my dick was broken, libido had got up and left after the attack on my team, but now... Fuck.

"Alex?" Micah asked. "You okay?"

"Honest?" I asked.

"Sure."

"I'm totally turned on. First time in a while. Like I thought I couldn't anymore, but..."

Micah looked stunned. "Really?" Then he frowned. "I guess being at war can do that to anyone."

It was that night with that thing that really broke me. And the death of my teammates. Now it was him turning me on, not being home or looking at some goofy sex toys. It was the idea of him. The fantasies a couple of videos had sparked in me, combined with his quirky casual attitude about sex and his smile. "You're not bothered?"

"No. But I lived most of my life overseas, so the American taboo on sex never really had a hold on me. Sex is fun and enjoyable. It's an act of consenting adults having a good time. Not something to be ashamed of. Does it upset you that your body is choosing now to react?"

"No. Just surprised... I mean I know physically there was nothing wrong with me. The doctors said it was likely psychological from..." He didn't need to know all the gory details. "My therapist said that time would help heal some of the emotional blocks..."

"That's good then, right?"

"Sure."

"Do you need to step out for a few minutes?"

No. I was a grown up. Could control my urges and all that.

"I'll be okay. I'll maybe put some stock away to get my mind clear?"

"Okay. Let me give you a little tour of the shop so you can start putting things away and getting familiar with the layout. People ask a lot of dumb questions, but most of the questions are where something is."

"Knowing is half the battle," I said with a bit of snark.

Micah smiled, seeming to catch my G.I. Joe reference. "I guess so."

CHAPTER 3

The shop layout was pretty easy since it was so small. Thankfully focusing on the layout gave my cock time to calm the fuck down. The register counter housed expensive jewelry, all custom artist pieces that were one of a kind. There was a wall of T-shirts and other commercial junk like mass-market voodoo dolls, incense, mugs, and plaques with funny sayings. That stuff sold well and needed constant restocking, Micah informed me. All made in China shit. Cheap knock offs that the tourists loved.

The rest of the shop was more interesting, with a bookcase full of local authors, wicca guidebooks, and a few hard to find old grimoires—which were locked behind glass on the top shelf. There were a lot of local artist items. From hand knitted shawls, and voodoo cat toys that benefited charities, to glass art, and metal sculptures.

Putting away the mass-market stuff was easy. Finding room for new artwork I left for Micah since he had a box of what looked like copper pounded jazz musicians standing about a half foot high. They were kind of cool, but I didn't see a single open shelf space to fit them.

There was a section of hand-crafted candles and soaps. Vials of essential oils, small containers of handmade lip balm and lotion. Even a section of prayer shawls and one of a kind shoulder bags decorated a corner near a mirror.

I found myself intrigued by a small section with a bulletin board marked with "Have you seen me" posters. There were dozens of posters, even a stack shoved in a folder almost an inch thick, fastened to the board. '411 Mysteries' the top of the board read in bold letters. A handful of books displayed on the shelf below it indicated it was a big thing, though I'd never heard of it before. I picked up one of the books and read the back. People gone missing without a trace in state parks for no reason. Small clues tied them all together, bodies found miles away, or even across the country, without shoes or clothes. People turning up months later with no memory of where they'd been; survivor tales of wolfmen feeding children berries. It all sounded like fiction to me.

"Feel free to borrow any books you want to read," Micah said as he added a few more to the stack beside the one I was looking at. "I do have copies of almost all of them in back that I keep for lending. Sometimes they get damaged, sometimes they never come back."

"I've never heard of this before," I said to him, holding up the book. "411 mysteries…"

"Wildlife parks are beautiful and dangerous places." Micah gave me a tight smile. "Interesting reading, right?" He walked away, and I wondered what that meant. I flipped through another of the books, this one was categorized by names of the missing. Stories of the lost. Most of them actually were categorized that way. It was the fourth book contents page that I was rustling through that I found midway down the page, "Micah Richards."

I blinked at it for a moment, thinking I had to be seeing

things. Only when I turned to the section, there before me was a picture of a "Have You Seen Me" poster with a photograph of a younger looking Micah on it. It had been dated over two years ago. Shit. Was that the thing that had changed his course? Was it polite to ask? I put the book down and returned to stocking, trying not to think too hard as endless questions cropped up in my brain.

A thousand horrors ran through my head of what might have happened to him lost in the wilderness. He looked healthy enough now. No external scars I could see. But I knew better than most that not all scars could be seen with our eyes, and the ones crisscrossing our souls were often the deepest of wounds.

There was a rush of customers sweeping through after five, and I stood beside Micah at the register while he explained how the system worked. It was actually an easy custom application. Items were scannable with a little QR code that Micah had been ticketing items with as he unpacked them. There was even a section for the tours, which was a little more complicated than a scan and pay system. Names had to be entered, IDs checked, and electronic passes issued via email. People were actually pretty friendly, and more than a handful bought art, despite the high price tags. I packed things up while Micah chatted. Sky came and went with customers, disappearing into the little back room for a while before both emerged again, sometimes the expressions were glowing, other times grim.

By quarter to six all the boxes were put away, including a new handful of books in the locked cabinet, of which only Micah had the key. The foot traffic had died down and Sky was at the register.

"Take a break," Micah told me. "There's food down the street if you're hungry, or feel free to park your butt in one of the chairs in the back. I've got to run two blocks over to pick up some books I won in an estate auction."

"Do you want me to come with you?" It wasn't dark yet, and the streets seemed bustling.

"I'm good. Take a break. Sky will handle the register. If she gets backed up try to help out. I should be back in thirty minutes."

I nodded and headed to the backroom and the large reclining chair stuffed in the corner. A break from people was nice, even if I hadn't been forced to socialize much. The book-case beside the chair was stuffed with copies of titles from the shop, including the book with Micah's story in it. I grabbed that one and flipped it to the section on his disappearance. He wouldn't have it in the store if he didn't want people to know, right?

I settled in to read. It started off with a story of a hiking trip with his boyfriend. The retelling made it sound like they had been very much in love, and while his boyfriend, Timothy, had been an experienced hiker, he was also ten years Micah's senior, and Micah had never been camping before. They'd only been out a day when Micah vanished without a trace in a public area with very clearly marked hiking trails.

Timothy claimed to have only turned his back for a few minutes. The small group of friends they'd been with had spread out over the area very quickly to search. And when that yielded nothing, authorities were called. Apparently, it had been a rather sizable manhunt, search and rescue there within hours with helicopters and bloodhounds. They found nothing. No footprints or discarded clothing. No sign of a struggle, and the police dogs couldn't find Micah's scent.

The police treated Timothy like a murder suspect, searching his bank records, home, car, and interviewing everyone who had known them. The media vilified him, even airing details about their videos despite the fact that neither man had ever shown their face in any of them. Ostensibly,

Timothy had been very careful to protect both of them from the public, but the media had disregarded all of that for the sake of sensational news.

The whole case sounded horrifying, suspicious, and plain weird. Seven people had gone on that trip including Timothy and Micah. All of them had been hiking that day. All of them remembered that Micah was near the back of the group with Timothy, as they all attested to seeing his bright blue jacket many times when they looked back. The trail had been a wide hike up, no cliffs, ridges, rivers or lakes, for some distance, just trees and boulders. Then Micah was gone.

Missing for over three months, presumed dead, until he showed up across the country with no memory of where he'd been, in the same clothes, missing his shoes and phone. The phone was never found, signal having died months earlier in an entirely different state. Fuck.

I'd gotten to the interview section of the report when I heard Sky's voice raised in the front, and jumped out of my chair like my hair was on fire. It was a tone of distress, and even though I couldn't make out the words, I still rushed to her aid.

Okay, so maybe I did have a hero complex.

There were three normal looking people at the counter, two women and one man, all as white bread as could be. They looked almost like missionaries or something. One of the women clutched a clipboard. "Trade with Mark," one of the women said. "It's not that big of a deal. I'm sure Micah won't mind."

"I'm not Micah. I don't make those decisions for him. And Thursday nights have always been his graveyard night. People reserve spots months ahead of time," Sky defended. "He's booked solid for tonight."

"I can take over his group for tonight," the man said. He was a middle-aged man with glasses and faded brown hair, unre-markable. "He can even keep the registration payments."

I stepped up to Sky's side and for a few seconds the group ignored me, but I cleared my throat and using my no-nonsense military voice said, "Can I help you with something?"

Three pairs of eyes snapped to attention, all having to look up to meet my gaze. "Not at all, sir. We're working on scheduling. This young man is being difficult." The improper pronoun was an intended insult, I could tell from the expression on her face. She looked like she'd come from a renaissance faire with her long blonde hair flowing over her shoulders and a floor-length dress in a white cotton with eyelets running down the skirt. The third woman was more ordinary in jeans and a T-shirt, but also appeared several years, or maybe even a good decade younger, than the other two.

"Skylar doesn't handle Micah's tour scheduling. *She* can help you buy something if you'd like, but you'll have to take scheduling up with Micah," I affirmed, taking Skylar's stance and putting more emphasis on the correct pronoun. I gave her a kind smile. "I'll handle the register now, if you'd like."

Sky glanced my way once and then took the opportunity to vanish into the backroom. The three continued to stare at me, like they were confused. "Do you need something else? To schedule your own tour led by Micah? Perhaps I can interest you in handcrafted metal jazz musicians? Or a deal on T-shirts? We also have a great selection of sex toys in the back." The three grumbled something between themselves I couldn't quite hear. "What was that?"

"Nothing," the man said. "We will speak with Micah later." They left after throwing me some nasty glances. I waited until they were out of sight to check the backroom. Sky was wiping her eyes, makeup a little smeared from crying.

"You okay?" I asked her.

"Sorry, sorry," she said waving her free hand and dabbing her face. "It's not a big deal. I haven't been... me... very long."

Ah, I understood. "You've been you all along. The world has only been acknowledging you correctly for a short period of time, right?"

She nodded.

"Don't let those freaks stir you up. Did you see that woman's shoes? Walmart special, right?"

Sky laughed. "Oh my God, yes. And those horrid pants? High waisters need to never come back into style. They didn't work in the eighties and they sure don't work now."

I nodded. "Now how about you go dab your eyes and I'll watch the front. If you need to take a break, I'm fine. I hear there are some really good donuts a few blocks away."

"Heathen," she teased. "They are called beignets."

"I speak French," I informed her. "French donut."

"You've obviously not eaten them yet. Shame on your brother for not giving you a proper tour of the Quarter."

"He's kind of a big deal. Homicide detective and all. Busy guy. More important things to do than drag his little brother around town for food. I promise to try them soon. Go take a break."

"You sure?"

"Yeah."

She leapt at me, giving me a tight hug before racing toward the bathroom to fix her face. I returned to the store, greeted a couple who walked in and went to straighten the wall of T-shirts, which Micah had told me seemed in perpetual disarray. Sky left, dashing out the main door, down the stairs and into the hot air of the early October day. The weather would turn soon, or so Lukas had informed me. One day it would be hot and sticky, and the next it'd be rainy and freezing. No snow. Or at least next to never, but tons of rain. I liked the rain. The white noise soothing.

The couple waved me down to ask questions. I hoped I didn't sound too much like an idiot when I tried to answer them.

"We read about the tours online," the woman said.

"He has great reviews on Yelp," the man said.

"One of only four certified tour guides in the city," I boasted, though I still wasn't quite sure what that meant other than he had more training and official authorization from the city.

"I'm Sarah," the woman said. "This is my boyfriend, Jared. We're from Washington State. You don't sound like you're from here either."

"I just moved here," I told them. "Was in the army. Living with my brother now."

"Thank you for your service," Jared said.

"You're welcome," I said automatically. The whole thing felt a lot like the old Catholic recitation of prayers thing. Said and copied without meaning, though it could have been my cynicism. "Micah has been a guide in the city for a while," I turned the conversation back to the shop and away from me.

"We looked at some other tours, the swamp tour, a voodoo thing, but the history on these sound really great," Sarah said. "Watched a few videos on YouTube. Snippets of his tour."

"There is also a Facebook group dedicated to pictures posted from his tours, of ghosts," Jared said.

I had no idea. "Really? People catch that many ghosts on his tours?"

"There are hundreds of photos in the group. And some crazy videos from his paranormal investigations, but he only does those a couple times a year," Jared said. "It's too bad we won't be here for Halloween since he does one every year on Halloween night."

"Crazy," I said. "Doesn't it scare you guys?"

"Nah," Sarah said. "I don't believe in any of that, but the photos are interesting."

"I've seen some stuff," Jared said, "that doesn't make sense. Doesn't mean I think the whole ghost thing is legit, but there's something out there. Maybe science hasn't measured it yet. They've barely figured out how the human brain works, and are still trying to map all the processes of what amounts to the jelly-fish inside our heads."

Sarah laughed. "He's a med student. Aiming for neuro-science."

"I have two family members with major mental illnesses," Jared said. "I think it's all about wiring and hoping to someday, maybe, help fix it. It's hard to see them in pain. Science has theories. Entire lines of pharmaceuticals that the theories are based on, but I think there's more to it. Same with people who see paranormal stuff. They can't all be seeing things. They can't all be crazy. Whether it's a different set of neurons that open people up to see different things, or pathways that are built up over time, it's fascinating, and so much has yet to be discovered. Some people want to explore space. I want to explore the human mind."

My heart flipped over thinking about his idea. "You think some people have different neurons? Maybe those neurons make them hallucinate."

"Maybe. There is a myth that humans only use ten percent of their brain, however, we have over one hundred billion neurons. We wouldn't have them if we didn't need them. We don't know what they all do yet or all the pathways that can be routed, but we do know that neural pathways can be rerouted purposely. Maybe some of those things can help us see into places we didn't know were there and haven't found a way to measure yet. Other dimensions or ghosts, or even thermal signatures."

"You're such a nerd," Sarah teased him.

His smile was huge. "I'm a bit of a nerd," he agreed.

"A bit?"

"I'm just saying, depression is often attributed with higher intelligence. Anxiety has direct links to the over-stimulation of the hypothalamus. I think we don't have all the details yet. So am I a believer in the paranormal? I don't know. Maybe."

"Wow," I said. Stunned by the whole idea. "I guess I never thought of it that way. Brain function and all." Though how many times had I been told it was all in my head? Maybe it was, in a different way.

"Anyway," Sarah said. "That's why we're here. Two weeks of exploring the most haunted city in America. Well, Jared's here for the ghosts, I'm here for the food."

"You should definitely sign up for one of Micah's tours then."

"His Facebook group says he always has new hotspots to give. Some of them tour with him once a month to find out where he'll take them next." Jared looked positively giddy with that idea.

"Well then we'd better sign you up," I said. "Maybe get you some gear like shirts and candles so you're ready to hunt ghosts?" The last was a bit of teasing but they both agreed that it would be great fun to play paranormal investigators while they were in the city.

CHAPTER 4

I talked the couple into a handful of T-shirts, a one of a kind vase, which they planned to give as a Christmas gift, and a leather-wrapped glass bead bracelet from the case which had a sticker price I'd been shocked by.

The bracelet had a little card with it talking about the different kinds of stones beaded in the leather and how the weaving, matched with stones, created a balanced design that symbolized strength, protection, and harmony. Sarah tried it on and admired how it fit on her slim wrist. "This is so beautiful."

"We'll take it," Jared told me.

The couple didn't bat an eye at the nearly $1000 order. I took the time to wrap everything carefully, even finding a box for the vase to help them get it home in one piece.

They signed up for the Saturday night ghost tour. Micah walked in the main door as I was finishing up their registration, his arms full of books, and Sky beside him holding two plates of what looked like mounds of powdered sugar.

"We're headed there next," Sarah said.

"Café du Monde," Micah said. "The beignets are good; coffee is a little on the bitter side. There's a great praline shop nearby in Jackson Square too. Cattycorner from du Monde. Made by culinary students so they are super inexpensive, but since they are supervised by pros, they always taste amazing." He set the books down as Sky took the plates of sugar to the backroom.

"We'll find it," Jared told him. "I love pralines. Am hoping to bring some home too."

Micah pulled out a small map of the quarter which I'd noticed most shops had, and drew on it, circling a small shop. "Lots of great artists in Jackson Square. If you walk it earlier in the day, you'll get free music and lots of locals who set up around the fence. Some of the prints in the shop come from there. And that's where the artist whose bracelet you bought got her start. They usually show up around eight in the morning and are done by five."

"We will definitely be checking that out. Thank you," Sarah said. "We look forward to the tour on Saturday."

"I'll see you then," Micah said. They left examining the map Micah had given them.

I turned the tablet Micah's way. "I did this right, yeah?"

He examined the order and payment. "Yes. Nice order."

"Huge order. Are they normally that big?"

"Nah. Only every once in a while. Mardi Gras is great for sales. I've always got the storeroom packed full in preparation. Most of it is mass crap that people buy, but collectors come through. We do start picking up this time of year, people buying ahead for Christmas. Halloween is pretty good for sales too. I do nightly tours the week before and after."

"I heard you do some ghost hunting thing on Halloween," I said.

Micah shrugged. "I do a drawing every year and pick six people to ghost hunt with me somewhere local. We film a lot of it and post it on YouTube. Brings in a lot of attention for the tours." Micah sorted the books, stickered them, then some went to the regular shelves and some went to the locked shelves.

He was hard to read. I couldn't tell if he believed in ghosts or was only using the idea of it as income. I guess it didn't matter much. Jared's words still pinged around my head. Maybe I wasn't crazy. Maybe my brain was wired to see things others weren't. Wasn't that the definition of crazy? I sighed.

Sky appeared with a plate, offering me one.

"I'm not sure that's food," I told her.

"It's not," she assured me. "It's divine nectar."

Micah laughed. "Eat them in back. It gets everywhere."

"Hush. You know you want some."

I took the plate and headed into the back area, away from everything before carefully picking up one of the dough pillows. Sky watched me as I put it in my mouth like she was waiting for me to faint from delight. It was all right. But I'd had beignets before in France. It was a bit like eating sugar-covered air.

"It's good," I assured her, wiping the powdered sugar off my hands. Sweets weren't really my thing. Though I'd tried red beans and rice thinking it was no big deal only to find I loved the stuff.

"More than good," Sky said. "Heaven."

Micah came in behind us and took one too. He pointed to spots of white on my shirt, but was spattered in his own a moment later. He brushed it off and looked at me. "You have powdered sugar on your face."

"Yeah?" I wiped at my mouth and chin.

"It's like glitter," Micah said. "Sticks in the weirdest places." He reached up and his fingers brushed the top of my lip on the left side. His intense gaze made my pants tighten again.

Sky snorted, a very indelicate sound for such a delicate looking girl. "The mess is part of the fun." She was also covered in sugar. I watched her devour an entire plate of the donuts in awe.

"Right?" Micah asked. "She eats more than anyone I know and still looks like a stiff wind could blow her over."

"I was just thinking that." I shoved the second plate her way.

"You sure?" She asked before reaching for it.

"Yeah. I'd rather have red beans and rice or gumbo any day."

Sky sighed sweetly and dug in. I checked the mirror in the bathroom before returning to the shop. No sugar on my face, and the semi-erection wasn't noticeable.

Micah dug behind the counter, pulling stuff out as I cleaned up the shirt wall again. "We should get going," he said as he glanced at the clock.

"Okay," I agreed. I wasn't even sure where the graveyard was.

"I'm taking Alex over to Number One," Micah told Sky. "You got the shop?" He had his hands full of badges, his phone, and a box of books. I offered to take the box, which he handed over.

"Of course," she said, obviously emboldened by the sugar rush.

I pulled my phone out of my pocket and sent Lukas a quick text that Micah and I were headed out of the shop and Sky would be closing alone. Maybe he'd get the hint and provide some company to the girl he liked. I added a little note as I thought it was funny, *Did you know Sky collects dildos?*

My phone pinged back seconds later with a *Really? Interesting.* I laughed and wondered if my brother would find a way to work that into their next conversation.

There was already a car waiting for us when we stepped back out into the heat. Micah opened the door and slid in. I followed, clutching the box.

"Evening, Micah," the older black man in the driver's seat said. He had Uber and Lyft stickers in the window. "Who's your friend?"

"This is Alex," Micah said. "He's helping out at the shop now, and with tours."

"Yeah?" The man pulled the car away from the curb. "'Bout time. Never liked you out at night alone. Too many crazies in this city. Not all of them living. Won't find cabs in the Quarter at night," he told me.

"Why is that?"

"Ghosts don't pay fares."

I laughed, but he appeared to be completely serious.

"I won't take anything from the Quarter after midnight, myself. You never know what will get in your car that late." He drove the entire way chattering about the importance of the tours for New Orleans and how Hurricane Katrina had changed the industry, and how the ghosts were a menace to the local cab driver population.

He let us out at a church. I knew it was Catholic by the many stained-glass windows. Inside the doorway, in a small entry before the big open area for masses, was a section of candles, statues of saints, and a display of brochures, including Micah's.

"The Catholic church is in on ghost tours?" I asked.

"They maintain the graveyard, so access goes through them. I pay them a fee from my registration income and they maintain the area. Technically they don't believe in ghosts, so the tours are graveyard history tours." He pointed out the set of brochures that actually talked about the cemetery tours, none of which mentioned ghosts. "The daytime tour is all history. Though I try to mix a few scary stories in with the history. It's easy since Marie Laveau's grave is here, and so is her lover's. He has a more negative history than she does. She's villainized in most stories, most likely because she was a woman and you know the church and witches. But most of the creepy facts are simply basic science. Like how the summer heat cremates bodies, and each grave has dozens sometimes hundreds of bodies in it. Beneath the crypts are big holes which are filled with only ashes."

"Gross and a little creepy."

Micah nodded.

"Marie Laveau," I said thinking back. "The Voodoo Queen, right?"

"Yes. Not all snakes and dead chickens. A lot of people have misconceptions about Voodoo. But it's another religion like Islam or Christianity. You'll find more white people practicing it nowadays than the African American folks it started with. Plenty of people in the Quarter claiming to be Voodoo Queens or what-not to try to drum up business."

"Do you subscribe to any particular religion?" I wondered. Did he believe in ghosts?

"Not really."

"What about the paranormal? Ghosts, tarot cards, and stuff like that?"

He glanced my way, his expression guarded. Had Lukas told him not to bring up certain topics? "I've seen things that have no scientific explanation."

I wondered about his disappearance. Did he remember any of it as he'd stated publicly, or was he keeping things, that no one accepted, quiet?

"The idea of ghosts is sad, anyway," Micah continued. "Who would want to stick around here after they died? And the concept of heaven and hell? You spend your short life struggling, trying to be the best you can be only to not get to heaven, if there is one, just because you hadn't subscribed to a particular religion? Sounds pretty narrow-minded if you ask me. Organized religion really is about controlling the masses. That's why philosophy has always been the bane of their existence. When people are highly intelligent, they often find holes in religion. The history of religion in general is one of control and fear. I think of myself as a spiritual person, believing more in self-awareness rather than any rules set by mistranslated texts."

"You seem to know a lot of history."

"I majored in history. Had plans to become a teacher. It's the reason I always kept my face covered when I did videos."

Had his disappearance changed that too? Was that why he was here running the shop now instead of teaching somewhere?

"That guy from the shop, Jared, is training to be a neuroscientist or something. Said our brains are still vastly uncovered territory." Or at least that's what I'd gotten out of his comments. "We don't know much about how it works, mostly it's speculation, and what little we do know evolves as they learn more."

"Truth," Micah agreed. "But if we spend all our time analyzing why we experience things in life, we have no time left to live it, right?"

Well fuck, that was a hard truth bomb too. "Right."

A couple came our way. "Looks like some of our group is here."

The group of twelve was actually fairly large. I understood why Micah limited it when we all gathered outside and he began checking people in. Everyone's electronic ticket was scanned and they were given a badge to wear around their neck, which was to be returned when the tour finished. Everyone was instructed that they would be signing in at the gate with the guards, and that Micah was responsible if they damaged something. So the unspoken warning was: "Don't break shit."

At the gate we were greeted by two guards who sat under a pop-up tent just inside the doorway. "Hey Micah," the older of the two said.

"Hey, Fred," Micah said. "This is Alex, the guy I told you

45

would be helping with my tours?"

Fred offered me his hand and I shook it. "Hello." They let us through and we all funneled into the first open area which looked out into a mini city of crypts. The white wall surrounding the cemetery closed out the rest of the world, as I couldn't even hear any of the traffic from the street nearby.

"Welcome to St. Louis Cemetery Number One," Micah said with a bit of a creole accent. "The first New Orleans city of the dead." Everyone laughed nervously and looked around. Though I didn't feel anything unusual standing in the late evening sunshine under a blue sky. Everyone had their phones out, snapping pictures, some videotaping small areas.

I listened as Micah talked about the walls, which housed the dead, and the tombs, speaking of individual stone houses of families with shady or interesting histories. Marie's grave was less intimidating than I'd expected it to be, but it was also maintained by the Voodoo Society or something, so it was clean, and white like most of the rest of them. Her lover's grave was a sort of dirty gray, and marred with a handful of Xs, looking older and beaten down. The stories Micah told about the two made for creepy romance tales that had everyone snapping pictures and examining the differences in the tombs.

From the outside, the cemetery hadn't looked that big. But inside, twisting and turning down small paths, listening to stories and examining plaques placed on the giant wall-like mausoleums, the place seemed huge.

Some graves were surrounded by fencing so people couldn't get close, others were nothing but piles of bricks. There was one toward the front, but off a narrow path, that had a temporary barrier in front of it and was still covered by a red curtain.

"As you can all see, this particular mausoleum is still in use as a body was added yesterday. The tomb is closed, but they will keep it blocked off for a few more days."

An eerie silence fell over the group as they stared at the red curtain. Almost as though they were realizing for the first time that we were standing in a real graveyard and not some made up petting zoo of ancient dead.

"The family that owns the crypt has been in New Orleans for a couple hundred years. There are rumors of witches in the line, though nothing confirmed. Those rumors of course started during the land wars in the 1800s. The city was a mess of cultures, poverty, starvation, and the rich trying to own everyone else. So not much has changed, right?"

The group laughed, and Micah moved the group along to the next big crypt and creepy story.

By the time we were back at the gate, the sky had begun to darken. Everyone chatted excitedly and Micah repeated his head count, retrieving all the badges. He pointed out a nearby tourist and visitor center and offered to walk the crowd over. The box of books sold quickly, everyone scrambling for a copy, which was a history of the cemetery written by a local author whom Micah claimed was a good friend.

We walked the group to the nearby visitor's center and then left them to explore the maps and gifts shops. I was starving. "Is there food close?" I asked Micah. "I'd even eat some of those sugar clouds if I have to."

Micah smiled. "How about some gumbo? It's a short walk but the food is good. We have to be quick and get back for the next group."

"I'm in," I agreed. We left the empty box with the gift shop to recycle, and he stuffed the badges in the pocket of his pants. We made our way to food with me thinking that maybe this would all work out. I'd been a little worried about these ghost tour things drumming up issues, but the cemetery tour had been nothing. Maybe the actual ghost tours would be different.

CHAPTER 5

F ood was good and fast, taking less than twenty minutes to eat and we were headed back toward the cemetery. The sun had set, leaving a chill in the air which made me wish I'd brought a coat. Micah's company eased the anxiety I'd begun the day with, and our conversation remained light, focused on the city and history instead of either one of our pasts. His smile, while guarded, was infectious and soothing, all at once. He had stories about everything, from each shop we passed to street signs, and every restaurant. Since I didn't mind listening, I asked an occasional question to spur on his memories over something and tried to absorb all the knowledge as best I could. Walking with him felt natural, and he treated me like a person instead of a freak. Maybe this job would work out okay.

"Anything different happen during the night tour?" I asked. The sky was still clear, revealing a full moon which was pretty in a creepy way as it illuminated the white walls of the grave-yard in the distance.

"Not really. Usually ghost hunter wannabes on the night tour. People look more for the scary stories and snap lots of pictures trying to catch ghosts," Micah said. "No flash allowed as it messes with our night vision. I have a flashlight on my keychain if needed. Some of the corners of the cemetery are really dark."

"Full moon tonight should help."

"Oh yeah, it actually makes it a little more eerie. Full moons are usually booked a couple weeks in advance. Not because anything different happens, but people think it sets a spookier mood. Did you know there are three days to a full moon? My night in the cemetery doesn't always land on one."

"Is that why that Mark guy wanted to take your night?" I wondered out loud.

"Mark? When was he around?"

"When you stepped out for those books. He and two missionary looking ladies were in and messing with Sky. I took care of them. Sent them on their way after they insulted her."

Micah laughed. "Missionary looking? Two wannabe voodoo queens and a guy who calls himself a voodoo priest. This is what I mean by white folks using religion to control people. At least I don't make claims of slaughtering chickens on the full moon to bring in sales."

"Good to know, as it would be weird to haul around chickens for you."

"Help! Someone please help!" The cry interrupted our banter and I whipped my head around to try to find the direction. It was coming from the entrance to St. Louis Number One.

Micah jogged that way, me racing after him, instinct kicking in. Was someone hurt? When we reached the gate, I recognized the man from the shop earlier.

"Jared," I said. "What's wrong?" There were no guards at the table in front. Jared was sobbing and begging for help, though I could barely understand his words. I took him by the shoulders and made him focus on me. "Jared, what's wrong? Where's Sarah?"

"Something was there! In the dark... It took her," he said panting like he'd been running a marathon.

"Jared, who? Where?" I asked.

He pointed into the cemetery. "That man promised a private tour to Sarah and me. Now she's gone. One second she was there and then something was standing in the dark. Then she was gone. Please..." Tears streamed down his face and he fought for air, hands on his ribs. "Please, help."

Micah looked at the sign-in sheet. "Mark took them in. They shouldn't have been let in at all. It's not their night." He headed through the gate whipping out the little flashlight on his keychain.

"The light on my phone is brighter," I told him, holding up my phone.

He shook his head. "Too bright. Ruins night vision. Stay here, I'll see if I can find them."

"Not a chance," I told him. If there was someone in there, he was not going in alone. "You're not going by yourself." I opened my phone and sent Lukas a text that there was an emergency at the cemetery and to send help before shoving Jared down into one of the abandoned guards' chairs with a firm command of "Stay here," and followed Micah into the darkness.

He was efficient in his search, shining the flashlight down the rows and calling out. "Sarah? Mark? Fred?" He obviously knew the cemetery very well.

No one answered. In fact the entire atmosphere of the place had changed, feeling heavy, and I struggled to suck in enough air. There was no sound inside, no birds or crickets, no passing cars or wind. It wasn't because we were moving so fast, though we were both jogging at this point, looking around tombs and down aisles. Twice I thought I saw something move and pointed it out to Micah. We'd trail down that path only to find nothing and backtrack. Why weren't they answering? The cemetery wasn't that big. They shouldn't have had a hard time hearing us.

Did Micah hear that buzzing? Or was it me?

It started as a low hum, so faint I hadn't noticed it at first. Now it drummed at my senses, like wings fluttering against my ears. My heart raced in time to the pulsing feeling like it was going to explode out of my chest.

Panic began to take hold in my gut. There was only one way in and out. Unless they climbed the walls. Had someone taken Sarah over the wall? I could barely hear Micah's voice anymore. It was like my ears were clogged. Spots trickled into my vision making it hard to follow him.

Micah lurched forward after shining his light down a path, and I chased after him as we both found the guard, Fred, lying beside a grave, very still. I leaned over him and checked for a pulse. Thankfully, I found one.

"Just unconscious," I said to Micah and turned the big man over. It looked like he hit his head. "I already sent Lukas a text, so help should be on the way." What was that smell? Slightly metallic. I looked over Fred again and he didn't appear to be bleeding.

"Do you smell blood?" I asked, looking around the small area we were in. I knew a half dozen yards away the tomb that had been open to add a new body stood, but didn't think they'd have left it that fresh. I would have smelled it earlier in the day, and it seemed odd they'd let people in the cemetery if that were a normal occurrence.

"I think it's from over there." Micah got up and tiptoed that way.

"Micah..." I called after him, leaving Fred's side to follow.

We kept moving forward, passing chalk markers written on some of the tombs that hadn't been there earlier in the day. The shadows grew thicker the further we walked, and so did the marking. That awful white noise filled my head, deafening me. I stopped twice to try to clear the noise, only to have it grow louder.

Micah stopped and glanced around a large sarcophagus.

"What?" I asked. Though the stink of death turned my gut, I'd smelled that a time or twelve in my life. Most vividly as I lay injured in the desert sand with my troop torn to pieces around me.

"Summoning ceremony." He motioned to a heap of dead animals that littered the ground. Their deaths had obviously been the result of torture since they were contorted in horrible ways. I swallowed back bile at the sight, trying to keep from spewing right there. It took a lot of willpower not to examine them and commit the horrors to vivid memory. Dead humans were one thing, innocent animals was a whole other that only added to the unsettled tension growing in my gut.

"What the fuck?" Nothing about this was normal. "Like one of those pretend voodoo fuckers killing animals for shits and giggles?"

"Maybe," Micah whispered. He tiptoed his way through the mess. "Wonder what they called."

Called? "Um..."

We passed another row of little houses for the dead, navigating around creepy baby statues that almost seemed to move in the dark. In this row all the crosses had been broken off the tops of the crypts. The discarded pieces of stone were flipped upside-down, making my head swim with the possibilities and terror.

The recently used tomb was open, red curtain ripped away, gaping hole of darkness where the marble plate was supposed to close it off. I couldn't see a body through the dark, but it looked like something black stained the edges of the tomb. Almost as though something had slithered its way out of it.

Micah stopped suddenly, forcing me to run into his back. I stumbled, trying to find my footing and felt something squelch under my boots. Looking down, I fumbled to organize my thoughts like I'd been put on a slow-motion roller coaster. The black liquid soaking my shoes made me gasp as memories hit me like an atomic bomb. The metallic sting hit my nose at the same time I caught the moving dark shadow from the side of my vision.

Unlike the other shadows I'd seen until now, this one wasn't human. The shape too large, shifting and undulating more like a worm than a person ever possibly could. My first instinct was to run, but I couldn't pull my feet from the bloody mess left by something more than an abused animal, or my thoughts from the chaos of disaster that swirled in my head.

The dark mass went through the stone walls, head a slew of writhing shadows, moving so fast I didn't know if I even had time to breathe. Horrors I'd seen once before in my life filled my head with memories. I saw it reach for Micah and I instantly reacted by shoving him away and taking the brunt of its touch.

The mass hit me like a slap of water, walloping me with an icy grip of pure freezing pain. I felt as though I'd been crushed by a glacier wall. I slammed into the ground hard and tried to suck in a breath, but got nothing. Everything around me frozen, my hands stung like they'd been gripping a bag of ice for too long, and my lungs burned for air. The night turned into a reddish-black haze as consciousness was stripped from me.

CHAPTER 6

I was dropped down into the memory of that day. Waking up under a hail of gunfire. The sound of the wind howled around like some sort of banshee of old storybooks. I crawled from my tent only to find the sky black with soot and the fierce pounding of another sand storm on top of us, the particles of sand like tiny shards of glass ripping at my clothes and skin.

Another man left the tent beside mine, took several steps toward the swirling mass of sand, and was suddenly yanked upward by the wind like an invisible giant fist wrenched him off the ground. Only a few seconds passed but he rained down over me in parts instead of a living person, blood and bone, clothes and hair, like an internal explosion, ripped to shreds. A storm couldn't do that. It wasn't possible. Bombs maybe, but nothing like that fierce whipping of the wind.

I struggled to breathe, feeling the weight of his blood drenching my skin and the scent filling my nostrils with the copper stink. The guy I shared the tent with came up beside me and I latched on to him, dragging him to the ground with me, holding tight as he fought to try to get away.

The howling continued, like a siren's call. Instead of giving me the urge to run, I felt like I should be heading into the darkness, reaching for that swirl of death. After watching the third member of my team explode, I buried my face in my struggling bunkmate's hair and held on, waiting for it all to end. Death or the sandstorm. I wasn't sure which, or that it mattered so long as there was an end.

He fought me, trying to answer the siren call coming from that whipping darkness. But I held on, using my weight to keep us locked down while I expected death to rip him from my arms any second and tear us to shreds.

He stopped struggling. I felt his hands on my face, which was odd as I didn't think he'd been at all cooperative that day. But soft fingers stroked my cheeks, brushing away tears I hadn't realized were falling. Then soft lips pressed against mine, and I breathed in the smell of spice and gumbo.

"Alex?" he whispered.

I opened my eyes, not realizing they had been closed and found Micah in my arms. We were both kneeling, covered in blood, but wrapped together, Micah sprawled around me like a shield. My arms were locked so tightly around him they ached with the effort, but he didn't protest.

There was a lot of shouting and bright lights directed on us so intensely I couldn't see beyond Micah's face. His hands cupped my cheeks, and he rested his forehead against mine.

"Alex? Look at me okay? Focus on me."

"Yeah," I said, throat hurting like I'd been screaming. I studied his face, the pale eyes and tiny freckles almost lost in the illuminating washout of color around us.

"You back with me?"

Had I gone somewhere? I thought of the memory. Maybe not a memory, but a full flashback. "Fuck."

"He's back," Lukas' voice shouted from somewhere beyond the lights.

"I'm sorry," I said immediately to Micah. I looked down at us. Was the blood his? Had I hurt him?

"I'm not moving until they lower their weapons," Micah shouted back. "Fucking police."

"Did I hurt you?" I hoped I hadn't hurt him, but we were coated in blood. My jeans and the back of Micah's shirt seemed to be coated. I also felt the heat of something running down my cheek. Micah held on tight enough that I couldn't really move. At least I could breathe again. "What did I do?"

"Nothing. You fell and hit your head."

"I'm bleeding?" Was that why my left brow throbbed?

"Yes, but it's not bad. Probably won't even need stitches, just bleeding a lot."

"Head wounds always bleed like you're dying." It didn't explain all the blood we were covered in. "Are you okay?" I tried to turn my gaze from him to see beyond, but his hands tightened on my face.

"Look at me, okay?"

I blinked at him, my heart doing a little lurch. "Did I hurt someone else?"

"You didn't do anything. But you also don't need that memory. So focus on me, okay? Your brother is coming. He'll sort this out."

I focused on Micah's face, a tremor of panic starting in my hips, a subtle shaking, and beginning to spread outward. It was a familiar reverberation of my spine that often spread into a full-on panic attack which would leave me gasping for breath and reality all at once. I had to fight to stay still when the urge to run filled my gut. The feeling of kneeling in congealing blood made my gorge rise and with it the morbid fascination of my brain to explain why, to see...

"You said I'm beautiful, right?" Micah said as my eyes strayed from his.

"Yes," I agreed, attention snapping back to him. I could almost see his freckles in the dark.

"Then keep your eyes on me. Wait for Lukas with me."

"Okay." I thought for a moment about the few seconds before the flashback had taken hold of me. Something had been there. Something, not someone. "Something was there," I whispered almost inaudibly. "A shadow..." With no face.

"Shh," Micah hushed me, still holding me tight. "Five things, right? You feel me wrapped around you? You see me? Hear me?" He pressed his lips to mine again for a few seconds. "Taste me? Smell me?"

"Yes," I breathed, focusing on him. I heard arguing, the lights shifted a little and then Lukas squatted beside us.

Micah made me turn my head to look at him. "See, here's Lukas."

"Hey, little brother," Lukas said looking relaxed and normal. "I need you and Micah to step out for a few minutes. Okay?"

I tried to look back again, but Micah held my face in a grip that belied his small size. "You don't need this memory," Micah said.

I blinked at him, brain starting to come back online. Someone was dead nearby, and it wasn't pretty. I could tell that much from the blood and smell of open bowels. "Did I do...?"

"No," Lukas said firmly. "But we need you two out. I'll have someone drive you to the station. They'll collect your clothes and your statements." He glared out into the darkness, raising his voice, "No one is shooting anyone here tonight."

Shooting? Was that why Micah was wrapped so tightly around me? Were they threatening to shoot me? Unarmed, injured, and confused? On my knees, bleeding, and they were threatening to shoot me?

"Slowly put your hands behind your head," Lukas instructed.

It took effort to release my grip on Micah, almost physically hurt to let him go. I did as Lukas said, moving very slowly and putting my hands up. Several cops leapt in and ripped Micah away from me, forcing me to the ground and cuffing me. What the fuck?

They hauled me up and dragged me out, a wall of blue standing between me, Micah, and whomever had died. The lights thankfully washed out all the dark shadows as they led me through the maze of tombs and out of the cemetery, to shove me in the back of a squad car. Micah was led to another. There was a sizable crowd lounging around, kept back by yellow tape and a few police officers. Lukas appeared beside my door and tapped on the window.

"Cooperate," he told me through the glass. "I'll be there soon."

I felt sick. How could I cooperate if I didn't even know what happened? This was exactly why they'd wanted me locked in a psych ward forever. I was crazy. I could hurt people. But Micah said I hadn't. He'd used himself as a shield. Did he understand how insane that was? He could have been killed. Did he have any idea how many people were killed a year by police simply because they had some sort of mental issue that the cops weren't trained to manage? My therapist had given me stats and guidelines on how to react around police if I could possibly help it. She'd also discussed the issue at length with Lukas, who promised to bring it up within the department.

I'd been in the wrong place at the wrong time. The only thing that had stood between me and accidental death by cop was Micah.

Micah. I sighed. Only a few hours after meeting him and I'd really fucked up. Probably lost the job. If he was smart, he'd avoid me like the plague from this day forward.

A pair of cops got in the front of the car and they steered the car toward the police station. I wondered if I was under arrest, but realized I hadn't been read my rights, and Lukas would have been all over that. Though the cuffs still bit into my wrists. I prayed the entire way that I wouldn't end up back in some psych ward, loaded up with drugs that made me sick, while they tried to erase who I was.

CHAPTER 7

The police station went by in a blur. They led me into a room, uncuffed me, took swabs from my hands and gave me scrubs to change into, demanding I give them my clothes, even my shoes and underwear. Without the clothes I still felt filthy, the stench of copper strong in my nose. Tendrils of my hair having escaped my bun were laced with drying blood. My forehead throbbed but didn't seem to be bleeding anymore.

I was freezing since the replacement clothes they gave me did nothing to ward off the chill of the evening's events. The cop that came in to talk to me asked only a handful of questions. He made it clear I was not under arrest, and they only wanted my take on things. Apparently we'd been recorded on the street level cameras entering the cemetery after Jared had called for us. They had our movements all the way up to entering the cemetery.

It didn't, however, sound all that good for Jared, as the detective was making it sound like the man was under suspicion for doing something to his girlfriend. Had that been her body in the cemetery? Was I covered in her blood?

"So you met Jared and Sarah at the shop earlier today?" The detective asked.

"Yes, they bought some stuff and signed up for the Saturday tour."

"How did they seem to you?"

"Seem?"

"Happy? Did they argue? Did they say anything about going out for a tour after they left the shop?"

"No," I said. "They seemed happy. They were going to get beignets. I didn't ask about the rest of their schedule. Did something happen to Sarah?"

"We're trying to find that out," was all the detective gave me.

"But there was a body?"

"Did you see anything?"

"Dead animals. Micah said it looked like a summoning ceremony."

"Do you practice the occult, Mr. Caine?"

It was odd to be called Mr. Caine. It made me think of my dad, or even Lukas. "No. I just started working at the shop, helping with retail work, and the walking tours."

"Is Mr. Richards a practicing member of the occult?"

"You'd have to ask him. I don't know him well enough to have that information."

"Did Jared and Sarah seem to be into the occult?"

"They were excited about the ghost tour stuff, but I think that's normal for tourists in New Orleans. The cab driver even talked about how big of a commercial industry it is for the city. Hotels use the idea of ghosts to lure in tourists, and it brings in a ton of revenue. I didn't get any other vibe off the couple other than that they were tourists."

"Did you see the tour guide Mark Gioness with them?"

"No, he'd left before they arrived," I answered. "I got the

impression he wasn't supposed to be in the cemetery as Thursday nights were Micah's. He had come into the store to argue with Skylar about switching days."

"How did he seem to you?"

"Um, I dunno. He and the two women he was with were mean to Skylar until I stepped in."

"Mean how?"

"Using the wrong pronoun. Trying to bully her into changing Micah's schedule even though she didn't have the power to do that."

"Who were the two women with Mr. Gioness?"

"I don't know. As I said, I started the job today. You'd have to ask Micah. It sounds like they are all tour guides." I did the best I could to answer everything. But when I got to the flashback it was all a blank.

"You don't remember falling?"

"No. Not really."

"But you saw the remains of some sort of ritual."

"If that's what you want to call dead animals," I said. "Who does that?" And people called me crazy. "Is Micah okay? Christ... What's wrong with people? Did you find Sarah? She seemed like a nice girl."

He didn't answer any of my questions. He asked only a handful more before I was escorted in the little paper slippers to the main area of the station. Sky was there holding a bag of something and talking to a police officer. She saw me and rushed over, throwing her arms around me in a hug that surprised me. Didn't she know I was nuts? Standing in the police station, in nothing but thin scrubs, and someone else's blood, I never felt more broken, vulnerable, and lost, even after my many psych ward visits.

Her hug was grounding. Real, though I didn't think I deserved it. But I was afraid to touch her back and get her dirty, both with the blood on my hands and the memories of my messed-up life. She seemed like a good kid. I was thinking that about a lot of people lately.

"Why hasn't anyone treated his head?" She gave the cops around us a scathing look. "Does anyone at least have a first aid kit?"

The cop she'd been talking too, took one out from under a desk and handed it to her like she was some sort of seven-foot soldier instead of a five-foot nothing princess. She took it, balancing it on top of the bag she was carrying. "I have clothes for you. Lukas asked me to grab them. Said they'd be taking your stuff since it was covered in evidence or something." She glanced back at the group. "Bathroom?"

They pointed off in one direction. Sky grabbed my hand and dragged me in that direction. I pulled her to a halt when she tried to drag me into the women's bathroom. She paused, stuck her head inside, then shoved open the door. It was one giant stall instead of multiples. "In," she said with that no-nonsense tone.

I followed her in and watched her lock the door.

"The ladies room is always cleaner in places like this," Sky told me as she set down the bag and began digging things out. "You'll have to kneel for me so I can clean that wound."

I stared at her for a minute but finally dropped to my knees and sat back on my feet, closing my eyes. I could have fallen asleep right there. The adrenaline vanished, exhausting me instantly. Sky began scrubbing my face. I smelled the tang and felt the burn of alcohol, heard water running, felt paper towels run over my skin. There was a knock on the door which startled me out of a bit of meditation.

"Who is it?" Sky demanded. I looked up to find her standing over me, looking fierce, ready to defend me. She reminded me of one of those little dogs who thought they were a big dog.

"Micah," Micah's voice came from the other side of the door. "Lukas says you have clothes for me."

Sky left my side to open the door and let Micah in. He was dressed much the same as I was in paper-thin scrubs that made us both look like we were going to jail today. Sky wrung her hands. "He's really quiet. Should he be this quiet? I need to find Lukas."

"He'll be fine," Micah assured her.

"I tried to clean the wound but it keeps bleeding. Should we bring him to the hospital?"

"No," I said firmly, fears of never being released again filling my head. "No hospital. I'm not crazy," no matter how much everyone else told me I was.

"No one thinks you are, sweetie," Sky said.

Micah closed and locked the door. "Are you nauseous or light headed?" he asked me.

"No. Just tired."

"Probably not a concussion then." He held his hand up in front of my face and moved his fingers around. I followed them lazily with my gaze. He nodded like I'd confirmed something for him, then picked up the first aid kit, finding a few things and making his way to me, kneeling beside me. "I'm going to clean it again and glue it shut," Micah said. "It might scar."

"I don't care." Scars didn't bother me. The idea of being locked in a psych ward again did.

"Clothes for both of you are in the bag," Sky said. "I'm going to find Lukas."

"He was talking to the sergeant," Micah said while he dabbed at my wound. "I hope giving them an earful about aiming weapons at an unarmed, injured man." He dried my head and probed at the wound a little. It ached, but more like a bruise than anything else. "This will hurt a bit as I have to press it closed and add the glue."

"Okay," I allowed, waiting for the pressure.

Sky left the bathroom, and I closed my eyes when the wound began to sting.

"It's a good thing you're not black," Micah said quietly.

"I am though," I told him. "Mom's as blonde as can be, dad's full African American. They are one of those ultimate poster-ready interracial couples. Two ends of the spectrum. Luke and I got frizzy hair and dark eyes out of it. We didn't have it as bad as some of the kids who did have dark skin, but no one really let us forget that our dad is black. Lukas's old police department knew and treated him like crap."

"Lucky," Micah said. "This city is full of racism and hate. Sad for a town that is such a melting pot of cultures."

"What about you?" I asked. I would rather focus on him than the pain and the disquiet still rattling around my gut.

"Hmm?"

"You're obviously Japanese, but I've never seen a blue-eyed Japanese person. At least not with real blue eyes. Contacts sure..." I was one of the few people I knew, who wasn't Asian, who could actually distinguish the different types of Asian faces; Korean, Chinese, Japanese, and Indian. It wasn't the skin tone as that could vary from city to city. It was the shape of the face, eyes, and cheek bones. Mix them up and it really became hard to determine, but I was pretty sure Micah's features were very Japanese. "What's your back story? What sort of mix stirred up a beautiful man like you?"

"Oh. Thank you. Mom is Irish. Red hair, blue eyes, and all. She taught English in Japan. That's how she met my dad. I have two aunts and an uncle on my mom's side who immigrated to America and grew up spending a lot of time here. Spent my life visiting places all over the world. Lived and studied in Tokyo, traveled to Ireland, and America, even spent a few years with my parents while they taught in China. It wasn't until I met

Timothy online that I moved to America. Sounds like you've traveled a lot too."

"Only while I served. Spent half a year in Japan on my first tour. My Japanese isn't that fluent though. It's better than my Chinese, but not by much. I pick up languages pretty fast, but it still takes immersion for me, at least a couple of weeks. My first tour was a lot of training and very little time off base. Second tour we did France. I'm fluent in French and Italian now. Third tour was all the Middle East. Thought I'd maybe get to go back to Japan someday, or even China, which is why I tried to learn Chinese. But stuff sort of happened..."

Micah blew on the wound. I could feel his warm breath on my forehead and knew he was drying the glue but it comforted me that he was close. "Life does that. Changes our direction sometimes."

"I'm really sorry," I said.

"For what?" He began putting away pieces of the first aid kit.

"This whole mess. I'll understand if you fire me. Disaster seems to follow me."

"You are not to blame for this evening, Alex."

"I flipped out."

"You had a flashback. I knew it could happen. Lukas had warned me. I've seen videos of people having full on flashbacks where they attack everyone who approaches them. Yours wasn't even a bad one. You pretty much dropped to the ground and held on to me. It wouldn't have happened if the circumstances had been normal. I do tours all the time and have never found a summoning circle or a body on any of them. St. Louis Number One is one of the best protected areas of the city. It shouldn't have happened. Had I even thought there was a possibility neither of us would have entered the cemetery." Micah shook his head, then he dug through the bag, sorting out what looked like clothing.

"Is Sarah dead?"

"I honestly don't know. They won't tell me anything."

"But you saw..." Or was the body too messed up to make out anything? My stomach churned at the idea.

"I saw blood."

And maybe more, but hopefully his brain wouldn't put it together. Having served and gone on actual tours in violent countries I'd seen my fair share of dead. It was never pretty. Funerals could dress it up, make it feel less horrific, but the prettiest part of war was a widow's tears. And there was nothing pretty about that, though it didn't stop the media from portraying it everywhere.

"I'm no hero," Micah continued, "just a tour guide who sometimes gets feelings that point people in the right direction to see stuff they wouldn't normally experience. What happened in the cemetery tonight was not normal. Even for me."

Maybe it was because of me. "Maybe I attracted something there." Maybe the thing that killed my troop had followed me here.

"Remember what I said about people influencing things because they expect it to turn out a certain way? Don't do that."

"But it's funny how it's never happened to you before and my first day it happens."

"Coincidence. You were with me the whole time. Not sure when you would have snuck away to bust up some animals and summon something."

"You keep saying that; summon something, summoning ceremony. You've seen it before? Know what it was?"

Micah shrugged. He stood, went to the door and locked it, then picked up his pile of clothes and set it on the edge of the sink. He began to strip out of the scrubs. I tried really hard not to stare, but couldn't help it. He really was everything that pushed my buttons.

Micah's body was slim and toned, not unlike what I'd remembered. Though he was a little more muscular than I recalled ever seeing in the videos. He was also hairless from the neck down. I wondered how much of it was due to his Asian heritage and how much was due to regular waxing. Either way, the smooth flow of his skin turned me on more than my exhausted body should have been able to at that moment.

"I've read about it. Even attended a few mock ceremonies put on by the historical society in alignment with the Voodoo society. I might not practice Voodoo but I can recognize the symbols just like people who aren't Christian recognize the cross. The symbols scrawled in animal blood were summoning symbols. Like they use to call spirit guides and such. Some of the voodoo priests and priestesses still use them, but most draw them with chalk instead of in actual blood. The city sort of frowns on using anything other than chalk to mark any public area."

He slipped into a tiny pair of bikini briefs and adjusted himself so everything lay smoothly. He probably felt my eyes on him, but said nothing, and didn't seem at all embarrassed. He washed his hands and face, even scrubbed at his feet before pulling on the rest of his clothes, a pair of jeans and another T-shirt. He found a pair of sandals and slipped them on before turning to look at me. "You're covered in blood," he said.

"Sorry." I frowned up at him, feeling inadequate, tired, and really lost. Emotionally wrung out from everything.

Micah pulled a wad of paper towels out of the dispenser and wet them down before beginning to wipe down my face. The water was cold and soothing. "You sure you feel okay? Your pupils are huge. At least it's both and not only one. If it was only one, I'd be insisting on taking you to the ER."

"I'm a little shaky?" I said really unsure. For all I knew it could have been him making me tremble. Or memories of something in the dark. Something that reached for him, almost took him. I wondered if that was what happened to Sarah. But that couldn't be right. It was all in my head. Those things weren't real. "I'm crazy," I said. "Seeing shit in the dark."

"You're not," Micah assured me. He scrubbed at my hair, but frowned as it didn't seem to be coming clean.

"Something reached for you," I told him. "I saw it. That's why I pushed you." Fuck. I'd forgotten about that. "Sorry, sorry. I didn't mean to push you. Fuck, well I did 'cause I saw something. But that's all in my head. They always tell me it's always in my head, fuck..."

"I'm fine. Let's get you washed up some and dressed." He tugged me to my feet and over to the sink. I scrubbed my hands, and had to strip my shirt off to rinse away some of the blood. My feet were stained brown with someone else's blood, knees too. The stuff on my hands, face, and in my hair seemed fresher. Mine, I hoped.

Micah handed me a pair of boxers and gave me the courtesy of turning his back while I stripped out of the flimsy pants and into the boxers. I also had an oversized T-shirt in black, a pair of dark green shorts, and a pair of flip-flops. I tugged everything on, feeling marginally better even if I still felt grimy. My manbun had turned into a giant poof at some point of the evening, looking more like a poodle's tail than a ponytail. But since my hair was soaked in my own blood, it was no use trying to fix it.

Someone knocked on the door again. "It's Lukas," Lukas said from the other side of the door. Micah opened it for him. Lukas glanced at me, looking me over hard, gaze finally landing on my forehead. "You sick at all?"

"No."

"I don't think he has a concussion," Micah said. "Though really he should have been looked at by an EMT."

Lukas frowned. He knew better than to suggest I go to the hospital. "I can't leave. I've got a murder to investigate. People to question, videos to review." He sighed. "You really shouldn't be alone tonight."

"I'm fine," I promised him. "Just really tired. Little bit of a headache."

"He can come to my place," Micah said. "You can pick him up in the morning. I can watch his head, make sure he doesn't start throwing up or anything."

Lukas looked at Micah. "That's not all I'm worried about."

"I'm fine," I assured him. Often having one flashback, meant that if I went to sleep, I'd be prone to waking in the middle of another. The whole process often left me floundering in a roller-coaster of emotion and flashbacks for a few days afterward. "I'll go home and lock myself in."

"He's fine with me," Micah insisted. "I'm stronger than I look."

"Sometimes he's not himself," Lukas insisted.

"Does he know anyone else in this city? Perhaps you'd like Sky to look after him? Or take him to the hospital?"

"No hospital," I reiterated.

Micah stared at Lukas, something passing between them. "I think I've experienced firsthand what he can do, and his instinct was to protect me rather than hurt me. You've already assured me a dozen times that even during his flashbacks he's never been violent," Micah said.

"That we've seen so far."

"Why would that change now?" Micah asked.

"You both could have been shot tonight," Lukas pointed out.

"Because of shitty police training. He didn't do anything. He fell. I tried to help him up and he held on to me."

"Which the police took as possible violence against you."

"Because they're stupid," Micah argued. "He was hugging me, begging me to stay with him. He was trying to protect me."

I blinked at them, not recalling any of that. "Was that all I said?"

"You said 'Don't go, you'll die. Please stay here,'" Micah said.

The memory always had me saving one of my fellow soldiers. I couldn't even remember his name anymore. When I asked, I'd been told a handful had survived. Not even who. I think they didn't want me talking to anyone about what really happened that day. Had I saved him? Or was that something my memory had created to ease my survivor's guilt?

Lukas sighed. "Fine. I'll pick him up in the morning. Let me find a rookie to drop you guys off. Do not give him any medication. He reacts to damn near everything. Even aspirin."

"Sorry," I said again, feeling awful that they felt they had to be so careful around me.

"Nothing to be sorry for," Micah said. He packed up the bag and handed Lukas the scrubs before tugging me out of the bathroom. Lukas went to find us a ride home. Sky had vanished somewhere. I hope she got home safely too.

"I'm okay going home," I told Micah. "I don't want to be a burden to you."

He studied me for a minute while we waited in the lobby area of the police station. Since it was almost midnight, it was pretty quiet, even though it was a full moon. "If it's okay with you, I'd rather not be alone tonight."

It took me a few seconds to catch up. But I realized in that moment that while I hadn't seen the body, Micah had. And he hadn't spent a few years in the military trying to desensitize himself to corpses. He looked tired, and gripped my arm tightly. He had also protected me from the police and likely been interrogated like I had. And still he stood in front of me looking calm and collected. Was it all a front?

"Sure," I said instantly, wanting to take care of him if I could. At the very least I owed him, though in reality I would have taken care of him anyway. It was instinct, and all my supposed "white knight" buttons were pushed with him, even if he really didn't come across as any sort of victim. "Kind of a crazy night, right? Probably more so than your norm."

He gave me a tight smile. "Yes. Much *crazier* than my normal evening."

Lukas pointed a duo of cops in our direction. They headed our way. "Looks like our ride." I offered Micah my hand. He took it and gripped it, then let out a long deep breath like he'd been holding it a while.

CHAPTER 8

M icah's home was a little garden apartment broken off
from one of the giant houses in the Garden District. It
was behind a gate and down a path that curved around the back
of the house. Attached to the house, it had its own little entrance
and sat on the corner, giving the two sides facing outward walls
of windows out to an elaborate garden. Inside, the curtains were
drawn so we couldn't see in. Outside there was a tiny patio with
little multicolor fairy lights installed on the square canopy set
over the patio furniture. A handful of potted plants bloomed,
mixed with fun lawn ornaments like light up mushrooms, and
waving zombie gnomes. The entire area looked like it took a lot
of time to maintain. Did Micah somehow manage that? Or was
it a perk of living in the little house next to the giant mansion?

The attached house was huge, and dark. It could have
starred in a haunted mansion movie, or one of those gore-fest
movies that kids who'd never seen real violence seemed to love.
During the daylight it probably looked like a grand old home.
But the silence of the early morning hours added a chill to my
bones that had me searching the corners for shadows that didn't
quite fit.

Micah unlocked the door and leaned in to turn on a light, then held it open for me. Inside was a bit of a surprise. It was small, there was no way around that. It might have been a drawing room or part of a ballroom or something in the house at one point with the high ceiling and thick crown moldings. It had a tiny loft area overhead, and a cottage ambiance with colors painted in white, pale blue, and sand that didn't feel at all New Orleans, but did make the place homey. His kitchen was little more than a corner with a tiny fridge, a single burner stove, a microwave, and a mini-sink. There was also a large appliance stuffed next to the sink that I suspected was one of those all-in-one washer and dryer things.

A small two-seater table was pressed against the wall next to the front row of windows. The rest of the space was a living area filled with bookcases, a futon/couch in a bright colored pattern, and a small flat screen TV mounted on the wall in the back. He didn't have a lot of furniture and what he did have was very minimalist, though some of the decorative items were really elaborate.

One overhead chandelier-looking light illuminated the whole space with LED crystals. Since the switch on the wall was a dimmer switch, I was sure it could be brighter. Tucked in the back corner under the window was one of those free-standing air-conditioner units. Thankfully it seemed to be working well because it was cool inside despite the soupy humidity outside.

If not for the loft, the place would have been a tiny studio. Maybe 400 square feet. Yet it felt homier than Lukas' place did, more lived in and personable. The stairway up to the loft was little more than floating bookshelves coming down the far wall. Architecturally it was stunning, but I worried I'd fall if I had to navigate those stairs in the dark.

"It's cute," I told Micah. "I bet in the morning the sun through the windows is nice."

He nodded, kicking off his shoes by the door and dropping the bag in a chair beside the door. I closed the door and flicked the lock out of habit, then took off my shoes and put them beside his.

A thump came from above, making me glance up toward the loft. A few seconds later a black cat came bounding down the stairs like it had done it a thousand times. It came our way, rubbing across Micah's legs in greeting.

"Hey, Jet," Micah said to the cat. Up close the black coat of the cat looked striped, with little rosettes in multiple shades of dark gray. He was also male and huge, maybe close to twenty pounds, sleek and muscled, not fat, and had short hair. I didn't know enough about cats to determine the breed, although I couldn't remember seeing a regular house cat that big before.

"You're not allergic, are you?" Micah asked me.

"I don't think so." I bent down and offered a hand for the cat to sniff, wondering if he'd bite me or maybe run away because I probably still smelled like blood. Instead he bopped his head against my hand and let me scratch him. "Never had a cat. He's friendly."

"Not to everyone." Micah looked around. "I think I'm going to jump into the shower, then I can make up the futon. You should probably shower too."

I thought for a minute of showering with him, but let that pass without speaking it. Okay, so sometimes my filter worked. "Do you want me to make up the futon? While you shower?" Were there sheets somewhere?

"Sure. In the drawers under the futon are some sheets and blankets." He glanced up at the loft. "There is no bed up in the loft. Too hard to get a mattress up there. I use it as a reading and craft nook, plus it gets really warm up there in the summer. Lots of pillows though. So if you want to grab a stack of pillows and some blankets and throw them down that would help."

I looked at the futon and realized that meant we'd either be sleeping in the same bed or I would be sleeping on the floor.

"It's bigger than it looks. Queen-sized sheets fit it." His cheeks pinked. "Sorry. I spend a lot on the shop. Would rather invest in that than a home I don't spend much time in since I work six days a week."

"Oh, hey, no judgment. I think this place is nice. Small, but nice. Never would have thought a place like this was in that giant house."

"They remodeled the whole thing after Hurricane Katrina. The entire house is made up of condos. This is the smallest of the bunch and the only one that has its own external access. I didn't want something that felt like an apartment. I also don't need as much space as a lot of people do. This was the smallest unit, and the cheapest."

"You rent or own?"

"Own," Micah said. "All the units are homesteads, no renting allowed. I wanted a place I could set up with space to work on my craft projects, and since the ceilings are so high in here, I thought the loft would work great for that."

That made sense. I wondered what the other condos looked like. "Are you okay sharing the futon with me? I can sleep on the floor. The rug looks soft and comfy."

"And full of cat hair," Micah said. He made his way to a wall that opened magically into a dresser that had been invisible moments before, pulling out clothes. "I don't mind sharing the futon. Sky stays over sometimes. She's a bit like sleeping with an octopus, legs and arms everywhere. But I'm used to her being around."

"Are you and Sky a thing?"

"Nah. She's really into your brother, and not quite comfortable with herself yet. I'm more into guys than girls, even transitioning girls. She's a bit too girly for me. She's saving up for top surgery so she doesn't have a place of her own. Does a lot of couch surfing. She's here probably two or three nights a week. Most of her stuff is actually at her cousin's place. They butt heads a lot, so she doesn't stay there much." He pointed at a door that seemed to lead to the bathroom. "I'll be out in a few."

"Sure," I said. He disappeared into the bathroom, closing the door, and I pulled open the drawer below the futon. There were half a dozen different sheet sets in the drawer, some of them very colorful and interesting, including a set with cactuses, and another with cat mermaids. Jet examined the contents of the drawer with me, glancing back in my direction with that cat judgment on his face.

"What?" I asked him. "I promise to keep my hands off." For tonight at least. We both could use some sleep.

I chose the mermaid cats and had to shoo him out of the drawer before closing it and figuring out how to get the back of the futon to lay down. A few seconds later it was flat, I stripped off the colorful wrap that appeared to be decoration over the plain brown cover, and pulled the sheet onto the bed.

I glanced at the loft and the stairs again, sucking in a deep breath before making the climb on my hands and knees, clinging to the small railing on every other stair. Tiny houses were a thing. I knew somewhere in the back of my head that they were a big thing in some parts of the country, maybe the world. Lukas watched a lot of random home improvement shows on the rare occasion he was home and wanting to get his mind off work. Sometimes they featured tiny houses. Micah's house was much like the tiny houses I'd seen on those shows. Only his space was more wide open, less focused on narrow room stacking and more one big simplified space with the loft. Having lived in Tokyo, Japan, likely Micah was used to living in small multifunctional spaces. I wasn't sure how I felt about it yet though I'd spent plenty of time crammed into tents with a bunch of other soldiers. It was different to have all the amenities of a normal home in such a small area.

The loft was exactly as Micah said, narrow, with a small section open to the rest of the condo. It was really just a big shelf built into the curve of the ceiling above the windows. There actually was a handful of short windows off to the side, also covered in thick window treatments. I could see how the sun might bake the space in the morning. A plush rug softened the wood floor, and small bookcases lined the area, some filled with books, others filled with fabric and yarn. There was a sewing machine on a short table near one wall, and a cat bed beside it, which was covered in black cat fur.

There was also not enough room to stand up, which explained why there were no chairs in the loft space. There were pillows set in specific areas that seemed to fit that section. Like one near the sewing machine that had a little back to it, likely to help Micah while he sat at the machine working. Another was a beanbag type. And two others seemed to be big floor pillows that I'd seen while dining at a restaurant or two in Japan.

In a set of cloth-covered chests near the stairs I found the pillows for the bed, and a handful of very beautiful and fun looking quilts. One of them was covered in spooky Halloween fabrics with skeletons, ravens, and witches. Another was a panel sort of quilt with pinups dressed as witches, zombies, and sexy maids on one side, the other side had half naked men fishing, camping, firefighting, and swimming.

I brought them both down in case Micah didn't want to share blankets. When I slept, I tended to burrow myself into the blankets, until nothing was left uncovered but the top of my head. It wasn't due to being cold, but more a comfort of the weight of the blanket. Both the quilts were thin, but big enough that I hoped they'd be that perfect wrap.

Lukas had bought a special blanket for me as a gift when I'd finally gotten out of the hospital. It was one of those weighted things that was supposed to help with anxiety. Which I really liked, but it was sort of small, so I couldn't wrap myself in it the way I liked. Usually it ended up pooled at my feet while some cheap Walmart quilt snuggled me like a burrito.

Jet jumped onto the futon and sat in the cat loaf-of-bread pose, staring at me intently. I reached out and stroked down his back, which he seemed to like. At least he wasn't growling or biting me. When I sat down beside him on the bed, he curled up next to me.

Micah emerged a few minutes later, clean, his hair very dark when wet, and wearing a pair of his bikini briefs. He pointed to the bathroom. "All yours. I put out towels for you, along with a fresh shower scrub, and toothbrush."

"Thank you." I leapt up from my perch on the edge of the futon and headed toward the bathroom trying not to stare at Micah. I couldn't help that my body responded to him. It hadn't done anything in months, and now it was doing the happy dance for one man who didn't seem to realize the effect he had on me. Not that he had to care, my body was my problem, I reminded myself. I darted past him and into the bathroom, closing the door behind me.

The bathroom was big for the space of the apartment, with a full-sized sink with drawers, a linen cupboard, a toilet with a lot of buttons, and a large, white, claw-foot, soaker tub. The walls and floors were tiled in bright sky blue, white, and a patchwork of colored mini-squares running in strips of three around the upper portion of the walls, and while there was a curtain strung on a rod hanging from the ceiling, it only covered a small portion of the bathtub/shower combo. The towels and stuff sat on a small bamboo bench near the shower. I used the toilet, figuring out that the buttons ran different for a number one or a number two, and there was even a bidet, which I'd never used before, but had seen overseas enough to recognize. Nice.

I made my way to the shower. Would there be hot water in a place this tiny after Micah had already used it? I turned on the spray and it was warm and soothing. I sighed, stripped out of my clothes, leaving them in a pile on the lush blue rug beside the shower. When I stepped under the spray, I worried for a few seconds that the liquid bandage wouldn't hold, but with the heat washing away the grime, I didn't care right then. The water turned pink and brown at my feet.

I used his shampoo and body wash, both smelling of honey and frankincense, sort of reminding me of Christmas. Once the water finally ran clear, I turned off the spray and dried off, using the action to focus my thoughts. The racing of my heart had eased, and exhaustion was tugging at me hard. But I felt... safe? Which was odd as I was in an unfamiliar place and ever since the day my base had been decimated, I'd never liked being someplace unfamiliar.

I tugged on the boxers, folding up the rest, then brushed my teeth and tried to work through the tangle of my hair. Surprisingly the wide-toothed comb Micah had left out for me slid through my hair like a hot knife through butter. What was this magic? There was a small tube of some sort of hair thing next to the comb. I glanced at the back of it, browsing the instructions, before adding a bit to my hair and working it through. It smelled nice, and seemed to ease some of the tight tension of my curls and soften my hair.

I gathered the mess into a ponytail, pulling it back as tight as I could. I'd have an afro in the morning anyway, but I was too tired to care right then.

When I left the bathroom, the overhead light was off and

Micah was curled up on the futon, wrapped up in one of the two blankets much like I planned to do myself. Jet sat at his feet, and the multicolored lights from outside filtered through the curtains on the windows, leaving the room pretty bright in a rainbow array despite the late hour.

I set my clothes on the chair with the bag and made my way to the bed. Micah held out a black piece of cloth for me. I stared at it for a minute trying to make it out.

"Eye mask," Micah said. "Helps with the lights."

I wondered why he didn't turn them off, but maybe the main house had control? Or maybe he didn't like waking up in the middle of the night to complete darkness. I took the mask, slid it on my head, resting the eye parts on my forehead and climbed in beside Micah. It took only a few minutes burrowed up in the blanket, listening to his soft breathing, and smelling the delicate Christmas scent of his body wash, before I fell asleep.

CHAPTER 9

The sound of some sort of animal chittering woke me. At first I struggled to figure out where I was. The black mask over my eyes blocked most of the room until I shoved it up and realized I was at Micah's. He was still sound asleep. His own eye mask firmly in place, and Jet curled around his head on his pillow, also sound asleep.

So what was that noise?

I sat up and pulled the eye mask off. The digital clock on the microwave read after three a.m., and it was still dark. The filtered lights still wafted through the curtains, making me wonder why Micah hadn't put room darkening ones in, though I imagined in the small space it might make it feel a bit like a cave.

The sound came again. A weird chittering I didn't recognize from anything I'd ever heard in my life. Not from years camping, or from the time spent serving my country. It was almost like a monkey, but that didn't sound right either. Was there such a thing as a hyena monkey?

I stared at the windows, searching the length of the curtains for a gap, only there was none. They were shut tight, even fastened at the edges with little hooks and strips of fabric. No real shape came through the curtains, only a hint of the lights in the distance. I stared for another minute before lying down again and pulling my blankets up. I hadn't been in New Orleans long. Maybe it was some weird bird or something. Would Lukas know? His apartment was in the middle of the French Quarter, up the stairs on the second floor of a row of apartments above art galleries and coffee shops. There were no trees or greenery to attract wildlife, just cobblestones and French architecture. He didn't have time for landscaping and gardens. So he might not know. The sound was more than a little unsettling, making goosebumps rise on my skin and my stomach flip a little with anxiety.

I stared at the window out front a little longer. Long enough to feel myself begin to fall asleep again. As my eyes began to close, a shadow rolled across the curtains outside, blocking the lights for a few seconds. I shot up, ready to race to the window and throw back the curtains.

Micah caught my wrist, nearly giving me a heart attack.

"Fuck," I said, pressing a hand to my chest.

"Shh," Micah said. "Come back to bed."

"Something is outside."

"Yes, and it needs to stay there." He had pushed the mask up on his forehead, and held my wrist tightly in his grasp.

"What is it? A bird? One of your neighbors?"

He sighed. "It's a discussion for another day, I think. Your brother doesn't want me putting thoughts in your head." He tugged at my arm again, and I gave in, sliding down beside him and turning to stare into his pale blue eyes, which looked like ice in the dim light of the room. The chittering came again, which made me tense. He didn't react at all. "You're safe. That's all that matters."

"Is it something that could hurt us?" I probably sounded like a little kid to him, but after the year I'd survived, the whole world seemed like a fucking death trap to me.

"Not really."

"That's not very reassuring."

He let go of my wrist and stroked my face. "We are safe. You are safe here with me. It's only a weird noise. You can think of this as a dream if it helps."

I shivered as the same feeling of that day in the desert filled my gut.

Micah lifted his blanket and curled closer to me, adding his quilt over mine. He wrapped an arm around my waist and tucked his face into my pillow beside mine. The warmth of his breath on my face was soothing.

"Put your mask back on," he instructed. I tugged it into place, sad that I couldn't stare at him while I drifted off to sleep again. If I could sleep after the weird noises continued outside.

"Lukas isn't here," I whispered.

"No. He's not," agreed Micah. "But the middle of the night is not a good time to put things in people's heads. Our brains are too vulnerable from sleep to process correctly. How about tomorrow when the sun is out and we have both had coffee and food, we discuss it?"

"Yeah?"

"Yeah," he promised.

The sound changed, becoming more like a scream, an animal in pain. I tensed, fearing it was Jet for a minute. "Jet?"

"He's right beside us," Micah said, his arm tightening around me. "Reach up and feel him if you need to, but leave the mask on."

I did reach up, petting Jet's wide flank and receiving a few licks in return. Was he unaffected by the noise? He didn't seem alarmed, though he stayed curled up on Micah's pillow.

"Focus on me and Jet," Micah said. "The more you think of the sounds the more they intensify."

"Self-persuasion?" I wondered. Was this more shit from in my head? No that couldn't be right, Micah heard it too.

"Only a little, but that doesn't matter. Now close your eyes. You're safe. I'm here. You're not alone. Sleep," Micah instructed.

I don't know if it was magic or something else, but I did close my eyes, sucked in a deep breath filled with the scent of him, the weight of his arm around me comforting, and I fell into a deep dreamless sleep.

K nocking woke me the second time, only when I shoved the eye mask off light filled the flat and the clock said it was almost eleven a.m. "Wow," I grumbled and looked toward the door.

Micah sleepily got up, pulling his own eye mask off and heading to the door, not seeming to care at all that he was wearing only undies.

He opened it and stood there, framed in the glory of the morning sun and I took a few seconds to admire his ass, the soft bubble sweetness that it was before looking beyond him through the doorway. The man that stood there was closer to my height, but other than that was very average looking, brown hair, brown eyes, wearing a T-shirt, jeans, and sneakers. A younger man stood behind him wearing shorts and a tee. The second man looked barely legal, hair a pale chocolate brown falling into his eyes and around his chin. His eyes were brown too, but he was pretty in a noticeable way.

"Tim," Micah grumbled, "Brad. Come in."

The younger of the two held up a bag, "Brought you breakfast." His smile was infectious. They came in and I rolled over to sit up and rub my face. "Hello," the young one said. "You're Alex, right? I'm Brad."

"Good morning, Brad," I said without much emotion. I'd need coffee before I could be intelligent and civil. It was still my drug of choice. Then my brain kicked in and began to work. Tim had to be Timothy; the guy Micah used to make videos with. And the young guy had to be the new boyfriend. Wow.

A dozen things snapped into place in that second. First, that while Brad was cute in a very young and unfinished way, Micah was plain hot in a cute real way. I examined the two of them, making a thousand comparisons and then tried to figure out what had been so great about Timothy. Well, other than the fact that he'd had a great cock. It was funny how jealous I was in that moment, like he had some hold on Micah's life, or that I did. A hundred things went through my head and I had to bite my tongue to keep them from spilling out. Stupid, broken filter.

"Coffee?" I asked as Brad set the bag down on the small table, pulling out bagels and cream cheese.

Micah went to the kitchen and opened a cupboard to reveal a coffee maker. It was one of the small drip kinds with a four-cup pot. "A cup or want a whole pot?"

"Oh my God, a whole pot or twelve maybe," I begged.

He filled the pot with water and grounds, something from a fancy looking bag I couldn't identify, and then pushed the 'on' button, then he vanished into the bathroom for a minute.

"You're hot," Brad said to me.

I blinked at him. "Thanks, I think. Sorry. I'm not awake before coffee."

"That's okay. We aren't staying long. Micah texted me earlier to see if I could open the shop for him. You guys are all over the local news. Maybe national since that girl is missing," Tim said. "Can't believe Mark is dead. He was a total twatwaffle though. Always up in Micah's business because Micah does his own tours."

I processed that. Sarah was missing. Mark was dead. So the body had been Mark's? Did Micah know? The coffee pot made a gurgling, almost finished noise, and I got up to make my way to it and look for a cup. I found something that looked like a soup mug and poured the entire contents of the pot into it. There was also a batch of almond milk creamer in the tiny fridge so I added that until it became a nice tan. The smell was divine. Not the Folgers crap Lukas kept at home and drank by the bucket full, but something with a butterscotch scent that made me sigh before taking a sip. The flavor of it rolled over my tongue, a sweet but smooth hint of butterscotch under the firm bite of a good bean.

I groaned. "Oh shit, that's good."

"That was hot," Brad said. "You ever do movies? Porn?"

I could feel his gaze on me. Did I have morning wood? I glanced down, no that was still not working, or maybe it had been the abrupt awakening that had dampened it.

"You'd be great in porn. I heard you were in the military. Do you still have a uniform? Those draw viewers in like a magnet. Plus you're good looking, thin, and only a little hairy. Lots of great muscle definition."

I gaped at him, the old Southern boy my mother raised waking up in me like a cat being rubbed the wrong way. "Haven't you heard? I'm crazy. Certified and everything by good old Uncle Sam." I took another long sip of the heavenly coffee, thinking I would have to interrogate Micah later about where to get some. "Wasn't useful anymore. Wouldn't make porn on a bet." Couldn't seem to get it up unless I was fantasizing about inappropriate things about my new boss.

"You know about Micah, right?" Tim asked.

"About his old job?" I asked.

"About what happened to him," Tim corrected. Was he implying Micah was crazy too? Because he'd vanished for a while? Was that why they'd broken up? Or was it because Tim had found a younger model?

"I know what I need to," I told him. What Micah wanted me to know was what I knew. The rest was up to him to share, even if I had been a little nosey and read a book with a story about his disappearance in it.

Micah reappeared with his hair pulled back in a ponytail and he'd found pants and a T-shirt somewhere.

"Did you want some?" I asked him, realizing I'd taken the entire pot of coffee. "Sorry... this is good shit. I took the whole pot." I offered the cup to him. He actually took it and took a long gulp before giving it back and going to the table of offered food.

"Is it true you found a body?" Brad asked him as Micah picked a bagel that appeared to be covered in salt then dug through the cream cheese for a minute.

"Almond cream cheese is there," Tim said. He pointed to the blue container. Micah picked it up and opened it to slather his bagel in it.

"Yes, there was a body. No, it wasn't pretty," Micah said before he took a huge bite of bagel. He sighed much the way I had with the coffee. He chewed and swallowed for a minute. "I can't tell you anything because the police are investigating."

"Was it gross?" Brad wanted to know.

"Yes," Micah assured him.

"Cool. Maybe there will be a real ghost in St. Louis Number One now."

Micah sighed. I wondered if I'd ever been that young, but in truth I had been, before my first tour. By the third, bodies were a regular thing even if I couldn't stomach them anymore. Some of those nightmares came back just when I thought I'd finally forgotten them. That last attack the most vivid of all. Sometimes I wish I could forget their faces, their names, and their deaths.

"Did you guys drive over?" Micah asked.

"Yep," Tim said. "Do you have stuff you want us to take to the store too?"

"If you don't mind. There are half a dozen bags, a couple of shawls, a box of soap, and another box of candles."

"Sure," Tim agreed. "I don't know how you find time to do all that."

"It's stress relief," Micah said.

Tim looked me over, seeming to frown at my lack of attire, but I probably had major bed hair too. He turned to study Micah. "You okay?"

"A little tired," Micah replied. "I'll have to call around to the people scheduled for last night's tour and see if they want to reschedule or if I have to refund people." He groaned. "It's going to be a long afternoon."

"We can handle the shop for a while. So at least that's off your plate. Are you still doing your normal ghost tour tonight starting in Jackson Square?" Tim asked. "I don't think I have enough memorized to do that for you. Sky is too flighty to do them. Not sure your new guy is up to the task either."

New guy sounded like more than purely an employee, but I didn't correct him. "Can I make more coffee?" I asked Micah, watching him eat. Mornings and food didn't work much for me, but the coffee was almost gone.

He stepped around me, and added more grounds and water to the pot. This time I took the bag of coffee from him to examine the label. Where was my phone? I needed to take a picture so I'd remember what to get. I scanned the room and couldn't recall if I'd actually gotten it back from the police last night. Maybe it was in the bag? And on that note, why hadn't I heard from Lukas?

"I can manage the tour. I have to make sure Sky is still okay closing tonight," Micah told him. "She was never meant to be full-time, but it seems to be working out that way. Her card reading brings in more, so I feel bad for needing her so much."

"That's why you hired Alex, right?" Tim asked. He looked me over. "To take care of some of your burden?" That sounded like a biting comment if I'd ever heard one. Though I must not have been awake enough to understand why.

I stared back at him. "What? Yesterday was my first day, you can't expect me to know how to give a ghost tour when I haven't even been on one yet. I can barely work the register. Five hours is not enough time to have the entire shop and city memorized."

"It's okay," Micah said. He put a comforting hand on my arm. "I don't expect you to be leading tours any time soon. I do eventually want you to be able to open or close without me, which will give Sky and me a more varied schedule. The shop is only open from one p.m. to nine. There's not enough morning traffic to justify opening earlier and I'm not a morning person."

"Amen to that," I said. Mornings and me weren't friends these days either. "Just give me a few days to learn the ropes and I can handle it."

"You okay with him?" Tim asked Micah like I wasn't there.

"I'm fine. Alex made a huge sale yesterday, over $1000 and I wasn't even there. I think he's going to work out fine. Let me go grab the stuff for the shop." He darted back to that mysterious hidden wall closet again, and pulled open a door, and then dragged out a half-dozen boxes. "Sorry there's so much. I haven't had a chance to walk any of it over."

"No worries. We've plenty of room in the car. Do you want me to put it in the storeroom so you can decide where it goes?" Tim asked.

"Yes, please. Thank you for helping out." Micah rubbed at his eyes. Since he'd been up texting people, he must have gotten up earlier and gone back to sleep. Brad and Tim trekked across the room and began stacking up boxes. Tim passed Jet, and Jet hissed at him.

"Back at you, little brat," Tim said. "Should have left you in the gutter that day I found you."

"Hush," Brad said. "He's a sweetheart. Just picky is all." He was allowed to pet Jet as he passed. Interesting.

The second pot of coffee finished, and I refilled my cup leaving some for Micah. He retrieved another cup and doctored up his own, leaning beside me at the counter and breathing in the smell before taking a long drag.

"What time do you think you'll be in to the shop?" Tim asked.

"I'll try to be there by five. I'll text you if I'm running late. The tour isn't until nine, and Sky will be there by three, so I have some time."

"Okay, see you later," Tim said, his gaze flicking to me again but he and Brad left without any fanfare.

"That was the ex?" I asked. "Great cock and all?"

Micah laughed lightly into his mug. "He can be a dick for sure, but Brad's a good kid. Tim is all right. He's a little bitter that he's in his mid-thirties and still has a desk job. He answers phones for a car insurance company."

"But you both made money on the videos, right?"

"Not so much the videos but the subscribers who sent us tips. We made a lot, really. Tim is not good with saving money. He's got a big house outside the city, a really nice car, and all the latest in electronics any computer geek could want."

"And a new boy toy to support," I pointed out.

"Yeah, there's that too."

"Are you okay with that? Him and Brad?"

Micah shrugged. "We didn't fit anymore. It wasn't personal. Tim is very reliable and nice. I trust him with the shop and he takes good care of Brad. Brad is a good kid, nice to everyone, sweet even while being a bit of a sex addict."

"You didn't fit anymore because of your disappearance?"

He was silent for a minute and I worried he'd get mad, but he nodded. "Yeah, maybe? I think it was more about what happened to him when I was missing than how I might have changed. The police, the media, even my family treated him like he was a killer. They were all certain he'd murdered me and hid my body somewhere." Micah let out a long sigh. "When he showed up at the police station in Reno... he was quiet, shut off emotionally, and bitter."

"Bitter that people treated him like crap while everyone thought you were dead?" It made sense, even if it sounded horrible. I couldn't imagine being treated the same way, accused of hurting someone important to me, only to have that person show up unharmed and prove them all wrong. "None of that was your fault."

"It doesn't matter. Pain comes in many forms and often makes a lasting impression."

"Do you remember anything about the time you went missing?"

Micah glanced my way, his eyes narrowed like he was hiding something, but I'd had a lot of time in the Middle East to learn body language and facial expressions. Searching for suicide bombers had made me wary of everyone. "Not really."

"The book said you were gone a couple months. Vanished from Chicot Park here and wound up in Reno?"

He nodded.

"I'm sure you've been questioned a million times about it. How about you share what you want to, and I don't ask?"

"I don't really want to talk about it at all. It feels like another lifetime ago. Everything. From before, to the day I simply showed up in Reno. I'd rather be who I am now."

Okay. That was something I understood. "If you need to talk, I'm willing to listen. No judgment. Been through my own shit, but I'm not going to push."

Micah gave me the ghost of a smile. "Thanks."

"I need to join your Facebook page, look at some of these ghost pictures people have taken to get ready for your tour tonight. Do you normally see stuff on the tours? Am I going to freak out?"

"I never see anything. Instead I point people toward areas that are known hotspots."

"None of the pictures are ever yours?"

"I'm too busy telling everyone stories to be taking pictures."

I took another big sip of the coffee and suddenly remembered the middle of the night noises. "It's bright out," I said.

"It is," he agreed.

"Captain Obvious, right? Can we talk about those noises?"

He looked at me, gaze searching my face for something. "Maybe it was a dream."

"I only dream of my time serving." I set the cup down on the counter. "Please don't tell me it's all in my head. I'm really tired of hearing that."

Micah sighed. "Lukas wouldn't want me putting stuff in your head."

"He's my brother, not my keeper." Except he sort of was. I sighed. "Can't you be straight with me?"

He gave me a wicked grin, the sort of thing I recalled from a handful of his videos, then stepped into my personal space and cupped my face with his hands. "Straight?" He inquired and kissed me lightly on the lips. "Is that what you really want from me?"

And of course, my dick was like oh hell no, it had a list of what it wanted from him, the fucking traitor. "You know I'm attracted to you, so that's not fair. I'm wondering if this is one more thing that makes me nuts." I pulled away from him.

"If I heard the same things would that make me crazy? Or simply validate that you're not crazy, but that there is something neither of us can explain that makes scary noises in the middle of the night? Is there really a right answer to this?"

I stared at him, thinking through all the scenarios. He was right, of course. Either we were both nuts, or something had been making noises in the dark. And wasn't that equally as terrifying, maybe even more so than actually being crazy?

"Managing the shop helps," Micah said, sipping his coffee. "People don't look at me like I'm broken because they assume I'm acting all dark and mysterious to bring in business."

"You're not broken."

"But aren't we all? Even if it's in small ways, the world shatters our exterior, cracks the shields we put up and sometimes allows something else to burrow inside. Those of us who look more put together? We have more cracks than most. You, who admit to being broken? Your cracks are big, sure enough, but few and mending them is easier when there aren't so many." He turned to stare out the window. "You're not crazy, Alex. The world is full of unexplainable things only because we haven't found a way to explain them. If you think of it that way, it's less scary."

"You have no idea what I saw in that desert..." My heart began to race just thinking about it.

"What if you let it go? Stop trying to reason through the whys and hows, but accept it as something that happened?" Micah asked. "Not everything in life has an explanation. In fact, most things don't. The memories will never completely vanish, but they might fade, and have less power over you."

"Is that what you have done with your disappearance?"

"Yes," Micah admitted. "It was either wallow in it or learn to live. I haven't been all that successful since I buried myself in work, but I'm hoping to change that and find a life again."

"You mean dating as well?"

"Yes. Everything. Going out and enjoying myself. Having sex. Maybe finding love. There's more to life than the job and distraction."

"Finding a life again would be nice," I agreed, liking his definition. Outside of the mental hospitals and couch surfing, learning to live sounded great. Was it an achievable dream? Or another delusion my brain wanted to cling to? "But as much as I'm attracted to you, we can't. You're my boss. That's a no-no in any culture. No matter how attracted I am to you."

"Lukas is your boss, not me."

I blinked at him. "I don't work for Lukas."

"You do, actually. Technically, I do too. Without him my visa would be up, and I'd have to go back to Japan. Immigration laws in this country really suck."

I gaped at him. "What? How? Lukas?"

"He's a silent partner for Simply Crafty. Helped me get the loan for the retail space and all the permits for the tours. New Orleans has laws about residency and shop ownership. Lukas has been here almost a decade and has residency as well as citizenship, so Lukas owns fifty-one percent to my forty-nine percent.

"Wait," I said. "Wait. So you didn't give me a job. My brother gave me a job."

"He's a silent partner. Doesn't really do anything business related other than collect a check and help pay some bills. I needed help at the shop and he asked if I could make it work for you. If knowing that helps me not feel like your boss, that's great. I want you to be comfortable."

I stepped away from him, feeling... something I couldn't quite define. Anger? Betrayal? Treated like a child? Was I that broken? Did Lukas expect so little from me that he had to be the one to give me work?

"Alex?"

"Sorry. I need a minute, okay? I'm sorting through a lot of stuff right now," I said. I felt his eyes on me, but needed to get my head straight first. Was I mad at him? Kind of. But what for? Had he really done anything wrong? He'd never interviewed me, let me walk along blissfully unaware that his benevolence was really my brother's. I'd never asked for all the details. Not his fault. But I couldn't help but be angry with him for bursting my hopes that I was finally getting set on the right path because I'd earned it, not just because of Lukas. I stalked to the chair and my stuff, then began pulling my clothes back on.

"Alex?" Micah asked.

"I'm not a little kid."

"I never suggested you were."

"I quit," I told him as I dug through the bag to find my wallet and phone. When I checked the phone there was not a damn word from my brother. So much for him picking me up in the morning. I had scathing things to say to him, but it was a bad idea. This whole thing was a bad idea. Hell, living some days was a bad idea.

"Alex, I didn't mean to upset you."

"No. I'm sure you didn't. But that's okay. We've just met, right? I kept thinking that it was all okay because I know you. But I don't really. You're some guy I watched on a video once. I overstepped by thinking we were friends. I forget that this world isn't about friends. Should have learned that at war when we suspected everyone, but I'm broken..."

"Alex."

"Thanks, Micah. It was nice meeting you. I hope things work out for your tour thing. It's probably not the best fit for me anyway since my brother doesn't want me entertaining any ideas that paranormal stuff is real." I left then, not daring to look back because I could feel the sting of tears in my eyes. Trust was hard. I'd trusted Lukas. I wanted to trust Micah, and now I wasn't sure where to turn.

I walked through Micah's garden, glancing over the area for any sign of what might have made the noise the night before, but everything was still and calm. Another fucked up memory I didn't need.

CHAPTER 10

The walk to Lukas' place took an hour because I got lost three times. Stupid Quarter all looked the same. I thought hard while I walked of a thousand things to say, or other work options, maybe I'd go home. Mom and dad still lived in the same house I grew up in. Mom loved the neighborhood, but worked long shifts as a nurse and was rarely home. Dad had trouble keeping a job, not because he wasn't a hard worker, but because the world was rigged against men of color, and he'd never gone to college. My mom hadn't cared. As kids we never cared. It wasn't until we hit our teens that the world opened our eyes to how narrow it was. He had been a mechanic for a few years until degrees and computers ousted him, now he mostly worked minimum wage retail.

Lukas and I had been lucky to be born white enough to pass. Outside of our hometown we could take advantage of that privilege. If I went back, I'd fall right back into the cesspool of hate that had me joining the army as soon as I was old enough in order to escape it. And look where that had taken me.

I'd been homeless two months after getting out of the army before a flashback had landed me in the psych ward. Two months on the street had been hell. The gnawing hunger in my gut. Constant fear that someone would steal the little I had, begging for scraps from strangers, and battling the demons in my head left me broken. It was hard to believe I'd been out almost a year. Free from the horror, back in the world with the knowledge to build a bomb or slaughter a group of teenage boys indoctrinated to murder, but couldn't get a job running a register or waiting tables. No skills, they told me, even after Lukas had given me an address and clothing so I didn't look like a hobo.

And didn't that all just burn. Pride. Wow. Something else I'd thought I'd lost in that desert. Only there it was, rearing its ugly head and demanding bullshit. When Lukas had come to visit in the psych ward and asked if I wanted a chance to start over, I'd jumped at it. I thought that I had no pride left to batter or bruise by accepting the charity of others, even if it was only my brother, but there it was. Fucking hell.

I stood at the base of the stairs that led up to Lukas' place and wondered why. Why I bothered? Why had I even lived that day? Why had I been spared? To be some slob living on my brother's couch?

With the clothes on my back and five bucks in my wallet I'd get real far on my own, wouldn't I? Maybe I would be better off if I checked myself back in. Though the sad fact of that was that even as a ward of the state, I could wait months to be put in some sort of house or facility other than the hospital. Overcrowded, and ignored, the crazy fell through the cracks. They tried a dozen meds to make me sane, all making me worse, adding akathisia, to hallucinations, to projectile vomiting, and nothing touched the depression.

"Crazy," I grumbled to myself. "Just like thinking some ex-porn star would ever want anything to do with you. No wonder his ex looked at me like I was dirt." I sat down on the stairs as I realized I didn't have a key to get into Lukas' place, though I knew I'd had one before going to the police station last night. Maybe I'd left it in the bag at Micah's.

"Fuck," I swore again. Angry at everything. Myself mostly, for being so damn worthless.

The overcast sky chose that moment to open up and down-pour. Fabulous.

I sat in the rain, hunched over, trying to protect my phone. The phone Lukas had given me, paid for, and even programmed. I sent him an angry text: *You bastard. I hate you. Why didn't you tell me I was working for you?*

I waited a while for a reply or for the rain to stop. Neither happened. Then I sent: *I don't have my key to get in... it's raining.* I sent it even though it sounded whiny to me.

The door opened at the top of the stairs and Lukas looked down on me, his eyes bloodshot. He looked tired, a deep-down bone-weariness that I'd been seeing a lot on his face since I arrived in his life. Coincidence? Maybe not.

I jolted upright, eager to get out of the rain. He held the door for me. I thought about punching him, yelling at him or something, but instead I entered the apartment and put my phone on his kitchen counter.

He closed the door. I could feel his eyes on me, but the room blurred. I shivered as the air-conditioning cooled the rain drenching my skin and clothes. Lukas reached out for my shoulder and turned me to face him. I wanted to be mad, rage and scream out all my frustration, but he wrapped me up in his arms and hugged me tight while I sobbed into his shoulder. The stress of the flashback always fucked with my head, making it hard to know which way was up. I was floundering, and that meant I said and did stupid things.

"I'm sorry," I kept saying over and over, although I wasn't sure what for. Being me, maybe. It wasn't the first time he stood witness over my tears. Hell, not even the hundredth time. It was what Lukas did, took care of me. And man, I felt so bad about that, about always being a burden to him.

"Can we talk about it?" Lukas asked after a while.

I pulled away. "About what? All the lies?"

"I have not once lied to you."

"Like you found me a job working for Micah, but I'm not really?"

"I said working with Micah. With, not for. It's not my fault if you don't hear what I say to you. He does all the business management. Makes the schedules, does all the training, and you'd call him if you were too sick to go in. I simply own a large virtual share of his shop so he can stay here. I actually thought the two of you would be a good fit."

I glared at him. "How are we a good fit? An ex-porn star and a broken toy soldier? We couldn't be more different."

"Don't give me that self-pity bullshit. You're only as broken as you allow yourself to be." Lukas said. When I started to interrupt, he held up a hand. "No, we're not debating this again. You think you're crazy. I don't agree."

"Seeing shadow men tear apart your entire base isn't crazy?"

"No," Lukas said flatly. "Do I understand it? No. Do you? No. Do you need to understand it to heal? I don't think so. What you need is to accept that there are things out there that defy explanation. Encountering them doesn't make you crazy. It might make you confused, but not crazy. You focus on that because of all the damn therapists. That's why I insisted on a new one when I brought you here. Someone who focuses on changing how you react to things rather than how you perceive things. Do you understand that?"

"I don't know..." I answered honestly. "I'm not sure what to believe anymore."

"Right! They did that to you with their drugs and supposed

therapy. Telling you to question what you saw, what you felt, what you knew, telling you it's all false. I think you see shit fine, but then you go and panic if you think what you see might not be the norm. There's no prize for being normal, Alex. If there is even such a thing as normal," Lukas said. He ran his hands through his hair making it stick up in ways I knew would drive him nuts if anyone else were to see. "I'm so tired. From the job and dealing with all your stuff."

"I never wanted to be a burden to you." I'd actually thought I'd be in the military for life. It was easy following orders day in and day out. Breaks between were hard, when I had to find ways to socialize and have so much down time, I didn't know what to do with it.

"You're not a burden. Fuck. I don't know why you didn't show up on my doorstep the day you got out. No, I had to find out almost a year later you were in a psych ward after mom and dad were asked if they wanted to take over your care or give up your freedom. You're not a kid. You're not nuts, and they were going to lock you away forever. No crime committed. Why would you let them?"

"It felt safer there."

"Safer from what? Yourself? Us? The world?"

I shrugged, not really having the answer to that.

Lukas sighed. "You need someone. Not me, not mom or dad. You need someone to take care of and to take care of you. I wanted you to have someone, something, to focus on. Micah is a good fit."

Was he nuts? "You're trying to set him up with me? Not only a job, but like a relationship?"

"Physical attraction is a good start, and I know you're already attracted to him. Plus you have a lot in common."

"Like what? We're both nuts? We both hear screaming in the dark?"

Lukas frowned. "Huh? When?"

"At his house at three a.m. He told me to go to sleep because if I thought too hard about it, the screaming would get worse. Does that sound like someone you want me with? Someone who might be as crazy as I am?" And that was the kicker wasn't it? I'd had a few moments of thinking maybe we did have that in common, not in the same way, but something from his disappearance that changed him in a similar way that I'd been changed. Our eyes opened even if we didn't want them to be.

"I thought two lonely people might find something in common," Lukas said.

"He doesn't seem lonely to me. He has Sky, Tim, and Brad for starters."

"Whom he keeps at arm's length." Lukas shook his head. "He may be sexually uninhibited, but he's very careful with his emotions. A good showman, but rarely giving anyone a true look at what he's feeling. Always has been, even before... And the disappearance only made it worse."

"You knew him before?"

"Not really. The Micah you meet now is very different from the little boy who went hiking with his boyfriend and vanished in the woods. Brad is more like Micah was. I only knew him because Micah and Tim volunteered at the gay youth center. That's where I met Sky too, though she wasn't a volunteer, she was a kid in need. But that was after... the search. It was tough you know?" Lukas said.

He sat down hard on the couch, and I sank to the floor at his feet. "We all responded to the search, nearly every cop in the state. Combed the area for weeks, going through it over and again. Nothing. Not a damn trace. People don't just vanish like that. Not in a forest."

"Micah said everyone treated Tim really badly."

Lukas nodded. "Of course. He was a suspect. Micah's

boyfriend, older by a decade, and collecting money for a porn channel starring the young, hot, and barely legal boyfriend? Plus being gay put him on a lot of old cop's radars. But nothing fit. It was the middle of the day. The group was together. They turned down a bend, Micah at the back of the group since he wasn't used to hiking, and he was gone. No clothing, tracks, or anything left behind."

"He says he doesn't remember it."

"Same song and dance he's been telling for years."

"You don't believe him?"

"I think he remembers more than he's willing to share, but since what he remembers doesn't make sense..." he deliberately paused, "he hides what he does remember. I went with Tim to collect him from Reno. He came home and the whole thing seemed to start all over. Everyone asking questions, demanding answers. Micah was thin, missing his shoes and socks, but wearing the same clothes he'd vanished in. It was bizarre. He was treated like a criminal for vanishing, and everything fell apart. Him and Tim's relationship, the channel, the money, and he was on the verge of having to go home."

"That was a bad thing? He made it sound like his parents were supportive."

"Of their kid being a porn star? Is anyone? If he went home, he'd have to become a teacher like his parents or find some other trade. Honor is still a real thing in Japan. Especially family honor. I've met his father, he's very traditionally Japanese. Micah is really creative and a bit scattered. He was doing one of those cosplay boudoir channels when he met Tim online. Making his own costumes and posing in sexy ways for paying fans. He doesn't do that anymore, but he has new projects all the time. Those are the things that make him happy, not technology and rule books set by family expectations." Lukas looked at me. "Sounds like someone else I know."

"I'm not crafty at all," I said, thinking back to Tim's comment about how Micah found time to do all that stuff. Candles, shawls, blankets. The loft craft area made sense when I realized that Micah used it to make things to sell in his shop. He said it was stress relief, and maybe part of it was.

"Right? 'Cause who built the tree fort out of those old barn pieces?"

It had lasted a couple summers. I was surprised he remembered it as we'd been kids.

"Then there was that Comic Con you went to when we were teens? The one where you became Optimus Prime by taping together and painting cardboard boxes? And who can dissect any weapon and put it back together in new and interesting ways? Do I have to remind you of a letter you wrote about receiving a reprimand for reconstructing pieces from broken weapons into the parts to fix a coffee pot?"

"Coffee is essential," I said. The Optimus Prime thing had been inspired even if it had broken the first day and I'd spent the entire con weekend gluing parts of it back together.

"My *point*," Lukas said, "is that you're just as creative. Mind always working, thinking, analyzing. I think that's why the rules of the military worked for you, as you could follow orders and still let your mind wander. It was a job that didn't take you away from having the freedom to think. Not everyone can do that. You needed someone else to set the rules so you could actually commit to them. Now you need another project, and maybe you haven't found your craft yet."

"You make me sound flighty."

Lukas looked at me incredulously. "No way? You think?"

"Asshole." Okay, I was a little flighty.

"Tell me about these noises?"

I shrugged. "Started off sounding like some weird monkey.

Then like an animal screaming in pain. I didn't see anything when I left, but I was sort of in a mood."

"Your flashbacks make you snippy," Lukas agreed. "But at least you realized it sooner this time."

"I will have to apologize to Micah. And I already quit, so I guess I'm back to the unemployment center again."

"How about you talk to him? Tell him that you were being a whiny bitch and really do want to work with him."

"I said not nice things."

"I'm sure he's heard worse." Lukas sighed. "You know after he came back," Lukas waved his hand like all the details were out there but he didn't want to rehash them. "Was found, or whatever. He'd moved into a tiny apartment not far from here, and called in a report of hearing screams. Early morning. A half dozen callouts over the next few weeks and no one found anything. The cops joked that his place was haunted. There's a lot of joking like that in this city. Other's commented that his disappearance had made him crazy, hearing shit in the dark and all that. He moved; same thing happened. He stopped calling the police. No one else ever heard what he did, but I checked in, even stayed over a time or two to see if I'd hear anything."

"You didn't?"

"No."

"But everywhere he lives he hears screaming?" That made no sense.

"I don't think it's always the same. It doesn't even happen every night anymore. When I stayed, he woke me up when he heard it, but nothing else happened. I didn't hear it at all." Lukas rested his head on the back of the couch for a minute to stare down at me. "Sky's heard stuff when she stays with him."

"And you believe Sky, but not Micah?"

"I believe all of you," Lukas said. "How many times do I have to tell you that I believe you. Not that my belief changes anything. Would I have seen the same things you did? Probably not. That guy Timothy, that Micah used to date, stayed over a million times at Micah's, says he's never heard a thing. Does that mean Micah is lying? Or is he just experiencing something that not all of us have access to?"

"I'm so confused right now."

"Yeah I get that, and emotionally drained. I can see it on your face. You don't manage stress well. I thought that this job would be low stress, some bullshitting customers and walking around the Quarter. Easy peasy." Lukas said.

"I didn't plan for a dead body."

"No one ever does," Lukas said. "How about you take a shower and get dry. You're shivering like a leaf. There's bacon in a bag in the fridge, maybe make yourself a sandwich. You're still so thin."

I wrapped my arms around myself feeling a lot like that homeless guy stuck in the ward that Lukas had come to see only to get mad because he thought they weren't feeding me. "I'm okay." Okay, that was a lie. "I should apologize to Micah."

"He sent me a text. I was wondering when you'd make it back home or text me. He wanted to make sure you were okay. Said you seemed very upset and he was really sorry that he caused you all this trouble."

"Um, I'm pretty sure the trouble started on my first day of work. Coincidence?"

"Or perhaps the meeting of two powerful forces in the universe."

I glared at Lukas. "When did you get so corny?"

"I think it was in the fourth grade when you told me you had a crush on Hayden Louis and were so mad that he was dating Sherry Matthews. You wanted me to try to date her so she wouldn't date him anymore. We pretended for months that Sherry was dating me and Hayden you. I got really good at role-play and corny lines about how Hayden thought your eyes reflected rainbows or some bullshit."

I gaped at him. "How do you even remember this stuff? What about this morning? You were supposed to pick me up," I reminded him. "Convenient time for your memory to stop working."

"I thought you'd be sexing up the porn star."

I wanted to. Badly. "I don't think we fit."

"Use more lube."

I choked on my own spit trying to find a reply to that.

"Hey you said you woke up twice... once in the middle of the night and then this morning, but didn't mention another flashback."

"Because I didn't have one."

Lukas looked me over, his gaze telling me a thousand things at once. "You came up swinging the entire first week you were here. Flashbacks nightly, the next morning a bear. Unfamiliar place, I think you told me."

"I'd just gotten out of a mental prison," I said and shrugged. "I was a little messed up."

"And one night with Micah and no nightmares, flashbacks, or waking up cussing all of humanity?" Lukas quirked a brow at me.

"It doesn't mean anything. I was tired. Had a stressful night."

"Yep," Lukas agreed while his posture said he knew I was being purposely obtuse. "Which usually makes you worse."

"What do you want me to say? That there's something about him? That he told me go to sleep and I did? That his presence relaxes me?" All while turning me on. And wasn't that all pure truth. Fuck. "What about you and Sky? Maybe we should prod at that relationship for a while."

Lukas laughed. "Right, 'cause you have room to give me

relationship advice? Go. Shower, food, and once you're human again we'll talk. Fuck, I'm so tired. Maybe we both could use a nap."

"Don't we need to talk about the case?"

"No. I'm not lead detective on it because you're involved and the department is a little pissed at me."

"Why?"

"Because while Micah was wrapped around you to keep you from getting shot, I was standing in their line of fire. Not all cops are that jumpy, but there are a handful that would rather have shot you and worried about the consequences later. Didn't matter that you weren't actually a threat to anyone. We need de-escalation training back, badly."

I stared at Lukas wondering in that moment how I'd been so blessed and cursed to have a brother like him. Protecting me from death and setting me up with an ex-porn star of whom I used to be a fan was something special. And his deviousness knew no bounds.

"Detective McKnight is very professional, by the book, and careful. He's had no complaints against him that have stuck, and does seem to get the answers we need. Did you tell him everything you saw?" Lukas asked.

Not really. As I didn't talk about the shadow at all. "Mostly," I admitted.

Lukas narrowed his eyes. "What did you see?"

I threw my hands in the air. "I don't know. I can't explain it and as you so often point out, I don't need to understand it."

"But what did you see?"

"A shadow," I said. "It reached for Micah. I pushed him away and it hit me instead. That's when I blacked out."

"Was this the same type of shadow as what you saw in the desert?"

Was it? No. This had been less defined. Weaker maybe? Or

just different. "No. I don't know how to explain it. I mean there were some similarities I think, but it felt very different... weaker, I guess."

Lukas sighed and said, "But you didn't see the body, right?"

"No. Not that I can recall. Just the animals..." That was enough of a bad memory even as vague as it was. At least all I'd seen had been a glimpse.

"Good. I'd rather you not have that as fodder for nightmares."

"I've seen plenty of dead bodies in my life," I defended.

"And how many of them still give you nightmares?"

A lot actually.

"That's what I thought," Lukas said, obviously reading the expression on my face. "Forget about bodies, focus on your new job."

"You want me to sleep with the cosplay boy toy." My body agreed with that idea too.

"Yep. You know you want to. Plus if you're both weird, what could be a better fit? Go shower, you're a hot mess and have nothing to show for it."

"I'm not weird," I said as I stalked to the shower thinking a thousand uncharitable things about my brother on the way. Lukas's only response was to laugh. Bastard.

CHAPTER 11

We actually ended up in his bed, which would have sounded kinky except that as twins we'd always been that way. Curling up together, even as teens. It wasn't sexual, more a comfort thing. Lukas needed sleep, and I needed to rest my brain in the safe proximity of someone I trusted. He told me he texted Micah that we'd both be taking a few hours of reprieve from peopling. I hadn't planned to actually fall asleep. Instead, lying beside Lukas, with my eyes closed and meditating, focusing on pushing aside the negative and focusing on numbers. Which is why I fell asleep.

The smell of spicy sausage and frankincense woke me up with my stomach growling. I opened my eyes to Lukas' bedroom, but with Micah sitting on the bed beside me, crocheting something. I think it was crochet as it was one hook thing instead of a couple of needles. My mom had done a little of both when we were kids. One of the guys on my second tour with me had been a knitter, whipping those two needles around in a frenzy that instead of having the team tease him, they joked about how he was some sort of ninja with them. He'd been very adamant about the fact that he was a knitter, not a crocheter. Though to this day I still wasn't sure why it was such a big deal.

I rolled onto my back and stared up at Micah.

"I programmed my number into your phone," he said. "And there's food out in the kitchen. Lukas had to go into work. He wanted you to eat, ordered you something before he left."

While I was shocked by the lack of nightmares from falling asleep again, I wondered at his presence.

"Are you feeling better? Lukas says the stress from last night really threw you off, and that I shouldn't take your quitting as fact." He glanced my way. "You left your key in the bag. It's out on the counter."

I studied his face, wondering a thousand things and where to begin. "Why would you still want to work with me?" I wanted to know.

He hesitated for a minute, his hands moving faster, creating some sort of magic that seemed to spit out rows of something, a shawl perhaps. "If we go on the walking tour, and I say I feel something, people take pictures in that direction. They don't really see anything until the pictures show them something. None of them feel the same things I do. They need the camera to *see* something."

I let those words process for a minute. "So you're saying you may not see ghosts or whatever, but you can feel them there?"

Micah frowned, staring intently at his work. "Yes? No? I'm not sure. I've never really talked about it before because everyone looks at me like I'm crazy. Even Sky and Lukas who have been on tour with me a half dozen times."

"But Sky has heard stuff while staying in your house at night? Lukas told me."

"I think that's different. That one, whatever it is, seeks me out." He shivered. "I don't go looking for it. The stuff on the tour... well I usually walk the route beforehand, find places that feel... different, and take the tour that way."

Well that would make for a pretty awesome ghost tour if Micah could sense where they were, though he said he didn't believe in ghosts. "What do you think you feel? Ghosts?"

"I'm not a believer in ghosts. I think whatever is after all of this," he paused to wave his hand over us, "is something more? Perhaps a higher plane of existence? What I feel doesn't make me think of people. Not in the same way. More like something else?" He sighed. "A lot of voodoo practitioners talk about veils and the weakness between dimensions, so maybe it's something from across the veil, if that is a thing. Sometimes it feels very faint. Other times it's so intense I can almost hear them talking to me, but they never feel like people."

"How do you feel them?"

"It's hard to explain. Like it starts in my stomach and then turns to jitters sometimes, or even a tingling on my skin. Like ants." He frowned. "Or bugs crawling." He glanced my way. "Do you think I'm crazy?"

"No," I didn't. Who was I to judge? "Were you always able to feel them?"

He shook his head. "Not until after the park."

"When you disappeared? Do you really not remember anything?"

"I remember hearing something. I remember seeing some sort of wavy break in the path, like when the day is really hot and the roadway has those heat waves you can see? Only it was in one spot. That's all I really remember. The police and therapists, and everyone say it was a dream."

"You were gone three months. Do you remember anything from that time?"

"Sometimes I dream of stuff. I don't know if any of that is real or stuff my head thought up," Micah admitted.

That was a lot like what was in my head. Had what I'd seen really been what I now dream? Or had my brain expanded it somehow? "Was what you heard similar to what you hear at night?"

He put the crochet down and stared into the distance for a minute. "Sometimes, yes. I'm not sure if the thing that comes at night is mimicking what I heard to scare me, or it really is the same thing. I don't want to know."

No wonder it scared him so much. If he went out into the darkness would it take him again? Had he escaped it somehow and now it followed him waiting for the right time? If it had taken him in broad daylight the first time, why not now? Maybe it was toying with him, enjoying making him afraid. That idea made me shiver.

We sat in silence for a few minutes, and he started his crocheting again. Stress relief, he'd called it. I could see that.

"Lukas said you've experienced stuff that can't exactly be explained. So I thought that maybe you would understand and not look at me like I'm pretending or eccentric," he said after a few minutes.

"I'm not sure what I saw." Not in the desert and not last night. "It was scary. That's all I'm sure of."

He nodded. "Sometimes when I prepare for a tour, I feel something that isn't right. Not in the way of 'there is something there that others might feel,' but something that makes me... afraid? Worried? Anxious? I'm not quite sure. Usually I change my route to avoid those spots."

"You didn't walk the cemetery before we went."

He shrugged. "I never feel anything in the cemetery. I think it's because I've always thought that who would want to hang around a place like that? If it is the dead or some higher consciousness, I'd think they'd want to listen to the musicians in the Quarter, or hang around the fun pop-up shops, or take a carriage ride. Anything would be better than hanging around a bunch of stone buildings which very few people are allowed to visit."

And that made sense. If I were dead, I probably wouldn't want to hang around a cemetery. "You never see anything. You feel it?"

"Yes. I mean sometimes I feel it so strongly that I worry any second something will pop up for me to see. Like last night in the cemetery when we got close to that new burial. I could feel something." He put the crocheting down again. "You said you saw a shadow."

"I guess? It came through the tomb, reached for you. It wasn't a reflection from your light. Didn't move that way. But I couldn't make out much before it hit me." It felt odd to tell anyone what I'd seen. Probably because I'd spent too long trying to bury those feelings, memories, and thoughts.

"It made you afraid?"

I sucked in a breath. "Yes. Afraid of what would happen if it touched you. It made me remember that day in the desert when my team died."

"But you don't know if it would have done anything."

"No. It just didn't feel right."

He nodded and started his work again. "Do you still want to quit?"

"Do you want me to?"

He smiled. "Answer a question with a question..."

"You're hard to read," I admitted.

He sighed. "It's habit. To withdraw. To keep people away."

"So how about you be plain with me? Lukas wants us to be a couple, not only to work together. I'm not sure if he told you that, but I really don't believe in pretending. I'm attracted to you, but nothing has to come of that. I'm not sure I'm whole enough to offer anyone anything in a relationship."

"Your brother is not subtle. I know his thoughts on us, and I'm not sure about all that. He has been talking you up for a while, even before you left the military. And I do find you attractive as well. But I'm not going to force the issue. I can get sex easily enough, but I want more than that. I want someone who is a friend and a partner. And I want someone who doesn't think I'm crazy or is annoyed by all my quirks, but maybe enjoys hot sex in regular intervals."

That comment made my dick stand up and wave. "Fuck," I grumbled. "Stupid body."

He looked at me, a brow quirked.

"I'm getting the 'hey, hello' from my traitorous dick again, don't mind me. I don't wake up with morning wood anymore, but apparently you say the right thing and it's like 'Let's go!'"

He laughed. It was a soft thing that I could really enjoy, smooth and rich, like a fine wine, with a bite of bitterness at the end as if he were a bit self-deprecating. "I like the idea of having someone in my life, even if we only work together, who maybe sees things a little differently."

"Someone else as crazy as you are?" I teased. "'Cause I've been called crazy for the stuff I saw in the desert."

"Not crazy. More aware, I think. People in general, often seem to sense something. Not everyone, as some people are completely self-absorbed. But I think even guys like Lukas, who are by the book and very fact oriented, often sense things. They call it gut instinct or whatever, but it's something. I think of myself as more sensitive to those instincts. Perhaps you even more so than me."

I thought about that for a while. It was a bit like what the guy Jared had said in the shop yesterday. Maybe my brain was simply wired different.

"You saw Mark's body?" I wanted to know, thinking in that moment he didn't really need that memory either.

"Just a foot."

I thought about that in a dozen ways at first. Just a foot. Nothing attached? "It was bad?" I'd seen enough blown up body parts in my lifetime to be okay with never seeing another.

"Didn't make sense at first. My brain was trying to put together what I was seeing, but it wasn't falling into place. Then you grabbed me. You wrapped your arms around me like a vice, holding me against you. If you hadn't, I probably would have seen more."

"But no Sarah?" Not Sarah's foot. I tried to recall if I'd even noticed what she'd been wearing on her feet. He probably would have noticed if the foot was more feminine? Smaller? Still in a shoe? Those were questions I didn't want to voice.

"I didn't see anyone else. Not until the police came. They took the guard away in an ambulance and another group of cops started screaming at you. I didn't know what else to do. You weren't doing anything wrong, and you were hurt. I tried to talk to them, but they were unreasonable. I'm grateful that Lukas arrived as quickly as he did or they might have shot both of us."

"Thank you," I said.

"It's part of my training to know how to react to mental health issues. Saw videos on the full audio and video flashbacks. They always say not to touch you, but I didn't want the cops to do something stupid, then you grabbed me and held on, telling me you'd keep me safe. Did you save the guy you remembered?"

"Yeah, I think so. They never let me talk to him afterward. He'd been a tent mate. One of half a dozen who all bunked in the same tent on rotation. I don't really remember much about him other than his name."

"But he's alive because you held on to him."

I had kept the storm from eating him. Funny thought that was. He'd been trying to get to it the whole time, following the pull of whatever, like Odysseus to the sirens. I had felt it too, heard the call, telling me to come, the offer of a million impossible fulfilled promises. Yet I'd stayed planted in the tent, watching helpless as the others climbed over us, exploding into blood and bone seconds later. The last man out I'd grabbed the leg of his pants, held on until I thought my fingers would rip off. All while he'd tried to crawl away. If he'd been of sound mind, he'd have kicked me away, or even turned and punched me in the nose to get me to let go. Same with the man I'd held to the ground with my weight. Both had survived. Though the second man had lost an arm. Funny how the memories came back so vividly when I wasn't trying to focus on them.

"Maybe you can teach me to crochet," I said watching him craft something so easily. "If it works so well for stress relief."

"It's a lot of counting," Micah said.

"I like numbers. It helps my meditation. When I'm having trouble relaxing, I count backward. Is this another shawl?"

"Yes."

"You sell the shawls you make in the shop?"

He smiled at me. It made something in my gut thaw, like maybe we'd be okay. "Prayer shawls. It keeps the church ladies from picketing my store. They come in and say 'look at that nice boy who makes prayer shawls to remind everyone what a temptation the darkness is, he's a good boy.' They have no idea."

I laughed, thinking of old church ladies browsing prayer shawls which were displayed less than two feet from the entrance to the little sex toy dungeon Micah had built. "You're devious."

He shrugged, looking pleased with himself. "The whole Christian thing never worked for me. Too much control and restraint against people being people. I'm gay. I like sex. I've been known to smoke pot and dance naked in the moonlight. Does that make me a bad person? I don't think so."

I thought of him dancing naked in the moonlight and would have liked to see that.

"You're thinking of me naked, aren't you?" he asked.

"Guilty," I admitted. "I'll watch you dance naked any time, but not in my brother's bed." I pointed at the bed.

"You can dance naked with me the next time. We'll do it at my place."

"Sounds like a plan to me." I thought briefly about whatever it was outside his house. Was it safe to be outside at night? That was a silly question as we'd gotten to his place pretty late. "Can you be outside your place at night? Is it a time thing? A place thing?"

"There's a structure," Micah admitted. "Usually after midnight, mostly after three a.m. though I have yet to find any reasonable explanation as to why that is. I've also found that putting stuff in the garden keeps them or it distracted."

"That's why you have zombie gnomes and stuff," I said remembering.

"Sky has picked a bunch of stuff. There are things in the trees to attract birds and fairies." He shook his head. "Not sure if she really believes in fairies or is more along the 'what the hell, it can't hurt' mentality, but whatever. The zombie gnomes are actually from your brother. I think they amuse him and since he doesn't have a lawn, he uses mine. A lot of the gardening is actually what he does on his days off."

For all Lukas's talk about not really being close to Micah, it sure seemed the opposite. "You and him are really not into each other? He has a thing for pretty. You're more than pretty enough for him."

Micah smiled. "I came on to him once. I think it weirded him out as I am firmly in the 'must protect' category. Like a kid brother or something. Not that it's impossible to break out of the role Lukas puts us in, as Sky started off that way too. She's more aggressive than I am. Lukas is also a bit more... formal, I guess? Traditional? It's hard to put into words because to me he feels like some of my father's old work partners. Respectful to the point you wonder if they are thinking bad things about you. Though usually that's just my paranoia. I think it's more that he can never shut the cop off."

"I don't think Lukas thinks bad things about you at all."

Micah shrugged and went back to crocheting. "He doesn't think bad things about you either," he pointed out. "He worries. A lot. Wants you to find solid ground beneath your feet."

"I don't think he can do that for me."

"No. But it helps if you have support from more than one person. Less pressure on Lukas too."

I thought about that for a few minutes. It made sense that growing my circle would give me more support and diffuse some of the tension on the rest. "Is that something you really want? To be part of my circle? Even if it means my troubles sometimes settle on you?"

"That's life, right? We all have troubles. I could use more friends. I know I have a hard time sharing. Maybe if we both do a little bit it will be easier for both of us?"

"Like when you're madly knitting in the bed next to me and I sit here wondering how I can help ease your stress?"

"Crochet," Micah corrected. "I suck at knitting."

"I know it's crochet," I told him, putting a hand on his knee. "I'm teasing a little. So why are you stressed? Last night? The graveyard rescheduling? Would talking about it help?"

He stared into the room for a few seconds like trying to decide how to answer. "I don't know. I feel uneasy. Like there's something coming. I can try to be prepared, which for me means locking down my life. An entire process itself that is broken. But I'm not sure how else to react. What if nothing happens and I'm preparing for nothing? What if something huge happens and my world falls apart again?"

"What if you lean on your friends and let us help you carry some of the worry?" I wondered.

Micah looked at me, his gaze meeting mine. "Do you feel anything weird?"

"I pretty much always feel weird. It's the fact of my existence now."

"But not like doom weird?"

That night I'd felt doom. When I'd watched that strange man-thing walk toward the base through the darkness. That had been growing doom in my gut. Right now, not so much. Worry was a part of my life. But doom, not so much. "Did it start last night? Or sooner?"

"I've had a few incidences in the past few weeks that aren't the norm."

"You've had the feeling before?"

"Yes," he admitted, but looked away.

"When? Did something terrible happen?" I asked before I realized where it was all coming from. "Maybe right before you disappeared?"

"I didn't know what the feeling was then."

"But you had it then? On the trip?"

"It started before we left. I also had it last year when Sky... well she went through something big. I sort of just knew. Went to Lukas for help. Wouldn't have found her in time if I hadn't. I think that day changed all three of us."

This was news to me. What had happened with Sky? The question must have been clear on my face because he shook his head. "Another time," he promised. "It was a while ago, but I think we're still pretty raw. At least Lukas and I. Sky seems to have moved on okay, but she's stronger than most people give her credit for. I think that's why Lukas worries so much about you. He's seen some of the ugliest of people in this world. He wants better things for you."

"I don't think I'm very strong."

"You are," Micah said. "If you weren't you wouldn't still be here. Me either. Sometimes life tests us in ways we never thought would matter, until it does, and we survive. We have to learn to thrive like Sky has. I'm trying. Just not there yet."

I studied him, his seriousness and the tension in his posture. Did he look tired? Was it physically or emotionally? I could tell he wanted badly to thrive, maybe to rise above. Honestly, so did I. Was there a life beyond the memories? There had to be, or else what was the point?

"Then best we get to trying, right?" I said.

Micah gave me a faint smile. "Sure," he agreed.

My stomach grumbled. I got up from the bed and made my way to the kitchen to find the food I could smell. "But food first."

CHAPTER 12

L ukas had ordered me a huge serving of red beans and rice and andouille sausage from my favorite restaurant. Leave it to my brother to keep me fed at least. "Have you eaten?" I called back to Micah. It was well past lunch but not yet three. "I can share." There was enough for at least three people, even if I was super hungry, which I was. I pulled a couple of forks out of the drawer and headed back to the bedroom with the container.

He glanced up from his crocheting like he hadn't heard my question. "Huh?"

"Food," I offered him a fork, and sat down, holding the container open.

"Oh, thanks." He took the fork and stabbed a slice of sausage, nibbling in between his crochet counting.

"What are you thinking about so hard?"

"The tour," he said. "I have a route, but I do try to change it often so as not to have a lot of repeating or people copying me."

"Tell me what to expect on the tour," I prompted as I ate. The food was the best thing about New Orleans in my opinion. Always something new, and a lot of favorites were easy access.

"We do a couple of regular fan favorites, like the dancing

girl at the Bourbon Hotel, Jackson Square and the French ghosts in the fog. Then there are a bunch of smaller areas that are more locally known that I hit up. I avoid two largely popular places: The Upstairs Lounge and the LaLaurie Mansion. Opposite sides of the Quarter. Often, we walk by the LaLaurie Mansion. There are always tours standing around it. It's really popular now that there was a TV show about some of the history. The Lounge, I avoid."

"Why?"

"The Lounge is very sad. It was where a bunch of LGBTQ people died in a deliberately set fire. Even after death they were treated horribly by the police and press. You can still look up some of the really disturbing photos the police took after the fire and let go public with horrible captions in the paper about how they deserved it or something. When I get too close to the building it gives me an overwhelming sense of sadness. I don't know if it's psychological since I know all their stories by heart and have seen the photos a dozen times. Or if their fear and grief still lingers. The LaLaurie Mansion is a whole other nightmare," Micah said.

"I think I heard of the Upstairs Lounge before. In one of those gay history of New Orleans videos I watched right after I moved in with Lukas. I was a bit worried about being dragged out into Jackson Square and burned at the stake for being queer. The pictures were chilling." Not as bad as what I'd seen overseas, but not much was.

"There is still discrimination by some people as most anywhere in the world. Most are friendly enough. There's even a sizable Pride celebration in the summer."

I nodded, having learned a lot of that from Lukas who the department thought was straight, but was likely as queer as I was. "What's the LaLaurie Mansion?" I tried to recall some of the reading I'd done on New Orleans and couldn't remember much other than basic founding facts.

"Lots of stories, some photos, but no one is absolutely positive of the truth. Only that the matriarch of the LaLaurie family was known for torturing black people and killing them. Even after slavery ended, she kept them and tortured them. There are pictures of some chains found in the back of her house. There was a fire once, as actually happens here a lot according to history, and those who were chained up, died. There's a story of the neighbors seeing her chase a servant girl with a knife. The girl jumped from the roof to her death to escape."

"That's lovely," I said, hoping he caught the sarcasm. "Lots of pleasant history here in New Orleans."

Micah shrugged. "It was founded on blood and to this day that vein continues to flow. It's why so many people come here trying to experience something paranormal. They can feel the convergence of ley lines and all the paranormal weirdness gathering like a hurricane building. The LaLaurie Mansion makes my skin crawl to even be across the street from it. In everyday life, I avoid it, taking other streets, and for tours I let them get close and stay back. We never linger long. The new owners have invited me to do a Halloween paranormal thing, but I've turned it down two years in a row. There's no amount of money I would take for setting foot in that house. Even standing close to it makes me feel like my skin is writhing. People often try to stop and ask questions, but I hurry them along as a lot of times getting too close makes me nauseous."

"Wow. Sounds creepy."

"It looks like a normal house from the outside. Sort of like the Sultan's Palace. Big with old architecture, but the Palace doesn't ever feel like much to me."

"I need to research this stuff," I said cramming the last of the rice and beans into my mouth. Micah had eaten the meat, but I was okay with sharing.

"Lots of books in my shop. But you'll probably learn more following me on tours about the little stuff; ghosts in cabs, serial killers, vampires in brothels, and fist fighting prostitutes."

"Fist fighting prostitutes? Will I be defending you from said prostitutes?"

"She's never touched me, though people have pictures of her in the French Market. She's not always there, but I do take people through there a lot as they find her story amusing. In life, she gutted a bunch of men with a butcher knife and there are legends of her demanding people fight her."

I gaped at him. "This town is really full of crazy dead people, isn't it?"

Micah laughed. "Live ones too. Bourbon street at night is always insane. And wait till Mardi Gras. I don't allow people with alcohol in hand on the tour, though it is allowed in open containers on the street. Usually people only try to show up drunk during Mardi Gras, the rest of the time people are sober and ready to be scared with a creepy story."

"Fuck. This city is so weird." I shut the container and thought about the previous day. Stress and me didn't work, but Micah said that wasn't the norm. If it was, he wouldn't still be operating a tiny shop, would he? "If you want me to still work with you, we can try again. Sorry if I wig out on your tour, but you should be warned it might happen."

"Can you tell me if something is bothering you when we're out? If I don't feel it, but somehow it feels dangerous or menacing? I wouldn't want to expose others to that." Micah leaned over to pull a bag up from where it sat beside his feet. He stuffed the crochet in it. "No matter how much of a scare they might think they want."

"Sure. Even if I see knife wielding prostitutes?"

"Especially if you see knife wielding prostitutes."

"But you don't believe in ghosts," I reminded him.

"Their existence persists anyway, whatever they are. Maybe they aren't ghosts but beings from a parallel dimension? Maybe a ghost is really the next stage in evolution for humanity, like a higher presence or something."

"Who hang around where they died?"

He frowned at me. "There is that. I tend to think those specters are really the residue of emotion. As humans we have an overabundance of emotion all the time. Seems only likely that it all goes somewhere instead of completely stopping. The universe could use that energy for something, right?"

"Sounds like some video game stuff to me. Who knows?"

He sighed and looked down at his crochet bag. "I need to bring this home."

"Okay. So let me find some comfortable clothes for this awful soup we call weather and we can walk this route of yours," I agreed.

"You don't have to walk me home. We can meet at the shop and then go the route."

"Nah, I need to get more familiar with the city. Can't do that if I'm only walking a half a block. And I'm excited about the tour. I also got a little lost finding my way home from your place earlier..."

"It's only a few blocks."

"Took me over an hour and a dozen wrong turns I'm sure. So it's probably best if I can see your tour during the day, maybe help get my bearings."

"Yeah?"

"Sure. We don't go in any of these places, right? It's only a walking street tour?"

"Correct."

"Then I think we're good. I'll tell you if I see any creepies and you tell me if you feel any crawlies." I got up and headed into Lukas' closet to find something to wear. I only had a handful of things that I'd gotten from a second hand store for cheap. Most of Lukas' things would fit, but his clothes were all stuffy detective. How did he not melt in this heat? "It's so damn hot outside."

"It will turn cold soon. The rain is usually the trigger. One day you're sweltering in the heat and humidity, then you're drowning in icy rain. You can wear shorts, if you want," Micah added. "I'm not picky about the shop. Though I'd prefer you wear a T-shirt from the shop."

"The one I got yesterday was Lukas's. I don't know if he has more." I found a pair of shorts in a bottom drawer and another drawer was filled with random T-shirts. A lot of which were from Simply Crafty. "Well what do you know?" I picked a shirt that read: 'Do I look like I speak fluent ghost to you?' It was black with white writing.

"That one glows in the dark," Micah remarked.

"Yeah?" I glanced his way as I put on the clothes, not caring that he watched. Did he see the scars? Judge that he could see my ribs? Or that Lukas's shorts hung a little loosely on my hips? I guess I was laying it all out there for him. We could be friends, or more, but only if we were real with each other. "Easier to find me in the dark later, then, right?"

"True," he agreed. "Wear good shoes if you have them. We have a lot of ground to cover. At least the rain stopped. Now it's just humid."

I sighed. Better than the sweltering desert, I suppose, and the shadow monsters who stalked them.

CHAPTER 13

As proof of how small the area of the Quarter was, we ran
into Jared in Jackson Square. He looked up and saw us
then waved his arms in our direction like he was landing a
plane. Since he was no longer in police custody, I took that as a
good sign that they didn't have anything bad to hold him on, and
wondered if they had found Sarah.

"Hey Jared," I greeted him. He looked tired, bedraggled,
and almost strung out. "Are you okay? Should I call someone for
you?"

He shook his head and stepped into my space, grabbing my
shirt. At first I thought he might hit me, but he kept shaking his
head. Tears fell down his face. "She's missing, man. It took her.
No one will listen to me. No one will help me find her. No one
believes me."

Micah stiffened beside me.

"Have you talked to the police?" I asked Jared. "Told them
everything you saw?"

"Yes. Fuck." He let me go and stepped back to scrub at his
face. "I should never have listened to that guy. He said that your
tour was boring history and we should experience the real thing.

Promised he would show us a voodoo ceremony. Sarah didn't want to. She wanted to stick to the ghost tour. But I convinced her to go. Now she's gone."

"What happened?" I asked. "What did you see?" Had he seen the shadow? Had it been the same shadow that reached for Micah that had taken Sarah?

"I don't know. Darkness? It was gross. I mean, I never thought he'd kill real animals. And he took something from the grave that was open. Gave it to that woman. Then it all went to hell."

"What woman?" Micah asked. Neither of us had seen anyone else at the graveyard, but maybe there was more the police weren't telling us.

"Mary Voodoo or whatever her name was. She said she was a descendant of Marie Laveau. She helped that guy with the ceremony. Sarah didn't want to stay when they started killing animals. We started back to the gate and called for the guy who let us in."

"Why did he even let you in?" Micah wanted to know. "With animals?" And since it had been his night, I wondered why they'd been let in at all.

"That guy said he had a deal with the guard. They paid him a stack of cash. Said it was so we could get a real experience." Jared paced. "The cops think I did something. But they have video of us entering the cemetery. They searched the whole thing and no sign of Sarah. That Mary woman was gone too." He shivered. "We were headed back to the gate and I felt something. God, I've never felt anything so awful in my life."

"Doom," Micah whispered.

Jared nodded, his eyes huge. "Sarah's hand was in mine. I looked back because she stopped, and something black rose up like a void and she was gone. It ripped her right out of my arms. I ran. That's when I found you guys."

"Did you tell the police all of this?" I asked, though I wasn't sure what they could do about voodoo ceremonies gone wrong and possible demons summoned from the depths. The scariest part was that it sounded a lot like what I'd experienced in the desert. Only Sarah wasn't killed, at least not yet, I hoped. Wouldn't the police have mentioned it if they'd found her DNA? If he'd been running from something and she'd been taken and killed, wouldn't we have found something away from the open grave? There was a reason my brother was the detective and I was the hobo. I hated mysteries. My brain often followed them off in a thousand illogical directions, meanwhile Lukas would be thinking about who took the girl and how to get her back. Common sense versus irrational sense.

"Yes, but they think I did something. They even suggested I go to the hospital to have myself looked at."

Because they thought he was crazy. Yeah, I'd heard that before.

"Have you slept?" I asked him. "Maybe gotten a little rest in case you've forgotten something that might help?" He looked like he hadn't slept in a week.

"No. I close my eyes and see it all over again. And there are reporters stalking around my hotel. My family is on their way down. I'm looking for Sarah. I mean, who would take her? I know I talk about paranormal shit being real, but I never thought... Fuck, this can't be happening!"

"Hey, it's okay. When does your family arrive?"

He glanced at his phone. "An hour or so. I tried waiting in the hotel, but I couldn't stop pacing and worrying."

Micah's silence beside me, worried me a little. "Let me walk you to your hotel room. I think you should wait till your family arrives. Maybe then you can get some rest? You look really tired. You can't help Sarah if you're too tired to think straight," I told

Jared. "She needs you rested and alert, ready to take care of her when we find her."

He blinked at me for a few seconds like my words were slow to make sense. "Someone has to look for Sarah."

"The police are looking for Sarah," I said. "My brother is one of those detectives looking for her. He's a good guy. He's going to do everything he can to find her."

"Yeah?"

"Yeah," I promised because I knew Lukas was doing his best to find her. It was how Lukas operated. "You told them everything, right?"

Jared nodded, his exhaustion making him look like a bobblehead with overexaggerated movements. "I don't think they believed me. That the darkness took her."

"You told them about Mary being there?" Micah asked.

"Yes," Jared agreed. "I told them everything. I want Sarah back. She's everything to me. I don't care if I never see a real ghost or even get my medical license, as long as I get her back."

Micah gripped my hand but didn't look at me. I wondered at the thoughts in his head at that moment, and how reminiscent they were of when he'd been found, but didn't push for answers in that moment.

"Let us walk you to your hotel. Are you staying in the Quarter?" I asked Jared.

"Yes. The Bourbon. We thought we'd see the ghost of the dancing girl..." Jared sighed and began to cry. I reached out and put a hand on his shoulder, steering him toward the hotel and giving him support all at once. It was less than a two-block walk. Micah led us silently, even deftly guiding us around a handful of press vans and reporters into the hotel. We got Jared to his room, instructing him not to let anyone other than his family or the police in. He agreed and sat down on the bed like the steam had simply been taken out of him.

"They will find her," I assured Jared. "Get some rest, okay? You can't help her if you're too tired to stand up."

He nodded again, laid down, and put his head on the pillow closing his eyes. Micah and I left, ignoring the handful of annoying reporters who asked questions we had no idea how to answer about a missing girl and a dead tour guide. I could feel Micah's tension as he gripped my hand and dragged me toward his place. He practically vibrated with the need to escape, yet didn't let me go.

Instead I followed and hoped that time would ease what he refused to share.

When we arrived at his place, I was surprised at how quickly we got from the hotel to Micah's, and realized how close Lukas's place really was to everything. I must have gone in circles earlier in the day because it was less than a ten-minute walk. Micah let me in and we both greeted Jet who rubbed his cheek on my leg. I knelt down to give him the scratches that he seemed to crave. He purred happily.

Micah vanished into the mystery closet rather than taking his crafts upstairs like I thought he would. I got up and followed, wondering how big a closet it was. Over all, he had a minimalist style to his apartment. Everything was clean lines, necessary, and put away. With the exception of the mermaid cat sheets which were still on the futon, though the bed had been pushed back into a couch position.

I knew the upstairs was a craft space because I'd seen it, so I wasn't expecting the explosion of crafts central in his closet when I followed him in. Like I imagined entering the wardrobe and stepping into Narnia might have been, it felt a bit like a different world. A treasure trove of well-crafted goodies, like a dragon's hoard of miscellaneous shiny things, clothing, and texture.

The room was easily twice the size of the bathroom, with built-in rods for hangers and drawers. There was a section of shoes, everything from a spread of bright sneakers to sparkling stiletto boots. The back wall appeared to be a mess of compartments filled with fabric, organized by color and perhaps type as several rows of rainbows arched through the shelves. The entire right wall a canvas of costumes and completed crafts. Including a section of quilts hanging from clips, purses and bags of all types both sewn and crocheted, and costumes that ranged from cute Japanese school girl to a section of full-length coats that made me think of all those old video games I'd played as a kid. The ones in which the badass MC had a stack of guns in his coat, and the coat would billow out around him as he fired, ringing him in badass glory. That sort of thing never happened in real life, logistics and the science of gravity, but in the gaming cosplay world, anything was possible.

Micah pulled out a drawer and added the bag of his crochet project to it. A coat, which appeared to be made out of dragon scales, caught my eye. Gray in color, I thought at first, only as I got closer and pulled the hanger free from the rod, the coat had an iridescent shimmer, like metallic threads woven through the fibers, changing when the light hit it in different ways. It was surprisingly light for how big and detailed the design looked.

"This is amazing," I slipped the coat off the hanger, expecting it to be Micah's size, only it was far too big for Micah's petite and lean frame. I pulled it on and was surprised that it was only a tiny bit too large through the shoulders for me. When I buttoned the front, I felt like I should be headed off to battle some supernatural war, flaunting my badass-ery as I went.

"Okay, I feel amazing," I confessed. "Like some game superhero. Do I look like I feel or like a nerd?" I struck a pose that I hoped would look superhero-ish.

Micah smiled, and his expression said nerd, though he responded with, "Superhero."

"Liar," I accused.

He held up his hands. "It fits you."

"Almost. If I hadn't lost weight it would fit perfectly. How come it's not in your size?"

"Because dragon scales don't really fit my personality," Micah said. "I'm more lace and ruffles."

"You can be whatever you want. Just because you are pretty, doesn't mean you have to only wear pretty. Not that I'm opposed to either, or nothing at all." I pawed through the cosplay side of his closet, finding easily a dozen jackets similar to this one. Some in faux leather, some in suede, and some in lace, all varied in color and size. I could have worn any of them and felt like a king.

"I like lace and ruffles. Dragon scales too, though on me it looks out of place. Maybe I haven't found the right design yet."

"How come these aren't in your shop?" I asked.

"They're new. And I've been playing with multiple patterns."

"How new?" I looked around the room at the hordes of costumes, quilts, and bags, which were in the dozens of each. "How do you find time to make this stuff and still work the shop full-time, then give tours?"

"I craft when I'm stressed," Micah reminded me.

"Which you're saying is every second of your life?"

"Lately yes. And I don't sleep much."

I thought about that for a minute, analyzing what I had learned about him in the past twenty-four hours. He always seemed a bit on edge, though hid it well. "So when the thing outside makes noise and wakes you up, you get up and work on stuff?"

"Yes," he confessed.

"When it woke us up last night did you get up and work on something while I slept?" That bothered me, as I had slept well for the first time in a while. Whether it had been from exhaustion or sleeping wrapped in the warmth of his Christmas scent that helped, I didn't know yet.

"No. I went back to sleep when you did. I woke up early to text about the shop and then back to sleep. I don't think I've slept that much in a long time."

"Do you do that when Sky is here and you hear something? Get up and then go back to sleep?"

"I try to go back to sleep. Usually she falls back to sleep and I find a project to work on because I can't sleep."

I stared at the closet of stuff around us. "You said the feeling of doom started a little while ago. A couple weeks?"

He nodded, fiddling with organizing a shelf.

"All of this is from the past few weeks," I deduced.

"Mostly. Some things are mine and I won't sell them. Some are experiments that didn't turn out right and I feel bad selling things that aren't perfect. But yes, I've been working on a lot lately. Trying to find a distraction."

A distraction from doom. Wow, did that sound creepy and difficult. Though I understood it. What if I felt the way I had that night in the desert for weeks at a time? I'd probably go mad.

He riffled through the hangers of costumes. "You can have the coat if you want. It was my first attempt at that pattern. Not sure I like it. I'd probably add more pockets, maybe use a mermaid print next time. I do like the cut of the shoulders and the length. A few of the other patterns have been a bit more complicated, but I'm not as fond of how they drape." His tone sounded strained even while he rattled off sewing concepts I wasn't sure I understood, but he wouldn't look at me.

"Micah?"

He bowed his head, his shoulders slumping, and I heard the faintest sniffle. Was he crying?

"It's my fault."

"What is?" I asked, trying to follow his train of thought.

"Sarah missing, Mark dead."

"No. Do not pass go, do not collect two hundred tears. You had just met the girl for a few seconds in your shop. And that Mark guy was bugging you for ages." Hadn't I felt the same thing? Like it was all my doing? Maybe Lukas had been right about it being a meeting of two powerful forces. Or maybe two weirdos like us.

"A lot of people have suggested that I'm cursed now. People meet me and fall on hard times like some sort of chain reaction. Tim and Sky, even Lukas."

I reached out and gripped his shoulder, turning him to face me. His eyes were watery with unshed tears and ringed with exhaustion. "This is probably going to be hard to hear because you're a video star and all that... but you're not the sole center of the universe. It doesn't revolve around you, people aren't cursed because they breathe the same air you do, life happens in misfortunes for most. Sometimes in clusters, sometimes it's coincidence, but it's not your fault. You are not the sun, moon, and stars, yeah?"

He gave me a strained smile. "Yeah? I'm a piece of shit, eh?"

"More like another grain of sand on a big rock like the rest of us." I held my arms open, letting him make the decision to be touched or not. Just because I wanted to hug and comfort him, didn't mean he'd let me. "I mean, if you look at things that way, then it could be as much my fault as yours. Since I'm probably cursed and I spoke to Sarah and Jared for quite a while, and silently wished bad things on that jerk Mark. If anyone is to blame it should probably be me. Though my therapist tells me not to 'should' on myself. How about we both agree to that? No 'shoulding' on ourselves." Which sounded a lot like no shitting on ourselves. Good thinking, even if it was hard sometimes in a world that trained us to always be striving for a 'should.' "You told me you've been doing tours for ages and nothing happens, then I show up. Maybe I'm the cursed one? You sure you want to hang around me?"

Micah hesitated for a minute before stepping into my embrace and laying his head on my shoulder. I wrapped my arms around him. Holding tight, rocking him lightly. He'd been through a lot, no one could be strong forever, and enough bad turns could make anyone think the universe was out to get them. I'd thought that a time or two myself, only to be reminded over and over again that, "I'm really not all that special. None of us are. We aren't saving the planet or humanity, we aren't changing the world, we are barely making it through each day. But you know what?" I asked him as I ran my fingers through his hair. "That's okay. We are doing the best we can being us. Even if it's seeing or hearing weird shit, that's a quirk of being us."

It made me think hard about what Lukas had said. I didn't need to understand what I'd experienced to keep going. And maybe knowing the truth would make it harder to move forward. "I thought for a while that if I leaned too hard on Lukas he'd leave, you know?" I said.

Micah tensed against me. Recognition, I think, of what he felt every day.

"We fear being a burden to others and so we bury our emotions and fears until it breaks us. I've been working on that. Trying to let it out more. Was a big ninny earlier today because I'd been letting the stress eat at me. But I had a big baby cry with Lukas and then a nap, which made me feel better."

"Big baby cry?" Micah asked.

"Crocodile tears and everything," I assured him. "Just because I was a soldier doesn't mean I don't cry. Hell, I've cried a lot, even while serving. Sometimes covered in the ash of human life you'd have tears streaming down your face, gun in your grip, trying to find a way to the exit, hoping to survive and die all at once." He looked up at me. I traced a thumb down his cheek, wiping away a shed tear. "You talked about thriving, right?"

He nodded.

"Let's work on that. Both of us. Find a balance between this," I indicated to the room that now felt more like a frenzy of trying to escape memories than a treasure trove, "to the beauty of this," I indicated the jacket I wore.

"I don't understand," Micah said.

"One complete project equals something a million people could never dream of doing. Maybe spending every moment trying to perfect it doesn't matter as much as the practice of making something and completing it if even one person enjoys it?" I looked around the space seeing a lot of incompletes. "How do you feel when you finish something?"

"Sad," Micah said. "Often like a failure because it didn't work out like I thought it would in my head."

"Yet, here I stand in a masterpiece, which I would wear proudly every day for the rest of my life if I could."

"You'd melt in this city." He was trying to distract me from the topic.

"Was this a failure?"

"It wasn't exactly how I pictured it."

"Yet I love it. And it's well worth melting in," I said putting my hands on my hips in a superman pose. "To feel like a super-hero." I grinned at him. "What's your favorite piece?"

His gaze went to the costume section. "A Lolita style Frozen dress that I did after the Sky thing. It's in her size, but I've been too afraid to show it to her."

I glanced at the shelf, having to think for a minute before the meaning of his words translated into something that made sense to me: Frozen, the kids movie; Lolita in cosplay fashion usually meant a dress with lots of layers of lace. There was a blue dress on the end that looked like it had tulle and stuff on it, sort of like ice. I reached for it and pulled it off the rod, holding it up on the hanger. Yeah, that had to be it. It was small enough to fit Sky's tiny frame.

"Looks like it would be the perfect Ice Queen adaptation," I told Micah. I turned the dress, marveling at the detail of layers of gem-like beads, lace, and a shawl that appeared crocheted from metallic thread. This dress had likely taken him weeks and here it sat gathering dust.

"Do you have one of those dress bags? We should wrap it up and bring it to Sky."

Micah gaped at me. "But..."

"You made it for her, right? Was it for any special occasion? A birthday or anything? Or more an 'I thought this would look cool on you' sort of thing?"

He flushed. "The latter."

"Okay. Do you normally give her stuff that you make?"

"She has a few shawls, purses, and a quilt."

"But nothing this elaborate?"

He glanced away and shook his head.

"Then let's bring it to her. I bet she is going to think this is the most amazing thing in the world." I ran my hand over the rows of costumes. "These are all amazing. You are very talented."

"There are people a lot more talented than me."

"Sure," I agreed. "That's the way of life. There will always be someone better than you at anything you do. But that's okay. You learn something from each piece, right? Even if it's about yourself? I should tell you about this Optimus Prime thing I created for a Comic Con when I was a teen. It was inspired, but really lacking in skill. Though I had a bazillion people ask for my picture. I felt amazing and like a fraud all at once."

Micah studied me. "You really don't think I'm nuts?"

"No more nuts than I am," I said. "Take that for the good or bad it may be. However, I think you're amazing, for your talent, your persistence, and your strength. Those are all good things, yeah?"

"I guess," he agreed.

"Is your lack of confidence why you don't do the cosplay pictures anymore?"

Micah shrugged, though I could tell from his posture that I'd hit the nail on the head.

"Lukas said you used to do sexy pictures before you started working with Tim."

"Tim convinced me there was better money in porn," Micah said.

"Was there?"

He seemed to think about it for a minute. "A little."

"But you enjoyed the cosplay thing more?"

"I've always liked dressing up and pretending to be someone else for a few hours." He pointed to me in the coat. "Feeling like a superhero, if you want to think of it that way."

"So why stop? You have all these costumes. How many are in your size?"

"Not many anymore. A few maybe, but I had my final growth spurt a year or so ago, which means a lot of the stuff is too small."

"But you obviously have the skill to make something that fits." There was even one of those dress dummies shoved into

141

the corner, which I thought would probably scare the bejesus out of me if I walked into the closet in the middle of the night.

"Sure."

"You don't make stuff for yourself anymore?"

"Not really."

I realized that it was a lack of confidence. How a man as beautiful as Micah could lose that confidence baffled me. He'd been a porn star, loved for the body that so few men had, being delicate and feminine, while just masculine enough to turn on most gay men. Had the disappearance stripped that confidence away, or something else? Perhaps the loss of his relationship with Tim or the constant noises in the darkness? I wasn't sure he had an answer.

"That's something to focus on then. I'm certainly no model, but maybe we can make a cool duo of something for some pictures. Is there an anime con soon? Even if it's only for walking around and feeling like I'm a badass, I think it's worth it." I thought about it for a few minutes. "I'm a little out of touch with what's popular, but I remember Devil May Cry, and I played Witcher for a while. I could totally do one of them. But I'll even wear a dress if you want me to."

"Okay," Micah agreed, though I think he wasn't really ready to talk about his designing yet. I wasn't going to push. Not yet. "And I don't know about any upcoming conventions. But I can make something."

"And can we give this to Sky? I can't wait to see that girl's face. Every girl wants to be a princess, right? Hell, I'd love to be a princess and have some hot prince rescue me from all the world's troubles."

Micah stuttered out a rough laugh. "Okay. I can make you a princess dress. I think Sky would rather be a queen."

"Honey, I'm already a queen, but I'd still be your princess," I said pointing at him.

This time I got a real smile. "Guys usually expect me to be the damsel."

I snorted. "Rescue me any time, babe. I've already done my service for the macho man brigade." I did a little YMCA dance.

He laughed again. "Wow..."

"Nerdiness a turn off?" I asked him. "Come on, there's a whole nerd-guy-glasses kink in romance novels. I could fit that. With some glasses and a better haircut. Ignore the exterior and focus on the dork underneath."

"Nerdiness is okay."

"Especially cosplay nerdiness," I clarified because that had been Micah's original passion and heck, I could be on board with that. His talent gave me all sorts of ideas.

"Yes," he agreed.

I did another little jig, swinging my hips and bouncing into poses of all the video game characters I could ever remember. "We should probably go though..." It was getting late. "How time flies when you're having fun, right?"

"It does," Micah said. "I still have to walk the route first, it's silly to go to the shop and then back out again into the heat."

"That's okay. I can carry the dress for Sky. If you're okay with giving it to her? You have a bag we can put this in to protect it? I don't want to get it all dirty." I thought about the coat I had on and the heat outside. "I'll leave the coat here, maybe you'll let me wear it when it starts to get cold? I don't want to sweat and cover it in my man stink right now."

Micah gave me a faint smile and said, "Sure." We wrapped up the dress and headed out to get something productive done for the day.

CHAPTER 14

Micah had not been kidding about ground to cover. We walked the entire Quarter and then some before arriving at the shop after five. Skylar waved and grinned at us from behind the register.

"Been busy?" Micah asked.

"A little. Tim and Brad left a half an hour ago. They helped get rid of the reporters. Good news is that we've had lots of sign-ups for your tours, and sold a bazillion T-shirts, which we need to restock. The new candles you brought in are gone too. Sorry, they smelled nice, so I put them out. The tomb shapes were a hoot, and everyone had to have one," Sky chattered away like she had all the energy of a rabbit on a B-shot. "Hi Alex, good to see you back. Your head looks better."

The glue was still firmly in place from Micah setting it last night. In fact he'd done so well I doubted it would scar at all. "Thanks, sorry it took us so long, we were mapping Micah's route for tonight."

"Oh, how exciting," Sky said. "Did you see anything terrifying?"

I had actually, but didn't want to share that. And it had been at the LaLaurie Mansion. We hadn't even gotten close, but from half a block away I could see waves of some sort of black mass pouring from the windows. At first, I thought it was a fire and pointed it out to Micah who had looked confused. Then one of the black masses turned, more like a person than the shifting smoke of a fire, and seemed to stare at me, the darkness that was its writhing face looking like a nightmare of snakes in the bright light of the day. I had no interest in what the place looked like at night and instead begged Micah to skip by it as fast as possible.

"No knife wielding prostitutes," I affirmed because I hadn't sensed anything in the French Market other than that there was a lot of food there I had yet to try and wanted to. I held out the wrapped dress for Micah. "Do you want to?"

He flushed and took it. "Maybe later?"

"Um..." I looked at Sky.

She looked between the two of us. "What?"

"It's something Micah made for you," I said. Was he worried she wouldn't like it? I couldn't imagine not being floored by the skill and beauty of the dress. Even if it had been made for me and I'd never worn a dress in my life.

"Really?" Sky eyed the bag. "What is it?"

I took the bag back from Micah and handed it to Sky. She laid it on the counter and zipped it open. Her squeal of delight nearly broke my eardrums.

"Oh my God!" She untucked the dress from the bag and held it to her chest like she was modeling it. "Is this for real? This is amazing." She looked at the door to the backroom. "I need to try this on. Is it really for me?"

Micah's face was red and he wouldn't meet her gaze. "Yes. I made it for you. It was some experiments in fabrics, design, and color. The bodice is expandable too, like a corset only less restrictive, for after your surgery..."

Sky leapt from behind the counter to wrap her arms around

Micah in a tight hug, which he didn't return. She didn't seem to care. She took the dress and headed toward the backroom. Then paused.

"Oh and so about the tour," Sky said looking guilty. "I mean, I didn't do anything, but Tim did and he said there were no limits. I began putting people on other days when I got here, but the damage was already done. I'm so sorry."

Micah tilted his head like he was trying to understand what Sky was saying. "Huh?"

"There are twenty-two people scheduled for tonight's tour," Sky said in a rush.

"Um..." Wasn't there a limit? Or was that only for the grave-yard tours? "That's a lot of people."

Micah sighed. "I'll have to cut a few stops off the trip. Too many people means too many questions and no time for photographs. I've never had a tour with more than fifteen at once."

"Some of them might be reporters," Sky added.

"What? Why?" I asked.

"Stupid, nosey..." Micah grumbled as he stalked his way to the backroom. Sky stared at me with wide eyes. I blinked at her wondering if I'd missed something.

"Reporters because of last night?" I finally asked.

"Partially, and partially because some of them remember Micah's disappearance. There are a few who regularly come by to bother him. Ask him if he remembered something or if he knows some other random person who went missing. Now with last night, it brings them around to start bothering him again."

"Because he somehow controls the universe? Dictates who dies and goes missing? Seems like a lot for one small Asian dude."

Sky nodded. "Read your cards earlier," Sky said. "They said not to go chasing shadows into the darkness."

I paused and glanced at her before saying, "Thank you. That's insightful. I'll keep that in mind this evening as I walk around in a dark haunted city with a paranormally sensitive tour guide. I'm sure there won't be shadows anywhere. If I do see any, I'll tiptoe past them instead of running."

Sky giggled. "Oh, sarcasm, I do like you." She rushed past me to disappear into the large unisex bathroom and likely change into her dress.

I made my way to check on Micah. In the storeroom, Micah angrily sorted through all the stock he'd had Tim and Brad deliver, and a few other boxes that appeared to have been dropped off by UPS. He picked up boxes, dumped them out and then began dropping stuff into piles. It was a reckless sort of movement I hadn't seen from him yet, but knew enough about body language to recognize. Anger had to be better than tears, right? I couldn't make the world leave him alone and stop reminding him of a time he wished had never happened. I knew that better than most, but I could remind him there was more to life than living in the past.

"Are you mad at me for giving her the dress?"

"No," he said, and it sounded like the truth.

Still his movements were tense and angry. Warning bells went off in my head. He was angry, probably more at himself than anyone else. It was that loss of control that made me mad at myself often. Like somehow, I should be able to lay all the cards right in the universe. Only we didn't have that sort of power, and I knew how frustrating it was to stand in the middle of the storm.

Reporters who made him feel like things were his fault sort of pissed me off too. He had already been blaming himself. I wondered if I hugged him again if he'd fall apart. Maybe he needed the break. I wasn't yet sure what he needed, so I thought to maybe try a bit of humor.

"Can I help or do you need a few minutes?" I asked. "I can go stand at the register and look pretty if you'd like, or you can vent and then we can put some of this weird shit out to sell to some quirky tourists. Too bad I didn't bring the coat. I could have stood out on the sidewalk and proclaimed my nerdiness to the world to draw in more business." I thought about that a minute. "Okay that might have scared people away..."

A smile cracked the seriousness of Micah's face. "Jerk. You are a giant nerd."

"Guilty," I agreed. "We could move the Holy Fuck out front and see if any Karens clutch their pearls and cry 'Well, I never...'"

He looked at me, fighting a full grin.

"Of course you never, Karen. That's why you're so uptight. Let me show you our collection of vibrators, I'm sure we have something to help you loosen up that tight ass and show you lots of things 'you never'. Straight people butt fuck too, right? Never mind, gross. Image in my head now. Sorry I asked and commented."

"Stop," Micah grumbled, trying hard not to laugh.

"Anyway, back to Karen, I do the bait and switch, showing her some alien impregnators which she'll have to buy, and then she will write some steamy chick romance that will make the best seller list like Fifty Shades only instead of some rich white dude, the Dom in this story is a giant alien dick. Oh, Narwal Dickmaster, my alien overlord, take me to heaven."

Micah laughed. "You're a total jerk," he remarked.

"For making you laugh? I'll own that. Better than serious, angry Micah any day, right?" I picked up an unopened box and began to pull away the tape. "Any more alien impregnators in here I should be looking for? Maybe a box of anal probes?"

"I already have a whole selection of those on display. Do you need another tour?" Micah asked with a devious smile.

"Did I miss those? Well, butter my buns and call me a biscuit, I'll have to do a full inventory on them later so I can recommend them to the tightest of assholes who enter the store. I'm sure there's plenty of lube to ease their transition to the dark side. We might not have cookies, but we have sex toys and I'll be damned if that isn't even better."

Micah was full out laughing now. "Oh my god, stop. Apparently put beans in you and you become some sort of sarcasm jukebox." He shook his head. "I need to write some of that down and put it on T-shirts."

"I'm a thirty-two-ounce refillable fountain glass of sass," I affirmed.

"You are," Micah agreed.

"So, no alien impregnators?"

"Tim and Brad bought all three," Sky called from the bathroom. "I told them it wasn't fair, but Tim said you'd have to order more."

I opened my mouth to spit out a reply to that but couldn't. Alien egg impregnators... Yeah, that was a bit out of my comfort zone. But maybe I had to start slow with small anal probes or cute androgynous boy toys who happened to make my winky stand up and wave.

Micah's eyes narrowed on me. "Are you thinking sexy thoughts about me again?"

"Um... maybe? I can't help that certain words in context with the idea of you and my memory of some old videos conjure up physical reactions I haven't had much of in the past few years."

"I have some alien dildos at home, fun shapes and all, but I don't like the egg idea thing," Micah confided. "I know they sell the idea of them being safe and that your body heat melts them down to liquid, but I don't want blue goo coming out of my ass."

Instead of blue goo I pictured my come dripping out of his ass and felt my cock awaken. Fuck. "Alien dildo?"

"There's a collection in the other room. Colors and unusual heads or even barbs."

"Barbs?" I could only picture thorns like on a rose bush.

"Some animals have them when they mate. It locks the two together to keep the seed inside. There's more science than that, but the toys are all about illusion, so it's simply a really hard-ending nub on a dildo. You're supposed to sit on it and grind into it to get the *barb* sensation. They also make a cock ring that your partner can wear with a lot of the same effect."

The idea of him riding me was all that filled my head in that moment.

He threw his hands up in the air in exasperation. "Seriously? I begin to doubt the excuse that you haven't been functioning until now." He pointed to the crotch of my shorts and my very obvious erection.

I tugged the T-shirt down, like it was somehow ever going to be long enough. My face burned with embarrassment and desire. "I promise I've not always been this sexually awkward." Okay that was a lie, and the years serving having nothing but alley meetings and fast fucks between tours with strangers, wasn't really experience. "Okay, I'm awkward. You sure you even want to take a step in that direction? It's fun flirting with you, but you know I'm a little messed up, and what if I'm bad in bed?"

He shrugged. "There are two types of lovers. Those you screw because you're physically attracted to them. They might be good in bed or bad in bed, doesn't matter so much because the physical attraction is there. Usually you get them out of your system, sometimes it takes a few days, but never lasts. Sort of like a fast spark and then it dies."

"And the second kind?"

"The kind you train. Those are the ones you want to keep, maybe because you like their personality or their lifestyle fits yours, so you educate each other on what you like, building a relationship through knowledge as well as physical attraction. That one is more than a spark, it's genuine interest in learning more about a person with a side of the physical desire."

"How do you know the difference?"

"Physical burns hot and fast, like a lit match, and then after a few seconds you have to put it out or get burned. You sleep with them once and are like eh, okay, and move on. Sometimes they last a few weeks before you realize you really don't like the person for more than sex. Relationships aren't really like that. Not for most. You might be attracted to someone, but life gets in the way. Unless you're cruising for a hookup, it's unlikely you're gonna have to screw that person right this second. If you walk away still thinking of them, even pass a few days and they are still on your mind, that's a training situation. And it either works or becomes the first type of lover. Not every lover wants to be trained. Either way you've had a good time."

It was a very different way of looking at relationships. I guess I'd had a lot of the fast ones in my life. The quick spark that leads to nothing. Never had a training sort of one. Hadn't met anyone I wanted to keep before, not in real life. I admitted to being curious about Micah. Not only sexually attracted to him, though that was a large enough factor on its own. Did I think we could mesh? Maybe. Was it worth a try? Again, I thought maybe.

Micah unloaded another box of T-shirts. "Choose some shirts to take home with you. So you have stuff for work." He looked me over and smiled. "Pick a smaller size than your brother does."

I glanced down. "If I pick a smaller size it will cling."

"Yep."

"And show everyone I'm aroused when you walk into a room," I pointed out.

"We'll see if we can strike a flame after work and fix that," Micah said.

"Huh?" Was he saying we'd be having sex after work? My body was like *oh fuck yeah*, we're on board. Maybe I was translating that wrong. Was he speaking a language I'd missed somehow while being overseas? Maybe it was an age gap thing. I'd always thought of him as barely legal when I'd watched the videos of him. Now I wondered, hoping he had been of age, or else I'd really feel like shit. "How old are you anyway?"

"Twenty-two."

Fuck. Ten years. I felt really old in that moment. At least he'd been over eighteen when he made videos.

"But I like older men, if you recall."

Again, back to the videos. I sighed and hung my head. "I've not seen this much action in most of my life," I confessed. "And we haven't done anything yet. I'm not sure we should. We work together. What if we are a lust flame or whatever?"

"Then we burn and burn out. It happens. Best to know now and be done right? I'm adult enough to work with you after we have sex. And maybe it will stop you from always getting wood around me."

Unless it made it worse. "Hmm."

Micah stepped into my personal space and put an arm around my waist, pulling us close. I had to look down to meet his gaze, and it was intense, a heat flashing between us with little more than a touch and a glance. His lips breezed across mine for a few seconds. A teasing pass of softness and the scent of peppermint on his breath. I had to admit that while his touch revved my body up to lightning horndog speed, his presence also relaxed me. I should have been worried about Sky walking into the room, or getting interrupted by a customer, or a thousand other things. But in his arms, looking down into that intense blue gaze? It didn't matter. He was my focus right then. Maybe that's what Lukas had meant about me finding someone to steal my attention?

I held on to him and realized that I was curious. Could we be something? More than a broken soldier interested in a guy he'd once watched in porn? Was it a fantasy? And did it really matter?

"I'm not sure what this is," I told him a little breathily. "Lust?"

"A spark," Micah agreed. "Time will tell if we can be more. Let's get this stock out." He pulled away and lifted a box of supplies. "Nothing sells from the storeroom."

I picked up the box of shirts and followed him out, a thousand things on my mind, but most of it centered on him.

When Sky emerged from the bathroom, she looked like an ice queen. She had pulled up her hair, and even done something with her make-up that made her look magical. It was a perfect fit. I took pictures and sent them to Lukas, and Sky danced around the shop, not caring that she was overdressed for working the close shift.

The small smile on Micah's face at seeing her so thrilled by the outfit made the entire afternoon worth it. Some of the tension in his shoulders eased. The trickle of customers who came in insisted on pictures with Sky, even texting friends to encourage them to stop by. It became a steady stream of people visiting to see Sky in full Queen mode, which increased sales as Micah and I restocked. It made for a busy early evening, and I felt pretty good about handling the register and answering questions. I hoped the tour would go as smoothly later.

CHAPTER 15

Lukas showed up briefly to bring us food. I was surprised by his arrival, but no one else was. Sky flounced around him in her dress and flirted shamelessly, while Lukas smiled and pretended his interest in her was professional. Either way I enjoyed the giant meal of banana fosters French Toast he'd brought me, with a huge side of that andouille sausage. Micah had some sort of bento box thing, and Sky a plate of beignets that she insisted on eating, but only after she pulled a T-shirt over her dress to protect it from powdered sugar.

"Did you know there was some Mary Voodoo or something in the cemetery too?" I asked him when he sat down in the back room with me while I ate. "Micah and I ran into Jared in the Square today. He seemed pretty distraught."

"I can't talk about the case with you. But we are exploring all angles."

I stared at him for a minute, parsing the brother speak before I continued. "I didn't see her. I don't think Micah did either. Is she missing too?"

"No. She's been questioned like you and Micah were. How

about you focus on the job and Micah, and let me focus on the case?" Lukas stole a bite of toast from me.

"Jared said she took something from the grave. And he saw the darkness take Sarah from him."

Lukas sighed. "Alex, stop."

I frowned at him. He was the one who wanted me to stop pretending I didn't see strange shit. Or was it something else?

"Whatever happened in that cemetery doesn't need to be anything but a short memory for you. Okay?" Lukas said.

"But Jared and Sarah..."

"Are people you met." He shook his head. "You and Micah are scary alike sometimes. You know that? Meeting people does not make you responsible for them. Not their actions or their fate. If they'd left the shop and gotten into a car accident, would you have felt responsible?"

"No. But I don't feel responsible for them right now either. Just worried and trying to help," I pointed out.

Lukas stared at me like he could see right through me.

"Okay, so I feel a little responsible. Plus Jared is a wreck and the cops are looking at him like he did something."

"It's standard procedure because most of the time it is the SO who has pulled some shit. It's not even a one-off, Alex. Almost every case of domestic abuse that ends in murder is some guy claiming they'd never hurt so and so. Did Jared do something? We don't know. The timeline is off, and we have them on video. We have Mary Lamont, self-proclaimed Voodoo Queen, leaving the cemetery before Jared came calling for help and the two of you ran up. We don't have a body for Sarah, or any video indicating she left the cemetery. But you know what all that means?"

I shook my head.

"Of course you don't. The police don't either. But it's our job to put the pieces together. Not yours." He reached out and put his hand over mine. "How about you focus on healing instead of worrying about stuff you can't do anything about?"

"Maybe if Micah and I talk to that Mary person? Maybe she'll remember something else?"

"Maybe you'll give yourself a heart attack from all this worry?"

"I'm fine," I promised.

"Then focus on the job. Learn about the city. See if the pretty boy is someone you want to spend some time with. Let me deal with the trouble of New Orleans."

"What if it's paranormal?" I wondered. Lukas didn't seem to be sensitive to it at all.

"What if it is? What would you do?" Lukas asked.

He was right. I didn't know. Just because I could see something other people might not didn't mean I had a way of proving it or even doing something about it.

"Exactly," Lukas said, understanding my expression as only he really could. "Now relax. Learn about the city. And try to stay out of trouble. Yeah?"

I nodded, even if my brain was twirling a million miles a second with questions.

The tour began in Jackson Square right in front of the gate to the little park full of statues. We arrived a few minutes after eight and Micah pointed out some of the local food places in the area that were good. The crowd began to assemble by quarter to nine, phones out and walking shoes on. At least it felt like they were taking this seriously. Micah frowned over an arrival or two, whom I assumed were the reporters. But he checked them in with a smile and a welcome. I stood beside him in a shirt that read: 'Ghost Security is more than fences around graveyards.' It was bright purple with white text that glowed in the dark. It clung a little. When I tried it on, Micah had made appreciative sounds even though the color was a little intense for my normal tastes.

"When everyone is here, let me talk first, okay?" I said.

Micah gave me the side-eye. "Okay?"

"Trust me."

He shrugged and continued greeting everyone. It was a big group. They fanned around us, a smattering of late teens, twenty-somethings, and all the way up to a couple with matching silver hair and a lifetime of likely well-earned wrinkles. Everyone looked a little nervous and excited. My focus was on Micah. He'd been clear during our walk-through that we had to keep the group moving, and occasionally pull the group back from wandering or asking off-topic questions that slowed the entire tour down.

Finally the last of them had arrived. I cleared my voice and waved my hands to get everyone's attention. "Welcome everyone," I said once they'd quieted down. "This is Micah, your tour guide and New Orleans haunted history guru," I indicated to Micah. "I'm Alex and I'm security. You'll notice we have a large group tonight, and I'll ask that you try to keep your voices low so everyone can hear Micah speak as that's why you're all here. Stay with the group. We will be stopping at each location so you can ask questions and take pictures. The tour lasts about an hour and a half. We can't promise you'll see ghosts, but if you see me chasing something, maybe run the other way, eh?"

There was a nervous giggle from the crowd.

"Keep the questions and comments respectful and we are sure to have an entertaining adventure. Now let's get started, okay?"

"Is it true one of the people on your tour went missing?"

One of the men in the back asked. Micah tensed. I put a hand on his arm.

"Not true. She was not on our tour. Any further questions about last night's incident will have to go through the police as it's an ongoing investigation," I said. "Now, we are all here for a tour, right?"

The crowd murmured its agreement. All eyes turned to Micah. He welcomed them and began the story about the Jackson Square ghosts. The night was overcast, but no rain or fog in sight, though the crowd searched the area for any sign of the four murdered men who were known to haunt the Square.

We made our way up Royal street, stopping at a few places to hear scary stories. The crowd snapped pictures of places, though I saw and felt nothing out of the ordinary. I kept to the back of the group, keeping an eye on the two guys I was pretty sure were reporters, and Micah. He was very engaging. His verbal story telling skills were intense as he projected his voice over the crowd, lowering or raising his tone with the story, even adding accented dialogue a time or two like a skilled audiobook narrator might.

I didn't see or sense anything unusual until we got close to the Voodoo Museum. Micah had told me on our earlier tour that people used to be able to visit the museum and take part in mock rituals, but there had been a fire, and the Voodoo Society had been trying to raise enough funds to finish the repairs for quite some time. So in short, the building was vacant, and locked up tight. When we'd passed it earlier, I'd seen nothing and it sounded like a sad story of how capitalism milked everyone for every penny by asking for more and more permits. Now the building seemed to glow with some sort of eerie light.

I frowned at it and wondered if Micah felt anything.

He paused a few feet from the building, letting everyone gather around him, and glanced my way. Was he getting that bug feeling? I met his gaze and he nodded. Yes, he felt something. "This is, or was at least, the Voodoo Museum you probably heard of in your research of New Orleans," he began.

I looked over the building trying to figure out if there was some scientific explanation for the building having a glow. Nothing close was lit with anything more than a streetlight. Nearby shops were closed. And I knew, because of Micah's comments earlier in the day, that the power to the building was turned off. Yet all the windows flickered with a faint light, almost like a fire.

Nothing seemed to move within. I wondered if we should call someone and let them know? Or was it something only I was seeing? The group snapped lots of photos, but no one remarked on anything in particular. I pulled out my phone and snapped a few pictures myself of the windows and the area where the top of the building met the skyline of the city, to see if later I would be able to distinguish any glow.

"Did you catch anything?" The woman nearest to me asked.

"Haven't looked yet," I told her honestly. "You?"

"Maybe?" She held up her phone and in the window near where Micah stood was some sort of hint of a face. Not a reflection obviously as no one was standing close enough for there to be a reflection. "I think the window is boarded up from the inside," she continued. "Maybe it's something on the wood?"

I glanced up at the window and didn't see anything there other than the glow, but it *was* boarded up from the inside. A big piece of plywood on that side protecting the oversized window from either vandals or people trying to look inside.

"I don't see anything now," I told her and stepped up to the window. Micah shrugged when I threw him a questioning look, assuring me he was okay with the time we were making on the tour.

The glass was solid, thick, with a sun-resistant coating of

some kind on the outside. I put my hand to the glass more to feel if anything was different about it, perhaps a texture or something that only came out in the photo. I heard phones snapping pictures around me, but didn't see anything other than the faint glow. I stared into the dark pane for a minute, the palm of my hand pressed onto the glass, feeling nothing really, then heat radiating from the center of my hand and intensifying. I yanked my hand away and blinked at the glass. For a few seconds I almost felt like something was staring back at me. Nothing I could actually see, but more a presence I could sort of feel.

Micah put a hand on my arm, which made me step back into the street away from the ruins of the museum. "Ready to move on?" he asked.

I nodded, though the sense of something close ran through my nerves like a rush of anxiety irritating my skin. Maybe that was what Micah meant by bugs?

I returned to the back of the group and followed as we continued the tour. We stopped briefly near the intersection of Royal and Charters to listen to the infamous story about the Casket Girls who legend said were vampires. The monastery overlooked the area with an intimidating white tower, boasting closed off windows and a large fence keeping people out. Micah knew all the history and talked about the myth of the girls and how it had exploded in the seventies after an incident that he hadn't been able to find real record of.

The third floor of the giant white convent in the distance looked still and normal to me, as it had on our initial tour, though most of the group took pictures.

"We'll stop by the entrance to the convent on our way back to Jackson Square later. That is supposedly where the two investigators were found after they were eviscerated by the vampires," Micah told the group. "Occasionally the convent holds tours inside. Though I have never seen the third floor. As far as I know it is still locked up."

The rest of the tour went much the same way. I didn't know how Micah kept all his facts straight. And no matter what questions were asked of him, he had an answer, even if it was simply to point them toward a historical reference website.

The brief stop we made at the LaLaurie Mansion made my gut ache. We weren't even close, instead staring down at it from half a block away. Even through the barely lit streets I could see another tour gathered around on the sidewalk in front of the house. Micah told several very sad stories about victims and ghosts while everyone took pictures and listened raptly. I examined the windows in the distance. Looking for the smoke creatures. In the dark it looked black. No glow. No movement. Just lifeless.

I thought for a minute or two that maybe what I'd seen during the day was a fluke. But the longer we stood there while Micah answered questions, the more the pain in my gut intensified. Almost like the siren song of that day in the desert. Only I recognized it for what it was now, the call of death. Or as Micah had put it, doom.

When we finally moved on, I breathed a sigh of relief as the further we got from the house, the more the feeling eased. We didn't see the dancing girl at Jared's hotel, or barmaids at the Dauphine. The night was quiet enough, though if I never had to walk by the LaLaurie Mansion again it would be too soon.

The French Market was our last stop, and very still in the darkness, an empty stretch of road with a few street lamps in the distance. I listened to the stories and chatter, watching the area. Movement caught my attention from near the end of the market area. We stood near the crossroads, street signs a few feet away, but I could only read one which said Gallatin. The long stretch of the Market that had been filled with vendors fading off into the darkness.

Down toward the end there seemed to be someone walking toward us. I blinked in that direction, trying to make out who it might be in the darkness. Was it someone who wanted to bug Micah for hosting a tour? I'd noticed he had taken a very different route from the handful of other tours we'd passed. Had any of them ended up in the Market?

I looked around at the group and wondered if anyone else had noticed. But they were all snapping pictures around and laughing lightly about prostitutes who could whip the asses of a bunch of stupid and likely very drunk sailors. I raised my own phone and took a few pictures of the group and the figure who ambled our way. The figure didn't really get any closer.

Micah was still talking, so either he didn't notice it or was ignoring it. And I didn't feel anything. Nothing. Not a sense of doom or even anxiety, not until I realized I could see a hint of light filtering through the figure. Not a person, I thought, keeping it to myself. Human shaped with a defined head and shoulders, the bottom half a bit more unfocused. Could it have been the prostitute? What was her name? Red something? I'd missed half the story. Would have to ask Micah about it later. But the story ended and questions trailed off. The figure was gone.

"Thanks, everyone, for coming. If you have a chance, please post a review of our tour online," Micah told them. "Does anyone need directions from here? I always feel like the Quarter, while very square, is somewhat confusing to newcomers." The older couple approached him for help, while the rest of the group began to scatter, except the reporters.

I approached them. "Can I help you guys with something?"

"Did you guys really find a dead body on the tour last night?" One of them asked.

"We weren't on a tour, and really weren't involved at all. Perhaps your questions would be better directed toward the police, as I believe they are still investigating," I said.

"Do you think Micah's past might have something to do with it?" The other asked.

"Since we have nothing to do with the incident, I think that question is moot, right? It's a bit like stumbling on a car crash. Just because we know how to drive doesn't mean we were involved in the crash." I used Lukas's analogy hoping they'd go away. "I have the phone number for the detective in charge of the case if you'd like to speak to him directly, but neither Micah nor I have anything to give you."

The men didn't look happy with my answer.

"Would you like the number?" I repeated.

"No. They won't give a statement to us anyway."

I shrugged. "Guess you're out of luck then. Have a good evening, gentlemen. I hope you enjoyed the tour. Please refer your friends." I made my way to Micah's side as the rest of the group scattered, heading off in different directions.

"I hope that we're done for the night," I told Micah. "'Cause I'm tired." I looked down at my feet. "Maybe I need better shoes."

"I used to wear one of those fitness watches," Micah said as we walked down Decatur toward the Square. "Some days I'd clock twenty kilometers. Used to come back this way every night and stop to get beignets, could eat two whole plates to myself. I think I overdid it since I don't care for them much anymore."

"Is it open all night?"

"Yes. Did you want to stop?"

"Nah. They were okay, but nothing to write home about."

"Do you want me to walk you home?" Micah asked. "So you

don't get lost?" He paused then added, "Or you can come home with me."

My heart sped up a little. "I'm not sure what the right answer is here, though I do think I should walk you home at least." I didn't like the idea of him walking through his dark garden alone, even if whatever it was only showed up after three a.m.

"But would you find your way home if you did that?"

"Maybe?" I reached out and took his hand in mine, liking that he didn't pull away. "Do you want me to go home?" I thought about that for a while when he didn't answer. "If I go home, will you be working on some craft all night instead of sleeping?"

He shrugged. "I usually sleep a few hours. But I do have some ideas of stuff to make for you."

"You've been hearing stuff nightly for the past few weeks."

"Yes. It's fine. I need to work on stuff anyway."

I couldn't help but grin at the thought of some cool new coat or costume. "You don't have to make me anything."

"No, but I have ideas. It's easier to get them out sometimes instead of keeping them in."

We walked a little further. Far enough that I was getting an idea of the area now. We'd have to make a choice on which way to turn soon. "If you're okay with me hanging with you, maybe I could stay over. Pet your cat or something." Man, was I awkward.

He laughed. "Jet loves you. He's a great judge of character."

"Doesn't seem to like Tim much," I said.

"I think it's because Tim doesn't like him. It's like he senses it. Tim has never really been an animal person. I didn't think I was either until Jet. No one really owns cats where I come from. It's more like the neighborhood cat. Everyone feeds it and it comes and goes as it pleases. Can't really do that here. It's not safe for Jet and a lot of people are very cruel."

That reminded me of the animal thing we'd seen in the cemetery. I didn't want to think about it. I squeezed his hand and let him steer us toward his place. Despite being after eleven there were still a lot of people lingering. We walked by the shop and everything was closed and dark, the sign gone from the walk.

"I hope Sky got home okay in her queen dress," I said. She had still been flouncing around in it when we had left for the tour.

"Lukas sent a text to say he was going to walk her home," Micah said. "You must have missed that in all your people watching. Did you get any good pictures? I saw you take a few."

"I haven't even looked." I pulled my phone out of my pocket and flipped it open, sending Lukas a quick text to tell him I was staying with Micah tonight. Maybe he was finally making good with Sky. "Made it through the whole tour without freaking out," I said. "Even after seeing a ghost. I'm pretty proud of myself."

"I'm proud of you too. Usually it's uneventful. Where did you see a ghost?"

"At the Market. Did you feel something at the voodoo place?"

"Yes, but it was mild."

I flipped through the pictures. Sure enough, at the Voodoo Museum, in the picture of the window beside where Micah stood, there was something. I wasn't sure what, but there was something. I tugged him to a stop and showed him the picture. "You see that? Or is it me?"

He examined the picture, brows knit together in thought that made me think I was seeing something in the picture he wasn't seeing either. "Sort of looks like a person. Almost like those Slender Man stories. Though those are all from a fiction piece that started about a decade ago, so not really long enough to even be an urban legend. I sometimes wonder if it is people's belief in things that create an alternate reality of some of these creatures."

"So you do see something. In the window?" I clarified.

"Yes. Mostly an outline. We can post the picture to the Facebook group. Let them debate it. There are legends of voodoo spirit guides that linger near where the veils are thinnest. Some of them would fit the description and this photo, but it's all hearsay. Stories of someone's best friend's brother's neighbor's wife... Did it feel dangerous to you?"

I had to think about that as we continued walking. "No? Not really. But the whole building seemed to glow." Which none of the pictures captured.

"Spirit guides aren't something that is supposed to be dangerous. Quite the opposite actually. I didn't notice a glow. Did it show up on camera?"

"Nope." Which irritated me. Did that mean my eyes were weird? Or my perception of reality?

"Did the LaLaurie Mansion glow?"

"No. It was dark. Black. Dead." Like a wormhole dropping into nothing, I thought. "Made my stomach hurt though, even if I didn't see anything." It was really nice to actually talk to someone about this stuff and not pretend everything was normal.

"Hmm," Micah said as he unlocked the gate to enter the garden surrounding his condo.

I got to the picture from the French Market. Yeah, there was something in that picture too. One of the ten I took, but clear enough to see the shape of a person in the distance. "Well, fuck. Maybe I am some kind of psychic live wire or something." I showed the picture to Micah.

"Could be a person," he said. "It's pretty far away."

"But you can kind of see the ground through the legs, right?" He enlarged the picture and moved it around a little. "I guess. Another one for the group." He gave me back the phone and we headed down the little path that would lead around the house to his place.

"I don't know how you can be such a skeptic when you experience so much," I said. "Therapists taught me to question everything, especially myself, and even I am at a loss for what this stuff is. Lukas says I don't need to understand it to accept it. Is that how you look at it?"

"I try to not look too deeply at any of it. Focusing on any of it seems to draw them in."

"But the idea of ghosts doesn't scare you. You walk around town where all the haunted places are and point everyone toward things they wouldn't normally see. And they don't scare you at all?"

"Ghosts can't hurt you. If that's what they even are. Ghosts by definition are in the past. A memory, or an emotion, or an old history, it's all before. The things people take pictures of are often the same. Repeating history? High emotion? I've done these tours for years and no one has ever been attacked," Micah said.

Or vanishes, I thought. But the noises outside his house late at night scared him. Memories of a different kind, much like that night in the desert.

"Ghosts sometimes touch people," I pointed out. "I've read about it."

"Conjecture," Micah stated unfazed by the idea of some wraith accosting him in the dark. "Plus why do they only come out at night or in old abandoned buildings? Why do we have to have all this special equipment to *see* them? I think because most of it is in our heads."

"We're all crazy," I supplied, suddenly feeling bad about myself again.

"Some more than most," Micah agreed.

I sighed, wondering if I should just go home. I was reasonably sure I could find my way back to it.

"Stop," he said.

"What?" I replied more lost in my thoughts than focusing on him.

"Thinking bad things about yourself."

"You just agreed that I'm crazy," I pointed out.

"We're both crazy. If seeing things makes you crazy, then me disappearing without a trace and coming back to hear strange creatures in my garden makes me crazy."

"That's a very specific type of crazy."

"Yeah?" He asked. "You studied types of crazy?"

After several long psych ward stays, I sort of felt like I had. "I'm not sure anyone really does, as much as locking it away."

"But you're not locked away now," Micah said. He turned and put his hands on my face, and I looked at him. "Stop putting yourself in that cage. It's okay to think, question, analyze, and even be afraid. It's what makes us human." With his warm fingers on my face some of the racing thoughts vanished, and having him right there was all that mattered.

"Live life, right? Instead of running away from it?"

He nodded and stepped away, instead reaching out to lace his fingers between mine. I gripped his hand as we walked through the array of pots. He paused and frowned. Some of the zombie gnomes were knocked over. They hadn't been like that when we had been by before going in to work. I stepped off the path and Micah gripped my arm.

"I'm going to stand them back up," I told him.

"We can do it tomorrow. Let's go inside."

"It doesn't have to be paranormal," I told him. "It could be a wild animal, or one of those stupid reporters. Who all has keys to the outside gate?" He might not fear ghosts, but whatever haunted his garden terrified him.

"Everyone in the building," Micah said, waving his free hand at the house. "Most don't come around the back of the house since they have a courtyard in the center of the house."

"Could have been one of them too. Maybe it was someone new who didn't know where the second path leads." I turned the flashlight function of my phone on. "Let me check the yard really quick."

Micah tensed, his hand squeezing mine hard enough to hurt.

"How about I walk you to the door first, then I'll check?" No reason to leave him standing on the sidewalk alone in the dark.

"No. Just no. What if it takes you?" And this was the core issue. Not fear of something being there, but fear of something being taken from him.

"Nothing is going to take me. I don't feel anything right now." And I didn't. No doom or skin prickles. Just the quickly cooling night air, exhaustion, and irritation at the thought that someone might have been creeping around his house. "Jet couldn't have gotten out, could he? Do you ever let him outside?"

"No. And he's never tried to get out."

"Maybe it was a big squirrel or something then." I tugged at his hand. "Let me walk you to the door."

"No. I'm going with you."

"Micah..." I could tell he was terrified about standing there on his own damn sidewalk this close to midnight. But he wasn't letting me go. "Okay. Turn your light on too. We'll cover more area." He agreed and turned on the light from his phone. With the two of them it was a bit like having a flood light spanning the entire yard. There were no unexplainable shadows, and when I righted the gnomes, no footprints or tracks in the dirt beneath them. Nothing else seemed disturbed, though the tension in Micah's shoulders didn't ease until we got to the door and he unlocked it with his key to let us inside.

Once inside, Jet mer-owed in greeting and Micah locked the door behind us. It was only then that I noticed he was shaking hard and breathing like he'd run a marathon. I shoved my phone into my pocket and wrapped my arms around him, pulling him into a tight hug. "I'm sorry."

"Don't ever do that again," he whispered. "Fucking Lukas does it all the time. He'd sleep on the floor, and I'd wake him up at the first sign of noise, only he wouldn't hear anything, but would then go racing out into the darkness. I'd be left in here, pacing, worrying. All my nightmares replaying over and over until he reappeared. Thinking, what if he vanished? How would I explain that? He's a cop. If they treated Tim horribly, and he's a damn boy scout, how would they treat me if a cop goes missing on my watch? And can you imagine how heart-broken Sky would be? And now I know you. If you vanished Lukas would go nuts. Even before I met you, I knew he would. You're all he talked about for a long time. He was so proud of you. If you were gone... Fuck."

"I'm sorry," I said again. "I was thinking less about actual boogeymen and more about the real sort of prowler kind. I didn't notice an alarm system earlier. Do you have one?"

"No." His hands gripped my shirt, like it was the only way he could stop them from trembling, and he pressed his nose to my collar breathing in the scent of me. I held him, rubbed his back, whispered apologies, though the whole thing made me a little angry. Not at Micah. None of this was his doing. More at the circumstances. At night he lived like a prisoner in his own home. Terrified of unexplainable sounds that not everyone heard, and stalked in the darkness by something he couldn't see.

I'd been thinking my own existence difficult, plagued by memories and dreams of a single nightmarish day in my past, while he lived in fear every day, tormented by something almost nightly. Dreaming of thriving while struggling to survive.

"Maybe we can take Jet and go to Lukas's place for the night. I don't think he'll mind," I said.

"It won't matter," Micah said as he pulled away and toed off his shoes to leave them beside the door. "I could be here or home with my parents and it follows me. Before Jet it would pull at the door knob, sometimes rattle the windows."

I looked at the cat who licked his paw like there was nothing important about him.

"Did you know that cats have historically been used to keep ghosts and all sorts of demons at bay? Across a dozen cultures and spanning through history all the way back to ancient Egypt. I think that's why Tim gave me Jet. Said he found him in the gutter somewhere. But Jet came to me chipped with Humane Society paperwork and a full medical record. Though I think he picked a cat because I don't have enough time for a dog and cats are more independent," Micah said.

It made me think better of the guy. Sure their relationship may have exploded from all the shit they'd both been through, but Tim seemed to be trying his best to still help out a friend. "He's a good guy."

"No reason to be jealous of him," Micah said. "Tim and I are over."

"I'm not jealous." I was jealous. Tim and Micah had a whole history, and so far Micah and I were what? A spark?

"You hungry? I can make pancakes or eggs or something. No dairy. I'm pretty allergic, but I can cook rice about a dozen ways. Potatoes too."

"Are you making ethnic jokes about yourself?"

"A little." He began picking up small things I hadn't noticed and putting them away. "I'm Asian but don't like sushi. So that one doesn't fit. I'm Irish and love potatoes. That one fits. Hungry?"

"Not hungry," I told him, watching him move. It was methodical. Like putting emotions into a box with each item he picked up. And perhaps it was. A way for him to build the wall around the anxiety that made his heart pound while we stood in the garden. "Tell me what I can do to help?"

He sighed. "I don't know?"

"Are *you* hungry?" I tried. I knew nothing about the layout of his kitchen or the possible contents, but I could cook and didn't have any food allergies that I knew of. Living on military rations sort of meant eating whatever you could.

"I don't know?" He asked again, unsure of everything in that moment. "I think I'm going to shower."

The only thing I'd seen him eat all day was part of a bagel and a few bites of sausage from the meal Lukas had ordered for me. "If I cook, will you eat?"

"Maybe?" He looked at me like a frightened bird, beautiful and injured. Micah needed focus too, I realized. Something beyond the fear.

"Where is your crochet? The one you were working on?" I tried to recall his closet layout and where he'd put it.

He shrugged. "It's one of many unfinished projects."

"Okay, what if I ask you for something? Give you something to focus on and finish? Will that help? I'll try to make us something to eat and you can start on the project."

He blinked at me like my words weren't quite making sense. I'd spent enough time overseas and in a psych ward to learn body language. His fight or flight mode was shutting down. Too much stress did that sometimes. Had that happen to me a time or two, so overwhelmed that I couldn't function, even breathing was hard when that happened. Sort of like a panic attack, only silent, a mental collapse inward.

I reached him in two long strides and pulled him into my arms, touching him, forcing him to feel me, breathe me in. "I'm here," I said. "You're not alone." His trembling hadn't eased. I thought about what therapy had taught me. Grounding, was one of the best ways to pull a person out of panic. That was all about the senses, but I'd always been very touch oriented. Which was why the weighted and textured blankets had worked well for my anxiety. I wasn't sure Micah had one in the menagerie of his crafts.

The second-best option was water. So I dragged Micah into the bathroom, stripping off both our clothes as we went. He didn't protest at all, which worried me, but his skin was cold beneath my hands and he shivered, even as I turned on the water to find it already hot.

It took a few buttons to figure out how to change the shower-head to use all three heads and more of a waterfall mode. Then I pulled Micah under that spray with me, wrapping my body around him for warmth and comfort. Letting the water trickle over our skin in a gentle rain. It wasn't sexual in that moment, though I doubted it would have taken more than a few basic thoughts to get me hard and ready for Micah. Everything about him appealed to me. Not just how beautiful and delicate he was, but how much my need to protect was fulfilled with him. Stupid white-knight syndrome. Why did Lukas always have to be right?

"You're safe," I promised him. "I'm here."

Micah clung to me like I was a life preserver keeping him afloat. The shivering slowed as I ran my hands through his wet hair, feeling it slide through my fingers. He accepted the small kisses I planted all over his face. And I wasn't sure he was hearing anything I said. I found his scrubbing sponge and added some body wash to it before working it to a lather and gently applying it to his skin.

He relaxed in inches along with my gentle washing. His shoulders, then his arms and inch by inch lower. He wasn't aroused, but neither was I. Instead he rested his head on my shoulder, eyes half lidded, exhaustion sapping the last of the panic from him. His breathing even, matching mine. I kept talking, nonsense really, but it didn't seem to matter.

"That's right, easy breaths. We'll get clean then find some food," I told him. If he didn't fall asleep first.

I turned off the shower and reached for the towels hanging on the drying racks. Micah didn't move, and almost seemed to be sleeping in my arms. I dried us both as best I could, still gifting him with small grounding touches and tiny kisses to the tip of his nose or ears. I should have thought to bring clothes with me when I knew I would be staying over.

"Do you have any clothes big enough for me to borrow?"

"Lukas has some stuff in the dresser. Bottom drawer," Micah mumbled.

"Do I need to ask again about you and my brother?"

Micah huffed at me, but I wrapped the towel around him and went in search of basics. "Sometimes I get afraid to be here alone. Lukas stays over if I text him and he's not working. Tim sometimes, too. I try not to ask them too often anymore because I don't want them more annoyed with me than they already are."

Lukas wouldn't have been annoyed at all by helping Micah to feel safe. I didn't know Tim well enough to judge that about him, but suspected it was much the same. Two years and still Micah didn't feel safe in his own home. I wondered if it was due to the nightly noises, or something more psychological. I suppose it could have been a little of both. I still clenched up when the wind howled. If it happened every night would I have grown immune?

I found a clean pair of boxers for me and an entire drawer of very adorable undies for Micah. I stared at the contents of the drawer for a minute, taking in the lace, fun patterns of super heroes, and even food stuffs, before grabbing the first pair near my hand. They were pale blue with colorful macarons on them.

When I brought them back to him, he slipped them on without comment or much thought. Bikinis. Very nicely fitted. Micah held out the towel for me, which jogged the slow-moving cog in my brain that said maybe I shouldn't be staring at him. I returned the towel to the drying rack and went to the kitchen to find food. Micah laid the bed back down and curled up under the blanket much like I often would when alone.

"Okay, so you take bachelor pad to a new meaning," I said after examining the cupboards. In the fridge there was almond milk, almond milk creamer, a newish carton of organic eggs, and a half dozen apples. In the pantry, which was one cupboard near the stove, there was a bag of rice, a jar of peanut butter, and a container marked sugar.

"Not home much," Micah said. "Usually I make fried rice or something."

I wasn't sure how to make that. Eggs and rice maybe? I did know how to make one thing with the few things he had, and figured why not, then dug around to find a flat pan that would fit in the tiny oven. It took less than two minutes to whip up a batch of poor man's peanut butter cookies. One egg, one cup peanut butter, and one cup sugar. It only made a dozen little bites, but that was all there was room for on the pan anyway.

"You like sweets, right?" I asked.

"Hmm," Micah grumbled.

"Was that a yes or a leave me the fuck alone?"

"Yes," Micah said. "I like sweets."

It took less than ten minutes in the little oven for the cookies to bake. Jet curled up with Micah, taking the spot right beside Micah's head and sticking his face under Micah's chin until he laughed. "Brat," Micah told the cat, reaching out to pet him.

"Does he need food or anything?" I asked, looking around the small space. There was an automatic fountain thing near the edge of the kitchen, but I didn't see food bowls.

"He has an automatic feeder for at night. It's upstairs in the loft. In the morning he gets wet food." Micah stroked Jet's back, his eyes closed and looking much like the cat in that moment, calm and content. That was much better than the panic earlier.

I took the cookies out and turned off the heat, found a plate and stacked them up. Then I poured a glass of milk for each of us and brought it to the futon. "Ever had poor man's peanut butter cookies?" I asked him as I set the plate down.

"I've had peanut butter cookies."

"These are a little simpler." I took one and tasted a bite. Yep, just how I remembered it. The peanut butter made the cookie very rich, the sugar taking the edge off it a little. "A lot of Europeans don't like peanut butter." Since he had a jar in the cupboard, I assumed he probably was okay with it.

Micah sat up and took a cookie. He took an experimental nibble. The cookies were small enough to be one bite each, but his expression softened. "Wow, that is very peanut buttery. Not all doughy like most cookies." He took a sip of his milk and finished the first cookie before taking the next.

"High protein. We always got peanut butter and sugar from the food shelf growing up. During the holidays we'd have the regular sort of peanut butter cookies with all the flour and stuff. I never liked those as much. I think because I grew up eating these, that everything else was sort of dulled down in flavor. When we got older and mom was making more money, she'd make the other kind, but neither Lukas nor I ate them, so she'd bring them to work or send them with dad. After a while she stopped making the other kind."

Micah ate another cookie. "We have cakes a bit like this. Super simple, rice flour, eggs, and a bit of flavor added in sometimes like fruit or tea. Mom cooked a lot when I was little."

"You still talk to her? Or your dad?"

"Yes. She calls once a week. I talk to them both. Dad is always trying to find me a job."

"You have a job," I pointed out, probably unnecessarily.

"One back home. He's tried to get me to teach English in a lot of places. That's not my world anymore. Not sure it ever was. He's even been trying to find me something teaching history. I'm not sure I can pretend to be that normal."

"I hear you there." I held up my glass of milk so we could do a pretend toast. We clicked plastic cups. "To messing up all on our own."

Micah smiled. "I think you're doing okay. You make great cookies."

"Thanks." I snuggled into the bed beside him. Once the cookies were gone, and milk empty, he put the dishes on the end table and reached for a remote that killed the lights. The apartment was silent, just the quiet whir of the air-conditioner. I wiggled closer to Micah, until I could smell his Christmas scent and reach Jet's furred side. Jet had a paw curled around Micah's arm. I reached out and petted the cat for a bit, closing my eyes and letting the texture ease the last of my anxiety away. I counted backward, expecting it to take a while to fall asleep, but it didn't. And even after all I'd experienced on the ghost tour, I didn't dream of deserts or fallen soldiers. I dreamt of cookies, cats, and cosplay boys.

CHAPTER 16

At first I wasn't sure what had roused me. The hiss of a cat was unfamiliar enough to have me jolting up in bed. I hadn't put the eye mask on and the room was its normal semi-dark with multicolored lights outside. Jet sat in front of the door, hissing and yowling at it, while the knob rattled.

I had to admit, heroics weren't my first thought. Instant fear carved agony into my gut. A glance back at Micah proved him to be awake and ghost white with terror. I threw back the blanket ready to get up and confront whatever the fuck it was and demand it leave us alone, but he grabbed my hand.

"Don't," he begged.

"You said it didn't do that anymore. Not since you got Jet."

"Apparently I was wrong." He climbed out of the bed, keeping his distance from the door but not letting me go. Instead he tugged me toward the loft.

"Micah?"

"It can't get in. All the windows and the door are painted with a mix of salt and holy water. Had the place blessed by both the Catholic church and voodoo priestesses. It's never gotten in." Yet he ran like hiding in the loft could turn off his terror. We stumbled into the small space above and Micah frantically dug into one of the chests for something, then found some sort of mat like thing and pulled it out. He laid it over the rug, then added a blanket to the top and got under it, holding it open for me. "Please," he begged when I didn't move.

I could still hear Jet's angry hissing from below and the vague rattle of the knob, but I crawled beneath the blanket with him. The entire loft was sort of like a big blanket fort. All it needed was a few little curtains to block off the rest of the main area. Micah curled up into my arms, trembling, his face buried in my shoulder, and his lithe body pressed against mine.

Of all the inconvenient times to wake up with wood. And of course, my hip hurt, perhaps from being overworked from all the walking, or even the climb up the stairs. The sound of the air-conditioner kicking in downstairs covered up the sounds from the door. I let out a breath I hadn't realized I was holding and let some of the fear go away. A thousand things could be at the door, or nothing at all. Micah needed reassurance more than I needed answers.

"You're safe," I told him. I kissed Micah's head, brushing his hair off his face and holding him close. He tilted his head, lips finding mine, not with the butterfly kisses I'd been giving him all night, but a fierce, possessive kiss which I couldn't recall ever experiencing before in my life.

His tongue dueled mine, mouth feeding at my lips like I still had the crumbs of cookies on them. I tried to mimic him, but gave up the battle and let him explore. He shoved me onto my back, straddling my hips and kissed me. That was okay. Well more than okay. My body was on fire with need for him, but I could live with kissing. He could have every bit of me in that moment if that was what he wanted.

His fingers stroked my face as the intensity of his kisses eased a little. He slid back until his ass was parked over my groin, and my erection nestled in-between the spread of his legs. Even with the fabric separating us, I could feel the heat of him, the shape of his crack and the swell of his balls where the head of my cock was nestled. I groaned, trying not to move my hips despite my body saying, *fuck yeah*. Each time I moved pain echoed through my hip, sharp and unforgiving.

"Fuck," I grumbled into Micah's lips. "Worst time ever for my hip to go out. Getting old sucks."

Micah chuckled a little and pressed a hand to my right hip. "This one?"

"Yeah. Cracked it ages back. Took forever to heal. Doctors said it would be weak for the rest of my life. Sometimes it feels like the joints don't fit together right anymore."

Micah put his other hand on my cock, stroking me through the boxers. "But the pain isn't bad enough to wilt this."

"Apparently not," I agreed. "It's only a little ache in my hip." Though I knew if I tried to move it too much it would really begin to hurt.

He sighed against my lips and kissed me again. "Can we have sex?" He asked, bluntly. "I'd really like to have sex with you."

"Um, okay?"

"That doesn't sound all that certain," Micah said.

I wasn't sure now, while something was downstairs scaring the cat, was a good time to get our groove on. Was Micah even awake enough to be in the right mindset? Was it fear driving him to want me? I thought about all the porn I'd watched in my life and the romance novels I'd read. What was it in the books that had always been a turn on when someone was afraid and seeking physical comfort? It was always the slow, discovery love making, right? I could do that. I probably wouldn't last long myself, but I was pretty sure I could get him off a time or two.

I reached up to cup the back of his neck with my hand and

bring him down for another kiss. This time I led a slow and sensuous dance, exploring the shape of his lips, and the taste of his tongue.

"Hmm," Micah grumbled. I wasn't sure if it was a good or a bad response, but he wasn't pulling away. "Don't want slow," he told me after a few minutes and a dozen similar kisses. "I'm not made of glass."

"I thought maybe I could worship you for a bit. You know, like they do in romance novels."

He tilted his head to look at me and I wondered how much he could make out in the pale light of the loft. "That's sweet, but I'd rather you fuck me."

"Not sure I can at the moment since my hip is being a bitch," I pointed out.

He seemed to consider that. "I can ride you."

Oh boy did that make my dick twitch at the thought.

"I'll take that as a yes," Micah said, obviously feeling my body's reaction against his. He leaned over to reach in a small cupboard and pull out a little zippered bag. Inside was a bottle of lube and a couple of condoms. He wiggled out of his underwear before I could protest and turned on a small lamp near the sewing machine. I sighed as I looked over his lithe body. The small ass, smooth legs, and generous cock made for a lot of fantasies in my life. None of which I'd ever thought I'd experience in person. He was hard and leaking, dripping precome onto my stomach as he tugged off my boxers.

I was not the same delicate perfection. My hips, legs, and thighs were scarred, hairy, and a little bony. My cock wasn't bad in size, thick, rather than long, and not the video ready sort that apparently Tim had been, but I'd never thought it wasn't enough. Our flesh bared, he sat back down, nestling my cock against his taint and leaning over me to take the lube he'd applied to his hands and press it into his own hole.

I wish I could have watched that bit, his fingers swallowed up by his own heat as he made himself ready. Only I wasn't sure I would have lasted more than a few seconds. As it was, with my dick trapped between us, the weight of him keeping a steady pressure against me, even as his hips wiggled a little, I struggled to hold back. I could feel him pressing his fingers inside himself with our bodies aligned so tightly together. I could feel the way his body trembled in reaction, tightening and loosening, and I could feel the rest of his fingers against my balls as he changed directions or added a finger.

There was a bit of frenzied anxiety in his touch. I knew that sometimes sex could ground people, though I'd never seen it in real life. It was like he was trying to use my body to ground himself, only it wasn't working. He panted for breath and didn't seem to want my help, though I didn't want him to hurt himself.

"Micah?" I asked, putting my hands on his cheeks and making him look at me. "Breathe, okay? I'm not going anywhere."

He pulled away almost fierce in his need. He reached down between us with his other hand and coated the head of me in slick. I gasped, my hips moving without conscious effort, pain spiking through my right side and easing some of the immediate need to come.

Micah opened a condom and slid it over me, then applied more lube before wiping his hands on a tiny towel that had been in the little zipper bag.

My stupid hip screamed at me, while my cock begged and twitched to be encased in Micah's warm heat in a fantasy I'd longed forever to fulfill. He frowned at me, an expression I didn't like to see while he sat over me like some avenging angel of sex and fantasy. He glanced down at my hip, then placed both hands on my waist and leaned forward to kiss me. I accepted his kiss again. This one more subtle, a pressing of lips, and mingling of air. I closed my eyes to savor the feel of him against me, his heat, and his touch.

"Sorry," he whispered two seconds before my hip exploded in a fire of pain as he pressed against it to shift the joints and something popped back into place.

"Fuck!" I cried out, but just as quickly the pain was gone and my hip seemed back where it belonged, smooth and only a hint of the prior discomfort. My dick was still hard so that was something. I stared at Micah, turned on and highly confused.

"Massage lessons come in handy every once in a while." He lifted his hips and stroked my cock which was now very excited to be given attention.

"Warn a guy next time," I grumbled at him.

"You would have tensed up."

Probably. And I'd have hurt more, which would likely have ended our play. I stared at his beautiful body, thrilled for the light so I could examine his perfect skin and gentle curves. He was paler than I, more cream than the tan I'd always been. And tiny freckles decorated his skin in light kisses that I'd never noticed before on any of his videos. It made me giddy to find there was something that not everyone knew.

I reached for him, hesitating a moment. "Is it okay if I touch you?" I'd met a few guys who liked to give but not be touched. Or receive and not be touched. But being gay in the military had been a delicate balance of a lot of fragile emotions.

"Yes," Micah said. He continued to stroke my cock, then positioned it against him. I trembled at the idea of what was happening. The pulsing heat of him against the tip of me, the shadow of my dick visible behind his balls and between those amazing thighs.

I put my hand in his hair, running my fingers through the softness as he began to lower himself down. He gasped when the head of me finally breached him, pausing and letting himself adjust. For me it was a teasing bit of fire. A strong warm grip around the tip of me. The muscles of his hole clenching around the underside of the glans. I grabbed at the blanket trying to stave off coming like it was my first time or something.

He slid down slowly. Easing up a little, sliding me in further, the look of concentration on his face, intense. I struggled to breathe fearing that letting out a full breath meant spoiling the moment and ending the pleasure.

Finally I was balls deep, awed at the beauty of our bodies meeting, mine deep inside him, encased in heat. He rocked from side to side slightly, ass resting on my hipbones, legs spread on either side of me. It was like he was searching for something.

"Tell me what you need," I said.

Micah shook his head, concentrating rather than speaking. He leaned forward, shifting the angle or something before he started to move. It was heaven. A dream. Like a porno happening to me right that moment all at once, and yet I felt detached because he seemed to be detached.

I caught his hips, stopping him despite my body demanding more, faster, harder. "Hey, maybe we should slow down a bit?"

He looked down at me with half-lidded eyes, glazed, not with lust, but more that earlier panic I thought we'd washed away in the shower. He wasn't seeing me. Was he imagining someone else? Had someone hurt him? I frowned, and lifted his hips to unseat him. He gave a small protest.

"I'm not even sure you're awake right now," I told him.

"Because I want to have sex with you?"

"Because I'm more than a blow-up doll."

He blinked hard at me and sat back on the rug, frowning as my words began to sink in. Some of the fear seemed to leak away from his face. He glanced around the small loft. Was he just now seeing it?

"Micah," I called.

"I'm okay."

I didn't believe that for a hot minute. "Talk to me. What's in your head?"

"Nothing."

A lie. Okay. It was fine if he wasn't ready to talk about it.

"Is this a one-off? I'm okay with comforting you," I told him, focusing on the broad picture instead of unspoken suspicions. "But if we're going to have sex, I'd like you to at least be emotionally present."

"Most guys don't want that."

"I'm not most guys." I pulled the blanket up around myself and lay back down on the mat. Micah sat a few feet away, either unconcerned with his nudity or unashamed of it. He was still hard, though I was quickly losing my erection. Maybe this too, was a sign that I was broken. Most guys would have jumped at the chance to fuck Micah. Emotional connection or not. I didn't want to look into his pretty blue eyes and think he was imagining I was someone else. Or that he was somewhere else. Or worse, reliving a past nightmare.

Some people fantasied about being in the middle of a porn video. I was beginning to think that wasn't the fantasy most people thought it was. After watching for over a decade I knew how much of an act it was, how unrealistic the positions and expressions were. It was one of the reasons I'd stopped watching pro stuff and gone to amateur videos, which was where I'd found Micah's stuff. I was looking for some realism. This wasn't it.

I opened the blanket a smidge for him. "We can still cuddle," I offered.

"But no sex?" Micah asked, frowning.

"I think not yet. Didn't you say something about flames burning out and all that?" My body revved up again at the reminder that I had actually been inside him for a few minutes

185

and been stupid enough to pull away. It wouldn't be a stretch to fan that flame back into an inferno.

"There's nothing wrong with sex," Micah grumbled.

"No," I agreed. "But is it really me you want here? Or am I just a warm body distraction?"

He stared at me for a while, expression blank, body slowly calming. I wished he would share his thoughts with me.

"Micah?" I asked again. I offered him the blanket. He reached across, turned off the light and crawled into the cocoon I'd made of the quilt. He sucked in a deep breath, holding himself at a distance for a minute before sinking into my arms. He did reach down and tug off the condom, depositing it in a small trash bin near the sewing machine. Then he buried his face in my shoulder and began to cry. Not gentle sniffles or silent tears, but ugly tears and harsh breathing.

"Do you want to talk about it?" I whispered into his hair.

"No," he said.

"Okay." I rubbed his back, told him it would be okay, though could only imagine all the avenues his brain might take him down. I dragged over a box of tissues and kept handing them to him as I kissed his head and whispered, "It's going to be okay," over and over. Was it a lie? Maybe. Whatever had been stalking him, had been doing it for years. If it hadn't stopped by now, would it ever?

I curled around him, using my body as a shield and my words as comfort. It was all I could give him in that moment.

CHAPTER 17

I woke before Micah, not really remembering when I'd fallen asleep. Our little adventure in the loft had been real and not a dream as we were both wrapped in the blanket and my cock a little crusty from dried lube. He slept pretty soundly when I opened my eyes to Jet staring intently at us both.

"Creepy," I whispered to the cat, annoyed by his intense gaze. He sat there, tail twitching like a little whip. Right, Jet got wet food in the morning. I glanced at my phone and realized it was after six. Despite the few hours of sleep, I felt pretty rested.

I carefully extracted myself from Micah and the blanket, leaving him wrapped up and curled around my pillow, and found my way to the bathroom. I washed up, put the boxers back on and found food for Jet before filling the coffee pot.

The water slowly seeped through the grounds while I stared longingly at the brew and thought about the early morning encounter. Not the door thing, that was its own issue that I planned to research on my phone as soon as I had a cup of coffee in my hands, but Micah. I still wasn't sure how to read his behavior. Had I been wrong to turn him away? Was I being a prude for wanting him to be in the moment with me? Or misreading his body language that there was something he was hiding from me? I'd been a toy soldier so long that I wanted more than to be jerked around, or even off. I wanted to get to know Micah, help him if I could.

At least he'd fallen asleep finally.

I sent a text to Lukas: *I think I'm not cut out for relationships.*

The fast responding text surprised me a little, as I thought he might be sleeping. *You've barely started one. Too soon to tell.*

We almost had sex. I confessed. Hell, to some religions we had sex, even if neither of us had come.

Almost? Did you take a taco break in the middle and forget to continue?

Jerk. I sent back. *I... felt like he wasn't present.*

The little (...) bubble showed up for a while, meaning he was writing or debating on writing, but nothing showed up. I got up to fill my coffee cup, and found my way to the little dining table off the kitchen.

I wrote, *Closed off. Porn star active, human mode off.* Twice I typed 'afraid' only to delete it, not sure if Lukas knew or even should know. Fuck, I didn't even know there was something more wrong. Well, more than some weird noise at night.

Defense mechanism. Lukas's message appeared.

Which had been my thought as well, though I'd done my best to try to make him comfortable. *Yeah. So that's why we only almost had sex.*

You're such a nice guy sometimes. You could have used that to overcome the first hurdle.

First hurdle? Since when is sex a first hurdle? And rude that you think I'd take advantage of anyone.

Most guys would have.

Good thing I'm not most guys, I sent back a little irritated. *I wish he would open up to me a little.* He'd tried. Sharing a bit about the closet, his crafting, and how he felt things other people didn't, but those were all things about him, not how he felt, emotionally. I didn't know if he was that reserved or I was missing something. He'd broken down and sobbed in my arms in the middle of the night, crying like his heart had been ripped out, but giving me nothing other than his tears. It made me wonder if it was I who had disappointed him, or life, or something he hadn't yet mentioned.

Time. Lukas sent back.

Maybe. But there were other problems I had to fix. *Need to research garden monsters. Talk to you later.*

Garden monsters?

But I closed the message window and pulled up Google. Micah had mentioned salt and holy water. I'd heard of those things. Wasn't sure how it corresponded with our nightly visitor, but I began to research anyway, hoping to at least give Micah a little more peace at home.

I spent over an hour searching, making notes, and planning, then made another cup of coffee, this time bringing it up the small stairs to Micah. I set it down two inches from his nose, which was the only part of him poking out from the rolls of the quilt. A few seconds passed, then his nose wiggled a little. Yeah, he was as much a coffee addict as I was.

"Morning," I said when he pushed the blanket off his eyes. "Brought you coffee."

He glared at me. "Please tell me you're not a morning person."

"Nope," I promised. "But already been up an hour or so. Was going to run some errands really quick, and I wanted to make sure you were okay with me leaving for a while. I can see if Sky will come stay with you for a bit."

"I'm fine," he said without feeling. How many times had I

said that same thing? It was a lie to cover up things too compli-cated to say.

"Yeah? How about you have some coffee, maybe a warm bath, and I'll bring you breakfast. What do you like?"

He frowned at me, half a dozen emotions flitting across his face too quickly for me to read. "You don't have to do anything for me."

"Nope. But I want to. So what would you like?"

"Those pancakes you had last night looked good."

"The French toast? Okay. I know where that place is." And it was on the way to the rest of my errands. Thankfully, most of what I needed was in the Quarter. "Are you going anywhere right away? Big plans for this morning?"

He shook his head and lifted it a little so he could sip from the side of the coffee cup. It was funny as hell because it screamed of laziness and coffee addiction all in one.

I leaned over and kissed the side of his face. He frowned at me.

"Can you rest a bit this morning? I'll be back in an hour or two?" I looked at my phone and it was almost eight. "Let me bring you breakfast."

"Why?" He asked. "You don't owe me anything."

"No. And that's sort of the point." My brain had been going over it for a while now. "You don't owe me anything either. Not for the job, or hanging out with me, or even for being my friend. You know that, right?"

He stared at me but said nothing. That's kind of what I had thought.

So I spelled it out for him. "You don't owe me sex."

"I want to have sex with you. I like sex," he said. "I find you attractive."

"Thank you." I nodded. "I find you attractive, too, and maybe soon, we can have sex. When we're both ready and in the moment. You said something about training and still thinking of each other after a few days? I'd rather be that than a spark that burns out."

"A spark would hurt less when you go," Micah whispered.

I curled up beside him, careful of the coffee and wrapped my arms around him for a minute. "I'm not going anywhere. Even if we are nothing but friends. I'm building a new life here and would very much like for you to be a part of it."

His expression said he didn't believe me. It made me a little angry. Had all his friends left him because of the disappearance? I knew he and Tim had broken up, but it sounded like they still had some sort of friendship. And he had Lukas and Sky now, yet he kept them at a distance too.

"You don't even know me," he said.

"No, but I'd like to. I think you're cute and quirky. I enjoy your snark when you let it out. I'm fascinated by your crafting skills, and I'm a bit of a cosplay nerd myself even if I'm out of practice. Lifelong friendships have started with less."

"Do you want to just be friends?"

I thought about that for a minute. "I want whatever we will be to progress naturally. Yes, I'm physically attracted to you, but I think we need to move at a pace that works for both of us. I've been out of the world for a while. Never had a real relationship before. I'd like to get to know you better and see if maybe we can find something more than a one-off. Unless you don't want that?"

Micah frowned at me looking confused. "I don't know what I want."

"Fair enough. But you know you don't have to pretend to be into me if you aren't. Maybe you have a thing for Lukas. And that's okay. We look alike, but don't have much in common. I would be a bad substitute for him."

"I don't want Lukas."

I stroked Micah's cheek, finding the sleepiness in his face adorable. "Okay. Rest," I told him, giving him another kiss on the brow and running my hands through his soft hair. "Snuggle with Jet for a bit, let me get food, and worry about everything else later. Okay?"

"Okay," he finally agreed.

I made my way out into the garden. Nothing was moved. The gnomes were still upright, and no tracks. There was no sign of anything near the door. It made me angry that something kept tormenting him. My research had given me ideas, all legends and conjecture, but I had to start somewhere.

Thankfully Lukas had the day off since: *Cops get breaks too.* And was there at the gate with his rarely used car. I needed supplies and a way to get the stuff to Micah's. It was okay if it was all a flight of fantasy, and nothing worked. I would keep trying. That was the point of being human, after all, trying.

Lukas helped me carry all my stuff to Micah's place, when we arrived after ten a.m. I had a huge bag of breakfast food for the three of us, and supplies which I spread out on the open floor of Micah's living room. He was awake, and dressed, but sitting on the couch crocheting something when we came in.

"Hey, Micah," Lukas said setting down a container of quick cement and two-gallon jugs of water which we'd had blessed by a priest. It was crazy how many people Lukas knew, and calling on a priest this early in the morning had been a trip. The man had shrugged and agreed with Lukas's request to bless the water like it was something he did every day. And maybe he did. It was the most haunted city in the USA after all. Or at least I thought it should be.

I spread out a drop cloth to keep the mess to a minimum and

handed Micah his breakfast. He put the crochet aside and opened the container, looking at the food with a bit of wariness.

"There's eggs and sausage in the other container too if you want something less sweet," I told him, pointing to my breakfast. I could eat either or drink more coffee and not be bothered.

Micah put both containers on the couch beside him to pick at them while I worked on mixing cement with holy water, salt, and crystals and pressing the mix into a mold. It was one of the big perks of living in a town of musicians and artisans, finding a place where I could buy multiple cat shaped molds had been easy. In fact, the set I had picked was the 'see no evil, hear no evil, speak no evil' set of cats. I also had a set of sleeping cats in different positions. The idea was to ward off the thing in the dark or maybe make it so relaxed and sleepy it left us alone.

Lukas ate his breakfast of eggs and pancakes while watching me mix. He'd chosen some of the colors of the crystals we'd picked up. Stuff crushed and made for decoration in grout, expensive, but he hadn't protested the cost. Nor had he told me the idea was stupid. He had in fact been willing to fund my entire monster buster kit for Micah's yard without question.

Jet parked himself on the edge of the drop cloth and watched as though he worried the cement cats were taking his place. After a few minutes Lukas closed up his container and pulled Jet into his lap. The cat curled up like it was his favorite place to be, tail flicking lazily and eyes closed as Lukas petted him.

The first batch of cats came out a little rough. Chipped in some spots, uneven, and not pressed perfectly into the mold, but that was okay. The second batch worked fine. I had to move fast because the stuff dried so quickly, but soon I had half a dozen of the little critters sitting on the cloth beside us. Micah had found his way down to the floor as well, mixing up colors of the ground crystals and water for me while I pressed the mix into the molds. Each set sparkled with the crystals, looking a little bit color-streaked with the white I'd chosen as the base. My goal was to fill his garden with the cats. A mix of legends meant to keep the supernatural at bay with salt, holy water, particular crystals, and cats. The glitter I'd thrown in there for a bit of pop.

Lukas had also picked up another set of gnomes as the shop with the molds was the same one where he normally bought his lawn decorations. These two gnomes were warrior gnomes, dressed for battle, in old armor and wielding swords like they were there to protect the garden. I planned to put them one on each side of the door with cats lining the path around them.

Lukas kept looking at his phone. He must have been texting Sky because she showed up after eleven with an arm full of boxes she claimed were fairy guardians to hang in the trees. Micah sat on the little bench under the tree watching the three of us decide where stuff would go. He sat in silence, crocheting, face filled with confusion, but not protesting.

Tim and Brad arrived before noon with a set of boxes as well. Theirs was one of those doorbell camera things, which Tim installed in minutes and linked to all of our phones. He added camera angles to view each area of the house and garden, five in total, which pulled up in tiny little screens on our phone or full-sized on Micah's computer.

Brad and Sky chatted as they hung dozens of little crystal 'fairies' from the giant willow tree, making it cast rainbows when the sun hit it. The fairies doubled as hummingbird feeders and would have to be refilled on occasion, but the wind through the giant tree made them dance and sing.

From what I overheard of their conversation, Lukas had told Sky that Micah had a rough night because I'd told him, and Sky had told Brad who had told Tim. It was a bit like a confusing game of telephone.

Lukas went over the specs of the security system with Tim

and I sat down beside Micah, worried about his silence. "Is this okay?" I asked him waving at the yard and all the changes.

He shrugged. "I'm not sure it will help." He sucked in a deep breath. "It's hard to hope anymore. It shouldn't bother me so much. It's just noise."

I took his hand in mine and squeezed it gently. He'd been tormented by the noise for a long time. I suspected it would eventually drive anyone a little crazy. Would any of this help? None of us knew. I think what mattered more in that moment was that we were all willing to try.

"Out in the desert that night, when my base was destroyed, the wind howled like some sort of banshee." I frowned. "I've been researching a lot of legends today. Anyway, I still tense up if the wind howls like that. If I heard it every night, or it intensified and got closer? I'd be freaked out too. I'm sorry that this is happening to you. I hope this helps a little."

"Sorry about last night," Micah said quietly.

"For what?" I asked, genuinely confused.

"The sex thing." He looked away. "I was trying to use you as a distraction."

"Ah. I don't mind being a distraction if that's what you need. I wanted you to see *me* while we were together. Does that make sense?"

He nodded.

"And you weren't seeing me, were you?"

"No. I was too afraid. It hasn't tried to come inside in a very long time. I thought maybe if I could turn my brain off and not think then it wouldn't matter."

I slid closer to him and wrapped my arm around his shoulder, pulling him into a sideways hug. I kissed his forehead again, then rested my chin on the top of his head. "This okay? Me touching you?" I clarified.

"Yes. I like that you don't hesitate to touch me. Like you're not afraid that touching me will curse you."

"You're not a curse."

"Hmm," was all he said.

Only time would tell. I didn't think he was a curse even if misfortune happened around him. It wasn't his fault. "Well, we've got the monster busting kit together. Blessed cats, infused with special earth protection crystals and pure salt. Guardian gnomes. Fairies to watch over your plants and trees, and technology for the modern stuff in case some rougarou comes loping to your door."

"I've seen some believable pictures of werewolves," Micah said of the rougarou comment.

"But not likely one in your garden as I suspect he'd make a bigger mess than knocking over some gnomes." I took his hand in mine and squeezed it. "Do you know what's best about all this?"

"I didn't have to pay for it?" Micah groused.

"Oh, you're a comedian. Funny. No, smart ass, the best part of all this is that your friends are here for you, trying to make you feel better."

"Even if I'm nuts."

"I heard and saw it too. So I'm as nuts as you."

He sighed, and turned his head to look up at me, expression thoughtful. "I like you."

I grinned at him. "I like you too."

"Aw," Sky said, overhearing. "Look at the feels." She rushed our way arms spread wide and wrapped us in a bear hug belying her small size. Brad laughed and copied her.

"Don't you dare," I told Lukas when he headed our way, a serious smile on his face. He did anyway, wrapping all of us in his huge reach and squeezing until we all groaned. Tim shook his head like we were all nuts.

"On the happy feels note, I have a bit of bad news to deliver," Lukas said when he let go.

I narrowed my eyes at him. "Really? Burst our bubble?"

He stepped away and held up his hands in surrender. "Not my fault. I'm the little guy on the messenger board for this one. The cemetery is still a no-fly zone today. The department says probably by midweek it will be clear. I know you usually have Saturday tours, Micah. Sorry."

"I already rescheduled or refunded people for today. Some are going on a ghost tour instead since they wanted the full moon atmosphere for the cemetery and today is the last day of it."

I hadn't even thought of that. Did that mean there was another legend somewhere I had to research and add to the garden?

"Tonight is the kid's tour," Sky said.

"Yep," Micah said. "And I'd like to show Alex how to close tonight. So it's okay that we only have one tour today."

"Is the kid's tour different?" I asked.

"Earlier. Starts at 5, is only an hour. It's focused for kids under twelve. Accompanied by their parents of course, but the stories are more PG and the route shorter. I focus a lot on history that the kids can relate to. Stories of other kids, more often who were heroes rather than victims, though they do like a good creepy story or two." Micah looked at me. "Are you up for an open-to-close shift today?"

I nodded, looking over the garden one more time. The path was lined with cats, fairy feeders, and monitored by cameras. I felt like it was as safe as I had the power to make it. And while I couldn't chase away the ghosts that haunted Micah's thoughts, I hoped to scare off whatever it was that lingered in his garden. Even if it was for a selfish reason like seeing him drop his guard a little.

CHAPTER 18

Opening the shop was as easy as it sounded. A three-step process of unlocking the door, disarming the alarm, and putting the chalkboard sign on the walk downstairs. The first few hours were stocking, ringing up the steady stream of Saturday customers, and preparing for the kids tour.

Micah plugged in his phone to a little speaker system and played pop music in the shop. I'd never taken him for a Justin fan but had to admit the tunes were catchy. Both Justins.

"Do you have a thing for Justins or for blonds?" I asked Micah.

"I have Taylor on this mix too. Some Pink as well."

"So it's the blonds?" I said giving him a big grin.

He glanced at my hair, which was looking good with the help of whatever his little supply of secret Japanese inscribed products were. "Yep."

The most recent of the Justin pop songs came on and I swept Micah up into my arms for a dance. I was an awful dancer, but that didn't mean I never danced. He laughed and tried to sway with me. We ended up simply shaking our asses around the store.

Customers laughed and waved when they came in, but no one said anything bad. The song ended and I wrapped an arm around Micah's waist, pulling him into a hug. We were both breathing hard and smiling. Micah's expression open and real. Not an act or a mask, but actual joy. I reveled in it, while gifting him with a kiss on the cheek, then let him go so I could attend to the customers.

Micah worked on creating a small backpack full of fun things for each of the registered kids. I stuffed them with stickers, a T-shirt, some well-marked allergy free candy, and a voodoo doll that was really a catnip stuffed cat toy. The pack was a little ingenious as it was all safe stuff that the kids would think was very unique and paranormal.

He also had a box of stretchy fingerless gloves made from shiny fabrics that looked like superhero-type designs. "What are these?" I asked pawing through the box. There was a couple of sets that looked like dragon scales. I pulled them out and found them stretchy enough to fit.

"Sometimes the kids get scared, even though I keep it low key. So they all get a set of superpowers to take with them, just in case," Micah said. "When the parents sign up the kids I usually ask if they have a favorite superhero. Sometimes the kids are autistic and either love or hate certain colors, so I always have a variety."

That was insanely thoughtful of him. The gloves went up over my forearms, fitting pretty snug. But if they were kid sizes that made sense.

"You can keep those if you want," Micah said. "There are only two different sizes and I try to make a few of each pattern so the kids all get what they want. I have more in back too if I run low. They only take a few minutes to make."

I flexed my arms pretending the gloves gave me magic

powers. "What do you think? Do I look like I have superpowers, or like I'm really constipated?" I asked him as I posed.

He laughed. "You're such a dork."

I couldn't help but smile at the ease of his laughter. Some of the wall was coming down around his emotions, and that thrilled me.

The kids began arriving at four thirty, all excited and eyes aglow as they prepared for hunting ghosts. Their parents took pictures as Micah performed a 'ritual' on each of them, blessing the kids with 'magic' to prevent ghosts from clinging to them. Each kid chose a pair of superhero gloves. I got down on my knees and flexed in poses with them, showing them how to ward off evil with the turn of their wrist. Okay, it was a little gay and over-the-top RuPaul-ish, but no one protested and the kids thought it was great. Then the group shopped until the last of the kids had all arrived.

Finally at five o'clock, with Sky behind the register to cover, Micah and I led the kids and their parents out into the Square to begin their ghostly journey. I quickly learned the reason that there had been no walk-through of the kid's tour was because there was nothing really scary that could happen on the kids tour. Micah told stories, mostly history, and answered questions.

"Have you ever seen a ghost?" One of the kids asked me.

"Yep," I told him.

"Were you scared?"

"No. Ghosts can't hurt you." At least I didn't think they could.

"Why do they stick around then?" Asked another girl who had been the sort of smarty-pants of the group so far.

"I'm not sure they do. I think they come to visit when they know people will be by." I had no idea if I was giving the right answers or not. Me and kids weren't a normal combination, though Micah seemed a pro with them. In fact, I'd never seen him so engaged as he was with the kids. No mask, no acting, just earnest storytelling.

We passed Lafayette's Bar and Micah told tales of pirates that had all the kids excitedly searching the streets for signs of men with peg legs and parrots. The plaque on the side of the building gave a brief overview of the property which made me think Micah's history was spot on. The path around the Quarter was short and detailed. There was not one boo-wiggly on the entire tour.

We ended up back in the Square, all the kids bubbling with excitement having taken pictures with their phones or their parents' phone and hoping for ghosts to appear. I called for them all to line up, "Superheroes present!" I called.

The kids formed an awkward line and we all posed. The kids with their backpack ghost hunting kits, T-shirts, and super-hero gloves, and me looking like a big doofus on the end in my gloves, which Micah informed me were mermaid scales not dragon scales.

"Mermaids are ocean dragons," I informed him. To which he shook his head like I was too much.

The parents and even Micah snapped pictures. I got hugs all around and Micah got smiles and 'thank yous' from the whole group.

Of all the tours so far, this had been my favorite. I got to see a very animated side of Micah as he told stories and answered questions that weren't all about gloom and doom. The unguarded version of him was a beautiful thing. A little raw, yes, but inspiring.

Once everyone had wandered off to find dinner I snuck up beside Micah and kissed him on the cheek, then took a hold of his hand and squeezed it gently.

"What was that for?" he wanted to know.

"For giving those kids an amazing night they will not long

forget. I didn't even know there was a kid's tour. I think I like this one best."

"Just once a week on Saturday's," Micah said. We walked together toward the shop. "I think I'm the only one that does them regularly."

Those kids had thought Micah hung the moon as they listened to the facts. "Bet if all their history classes were like that, they'd be top students in no time."

Micah smiled. It appeared genuine this time. "I had a history teacher as a kid who told us stories about our school being haunted. Me and a couple other kids often tried exploring the school at night. Got in trouble more than once for being there when we shouldn't, but we never saw anything. I remember his stories though. Maybe that's why I became a history buff."

"Haunted school, eh? You were even hunting ghosts as a kid? Weirdo," I teased.

He shrugged. "It was all a game back then."

It was still a bit of a game now. Cat and mouse. I'd posted my pictures to his Facebook group and watched the comments and speculation rise without getting involved, since Micah suggested I leave all of that to the group.

"Kids don't expect the same things as adults do. Adults want to be terrified. They want to be uncomfortable, even if it makes them angry sometimes. Kids want to feel like there is a purpose to everything. Purpose means safety. That's why I try to keep it very positive for the kids."

"Well I think you did an amazing job." And I'd gotten to see the real Micah, unguarded and joyous, which was a thing to behold. "How come they are only on Saturdays? The kid one?"

"Weekends are easier if kids are out of school or on vacation with their family. Earlier in the day people are on bayou tours and stuff. I found Saturday night at five is the most accessible for families, though I've been known to do exclusive tours if someone is visiting and can't make the Saturday. Some people bitch about exposing kids to the 'occult,' but I think it keeps their minds open, questioning, exploring, and learning," Micah said.

"That makes sense to me. Obviously the parents who bring their kids think so too."

"Most of the time. I've had a few complain because I didn't focus more on the church, and then others complain when I focus too much on church history. Nothing is ever perfect."

I tugged him closer and wrapped an arm around his waist so I could draw him in for another hug. "Sorry," I said. "I needed to hug you. Sometimes I'm touchy-feely."

He accepted my hug and returned it with one of his own. "I'm okay with touchy-feely."

We separated and walked a little longer in silence, but Micah tugged me away from the street that would have taken us back to Simply Crafty.

We walked by Café Du Monde and I admitted to myself that the smell of pastry and sugar made me hungry. "Are we in a rush to get back?" I asked him as we passed the shop that made pralines.

"Not really. Sky has the shop until we get there."

"Good," I said, pointing toward the praline shop. "Can we get some?" I asked as my stomach rumbled. I needed to get better at eating regular meals.

He narrowed his eyes like he was on to me. "Okay."

I sighed happily and raced toward the shop. We ate, nibbling pralines and ethnic food from the open market area, while browsing a few shops on the way. I'd found the shop Sky had gotten her fairy light feeders from and used Lukas's credit card to purchase a handful of large, handmade, dreamcatchers with elaborate colors, beads, and wrapping, with the plan to put them around the windows in Micah's house.

"I'm going to owe Lukas all of my upcoming paychecks," I told Micah as he raised a brow at my purchases. "But I figure we should cover the bases of as many religions as we can, right?" The little money I got from my military medical discharge was already going to him no matter how much he complained about it.

Micah shrugged. "I guess." He obviously had no expectation of anything helping. But that was okay. I had enough hope for the both of us.

Back out on the street Micah looked longingly at a quilt shop nestled into one of the bottom floors of the rowhouses across from the boardwalk where we'd been. "Let's go in," I said steering him that way.

"I don't need more fabric." His cheeks flushed pink. "I'm already a bit of a fabric hoarder." Though from what I'd seen he didn't have all that much and it was very well organized. Unless he had a storage unit somewhere full of the stuff.

"Who said anything about need?" I asked him. "Plus you have me to design for." It didn't take him much convincing because he walked with me to the shop, and we left with me carrying two large bags of fabric. My favorite was actually a bit of quilting cotton made to look like it had rows on rows of multi-colored baby dragons in funny poses on it. We'd only gotten a yard since it had been very expensive, but I was in love with it. Micah had also chosen a fabric that looked like leather at first, with intricate designs etched into it, only it wasn't leather. I gladly carried our haul of stuff.

"I could totally see a cool coat or even a kilt out of that one. I've never worn a kilt," I said. "But I've always thought it would be badass to wear one."

"The correct way?" Micah asked.

"Meaning no underwear?"

"Yep."

"Sure, though I worry a breeze might freeze my balls."

"Not until December here in New Orleans, but I can make you a kilt."

"I want to stop by Mary Lamont's shop and see if she knows what Marc took," Micah said.

Admittedly it took a few seconds for my brain to latch onto the meaning of his words and the direction of his step. I tugged him to a halt and he turned to look up at me. "Say what?"

"I want to know what Marc took out of the grave, and what the hell they were doing in the cemetery on my night. They closed the cemetery because of her. I think she owes me an explanation." Micah pulled free from my hand. "You don't have to come with. You can head back to the shop if you want. I'll be there in a little bit."

"Um, no. You realize that her buddy Marc was murdered after she took some possible possessed item from an open grave after slaughtering animals and you think I'm going to let you visit her alone?"

"You don't know she actually took anything from the grave."

"I believe Jared," I said. "Just like I believe him when he said the darkness took his girlfriend. I'd rather the darkness not take you too."

Micah flinched. "I'm not going anywhere and it's light out," Micah said pointing up to the sky. Though the sun was fading. "There are people everywhere. Her shop is right off the board-walk. She lives above it, though I know she does Saturday night ghost tours too. I hope to catch her before she goes out. I need to know what's going on. Were they trying to get me in trouble or is this unrelated to me at all?"

I didn't point out that the last time he'd gone missing it had been light out, though it was on the tip of my tongue. "I don't think it sounds related to you at all. More that they wanted in the cemetery on your night because it was the full moon and an open grave."

Micah stared at me for a minute. "You think that's why?"

I shrugged. "Who am I to explain the mechanisms of crazy people. They tortured animals in a public place after convincing some tourist couple it was a history tour. That tells me something is off in their head. Maybe they lured Jared and Sarah there to use them as sacrifices too."

"Voodoo does not condone human sacrifice. That's a bad stereotype."

"And you said that these people don't really seem to be practicing Voodoo," I pointed out. "So forgive me if I don't trust them to be on the up and up."

We glared at each other for a minute, and I had a moment to wonder if this was what a fight would feel like between us. Only I didn't want to fight. But I needed him safe. "I don't trust her," I finally said.

"I'll be fine. I've met with them before." He walked around me and headed toward Decatur Street.

"For all you know they could be hiding bodies in the cemetery on their nights."

"I think the guards would have noticed," Micah said. "Plus Mary isn't all that big. I could take her in a fight."

"What if she had a gun or some weird magic spell," I stepped into his path to make him pause again.

Another shared glare. "I don't believe in spells."

"But guns. Guns are very real and dangerous, I assure you." I had way too many horrific memories of what guns could do.

He threw his hands up into the air in exasperation. "She won't hurt me in a public place. That would be stupid."

"And criminals aren't normally known for high intelligence. All I'm saying is that you're not meeting with any of them alone again," I insisted.

He folded his arms across his chest. "It's only a block down the road."

"Then you won't mind me tagging along. At least I can still carry your bags."

Micah narrowed his eyes. Nothing I said was fooling him at all.

I sighed. "No way I can talk you out of this, right?"

"Correct," Micah agreed.

"Fuck," I swore, then reached out to grab his hand. "Lead the way. Let's get this madness over with already."

He gave me a brilliant smile which both made me hard and terrified all at once. That smile felt like an omen of heaven and coming doom. Fuck.

He guided us through an alleyway and across a street. Her place was much different than his. Instead of the bright bohemian feel with added snark of Simply Crafty, Mary's place was dark and cluttered. Every bit of shelf space was covered in tiny statues, incense holders, and knickknacks. Nothing cute or precious like you'd find at a Hallmark. Instead it was endless skeletons, monsters, and zombies. There were no fun T-shirts or hand-crafted shawls, just cases of Tarot cards, bongs, elaborate 'ceremonial' candles, and daggers.

The entire vibe of the place was dark and creepy. A handful of old dolls sat on shelves around the top of the room, staring down with blank broken faces. Statues of demons and skeletons danced little jigs in every corner. And there were half a dozen mini altars set up with tiny notes taped near them explaining which spirit guide or deity they were for. All of them requesting offerings, and had bowls filled with coins, rings, and other trinkets.

"No wonder people come to Simply Crafty," I told Micah. "This place puts the capital S in somber."

"She calls herself a Voodoo Queen. Says all of this is part of her practice," he told me while we navigated the shop. There was no one at the register, no one that I could see in the shop at all. Maybe the back room somewhere? "At least she doesn't have live snakes in here anymore. Something about zoning laws. She had to get rid of them. I think it was mostly because the neighbors didn't like them."

"You don't believe she's a voodoo queen?"

"Lots of people practice rituals. Catholic priests practice rituals all the time. Do you think they really talk to 'God'? I think the same goes with the voodoo people. They practice rituals and proclaim they hear voices from the other side. Mary tells people she can talk to the dead. Uses it to get more money out of them. I think using people's grief to extort money is wrong and I haven't made my feelings on it a secret. Did you know when I went missing, she called Tim and tried to talk him into paying her to communicate with me?"

I gaped at him. "Are you shitting me?"

Micah shook his head. "Nope. Tim didn't take the bait, but he said it made him feel horrible and he cried for days thinking that I was dead because some hack psychic claimed she could hear my voice 'on the other side.'"

Maybe he had been on the other side, I thought briefly. Who knew where he'd been taken. Did that mean some random woman who thought she could talk to the dead had actually heard him? I wasn't sure I believed in all that, which was funny because I might have actually been seeing dead people a lot lately.

He stopped and frowned at the shop. "Where is she?"

"A storeroom maybe?"

Micah wove his way through the maze of tightly packed shelves to a little curtain area which led to a bathroom and a small room with a microwave and table. No one was there.

"You said she lives upstairs. Maybe she ran up for something."

"Even I wouldn't leave the shop empty for more than it took to use the restroom," Micah said. "Plenty of opportunistic thieves in New Orleans."

"Maybe she has her stuff cursed so if anyone steals it they bring it back?" I half joked.

Micah looked thoughtful. "Maybe. Wonder if I could figure out a spell like that."

"You'd have to believe in it first, right?"

"Minor technicalities," he said and headed back out the door and around the side to another door. That outside door opened and led up a flight of stairs to another door above. The door at the top of the stairs was ajar. "She never leaves her place unlocked."

"Let me call Lukas so he can send the police out for a wellness check," I said stepping into the little entry beside Micah. The door closed behind us and the feeling of heat and humidity seemed to close in. I pulled out my phone and wiped sweat off my forehead. It shouldn't be this hot in such a tiny little dark space.

Micah shivered as though he were cold and glanced up the stairs. "Do you smell something sweet?"

I sniffed the tiny area, but only smelled sweat. "No. Are you cold?"

"Freezing."

While I was burning up. It made me think of standing in front of the voodoo museum with my hand on the window and it began to burn. "We should go." That little feeling of doom began growing in my gut. There was some kind of energy here, that much I could tell. If Micah had been experiencing this for weeks, I could understand why he hadn't been sleeping.

"I don't feel anything on my skin," Micah said. "Just cold. Do you see something?"

I peered up at the partially open door and really hoped I didn't see something. "No. And I'd like not to. This whole 'tuned into the supernatural' is new to me."

"Is it? Or are you just now realizing what you've always experienced and brushed off might be something more unexplainable?" he asked, his expression curious.

"Fuck..." Now I was going to question everything I ever remembered. "I'm not sure you're good for my sanity."

He put his hand on my arm, his fingers cold as ice on my overheated skin. "I'd like to think I help bring clarity to chaos, but it might be the other way around." Micah took a step up the stairs.

I set the bags of our stuff at my feet and tried to pull him back. "Let's wait for the police."

"What if she's hurt? She's not young. Maybe she fell and hit her head or something."

"And doesn't own a cellphone?" I sighed and moved past him up the stairs. "Wait here."

"Right," he agreed, following me.

I groaned. "You realize it's a soldier's instinct to keep you safe, right? I'm not trying to be an asshole caveman. But you really should stay down here."

"And you realize I'm not five, right?" He threw back obviously not willing to stay behind.

"Don't touch anything," I told him, as I turned on the light on my phone and squeezed through the narrow opening in the doorway. The apartment upstairs was as chaotic and cluttered as the shop downstairs, filled with dolls and statues of things I'd never want anywhere near my home. The walls were brown or red, and windows so tightly closed against daylight that it made the apartment look more like a dungeon than a home. The few pieces of furniture were ancient, like something pulled out of a museum or an antique shop for people who loved creepy old things.

The entire place was maybe twice the size of Micah's, but felt smaller due to the clutter. I glanced carefully in each room as we passed, pausing when I saw a blond head that made me jump back two feet and shriek like a newborn baby.

"Fuck," I said, my hand over my chest. "Mary?" I called, easing back around the corner, Micah close behind. If my shriek hadn't woken her, I wasn't sure anything would. My heart thudded in my chest, racing like we'd just survived a head on collision. "Not good for my heart either," I muttered.

"Or my eardrums," Micah added.

Throwing my snark back at me. The little shit... If we weren't standing in the house of the creepy lady, I'd have kissed him stupid.

Mary, if it was Mary, appeared to be sitting at a small desk, half slumped over it like she'd fallen asleep there. But the light made her look eerily still in the dark room. Her long flowing dress splayed around her feet more in display than careless sleep, and the sweet smell, I finally noticed, was coming from her, or at least the desk. Something with nutmeg, cinnamon, and a bit of sugar.

Her blond hair was spread out around her head like a halo and since she was face down, I couldn't tell much about it. I reached out carefully to touch her shoulder, hoping she'd wake up and rage at us for being in her space, but had to step forward a half foot to make contact.

Two things happened at once. First the sticky sensation of something thick and viscous under my shoe made me wince, and second my hand on her shoulder made her fall away from the desk like a rag doll, flopping to the ground beside it with a thud.

Micah gasped, fingers digging into my shirt and side as he clung to me while I tried to make sense of what I was seeing. Blood coated her face like she'd been crying the stuff. It soaked the hair at the side of her head by her ears and even trickled down her upper lip. While she appeared lifeless, I feared she might actually still be alive and carefully leaned over to check for a pulse from the nearest wrist.

I counted, waiting, straining to feel anything or hear beyond my own trembling breath. There was nothing. She was gone. Her skin had already begun to cool, though she was still pretty pliable. Not long dead then. I stepped back, pushing Micah out of the room with me and dialed Lukas instead of waiting for his text reply. Two bodies found in a few days didn't look good for us, and I wasn't taking chances.

CHAPTER 19

The police descended again like locusts, swooping in and dragging us outside for questioning, scouring the place of everything, even hauling things out in boxes. At least we didn't have to go to the station this time, instead we sat on the sidewalk and answered questions with all the neighbors.

"She was taking her mail upstairs," one of the neighbors said. "Saw her not an hour ago." The nearby shop sold T-shirts and other mass market stuff. The Cajun man had told the police that he was keeping an eye on the shop while Mary had gone upstairs, though there were never many customers in Mary's shop before dark.

I watched as they carried Mary out in a body bag and wondered a thousand things. Some of the cops murmured that she might have poisoned herself, or mixed up the wrong concoction. A few implied she'd been a witch of sorts and her potion to keep her alive and full of power had accidentally killed her. It was stupid and made me mad enough that Micah had to grip my hand to keep me from screaming at them.

One of my biggest pet peeves is disrespect of the dead. I'd seen it a dozen times at military funerals. People were either severe in their respect or completely disdainful, and commenting things about how he or she must have gotten himself blown up. Often followed by the comment "When I served we never..." and then some bullshit about the handful of much easier weapons they'd had. Now it was all bombs made from spare parts and sprays of bullets from one hundred plus round capacity magazines. Nothing was simple about modern war, but death.

"Would they say the same stuff if it was you or me?" I asked him. "No, because they'd be saying stupid shit about how we got what we deserved because we're queer." We sat close enough together that no one would mistake our relationship as simple co-workers. Especially not since Micah had his arm wrapped around mine, his cheek resting on my shoulder, and his hand firm within my grip.

"Give me some shit about how my pansy ass could never have served our country properly..."

Micah lifted my hand and kissed the back of it. "Hey," he called.

I looked at him feeling like I wanted to kick some cop ass.

"Dead bodies make you cranky, yeah?"

I narrowed my eyes at him. "Most people don't see dead bodies in everyday life. I'd think it would make anyone cranky."

"Okay," he agreed. "But getting mad at the cops is going to help who? Remember, your brother is a cop and you don't want to make his co-workers pissy with him because you were pissy with them."

Lukas was not on duty, though he'd shown up when called. Since I was once again involved, even if it was simply finding the dead woman, he'd been shoved to the sidelines of the case again. Which I didn't think made him all that happy. He had also not been thrilled that we'd been there at all. But since Micah and Mary Lamont worked in the same industry, part of four, well now two remaining tour guides certified by the city, it was stupid to think they'd never speak to each other.

He'd given me the side eye that said he didn't believe we had come to talk shop at all, but left me to the rest of the cops for questioning. While we hadn't been stripped and taken anywhere, the questioning had been brutal. Probably a half dozen guys asking the same things over and over. Micah and I were separated, though I kept him in my line of sight. We told as much of the truth as we dared. Just that Micah had come to ask why Mary had been in the cemetery on his scheduled night. It was a simplified version of the truth, but still the truth.

We were finally released right before eight and told to stay out of the cops' way. "That's the plan," I told them as I dragged Micah with our batch of retrieved shopping items toward his shop. They'd taken my shoes again, since I had blood on them. Lukas had given me his since he had more than a dozen to choose from after sending a rookie to grab him a pair.

I would have stopped to talk to him, but he waved us off, with a comment of "Later."

At the shop Sky looked at us with wide eyes while Micah stalked to the back room to drop off the bags of stuff that had been searched a dozen times.

"Another body?" Sky asked.

I wondered how she could tell, but then I realized there was blood on my shirt.

"Dammit. This job is hell on my clothes," I said, trying to make light of it. I followed Micah to the back room and stripped off the shirt, throwing it in the basket in the small washroom, and washing my hands and face.

"Still think I'm not a curse?" Micah asked standing in the doorway watching me.

"No more than I am. Hell, maybe it's the combination of the two of us together that fucks people up. We could offer our services as political assassins. Drop us off in a random country and watch their world erupt."

"You're not funny."

"No?" I asked, drying my hands and crossing the room to tower over him. I grabbed his waist and pulled him against me, staring down into those wide blue eyes.

"No," he breathed, though it felt like a lie. He relaxed in my arms a little, tilting his head up. I rewarded him with a gentle kiss on his forehead, then one on each cheek before finding his mouth and teasing his lips with my teeth. His mask had gone back up while the cops questioned us, but I was beginning to see around it now, the small breaks of emotions he let through when less people were around.

"It doesn't have to be anything supernatural."

"Sure," he said. "Just dead people everywhere."

"Um, don't we live in a city full of dead people? Graves above ground, ghosts, and all that jazz? Oh and real jazz too. Didn't you tell some story about ragtime—the actual menstrual cycle ragtime—, prostitutes, and the growth of jazz?"

He gave me the narrow eye of judgment again. "Your brain is like a sponge."

"Thick and sopping wet?" I inquired teasingly.

He sighed and started to complain about my sarcasm again, but I kissed him soundly instead. Not a gentle play of control, but a full dive into his mouth with my tongue kiss. He relaxed into it, closing his eyes and returning the exploration with his own. We stayed together that way for a time. In the moment with each other. Not only was it calming, but clarifying. The chaos around us be damned. "I hope we're more than just a spark," I whispered when the kiss ended and I rested my forehead against his.

"Yes," he agreed. "I think we are."

And that was the best news I'd heard all day. I pulled away

to do a little dance. "Micah likes me, I like Micah, woot woot," I sang a little made up song and probably looked like an epileptic chicken while I danced.

"Dork."

"You had one hundred percent disclosure." I pointed at myself. "Crazy man."

He gave me a half squint. "I don't get you."

"What's to get?"

"You play broken pretty well, but you're one of the calmest, most put together guys I've ever met."

I grinned. "Really? You must know some really messed up people then."

He mock-growled and shoved me away, then made his way back to the main part of the shop to plug his phone in.

"Can we listen to some rock?" I called after him as I went to find another T-shirt. "Instead of Justin Fest?"

He turned up the volume and restarted his Justin playlist. At least there was a little Maroon5 mixed in. I hid my grin and went back to cleaning up shelves and organizing stock in between helping customers, while watching him sway sexily to the music.

Sky took a handful more Tarot customers, and I danced with Micah around the shop. The scent of incense was becoming familiar and I really was starting to know where things were. Watching Micah's cute little ass wiggle around the store turned me on and made me smile all at once. He wasn't focusing on the one terrible event of the day, which I thought was a step in the right direction.

A text noisily interrupted the music and was persistent enough that Micah finally had to check it. He stared at the phone for a minute, then glared.

"What?"

He held up his phone and in a text from Tim was a little

video of the front of Micah's house. A giant orange tabby cat wove through the garden décor of cats like he owned the place.

"Huh... No wonder Jet was hissing and spitting. That tom is encroaching on his territory." I took the phone and zoomed in and out to watch the cat.

"A cat did not rattle the doorknob," Micah said, indignant, his cheeks pink.

"Maybe not, but this guy may have knocked the gnomes over. I wonder if he belongs to one of your neighbors." I thought back to the first night and the horrible noises coming from outside. A cat? Maybe. Somehow, I didn't think what Micah had been hearing for the past two years was a cat, following him from place to place. Though having a more benign answer certainly eased some of the stress of worry over him being home alone at night. "Maybe Jet wants a friend."

Micah folded his arms across his chest and frowned. "Tim probably thinks I'm some total moron."

"Does it matter?" I asked. "Is he going to stop showing up when you call?"

"No," Micah admitted. "Probably not."

"Then he's a friend and that's all that matters." I turned off the video and handed the phone back to Micah. "We'll have to plant some catnip in your garden to keep your visiting friend stoned. All is well."

"Jerk," Micah grumbled. "I haven't simply been hearing a cat in my garden."

"No," I agreed. "Maybe not only him, but he might be part of the problem. The yowling could have been him the other night. Or another cat in heat."

He crossed his arms over his chest and looked away from me. The mask was back and impenetrable.

"Don't be mad at me," I said. "I'm not doubting you. Hell, I heard stuff too. Was it all this tom? Maybe? Does it matter?

That thing outside, whatever it is, you said it's deterred by Jet, right?" At his nod I continued. "So maybe having this big orange brat wandering about will help keep it away too."

Micah dry washed his face with his hands. He looked tired.

"Don't be like that. Don't dwell on this. Whatever it is. Good, bad, or nothing." I snatched the phone back from him, plugged it in to the speaker, and hit his playlist again. "Dance with me."

"You're an awful dancer," Micah said.

"I know but didn't you say something about training?"

He let out a dramatic put-upon sigh. "Try not to step on my feet," he said and proceeded to try to teach a soldier with two left feet how to dance.

We closed the shop at nine without any fanfare. Micah put the cash in a safe in the back, we armed the alarm, and locked the door. Sky had left a half an hour earlier, eager to be somewhere more exciting on a Saturday night I was sure. I carried Micah's bags from earlier in the day as we headed toward his house.

"Shop is closed tomorrow."

"Yeah? For church reasons?"

"Nah, 'cause even I need a day off. I find people are less offended by the store being closed on a Sunday because they think it's church related, not an 'I'm staying in bed' thing."

"Smart," I nodded. He let us in through the gate and down the path. Nothing was out of place, but now that I knew there was a resident yard cat of the real variety, I was a little less intimidated by the shadows.

"So listen..." Micah began.

My gut clenched. "Is this the 'it's-not-you-it's-me' speech?"

Micah laughed and shook his head. "Wow, you're quick with the snark. No. I'm thinking that maybe we can take a break tonight? I could use some time in my own head. There's been so much going on, and I need to sort it all out."

"Oh, of course." I held out the bags of stuff for him. "You're not going to do anything crazy like go examine graves in exclusive graveyards or dig through a newly dead lady's trash for clues of what she stole from said graveyard?"

He gave me narrowed eyes. "Eerily specific plans for pulling them off the top of your head. Are these things you plan to do?"

I'd thought about them, but was pretty sure Lukas would kick my ass if I so much as set foot in that direction. "Nah. Might do some more research on Lukas's computer. Lukas might actually hang me if he catches me stepping into this again. I should have thought to borrow some books from the shop. Since I have tomorrow to myself. I could read and catch up on all the fun New Orleans lore."

"I think Lukas has most of them anyway. Used to buy stuff while he was pretending that he wasn't actually there to check on me or Sky."

"Buying stuff from himself? Since he owns the store and all..." I laughed. That sounded like Lukas. "And he said I have a hero complex."

"I think you're more alike than either of you believe." He grabbed the front of my shirt and tugged me close, then leaned up to kiss me.

"What? Oh," I said returning his kiss which started out with little brushes of the lips and quickly turned to a heated duel of tongues. At some point I must have dropped the bags because I found myself wrapped around him, pressing my heat to his and wishing we were inside right that second to continue what I'd put a halt to last night.

He released me, but sighed sweetly into my lips. "Weren't you the one saying you wanted to see if we were more than just a spark?"

Yes. Dammit. "Was that me?"

"I really am only going to get some sleep," Micah said. "There's a lot in my head from the past few days I need to work out."

"Sleep or feverishly work on projects?" I clarified.

He shrugged. "Not sure yet, but it doesn't matter." He stepped away and picked up the bags I'd dropped. "Can you find your way home okay?"

I wanted to watch over him, but knew he was right. "Yes. I've got the route down now."

"No chasing shadows on the way home," Micah said.

I put my hand over my heart. "Straight home, sir."

He glanced my way and nodded before heading to his door. "Text me when you get home? So I know you're safe."

"Of course," I promised. "I will go once I'm sure you're inside."

He nodded and unlocked the door. A moment later he was gone and I did a quick search of the yard, looking for anything out of place before heading home.

CHAPTER 20

Lukas's place was dark and quiet when I got in. I texted him to let him know I was home and would be asleep on the couch if he got in late. Not that I ever heard him come in anyway. He was a bit like a ghost in that regard.

I made another batch of poor man's peanut butter cookies, leaving the ones I didn't eat out with a note for Lukas, and made up the couch. It was the first time I noticed, that in Lukas's pile of top sheets, there was one with gnomes on it. It was a sort of creamy white with blue China plate sort of print. The gnomes had looked like people at a glance, but up close, the big noses, beards, and pointy hats were unmistakable. Which meant this was probably Micah's handiwork.

I found my phone and took a picture of a closeup of the print. *Is this your work?* I sent to Micah. *Oh and btw I'm home.*

The (...) appeared for a moment. Then, *Yes. It's a running joke. He even has gnome boxers somewhere. Christmas ones. It was a fabric I found on clearance at a thrift shop and only had enough for something small. The nose of one of the gnomes goes where the...*

I laughed at the idea of my brother wearing a big gnome

nose on his dick. Had he ever worn them? *You made my brother boxers?*

Boxers are easy. Fifteen-minute project. I make them for everyone. Expect them for Christmas at the very least. Even Sky has sleep boxers.

I could use some boxers that fit, I allowed and thought about the fabric choices we'd made in that little quilt shop. *Could maybe have boxers with little dragons on them?*

Already started on something with that one. Sorry. I hope you don't hate it.

I will like anything you make me. Aren't you supposed to be resting? I made my way to Lukas's room and the wall with three —five shelf bookcases, full of stuff. The first was all police procedural stuff, manuals, and forensic guides. The second was fiction like Harry Potter. The third was a mix of everything else, but he did have three whole shelves dedicated to the paranormal. I pulled out a few books on New Orleans ghost history and the one with Micah's 411 mystery and took it to the couch.

Micah's reply said, *Am resting. Jet curled up with me.* Two seconds later a selfie arrived with a close up of Micah in bed with Jet perched on the pillow near his head. I couldn't help but smile.

You'll call if you need me?

Yes. Don't scare yourself too much with ghost stories.

Ghosts aren't real anyway, I reminded him. *Or so you keep telling me.*

The (...) appeared for a minute. Then, *But the idea of something else, unclarified and unexplained, is pretty scary sometimes too.*

That was true enough. *Best remember you're not alone then? That your friends are just a call or text away.*

Yes. Thank you.

I smiled at the phone. *Night.*

Night.

I actually fell asleep fairly quickly. Reading straight up facts about ghost stories wasn't as exciting as listening to Micah retell the tales of them. However, I dreamt of searching the city for something. My heart pounding in fear as I turned corner after corner only to find nothing. It was a growing sense of panic that made my heart race and sweat trickle off my brow. I turned a corner down an alley I didn't recognize and felt someone grab my arm.

I came up swinging.

"Fuck!" I heard the curse before it made sense that it wasn't me dropping the F-bomb. I blinked half a dozen times, worlds meshing and finally separating. Lukas stood a few feet away, hands up in front of him. I was sprawled halfway across the kitchen counter like I'd tried to get to him.

His apartment, not some random alleyway. The sun shone through the windows. Had I really slept so long? Was all that a dream? My heart still raced and I fought for a full breath.

"Sorry," I said.

"You were sleeping hard until about an hour ago when you started making noises. I thought I'd try to wake you up before it got too bad," Lukas said. He was dressed in cop chic again.

"Did you even get any sleep?"

"Yeah. You were out, so I went to bed. I'm headed back in. Are you going to be okay?" The unspoken 'if I leave you alone' hung in the air without needing to be said.

"I'll be okay. I was going to catch up on some reading today." I dropped back onto the couch, tired now that the adrenaline from the dream was fading.

"So not one nightmare while you were with Micah?" Lukas wanted to know.

"Not that I recall. He didn't say anything about me making noise in my sleep." I glanced at the microwave clock, it was after seven a.m., not that late. "He wanted time in his own head last night. I hope he didn't text me and I slept through it." I glanced at my phone. Nothing. Was it odd how sad it made me feel to not see anything from him?

Lukas leaned against the counter. "Thanks for the cookies, by the way. Man, did they bring back memories or what?"

"Right?" I tugged my boxers up as they'd fallen partially down my hips.

Lukas noticed and glared. "If I leave you some cash, can you maybe go get some clothes that fit you?" he asked.

"I have clothes," I protested, not wanting to spend more of his money.

"Clothes that fit *you*, not me. You're wider in the shoulder than me and narrower in the hip. You can't keep wearing my clothes hoping our bodies will suddenly be the same."

"We're identical twins," I reminded him.

"Which doesn't mean we are actually identical. You're a half inch taller than me, and I weigh a good twenty pounds more than you." He glanced at my hair. "Maybe get a haircut? Though whatever Micah did has been helping."

"I have been doing my hair," I said. "Some product Micah gave me, but I've been taking care of it."

"Okay, so maybe a trim, then. And clean up the beard a little? Clothes that fit? You have a respectable job now."

"Working for you."

"And a hot ex-porn star."

I sighed. "Aren't you supposed to be finding a missing girl or something?"

"I'm homicide, not missing persons. The dead guy is my jurisdiction."

"Is that why nothing gets done anymore with you cops? Right hand not talking to the left?"

"I'd bitch at you if you weren't so damn right." Lukas pulled his wallet out of his pocket and took out a stack of cash. "Shopping, yeah? Don't buy clothes you think I'd like, buy stuff for you. You still have the credit card I gave you? Use that too."

"What if I want ballgowns and wizard cloaks?"

He shrugged. "Okay, if it makes you happy." He glanced at the clock. "Gotta go. Don't find any dead people today."

"You're not funny."

"Shop," he said as he waved the money at me.

I sighed, taking the offered cash and watching him leave. Shop. Normally I hated shopping, but it had been fun yesterday, though I hadn't been looking for clothes for myself. I unlocked my phone and stared at the blank text window for a minute or two before sending Micah: *I hope you're okay.*

A minute passed with nothing. Maybe he was still asleep.

I'm supposed to buy clothes, or so Lukas has ordered. Where should I go?

I got up and made my way to the shower to wash away the sweat and the dream. I'd almost forgotten what the nightmares felt like, but waking from it reminded me of that overwhelming weight in my limbs, the drowning pool of depression, and the mental exhaustion. I felt like I hadn't really slept at all. A few days with Micah and I'd almost felt normal. It was a little scary to get a glimpse because what if Micah didn't want me around anymore?

By the time I exited the shower and dug through Lukas's clothes to find something that didn't make me look like an emaciated hobo, there were a handful of texts lighting up my phone.

Lots of shops off Decatur. Great thrift shop near Ursulines and Royal. Not far from LaLaurie Mansion. Tiny but good selection.

You okay?

Yes. Sewing and thinking.

I wasn't sure that was okay, but since he didn't seem to be inviting himself along or asking for my presence, I decided he probably still needed some space. That was okay. Apparently I needed clothes.

On the way to the thrift store I found a barber shop who was willing to turn me into something presentable. The barber cleaned up the beard, trimming it down and softening it, and took enough off my hair to make me look somewhat distinguished. The older black man gave me a long lecture on hair care, and a handful of products to help me keep the 'fro tamed during the humid New Orleans days. I thanked him profusely and took a selfie in the barber mirror, forwarding it to both Lukas and Micah, then headed for the clothing shop.

I'm glad you didn't cut it short. Micah wrote back. *Or shave off the beard.*

It's super soft, I sent him, stroking my beard and marveling at the texture of it. Who knew there was stuff that could make your hair as soft as satin? Having the beard trimmed this short it always felt prickly to me, only now it didn't. I had purchased a half-dozen products from the barber after he'd used them on me. Having never been all that into 'self-care' in general it would be work to create a new habit, but since it made me feel good, I'd try.

There were a dozen small boutique style shops in the area selling T-shirts and tourist gear, and I recognized the shop Micah had mentioned immediately. It was a mash of crowded racks, heaped with well-loved clothes, while still being very organized.

A plaque beside the entrance told a story about a lover's quarrel which had ended in tragedy, leaving the disgruntled couple to forever haunt the shop. The story was pretty recent, from the late seventies. I laughed at the silliness of it, a haunted clothing store. If there was something I would do in my afterlife, it would not be hanging around a thrift store. I took a picture of the plaque and sent it to Micah.

Never felt anything there. Micah replied. *But know the story. Murder-suicide. Sad.*

"Can I help you?" A young woman asked me. She must have been an employee, though didn't have a nametag. Her clothes were kind of thrifty cool, dated, like she'd picked the best stuff from the seventies and eighties and meshed them into a neat outfit. Her dark hair was long and flowing, pushed back by one of those cloth headbands.

"I need some clothes that fit," I told her and tugged on the shorts I was wearing, which were held up by a belt that really didn't go with the shorts.

She gave me a warm smile that eased some of my anxiety over shopping for clothes. "Sure. Follow me."

She led me to a section in the back of the store where there was a little changing booth and several crammed-full racks. One whole rack appeared to be jeans, pants, and shorts for men. I went to the size I knew Lukas wore and down one.

"Feel free to use the changing room to try stuff on," the woman told me.

"Thank you," I said, watching her weave her way through the racks. The store seemed otherwise empty, and bigger inside than I'd thought from seeing the outside, though not larger than Simply Crafty.

I pulled a handful of things off the rack and headed to the changing room, finding quickly enough that I was not one size, but two sizes smaller than Lukas. Jeans felt odd. Very restrictive.

Had it been so long since I wore them? I liked the shorts better, and a handful of cargo pants in cream, green, and khaki, with giant pockets and wide legs. I took a picture in one of the pairs and sent it to Micah.

These hide my chicken legs well, but fit through the waist and ass. What do you think?

I took pictures from the side and front, so he could see that it didn't hang off my butt or slouch on my waist. They were comfortable when I bent or moved.

As long as you have some color on top, they look good. Micah sent back. *I can add some designs to the pockets. I have an embroidery machine.*

Designs? I thought about that. *You mean like flowers or something?* How gay did he think I was?

Was thinking dragons or anime characters.

Okay, that was a cool idea. I tried on the rest of the pairs and added the batch to my must-have pile. The T-shirt rack was easier to sort through as I looked for solids in the size I'd picked from Micah's shop. Though I did aim for more color than I normally would have gravitated toward.

Someone had left a sequined dress on the shirt rack. It was pink, with sequin that turned silver when rubbed in the other direction. I picked it up, thinking funny things about something this slinky. I knew nothing about women's sizes but it looked like it might fit, so I brought it to the changing room to try it on for shits and giggles.

The inside of the dress was scratchy and I had to tug to get it into place, then smoothed the sequins down to pink. I took a picture and sent it to Micah.

What do you think? Should I become a drag queen?

You're fabulous. He responded. *But pink isn't really your color.*

Rude. I wrote back, then wiggled out of the dress and back into my regular clothes. I found another rack with dresses on it and tried on a yellow sundress. *How about this one? Not a kilt but I like the breeze on my balls.*

I received the laughing emoji back with a: *No yellow either.*

"He's so picky," I said to no one in particular.

My phone buzzed and there was a picture this time, of a skirt, black with rainbow colored scales between the pleats. I think those were pleats. It took a minute to figure out that I was looking at a kilt. Had Micah made that for me?

That's amazing, I sent to him.

Another picture appeared. This one a selfie of Micah, standing in front of a mirror, in what I thought was his closet, dressed in a Wonder Woman type outfit. Instead of a skirt he wore super tight hot pants that outlined everything, while showing nothing. The pants were a mix of golds, blues, and reds, made to look feminine, sexy, but leaving a lot to the imagination. Was his ass always that tight or had the fabric added shape?

Wow! I wrote back, adding the matching emoji, giant heart eyes bulging.

Another picture, this one a very suggestive pose hinting at naughty things as he bent forward and glanced back to take the picture, like pinups of old. My cock hardened and my stomach did a somersault of need.

Started it a couple months ago. Finished it today.

Was this the sort of thing he'd done before he started porn? Outfits and photos that were on the edge of sexy? Fuck.

I'm giving you the happy high five. I wrote him.

He sent the laughing emoji.

Seriously though, you look amazing. And happy, I thought, studying his expression. Sure, in the second one he was posing with a wink and an exaggerated purse of his lips, but the first one looked like he had a little smile on his lips. *Do you have more like this? Stuff for you that you haven't finished?*

Sure, he wrote back. *I get stuck sometimes. Couldn't figure out how to finish off this one until I was working on your kilt this morning...*

Hot damn your ass is fine in gold lamè.

He sent back a blushing emoji.

If sewing for me inspired him, I'd have to make sure he had more to keep him busy. I found a section in the back that had fabrics piled up, a mess of stuff really, but a few fun and vintage prints.

"Do you want a shopping bag?" A female voice startled me since I'd been so intent on the fabric. I glanced her way, surprised that it was a different woman than before. This one was younger and blond, dressed in jeans and a flowery top. She motioned to the pile of clothing tucked under my arm. She held out a mesh bag for me.

"Thanks," I said, putting the stuff in the bag and slinging it over my shoulder.

"Need help finding anything?"

"Oh, no, thank you. Your other employee already pointed me in the right direction," I assured her and went back to digging through the fabrics. She appeared confused for a minute before walking back to the counter.

I found a couple of neat prints, some with Halloween stuff on them, that I grabbed before heading to the front. The woman rang me up and I was surprised that the whole batch barely cost me forty bucks. Three pairs of slacks, four cargo pants, a half dozen pair of shorts, and five T-shirts, plus three hanks of fabric. I even bought a reusable tote so I wasn't adding to the whole environmental plastic bag issue.

"Thank that other girl for me, will you?" I said looking

around for her. "I'm normally intimidated by shopping for clothing, but she showed me right to the correct rack."

"What other girl?" The girl at the register asked. Her nametag read "Eleanor."

"The gal in the seventies clothes? She met me at the door? Long dark hair?"

Eleanor gaped at me. "I'm the only one working today."

I frowned. "No. I saw that other girl. Maybe she was a nice shopper?"

"You're my first customer today." She pointed to the clock and the hours posted on the wall. The store had been open less than a half an hour.

"Um..."

"I've heard of people seeing the ghost, but never so vividly they thought she was real," Eleanor said.

"That was not a ghost," I said. "I talked to her, she answered."

She shrugged. "I don't know who else it could be."

Fuck. I looked around the store, even did a full walk-through, searching the single bathroom and glancing in the tiny backroom. No one. The cashier watched me like I was nuts and she was waiting for a reason to call the cops on me. But the other girl was nowhere to be found.

I took my purchases, thanked the cashier and made my way out of the store still looking for the other woman. Maybe it was a hoax to try to draw more people in. Could she have darted out without me seeing her? Why go through the trouble? And what if I was seeing full body apparitions now?

Had a ghost help me pick out clothes, I wrote to Micah.

He sent back a question mark.

Long story. I wasn't sure how I was supposed to feel. Afraid? Not really. She didn't seem menacing. There had been no shadows or skin prickles. I hadn't felt anything different at all.

Except calm. As soon as she had smiled at me, my anxiety about shopping had eased. Well fuck.

I headed out of the shop and made my way down Ursulines, avoiding the LaLaurie mansion, but stopping outside the church to admire the architecture for a minute.

You can come over if you want. Micah sent me.

My heart skipped a beat. I wanted to race to his house and check on him, but knew I had to tread carefully. *I should wash this stuff.*

You can use my washer.

I smiled. *Sure. Have you eaten? I can bring food.* Because Micah didn't keep food in his house.

Ate the last of my eggs last night. Food would be good. There's a small grocery on Bourbon and Canal near the back of the church, right past Walgreens.

I google mapped Walgreens to point me in the right direction. *Okay, let me get food and I'll head your way.*

Hanging with Micah seemed like a better way to spend the day than reading alone. I ran into the Walgreens and got a package of boxer-briefs in my size, now that I knew my size, then found the grocery and filled up on stuff that looked good, while avoiding dairy, as I recalled Micah saying he was allergic. I sent him pictures of random foods with funny names.

Butt rub. A spice mix for ribs.

Cock flavored. A type of soup.

Cream between. Oreo-like generic cookies.

OMG! He wrote back. *You're such a perv.*

It's just food, I sent back adding a picture of Crunchy Nut Balls to the mix. *Are you hungry for some balls? Not my fault if you're thinking of sex.* I got the laughing emoji back in reply which made me smile.

CHAPTER 21

Of course not having thought ahead, meant I had a half dozen bags and was dying by the time I got to Micah's door. He opened it before I could ring the bell and took some bags from me.

"Thanks. I thought my arms were going to fall off."

Micah spread everything out on the futon and small counter space. While I was sad to see he was no longer in the Wonder Woman outfit, his shorts and snug T-shirt didn't lessen his appeal at all. I stepped close and grabbed him for a hug. He relaxed into my embrace and kissed me lightly on the lips before letting go so we could unpack.

"I got stuff for sandwiches. Read all the ingredients. Made sure there was no dairy." I helped sort the groceries into an assembly line for food and built a sandwich. "Wasn't sure what you liked so I got a little bit of everything I like." Including avocado, mustard, and bean sprouts. My sandwich was almost two inches thick by the time I put the top on it.

Micah's wasn't much different than mine, though he left off the mustard. We ate in relative silence, sitting on the futon, while he sorted through my clothes, and I told him about the ghost sales clerk.

"I've never heard of them making up stories to draw people in," Micah said.

"She talked to me, pointed me in the direction of the racks and the dressing area. I thought she was real since she didn't look see-through or anything. It wasn't some passing by of a specter. She smiled and I was calm. Like magic."

"Maybe her energy was stronger than most, or maybe someone was playing a hoax on you. Though I don't know why they'd waste that sort of energy on hoaxing anyone. I shop there pretty regularly. Upcycle a lot of their older pieces. They seem to be doing okay financially." He found the fabrics and ran his hands over them.

"I thought they looked nice," I said. "Don't know if there's something you can do with them." One of them sort of looked like alligator skin, though it smelled like vinyl. The pattern was too regular to be the real thing, but the effect was cool. I'd been attracted to the shiny black iridescent effect of the design.

"We'll think of something." He got up and began putting my stuff in his little washer. I was surprised at how much actually fit. "It's thorough but takes a while," Micah said. "Laundry usually takes me all day."

I finished my sandwich and picked up Micah's empty plate too, taking them to the kitchen and washing them. He didn't have a dishwasher, but since he lived alone, that made sense. He did have a small drying rack which he pulled out of the cupboard and set beside the sink.

"You still working on stuff?" I asked.

"Yes. I need to measure your waist to get your kilt the right size. I really don't have any plans other than working on a few projects today. Sorry I'm so boring."

I laughed. "Um, I'd rather watch you sew than shop with

ghosts again. It makes me wonder how many ghosts I've passed by in the street and thought were regular people."

"I still can't believe that. I've been in there easily a hundred times. What did she look like?"

"Girl from the seventies with long brown hair. I thought she was simply doing the retro thing really well."

He shook his head. "Never seen her. You really must be a magnet for weird."

I gave him narrowed, suspicious eyes. "Good thing you like weird."

He grinned. "I am weird," he said and headed toward the loft. I followed, bringing the new fabric with. In the loft, Jet was curled in his bed, the sewing machine setup sat in the middle of the floor space, and a long white plastic sort of cutting mat lay sprawled near the machine. I found my way to a cushion beside Jet that felt a bit like a beanbag chair. Micah dug through a drawer until he pulled out a measuring tape, then came over and wrapped it around my waist. He wrote some number down on a little piece of paper next to his machine.

"Oh, here's that fabric we got yesterday." He unfolded the bit of fabric with the dragons and it took a minute for me to figure out what it was. It looked like a pillow case, with draw-strings on the end. "It can double as an overnight bag. Carry your clothes and your pillow." Micah's cheeks turned pink. "For when you want to stay over."

I grinned at him and took the case, examining it. "This is great!" And I knew where he kept extra pillows. I crawled to the chest and dug through the stack of quilts until I found a spare pillow, then stuffed it into the case. A perfect fit.

"Pillow cases only take ten minutes or so to make," Micah said, again dismissing his skill and creativity. "I wanted to make something you could use."

I leaned over until I could brush my lips across his cheek

and said, "Thank you. I love it." I curled up around the pillow in my new pillow case and watched him sew.

He was very focused, turning and cutting or pinning something over the mat, then back to the machine to run a line of thread. He changed colors easily, the rough outline of the kilt coming together until he finished up a final stitch and held it up for me. He had used the leather looking material we had picked up yesterday. The tiny hexagons made the fabric look expensive and very custom. The folds of the fabric opened to reveal the design, like the intricate folds of a wing of some fictional beast. The multi-colored sections between shimmered iridescent with scales more defined than the mermaid patterns I'd seen him use. I was in love and hadn't even gotten to touch it yet.

"Nice. Can I wear it already? Or does it need to be washed first?"

"I prewashed the fabric before cutting. Try it on so I can make sure I got the waist and length right. It should fall right above the knee."

I took it expecting it to be heavy only it wasn't, feeling more like a pair of shorts than the leather look of the fabric. I slipped off my shorts and slid the kilt on over my boxers. It zipped shut, and fit perfectly, resting on my hips, not pulling down, even though the weight of the fabric kept it draped. I swung my hips, testing how it felt.

"I thought you said you were going to wear that the right way?" Micah said, staring at me, brow raised.

"Oh, right," I said, and shoved my boxers off. I expected it to be weird or that I wouldn't like the fabric around my cock, or that I'd feel a substantial breeze, but even wiggling my hips around, other than feeling 'free' and loose, it wasn't an unpleasant sensation.

Micah fiddled with the hem of the kilt, frowning at it for a minute.

"It's fine," I said. "I like it the way it is, remove your frowny face."

"The hem is a little crooked."

"Who else is going to be on their knees at my feet to notice?"

His cheeks turned pink. It was a look I was really starting to love on him. I pulled my kilt out of his grasp and returned to my little chair. "Carry on," I waved a hand at him. "Don't mind me. I'm going to lounge in my new kilt on my new pillow case and watch the magic happen."

He glanced my way, studying me a minute before digging out the next project. I didn't ask. He didn't offer explanations, though the tension in his shoulders eased the longer I sat there. He actually began to cut the vinyl piece I gave him into squares. I watched him change the needle and find a dark thread that looked really thick.

"Will you start modeling again? Those cosplay pictures, I mean."

"Maybe," Micah said absently. "I'd have to find a new photographer. My old one was in Dublin." His tone had a tiny lilt to it when he said Dublin. The first touch of accent I'd heard from him. It was adorable.

"I think you should. If it makes you happy."

"Maybe. I like making the clothes, but really didn't like looking at the pictures, though they were well done. We are always the most critical of ourselves and I could find a million flaws in a glance. But I had a pretty big following."

"I'd follow you anywhere," I admitted.

He gave me a chagrined smile.

"Not lying," I said, nestling myself into the cushion. "Even if it sounds cheesy. I'm fascinated. Can't wait to see what you design next. There's a whole lot of magic in your head. I don't know if you understand how amazing that is."

He ignored my praise and went back to his crafting. Again it was a bit like magic watching him work.

"Is there a method to your madness?" I asked. "You make certain things when you're in a particular mood?" Right now he looked calm, almost at peace.

"When I need a distraction, I work on more complicated projects, like cosplay, or designing a new pattern. Those things require a lot of focus and concentration, no real time to think about something other than the project. When I quilt or craft it's more to think. I've done so many quilts, bags, boxers, and other basics that they are sort of mindless repetition. Something to lose myself in the motion while my brain wanders a thousand puzzles."

And somehow that all made perfect sense. The nighttime frenzy of costume making in response to noises in the dark, and daylight crafting for reflection. He was beyond fascinating.

"Today you're in craft mode. Thinking?" I said.

He nodded. "My brain is loud." He glanced at me. "I don't know if everyone's brain is loud, but mine is always thinking, talking, analyzing. It's exhausting. This..." he motioned to his sewing, "seems to slow it down a little."

I had no idea what he was making, it was simply pieces of black vinyl and thread. Then it started to come together as a large tote bag. By the time I watched him sew in the lining and add the handles, I gaped at it. The bag looked like something you'd find in a high-end catalog for over a grand. It wasn't a purse so much as an open-top tote big enough for a computer and a bunch of books. He added a little key fob to the side, and a large wooden button to the front as a latch before stopping to examine it then passing it my way.

"Um..." I said, floored by his ease and talent to make something amazing out of very little. Completed in less than an hour out of a fabric hank I'd spent no more than ten bucks on. No pattern necessary.

"It's a simple pattern, but with the right fabric can look really unique and high end," Micah said. "You seem to need a bag to carry your books and stuff, maybe some extra clothes." He flushed. "More than a silly dragon pillowcase. I was thinking more fun than practical with that."

I hugged the pillowcase. "I love the pillowcase and the bag. Wow, fuck, you are like magic or something."

He waved a hand at me, then went to another drawer and began pulling out rolls of what looked like cut strips of fabric wound into a cake-like shape. "Pick one."

"Okay?"

"One roll turns into a blanket," he explained.

Oh. "That simple, eh?"

He gave me a wry grin. "It's a little more complicated than that, but you don't need to worry about the details. Pick some colors you like. I don't have a specific project I need to work on right now, so this is something small to help clear my head."

That worried me. "Anything I can do?" I prodded, hoping maybe to ease his need for distraction a little.

He shook his head. "Pick a jelly roll so I have something to focus on while I'm sorting things out. Think of it like Tetris. The pieces drop and I have to find places for them. Sometimes I have enough room to fit things together to make it vanish, other times it comes too fast and I get backed up." He gave me a side eye. "I'm a little backed up. Mentally speaking."

I grinned at him. "Glad you cleared that up." I chose a roll that looked like a mix of green, brown, orange, and yellow. It made me think of leaves. He picked it up and began pulling it apart into long strips and sorting it into sections six strips at a time. "You'd tell me if there was something I could help with, right?"

He glanced my way, sewed a few strips together before finally pausing and saying, "I don't want you to be mad."

"I have no reason to be mad at you."

"Everyone gets mad at me for some reason or another. Either because I don't listen to what they say, or don't believe what they say, or a little of both. But I'm just being me."

I thought about that statement for a minute and could identify with it myself. It mirrored Lukas's comment about me being flighty. Maybe Micah was a little flighty too. And that was okay since he seemed to work through it fine and get things done. "Being you is not a bad thing."

He sighed. "It is sometimes. I went outside last night. Sat in the garden."

"Like late? Or early I mean? When the noise usually comes?" That shocked me a little as he'd been so terrified of it.

"Yes. I needed to... I don't know, face it or something. I've been running scared for so long, hiding from what I feel and hear because no one ever believes me. Even Sky who hears it brushes it off as something that can be explained or simply noise. And then the video of the cat—but it can't have been the cat the whole time. I've only been here a year, and the other places I lived were all over town."

"I did think of that," I told him. "I wanted to give you some sense of peace that maybe it wasn't something terrifying in your garden waiting to snatch you up the moment you let your guard down." I thought about him sitting out alone in the dark last night and it made me worry, though there he sat, unhurt and seeming more confused than afraid. "What happened?"

"Nothing," he admitted.

"Was there noise?"

Micah nodded. "I waited until I heard something before going outside. Even checked the cameras Tim installed, but there was nothing. I waited for it to happen again and when it did, I went outside and there was nothing..."

How frustrating and relieving all at once.

"I sat down beneath the tree and waited, terrified, but not willing to keep running away. For the first few minutes I thought my heart would explode with fear. But there was nothing. It makes me think it might really be something wrong in my head."

"I've heard it too," I reminded him.

He looked at me, his expression very serious. "But each time you've been willing to check it out, run toward it instead of away."

"That doesn't mean I wasn't afraid. It may mean I'm stupid. I mean who runs toward danger?" I tried to joke.

He wasn't that easily distracted. "When you saw something scary in the desert you didn't run away."

"No, but running away would have gotten me killed," I said, telling him what I believed true from that day. "Only staying put saved my life and the lives of the men I held on to."

"But you were afraid?"

"Terrified," I agreed. "And without choices. We were in the middle of nowhere."

"An entire army of soldiers and helpless," Micah said.

"Not exactly an entire army. A unit."

"But all trained with guns and self-defense."

"Of course. Our troop was pretty well seasoned. I think the newest guy in was on his second tour."

"But they all died and you didn't."

"There was a storm. A sandstorm, I guess. And I saw something in the swirling wind." I thought about that terrifying vision that I'd blocked from so many of my memories only for them to replay in nightmares. It was a faceless man, or creature, like something out of a horror movie. Not real, everyone told me.

I'd been the only one who had seen it, so it had to be all in my head. "The weather reports from that day claim there was no storm, yet everyone died, ripped to shreds. The army says I misremembered a missile attack, but I know what a missile attack looks like. This was something I had never seen before." I watched him as he went back to sewing strips and worrying at his bottom lip in thought. "This is not a competition of who is braver, Micah. I would never have willingly gone out into that storm. I reacted on instinct and really most people would think I was a coward for staying in the tent when everyone else ran out to die."

"Because being dead is better than being a coward?" He squinted at me. "You saved two men."

"By laying in the doorway of the tent and sobbing like a baby." Holy crap did that hurt to admit. How long had I swallowed that bitter pill of reality, hiding it from everyone because it made me feel worthless, weak, like, "A coward."

Micah crawled to me, leaning over me to kiss me lightly on the lips. "Surviving doesn't make you a coward. Doing what you have to do to survive doesn't make you a coward. You saved two men. It's not like you threw them to the wind to save yourself. You held on to them, kept them safe."

Tears pricked the corners of my eyes and I swallowed hard. "Fuck, I thought I was over this."

"Survivor's guilt?" He asked.

I nodded.

"Not sure it's something anyone gets over." He glanced down and sighed deeply. "You know when I got back, from wherever, I had family members of others who were still missing show up to ask me questions. Like I could somehow point them in the direction of the person they lost. Some had found their loved ones dead and I felt like they were mad at me for surviving, for being found. And everyone expected me to have answers. Only I had more questions than answers. I'd lost time, and I quickly found out, everything else. Lots of people still think I'm crazy. Some have said that I'm not really me, but some replacement person, like a changeling or something." He bit his lip, then pressed his face into my chest for a moment, like he could somehow bury his memories in my arms. "I feel like me," he said when he looked up. "How do I know if I really am me?"

I blinked at him. "You are you," I said. "Maybe not exactly the same you that you were before you went missing, but I'm not the same guy I was before that desert attack either. Life changes us. Sometimes it's for the good, sometimes it's for the bad, most of the time we're different. Not good or bad. Just are. And that's okay because we're still here."

He sat up and frowned, his expressions so much less guarded than they'd been a few days ago when I'd first met him. "When you told me you cried as a soldier, I thought maybe it would be okay. That if I was afraid, it was okay."

"It is okay to be afraid sometimes. You shouldn't have to live your entire life in fear."

"That's why I went outside. I thought that maybe I was being afraid of nothing and I'd let my entire life change because I was living in fear. So I went outside, sat in the garden, and nothing happened."

"I have to say I'm happy that nothing happened." My gut ached at the idea of him going missing again, taken by some boo-wiggly or something. "Maybe all the changes in the garden helped."

"Except I heard the noise before I went out."

"So maybe it's not really dangerous?"

"That was my thought as well. But it makes me sad."

"Why?" I asked.

"Because I've lived the past two years like I was imprisoned.

A prison of fear, pretending to be normal, but waiting for the next monster to grab me."

"Okay, but you can't change the past. You can only change how you react in the future. What will you do if something makes noise in your garden again?"

He shrugged. "If I keep facing it, will it go away? I worry it will intensify."

"How about we keep going day by day and see what wonderful things we can make of them, instead of worrying about a lot of 'what ifs,' yeah?" I waved at the mess of fabric strips he still had laid out. This also was organized chaos, much like everything seemed in his life. "What are you making now?"

"A quilt top. I'll have to send it to the longarmer. I don't have a machine that can do that, though I've taken classes on it. I want you to have one big enough you can wrap yourself in." He sighed. "I can't justify spending over five grand on a sewing machine."

"Maybe if you do your photo things again you can save up for one," I said. "Maybe even sell some of your cosplay designs?"

He looked at me, and it was a thoughtful stare. "I never thought to sell the designs. I *do* have a lot of original stuff."

"Well, there you go," I said and waved my hands at him like I'd pulled some magic trick out of a hat.

"Hmm," was all he gave me and returned to his sewing. Watching the strips fly through his machine was very relaxing. Even the whirring sound and his little snips with the scissors and rotary blade, soothed the anxiety I hadn't realized being separated from him had caused. Though I'd spent the previous night worried about him being by himself, and then this morning his silence had worried me. I had to admit that having a full stomach, being curled up in the cushy chair-cushion, wrapped around my pillow, watching Micah, I was so relaxed, happy he was there, and feeling safe, that I began to doze.

I must have actually fallen asleep because when I woke up it was to have Micah curled around me and Jet on my pillow. At least this time I felt better rested. I stretched a little, which woke Micah.

"Sorry," I said.

He didn't try to get up, only slid his arm around my waist and kissed my jaw. "A nap was good," he said. "Sunday naps are always good."

"Yeah?" I kissed the tip of his nose. "Did you get lots of stuff done?" His little sewing setup was put away and I couldn't see any other projects sitting out.

"Enough to clear my head."

"That's fantastic," I said staring down into his pale blue eyes. The mask was gone, his expression sleepy, but rested. "You're so beautiful."

His cheeks pinked again.

I put my hand to his face and ran my fingers over his soft skin. It was odd how I thought we'd been mismatched, him far out of my league. Only there were a lot of little things that fit. Was that why Lukas had wanted us together? He'd seen the ways we would mesh?

"Why the frowny face?" Micah asked.

"Wondering if Lukas saw some of our weirdness and thought we fit that way, or it was luck. Well, I mean if you are interested, 'cause I'm interested." And again, I was tongue-tied.

"Remember what I said about the training thing?" Micah asked.

"Um, sort of?"

"When you can't stop thinking of a person, that's a training situation."

"Well I can't stop thinking of you," I admitted. Worrying about him was a huge part of it, but his presence helped me relax, and I was fascinated by the little things he did, whether it was his endless knowledge of history, his skill with crafting and a sewing machine, or the fun way he engaged with kids.

"Me too," Micah said. He kissed me, lips to mine, soft at first, an exchange of breath, and finally tongue. I sank into his mouth, enjoying the feel of him, the warmth, and the flavor of his interest.

We dueled a while, him sprawled beneath me on the little cushion and my pillow. Jet, obviously annoyed by us moving, wandered back to his little bed and promptly fell asleep. I rubbed Micah's stomach, keeping my hand above the waist, but running my fingers under his shirt to memorize his skin.

"You can touch me," Micah said. He guided my hand lower, to the button of his shorts. "I want you to touch me."

"Yeah?" I said, kissing his nose and then his lips again. Breathing in the scent of him, and the thought of us together for real this time, made my heart flutter. Fuck I wanted him so much. Physically, yeah, but not only that. I needed to know everything about him, to take care of him even if he grumbled, and sit with him while he created. Sex would be icing on the cake. I couldn't help but lick my lips at the thought of tasting secret parts of him. "You with me this time?"

"Mhmm," he agreed, returning my kisses. His hand found my thigh beneath the kilt, running soft fingertips along the inside in an almost ghost-like caress, and I couldn't help but let out a long sigh. "Sensitive," he said.

"You have no idea. I could blow any second," I admitted, hard as a rock and feeling like I didn't need much stimulation for him to rock my world.

He gave me a wicked little grin. "You could blow me."

The idea of my mouth wrapped around his cock, sucking him down... "Fuck, I really am going to come before we do anything."

He laughed and the sound was glorious. "I like that I turn you on."

"I would think you'd be used to turning guys on."

"It's not the same. Most guys are turned on by the thought of someone touching their dicks."

"I'm turned on by everything you," I said, laying it all out there.

He nodded. "Exactly."

The material of his shorts rubbed against my thigh, and even that was sensual. "I think we need to get you a kilt too," I said. "Easier access." I flipped open the button of his shorts, pushing them down a little to tease the skin of his lower stomach, then traced his hipbones, skipping over his bikinis and cock to caress his thighs as he was doing mine. He trembled beneath my touch, letting out a long breath and watching me intently. "You're sensitive too."

"In a lot of places," he promised.

"I look forward to exploring them all," I said.

"Not cheesy at all," he teased.

"Not purposely, but you knew what you were getting up front with me. And it's not a line. I really do want to explore every inch of you." Inside and out I thought. Not only the sweet lines of his body and trails along his flesh, but his mind and the million avenues of knowledge and creativity.

"Then let's get started, yeah?" His lips captured mine. His hand found my cock, which nearly jumped into his fingers with the need to be touched.

"Fuck," I groaned into his mouth. "I'm not going to last long if you keep that up."

"We have all day," Micah said. "Plenty of time for recovery and multiple adventures."

"I am worried I am going to disappoint you," I confessed. Micah was a former porn star. He knew a lot about sex, right? I didn't. "My experience is quick back-alley or bathroom stuff. I know sex isn't like porn. But that's where most of my knowledge of it comes from."

"Real sex is messier. Sometimes funny, bumped noses, premature ejaculation, or laughing yourself silly. That's all okay as long as you're having a good time and it helps to like the person you're with."

"You like me?" I asked.

"I do." Micah guided my hand back into his shorts and helped me cup his balls through the fabric of his bikinis. The weight of him in my grasp made me feel like I was holding something precious. Not because it was his sex, but because it was his trust.

"You know how you like to be touched, right?" he asked. "What sort of things make you feel good?"

"Sure, I guess?"

"Start there," Micah instructed. He pushed the shorts and underwear down so they framed his cock, and I marveled at the beauty of him. Micah wrapped my fist around him, his hand over the top and began slow strokes. His sigh was deep, cock weeping in my grip, and I couldn't help but smile at what I could do to him.

Our lips met, his hand gripping my hair to feed our mouths together. I devoured his passion, enjoying his dominance a little more than I thought I would. A groan escaped me when he twisted my head a little to give him a better angle. "Fuck."

"Yeah," Micah agreed.

He shoved the kilt out of the way and tilted our hips so the two of us could slide together. The heat of his cock against mine, both of us leaking precome, with his hands wrapped around us, tight and pumping. I groaned and had to fight to keep my eyes from rolling back in my head from the weight of the pleasure.

My hips moved on their own, thrusting in time to his

strokes, chasing the heat and friction of his hand and cock against mine. I couldn't really think beyond the sensation. We battled with kisses and writhing bodies, both of us making sounds that porn could never truly reproduce. His hold on my hair just this side of painful, but so fucking good, I couldn't help but fight it a bit, adding to the intensity.

He bit my lip, not a playful nip, but a quick sting of pain that blossomed into pleasure I hadn't expected at all.

"Sweet Jesus," I grumbled, the world spinning as I came, spurting over his fist and coating both of us.

He raced to catch up, fist pumping, hand still closed around mine, though I felt like I was useless at that moment to help. Then he was coming too, his soft cries a melody to my satiated body.

We both breathed heavily, trading kisses while our heart rates came down. My lip ached a little, though Micah lapped at it, sucked it, and gave it small kisses. "Sorry," he whispered. "I didn't break the skin."

"Nothing to be sorry for," I assured him. My brain began coming back online. Who knew I had that little kink? How could something so small feel so huge? He reached over and picked up some sort of spare towel or something and wiped off his hands and our spend.

Micah kissed the tip of my nose like I'd often done to him. "Okay?"

"Yes?"

"Is that a question?"

"Been a long time since I came. I think I had an out-of-body experience. You have a book about that somewhere?"

He snorted, which made me laugh and wrap him in a tight hug, to cover him with endless kisses. We curled up on the cushion together, laughing, kissing, and enjoying the moment.

"There are actually a few in the shop. Though I think it would be better if we practice and experiment ourselves."

"What do you have in mind?"

"I'd love to show you my toy collection."

"Let's nap, then I'm game."

CHAPTER 22

I was making another batch of cookies when someone pounded on the door. Micah frowned at the crochet project in his hands, but got up. We'd had an easy afternoon of sweet sex, cosplay idea discussions, and now food. I'd already fed him paninis for dinner—not even I could mess up a sandwich—but he'd requested more peanut butter cookies.

Micah opened the door. I expected Lukas or Sky, maybe even Tim, but it was Jared who pushed past Micah and into the apartment.

"Hey," I said, stripping off the oven mitts after taking the last batch out of the oven, and getting ready to tackle him if need be.

"You gotta find her," Jared pleaded with me. "She's in the cemetery. I know she is. I keep dreaming of her."

"We're not allowed in the cemetery," Micah said.

"Did you tell the police?" I asked. "They can get into the cemetery. But Jared, if she was there, she would have already been found."

"No one is listening to me." Jared tugged at his hair. "That other lady didn't listen. I told her to put it back, now she's dead. We need to put it back."

"Put what back where?" The question itself made no sense to me.

"A wedding ring. It had been put in the grave. That tour guide took it out, gave it to Mary, Mary is dead. We need to get the ring and put it back." He paced and both Micah and I stayed out of his way. "They will give me Sarah if we put it back."

He wasn't rational at all, and I understood. He'd been though a lot in a few days. I wasn't sure how to help him. "Did your family arrive, Jared?" I asked. He needed handlers before he did something stupid and got himself shot by the police.

He waved his hands as if none of that mattered. "They want to organize a vigil. My mom looks at me like I did something. My own mom." He tugged on his hair again. "I need to find Sarah. I close my eyes and I can hear her. She's calling for me. She's afraid. I need to bring her home." He dropped to his knees and Micah lunged to catch him, but I held up a hand to keep him back and shook my head.

"Jared, let me call someone for you. Have you slept?"

"Can't sleep. I have nothing but nightmares of the darkness eating her when I sleep."

I was beginning to think that maybe it was better if he was under more extreme care for the moment. I pulled out my phone and texted Lukas.

"I never wanted any of this. We thought we would have a little fun before I'm buried in four more years of endless work, internships, and tests. It was all supposed to be fun and games. Stories. It wasn't supposed to be real."

I patted his back and nodded for Micah to wait by the door in case Lukas showed up. "None of this is your fault," I assured Jared. "Sometimes bad things happen to good people."

"Sarah needs to be safe. They can take me instead. If I can't get the ring, they can take me instead." He sat there rocking, repeating the same thing over and over, looking disheveled, exhausted, and so lost. I knelt beside him, keeping up the physical contact, patting or rubbing his back, squeezing his arm, and talking to him trying to keep him coherent. So far he hadn't shown any violence toward either of us, but if he did, I'd rather he come at me than Micah.

Micah waved at me and a moment later opened the door. Lukas swept in with a couple of uniformed cops. I put my hands up and shook my head. Jared wasn't being violent. There was no need to arrest him.

"They're going to take him to the hospital, make sure he's hydrated," Lukas said and I heard his unstated 'among other things.' "I've already got people trying to find his family." Lukas crossed the room and crouched beside Jared and me. "Hey Jared, remember me? Alex's brother?"

Jared looked up and blinked hard like maybe he wasn't really sure where he was. "The police detective, right? Did you find Sarah?"

"Not yet, but we're looking. I'm a little worried about you buddy. This is Hartly and Mote," he said, motioning to the uniformed duo. "They are going to take you to the hospital."

"I'm not sick," Jared protested.

"Maybe not, but I think you need some fluids. Have you been drinking water? Eating? Taking care of yourself?"

"I have to find Sarah. She's so scared."

"I know, buddy," Lukas said, using his soothing good cop voice. He helped Jared to his feet. "But you can't help her if you're not feeling good. You have to drink water, eat, get some sleep, and let your family know where you are."

Jared's eyes were huge, pupils blown wide. I wondered if

someone had tried to give him something to make him relax and it had backfired like it normally did with me. "Did you take anything, Jared? Like to help you sleep?"

"My mom gave me some of her Ativan." He fidgeted, his hands trembling hard. He looked like a junky jonesing bad.

"Only one?" I asked.

He shrugged. "I don't remember. Feel like my skin is on fire. Like I need to rip it off to be comfortable again. But I gotta find Sarah."

Lukas looked at the two uniforms. "Get a bus over asap. He's having a reaction to medication." The same sort of reaction it gave me. Only I'd ended up seizing, and nearly choking on my own vomit from the stuff.

Jared's trembling got worse and he could barely stand. I held him up and prayed that he'd be okay. "Maybe some water would help," I said. "If he's dehydrated, the stuff will have concentrated in his system." I was more than a little angry with his mother, a woman I had never met, for giving him a benzo without knowing the risks. Had they taken him to the hospital at all? Didn't mental health issues run in the family? Wouldn't it have been smart then to take him for monitoring rather than give him someone else's meds?

Micah got him a glass of water and handed it to me. I tried to get Jared to drink some, but he couldn't really get it down. That worried me a lot.

He struggled for air, which had the cops panicking, but it wasn't a physical shut down of his lungs. This was a panic attack of the epic, medically induced kind. Micah took the water back. I sighed and wrapped my arms tight around Jared.

"Hey, buddy, just focus on me, okay? Breathe. Listen to my voice." I rubbed his back and kept in his line of sight. "You're safe. Everything is going to be okay." Lukas kept everyone back likely because he'd dealt with my panic attacks a dozen or so times. Telling Jared to breathe, and counting, seemed to help. Saying his name over and over, startled small breaths from him. He fought the panic so long I thought he'd pass out from lack of air, but finally he sucked in a ragged deep breath.

"Like that. Good. Breathe. It's going to be okay," I said.

"Sarah..." Jared wheezed.

"We'll find her," I said, not worried about the words being true or not. He wouldn't remember them in a few hours anyway. In his face, with his blown pupils, blood drained skin, and wide eyes, I saw myself. After a thousand nightmares, dozens of drugs, and endless days of being told I was insane. The human brain had a wonderful capacity for forgetting pain. Sometimes a memory of it would flare, but never enough to quite be the same as that first time. And that was a blessing, I thought as the EMTs arrived.

I let them take over Jared's care and made my way to where Micah stood, apart from the craziness going on in his living room, arms wrapped around himself like he was trying to keep his own body from exploding into panic. I tucked him into my embrace, his face against my collarbone, and body curled into mine, shielding him from unpleasant memories as best I could.

I wondered if he was thinking of Tim, and how he'd been treated when Micah had gone missing. Or if the scattered memories of his time in the ether rose up. My gut churned with the thought of his pain. Funny how quickly I'd latched on to him. I hoped it didn't scare him away. I was kind of attached now.

The cops and EMTs left. Lukas stood beside the door, looking tired.

"There's no ring," Lukas said. "I don't know where he got the idea, but there is no ring."

I tilted my head to process what he was saying. Jared thought he could get Sarah back if he returned some ring that Marc and Mary had taken from the grave. But if there was no ring... "Was something taken from the grave?"

"The family says no," Lukas said.

I wondered about that. Had they been there? Searched the grave, which by my understanding was full of old bones and ash? Somehow I didn't think so. Maybe they hadn't buried whomever with anything important. Or maybe they were hiding something.

"Stop," Lukas said. "I can see it on your face. Stop analyzing this. It's not some paranormal mystery. It's a missing girl."

"And two dead tour guides," I pointed out. "What if Jared is sensitive?"

"What if he is?" Lukas said. "What does that change? Will finding some magical ring, if it even exists, bring Sarah back? Back from where? Think about this logically, Alex."

"And when logic fails, what is left?" I asked. "You're the one who said I shouldn't distrust what I see."

"But what did you see? A shadow in the cemetery? How does that help us bring Sarah back? Or answer for the death of two people?" Lukas sighed. "I don't want you to go down this path."

"I'm already down this path," I defended. "Not by choice. A girl is missing. Everyone thinks Jared did something, but you have him on camera with date stamps."

"That doesn't mean he didn't do something to her. We always suspect the significant other first. It's how life works."

And wasn't that a shitty fact of life? "But you haven't found her body."

"Maybe it's in a tomb we didn't notice was opened? It's not like we can go and start opening them all."

257

I remembered back to the daytime tour and what Micah said about most of the tombs being sealed. It wasn't like that was something easy to do, to open a sealed tomb and reseal it. "But the cops would have noticed if something was tampered with, right?"

"This is not your problem," Lukas reiterated.

"Stop," Micah whispered. His hands gripped my shirt but he hadn't pulled his face away from my collarbone. "Stop, please. Don't fight."

I hugged him and kissed the top of his head, purposely looking away from Lukas to try to hide my irritation.

"Look," Lukas said and paused, seeming to think for a minute, "keep your distance from this, okay? I don't know what this is. Or why it's happening. But I really don't want either of you hurt. Okay?"

"Okay," I agreed. I didn't want Micah hurt.

"Has anyone gone into the cemetery?" Micah asked. "Maybe it's not paranormal." He looked at me. "Maybe Jared really hears her and she's stuck in there. The walls are high and if the gate is locked, she would have no way to get out."

Lukas frowned. "I don't know..."

"Common sense would say that someone should at least check instead of everyone calling Jared crazy," Micah said. "I think the two of you should be the last to call anyone crazy." He pulled away from me and stalked to the door to tug on his shoes. He was really taking this not being afraid of life thing seriously.

"We have patrols doing drive-bys," Lukas defended.

"And how are cops in cars going to hear a girl crying from inside a cemetery?" Micah asked. "If people reported hearing her would the cops claim it was some ghost bullshit and ignore it?" Lukas's expression said that Micah hit that nail on the head. I grabbed my shoes too. If he was going, so was I.

"This is silly," Lukas said.

We both looked at him and he threw his hands up in defeat. "Fine. Fucking fine. We can walk around the outside of it and if we hear something, I'll call someone in to unlock it. And if we hear absolutely nothing then I get to tell you both 'I told you so' and 'stay the fuck out of police business.'"

CHAPTER 23

I t was almost nine by the time we got the Uber to the cemetery. Lukas had suggested he go get his car, but Micah wasn't willing to wait. And since Micah wasn't willing to wait, neither was I.

We walked along the perimeter, no one else around and the street stretching empty as far as I could see. Micah put his fingertips to the wall and trailed them over the stone, walking ahead of us and listening hard. Each time Lukas said something, Micah shushed him. I was actually enjoying how much that annoyed my brother, but followed the two of them silently.

The waning full moon was beginning to edge between the clouds, and everything was silent. No birds or bugs that I could tell, which seemed odd. I didn't really feel anything unusual, just the humid night air and worry for Micah. And I wondered about Jared and a possible ring. It seemed like something out of a movie. Silly almost.

On the ride over I'd Googled the most recent burial in St. Louis Number One. It had been a woman who had passed. She'd been fairly old, in her nineties, and long widowed. Nothing about her obituary screamed of spooky rituals or

Hoodoo—the real word according to Micah for what Marc and Mary had practiced—paranormal vibes. She sounded like someone's grandmother, ordinary, though somewhat long-lived, and normal.

"Normal is relative," Micah had pointed out. "And being someone's grandmother doesn't mean she wasn't some sort of practitioner. Lots of practitioners are people's mothers or grandmothers."

"True," I agreed. "However, I'm more inclined to think it was something the other tour guides did."

"I wonder if Abigail knows anything," Micah said.

"Who?"

"I think you met her briefly," Micah said. "The same day you met Marc and Mary. They were usually together. Though Abigail is much younger than them. Abigail is Mary's niece. Though I don't think they were close. More a business relationship. I remember Abigail telling me once that Mary took her in as a teen and she had been working for her ever since."

"She's already been questioned by the police," Lukas said. "Claims she knows nothing." Only his comment made me look at him because it sounded detached, careful, like he knew more than he was sharing.

"Claims? But maybe was on video near the cemetery?" I deduced.

"Maybe," Lukas shrugged. "She did have access like the rest of them did." He wouldn't look at either of us or answer any questions during the rest of the drive.

At the cemetery I wondered about some of the legends I'd read while researching Micah's garden monster. "What about wraiths?" I asked Micah in a half-whisper. "Could a wraith have taken Sarah?" Did he believe in cryptids? Or simply that something spooky haunted his garden? Maybe he was humoring me and all my paranormal research by letting me put weird stuff in his garden.

He glanced my way and shrugged. Curiosity about the unknown did not make someone an expert, I was beginning to understand that. "I think legends are a way for humans to explain to each other the unexplainable. How much truth there is in them, is unknown, but someone at some point experienced things that created the legends. And legends only become legends through repetition. Does that mean it happened a lot? Possibly, or it was a really good story that people didn't mind repeating."

"More likely a way to scare people into staying out of trouble," Lukas grumbled.

"Like modern police work?" I asked him. "Because how many people fear the police now instead of trusting them?"

He glared at me.

"I know it's not your fault. Stating a fact." And being back at the cemetery made me mad with the reminder that I'd almost been shot after falling down and hitting my head. "Ruling through fear has never meant the betterment of societies." I knew that from experience while working in the Middle East. People hated and feared us, though we were supposedly 'protecting' them. In truth, we were there because of a war propagated over oil reserves and money. Some of the soldiers were die hard believers that we were protecting our country by destroying other people's lives. But I'd known many who knew the truth, though by the time I'd realized it, I'd already been halfway through my second tour.

Life did have a way of changing us. Not better or worse. Different. I looked at Micah who was walking close to the wall, hand tracing the white concrete, face tense with concentration. He felt something. I knew that from the set of his shoulders and his focus on the wall. And I knew it gave him a war of emotions as to what to feel about this sensitivity that he'd developed after his disappearance. Did that mean he wasn't still Micah? I didn't think so.

"You okay?" I asked him.

"Cold," he said. He glanced my way. "Are you hot?" Like when we'd been standing in Mary's entryway.

"No," I told him. I didn't feel much at all right then. "I mean nothing that the weather can't account for." The evening was warm and soupy. The scent of rain on the wind and the buzz of cicadas dancing through the night like a frenzy of earthen melody reminding us the city was seconds away from nature.

He frowned, but continued walking, hand on the wall, feet carrying him toward the main entrance. We rounded the corner to the gate and I had to glance twice at the door, which was closed, because it looked like it was encased in dancing shadows even though there was no moving light nearby.

Micah shivered. Was he feeling those creepy crawlies again? He went to the door and turned the knob, I think expecting as Lukas and I likely did, that the door would be locked, only it wasn't. The knob turned and the door creaked open.

"No," Lukas said, shaking his head. "I fucking hate this town and all the vandals. Let me call it in. It's supposed to be locked."

Micah barely spared him a glance before shoving the door out of the way and heading inside. I frowned, and followed.

"Alex," Lukas hissed.

"What are you going to do? Arrest us? I'm not letting him go in there alone. Do you know anyone who knows this cemetery better than him? He probably has some of the names on the graves memorized," I pointed out.

"Most of them," Micah said.

I followed Micah while I could hear Lukas talking on the phone to dispatch, but the sound of his voice faded away. Micah veered straight toward the grave that had been open. I followed and strained to hear anything other than our footsteps and breathing. The cicadas had gone oddly silent the second we stepped inside. Too far away perhaps? There weren't really any trees or anything other than stone and concrete inside the cemetery. Nothing for them to eat, but I thought we might hear crickets or something. Even the wind seemed to have died down. Creepy.

Was Sarah still here somewhere? The grave still had a red curtain around it and was cordoned off with yellow police tape. No one had been by to clean up the blood. It was dry and still tickled my nose with an old metallic scent. The animals and body were gone, but the entire area still felt eerie with an underlying vibe I couldn't really pin down.

Micah didn't try to cross the tape. Though he did examine something that appeared to be scrawled on the side of the tomb. It looked like gibberish to me.

"That the Voodoo stuff?"

"Hoodoo, I think," Micah said. "I'm not an expert."

"Any idea what they were trying to do?"

"Open a portal maybe? That sort of seems to always be the Voodoo idea. Open a portal to spirit guides to answer questions, or to the dead to speak with past loved ones, or even demons to learn about the future."

My heart raced at the idea of demons—put in my head by a childhood growing up in a Southern Baptist Church. "Like fire and brimstone demons?"

"Did you know there really is no such thing as hell in the Bible? Or demons. Just angels. Like the Christian God fucked up with his angels and tried to create humans to replace them, and the two species have been at war ever since," Micah said. "Lots of books taken out of the Bible by the Catholics who wanted humanity to only believe so much. Most of those removed books are about paranormal stuff including angels who came down to slaughter humans for being created by God."

"Um... I'd find fighting an angel pretty scary."

"I think the fear is the point."

"So they summoned an angel? Or are you saying demons are angels?"

"Yes, and maybe yes? Theory. Philosophy. The point is fear."

My head spun with the ideas. Too much. And yet, yes it all made me afraid in a way. Of a lot of things. Not the idea of hell, but of something scary out there to kill us for spite? Wasn't that the concept of humanity? All of our jaded emotions could make humans do things like lie, steal, and murder? "If angels are more fucked up than humans, I think we all really have reason to worry."

Micah nodded, "Right?"

We stood there in the dark for a minute, the air cool against my skin. I'd forgotten I was still in the kilt, but no one, not even Lukas, had commented. "I don't see or hear anything." Still didn't feel anything odd other than the eerie silence which could have been from standing in the middle of a concrete cemetery on the edge of downtown.

"Let's look around a little. Jared said they were on their way out when she vanished," Micah said.

"And she what? Tripped and fell into a giant mausoleum?"

He gave me an irritated stare.

I put my hands up in surrender. "Okay, let's look."

"And listen," Micah said. He led us down a zigzag through the rows, slowly weaving a way through the mostly paved walk, but turning us over the dirt area too. We stopped every couple of feet to listen. I closed my eyes each time, trying to focus on the sounds around us. If there was a girl somehow trapped in a tomb here, would we be able to hear her through all the marble?

In the far corner near the multi-mausoleum thing, Micah stopped since we had a wide view of the area, down several paths, even though it was dark. I closed my eyes, focusing hard to the sounds of the night.

Something faint in the distance made me pop my eyes open and search for it. Was it Lukas? It hadn't sounded like Lukas, the timbre had been higher, like a woman. "Did you hear that?" I asked Micah.

His gaze was focused in the same direction. "I heard something."

We headed toward the sound, stopping again after a few feet to see if we heard it again. It was so faint. Not a scream or anything so defined, more a faint moan. We wove our way around and down two other little pathways.

I nearly tripped over my own feet when I saw something move in the distance. "What was that?" I asked Micah pointing in the direction.

A shadow moved. Not our shadows. Was it Lukas? "Did you see that?"

Micah shook his head, frowning. He rubbed his arms like they hurt. "Feel something. My skin is on fire. Did you maybe see Lukas?"

"That was not Lukas we heard unless someone kicked him in the balls." I heard the faint moan again and decided to race toward the sound. "It's coming from over there." I pointed. Someone was hurt. Someone was there and needed help. Instinct pushed me to run faster, despite the uneven ground and rows of scattered stones in my path. The nearly full moon lit enough of the area that I could see where we were going even if it was all darkness and shadow. There were no lights inside the cemetery.

"Sarah?" I called for her. Was she stuck somewhere? After a few days without food or water she'd be pretty weak.

Was she really here? I thought I caught a glimpse of something around the edge of one of the big stone monuments, movement of some kind, not black, but more liquid than I thought a person's shadow should be. But when I rounded the corner, there was nothing. No shadow, nothing out of place, no Lukas, and no Sarah. I frowned, slowed to a stop and checked the two connecting paths. Nothing.

"Dammit," I cursed and turned back to find Micah. Only when I found the path I'd run up, he was gone. "Micah?" I called. For a moment I feared he'd gone off to some little corner to search on his own. As I traveled back to where I'd last seen him a feeling of dread built in my chest. He wasn't there.

"Micah!" I yelled, praying for an answer.

Nothing.

"Fuck!" I ran like a madman then, focused on the search, moving around the cemetery like I was trying to outrun a fire. I took every path, retracing steps and searching every corner. "No, no, no..." The cemetery wasn't that big. It looked big from the outside, but it really was a big rectangle surrounded by a high white wall. One way in and out. Lots of corners and tombs to hide behind, but he had no reason to hide, and I should have heard him, his steps, his breathing, or even the movement of his clothing.

He was gone.

I heaved for breath, searching the same areas three or four times until my lungs burned, and my side ached from all the running. A dozen times I dialed his phone, praying to hear his phone chime or have him answer, only there was no reply and nothing but silence stretching across the distance.

I found my way back to the gate, praying Micah had made his way out, or maybe even that Lukas had found him and dragged him outside. I panted and felt tears streaming down my face. My brain raced through a thousand horrible options.

Lukas stood with a couple other cops outside the gate. He looked up and waved me over, clearly angry with me. "Where's Micah?" he demanded.

"No, no, no, no..." I felt every last bit of my resolve vanish in that moment in the realization that he hadn't come outside to wait for me. "I only left him for a second." The panic attack that hit me then was almost welcome, as it came so fast and hard that I passed out, blissfully yanked down into a dark place where new boyfriends weren't stolen by cemetery monsters.

CHAPTER 24

I came to lying on the sidewalk with a handful of EMTs fussing over me. They had an oxygen mask pressed to my face and while the clean purity of it felt good, my lungs ached. I pushed the mask away and tried to breathe. The lights of police cars lit up the night almost as bright as daytime. Lukas stood nearby, and there were police streaming in and out of the cemetery.

"Lukas?" I called for him. Micah wasn't in there was he? They hadn't found him dead too, had they?

Lukas glanced at me, said something to the other detective he was talking to and headed my way.

"Micah?" I asked Lukas the second he got close enough to hear me.

"We're looking." His expression was guarded, tired, and sad. "I saw you both go in."

"He was right behind me. I heard something. Ran toward it, didn't find anything, but when I turned back, he was gone." I reached for Lukas's arm. "Are they looking for him? Did they find him?" Was he dead?

"I've got over a dozen cops in there looking for him. Hell, my sergeant thinks I'm nuts, but I have them searching every grave for openings that might have the girl stuck somewhere. If you had waited, neither of you would have been in there." He ran his hands through his hair. "Fuck, Alex. What happened? When will you fucking listen to me?"

I flinched. "I didn't want him to go in there alone."

"But you couldn't have convinced him to wait outside with me until we got some units here?"

Tears burned my eyes. "He's gone. What if he's gone again..." Maybe not even three months, but forever? I couldn't bring myself to voice the thoughts. Was it my fault? The day together had been amazing. Small things. Sitting with him while he made projects and worked stuff out in his head. An afternoon nap followed by sweet sex. Dinner and snuggling, time playing with Jet and a laser light while Micah smiled and watched from his place on the futon. For a few hours I'd felt normal, like there was a chance to find happiness even though we were both a little weird.

"Don't freak out, okay?" Lukas said. "Tell me what you remember and the last time you saw him. I've got people looking."

The EMT pressed something cold to my cheek. It hurt. I must have fallen and landed on my face again. At least I didn't seem to be bleeding. The cold pack helped ground me even while my mind raced in a million directions.

"You with me?" Lukas asked.

"Trying," I said, fighting down the panic. "You have to find him."

"We're looking, now tell me what you remember."

I closed my eyes and gave him everything. Detail by detail from the second we entered the cemetery, from finding writing on the side of the open crypt, to not hearing bugs, and following shadows. I recalled details this time around that I hadn't before. The shapes of certain graves, the sound of Micah behind me as I ran toward that last shadow, and the abrupt silence. He had turned down another path, I realized. Having felt or heard something he hadn't shared. It had only taken a few seconds. When I finished the retelling, I bowed my head to my knees and sobbed. He was gone. Something had taken him like it had taken Sarah.

Lukas's sigh was deep and tired. "Can I have someone take you home to my place? I'd feel better if I knew you were home safe."

"I need to find Micah."

"And I have people looking for him."

"That worked out really well, last time, right?" I threw back at him feeling the need to hurt because I felt like I was bleeding inside. That quickly Micah had become important enough to me, to make me bleed when he'd been ripped away. Fuck. "Sorry. That was an asshole thing to say, and I didn't mean it."

Lukas took my face in his hands and made me look at him. "Stop. All this shit in your head. Stop. I thought you'd help each other, not tear each other up."

"You didn't expect him to go missing again." But I had feared it from the moment I heard that thing in his garden.

"Let me have someone walk you home. Get some rest."

I pulled away and stumbled to my feet, feeling a little unsteady still from the panic attack. "Maybe he got by us somehow and went home?"

"I already sent officers that way to see if he was there, and I have his cameras linked to my phone, remember? So do you." Lukas reminded me.

I nodded and backed away. "I'm going to go check."

Lukas frowned at me. "Alex..."

"It's okay. I'm going to check his house and head home."

"Promise me," Lukas demanded. "His place and then home. I'll send cops around to check on you."

"Sure," I said, not really promising anything.

"Alex," Lukas called after me.

"I'm fine."

"I need you safe."

But I was safe. Something had taken Micah and probably Sarah, leaving me behind. It was Micah who wasn't safe. "I'm going to Micah's. I might wait for him there." I walked away from Lukas, ignoring his protests and pulled up the video on my phone. I headed down toward the Quarter. It was a bit of a walk, but not horrible. It gave me time to search the cameras' past feed for any sign of anything odd. I watched the video of Micah from last night. How he sat in the garden, tense with fear, while nothing happened. He seemed angry with himself when he finally went inside.

Then from the past few hours I saw us leave on camera, but nothing afterward, not even the orange tabby that had been visiting his yard previously. No sign of Micah. I didn't head toward his house or even Lukas's. Jared's words replayed in my head. All this over some stupid ring. What the fuck were they even thinking? Would the police even know what to search for in Mary's shop? Her place had been filled with clutter; how would they even know?

I turned in that direction instead and wondered how I would know if I found it. Would it glow? Was there even a ring? And why would a dead person care? They couldn't take money with them to the other side. Maybe it was some sort of magic thing. Was magic real or simply a state of mind? I wasn't qualified to make those philosophical leaps, though my brain did try.

A few blocks away I saw smoke and my stomach lurched in worry. For a moment I thought it might be from the LaLaurie mansion again. Only it was the wrong direction. The flashing of lights as I neared pushed me to run. Fire poured from a row of shops, centered on Mary's Voodoo place, but spreading outward. The man who owned the shop next door to Mary's stood there looking heartbroken as he spoke to a police officer. Firefighters worked on the blaze trying to keep it from spreading further.

I noticed another woman standing away from the crowd of gawkers, and vaguely remembered her from that first day in the shop. Abigail. I made a beeline for her. She barely glanced my way before I planted myself in front of her, and unlike the man who owned the shop next door, she didn't look upset by the blaze.

"Was the ring in there? Or whatever your aunt took from that grave?" I demanded of her.

She frowned at me. "Who are you?"

"Alexis Caine. I work with Micah. I need that ring."

She waved her hand at the blaze. "Everything is gone."

"Did you set the fire?"

"Fires happen a lot here," was all she said. "I'm not sorry to see it go, though I do feel bad for the neighbors."

I could have strangled her at the very thought of it. Was the chance to get Micah back burning to ash right that second? "What did they do at the grave?"

Abigail shrugged. "It never worked. I knew it wouldn't work. That was why I didn't go. Aunt *Mary*, that wasn't her real name, wanted proof that she was related to the last remaining LaLaurie. She wanted the Mansion to use it as a tourist attraction."

I tried to make sense of that. "Wait, so the woman that died

was a LaLaurie?" The name hadn't been the same. And from
what I remembered of the cemetery there wasn't a tomb that
was specific to the LaLauries. Or maybe that had been to keep
the vandalism down.

"Married half a dozen times and tried to bury her lineage.
Mary and I were supposedly related too, but I don't need that
legacy, thanks. Bunch of psychos. She thought if they could
prove lineage then they could go to court and get the mansion.
Strong Catholic woman didn't believe in cremation, but if they
left her in the grave long enough the heat would do it for her.
Marc thought if they could get DNA they could test. They
thought it would make them rich. Mary requested a DNA test
lots of times, but that old bitch wasn't having it. Now that she's
dead, they figured they could take it."

I gaped at her. "What the fuck is wrong with you people?"

Abigail shrugged. "Not me. I didn't want it. That family is
cursed and I want no part of it."

"So there's no ring?" I clarified. "They took a bone or something from the grave?" How gross was that. That they would
take something from a newly dead body for a DNA test. The
entire thing made me seethe with anger. Sarah and Micah were
missing because someone wanted control over a haunted house?
"All of this over a fucking house?"

"That place makes the new owners a fortune. And I don't
know what ring they'd be talking about. I know they wanted to
open a portal to a guide that would help them get back the
rights or something. It was always some mystic bullshit with
them. Spirit guides and portals. I hate this city and its paranormal crap." Abigail looked away. "Mary said she'd give Marc
a cut of the earnings. Not me, of course, because I was her
niece and she expected me to help. Except I didn't show up for
their little ceremony killing chickens and squirrels." She glared
into the flames. "I'm done with all of this. The mystical bull-

shit, death, ghosts, and all of it. I want a normal life. Let it all burn."

I stared at her for a minute, a thousand thoughts swimming for foothold and only one thing finding its way up. Micah. I needed to get him back.

The shop began to collapse inward, the fire eating through enough of the structure to cave the roof in. The sound of sirens and flashing lights seemed to give me a moment of suspended animation as I stood there, lost and unsure what to do. The chance of getting Micah back was very likely going up in flames, even if I'd known what to search for to begin with. I turned away from the fire, headed somewhere, though I wasn't sure exactly where in that moment.

I thought about heading to the river, even briefly about throwing myself in and letting the water take me. But where would that leave Micah and Lukas? Even if Micah never returned, Lukas would forever blame himself for not insisting someone walk me home. I sighed, so lost in thought I didn't realize I had wandered back to Micah's place until I stood at the door. I didn't have a key to get in. Did Lukas have one? We'd have to get Jet and take care of him until Micah reappeared. If he reappeared.

I sat down under the tree, heart heavy, lost in confusion, and so alone that it hurt to breathe. What if he was gone forever? We barely knew each other. It shouldn't hurt this much, my rational brain told me. Rational didn't matter much in ways of the heart. Was I in love with Micah? This soon? It sounded more like a romance novel than possible reality. But how else could I explain the tightness in my chest at the thought of him being gone forever. A few days wasn't long enough, not to love him or to lose him.

Training, he'd mentioned often. That was what relationships were built on. When you thought about someone for a while and had to learn to make things work. No one simply meshed together like magic, no matter how attracted. That made sense to me. I had looked forward to discovering more little details about him. The idea of waking up with him every day, of having that tiny smile directed at me, and his crafting frenzy calmed by my presence made me giddy. The idea of having lost all that? Agony.

Fuck.

Leaning back against the seat, I closed my eyes and tried to remember the good things. His smile, the teasing way he laughed, or the devious glint in his eyes when he talked about his silent war with the church ladies. Most of all was the thought of him wrapped in my arms, while he cried, slept, or made delicious sounds while we made love. Those moments holding him made me feel real again. Alive.

I prayed in that moment, like I never had before in my life, not to a single God or even anything specific, but to everything supernatural that might exist. *Please bring him back to me*, I begged. *Take me if you need to, just bring him back.*

Would anyone hear? Did anyone care? Was there a higher presence or was life the chaos it appeared to be. No fate, no higher power in control, just a couple billion drunks at the wheel. I sighed and lay down on the bench, curling up into a fetal position and staring into the unmoving darkness. Everything was still. No birds, bugs, or shadows. Quiet. Lifeless, I realized in that moment. Like I felt right then.

I sighed and began to count, trying to ease the anxiety and panic to think straight. Was there something else I could be doing right then? Anything to help Micah? A glance at my watch said it was nearing midnight. Where had the time gone? Would the shadow come out? Was there a shadow in his garden or was it something more sinister?

The counting helped. I could feel my heartbeat begin to

slow a little and my eyes drooped with exhaustion. It was work to keep them open and I blinked a few times when it seemed like the gnomes moved. A flicker at first, then the arms gave a little twitch before the head turned. Only that wasn't possible. A dream maybe? If I'd had more energy, I would have bolted upright and stalked across the distance to learn the truth even if it terrified me. But I couldn't find the strength as once again, my limbs felt weighted and heavy, as often happened when I napped,. A doctor once told me it was a mild form of sleep paralysis, nothing to fear really, just a slow awakening of the brain after or right before sleep. Only as I lay there in the darkness, sleep dragging me downward, the garden seemed to come alive. Gnomes, cats, and shadows extending to encase the area in movement. It should have terrified me, watching the change metamorphose the entire garden into a moving, thriving, thing. Would anyone see it on video? Or was it another weird side effect of that day in the desert?

I fought to keep my eyes open, muttering Micah's name into the darkness as the weight of something more powerful than sleep dragged me down. "Bring him back to me," I begged, stretching a hand toward a large shadow. "Please."

It reached for me with a spectral darkness of writhing shades, shifting and changing into something with defined shape, but making my heart race, even while I still couldn't move. A child with black eyes molded itself out of the darkness, the wavering of shadows giving it form. I blinked at it, fighting for strength to awaken, or move, or break whatever spell it had me under.

"If you want him back, you have to help him, otherwise he's lost to both of us," I whispered through heavy lips. Did the child care? Was this my demon or Micah's? Was it even there or my brain playing tricks on me? If it was Micah's, it had spent years tormenting him, did it want him gone or was it all an elaborate game?

I couldn't stay awake, even if the terror told me it was a good idea to not let it touch me. If I got Micah back, that was all that mattered. Lukas would take care of him if I were gone. "Save Micah," I whispered to the darkness. "Save Micah. Take me instead."

CHAPTER 25

The abrupt change from the garden to the desert sand storm jarred me to the bone. From near sleep to a battle for survival, I suddenly found myself sitting in the doorway of the tent, staring into the ripping winds, confused by the change, and assaulted by the elements. Was it a dream?

It felt real. The howling of the wind, the sound of the sand pelting on the tent, the heat wafting off the hot desert in waves of distorted color, and the giant mass of wriggling darkness beyond. I couldn't recall it having been that clear before. All the dreams had lost its shape in the swirl of air, grit, and darkness. Now I could almost make out its face, not unlike that man who'd walked toward our base in the darkness.

The locals had called it a jin. I knew from my research that jin weren't the genies of storybooks. They didn't grant wishes and weren't benevolence of any kind. According to legend, jin were mortal creatures, though longer lived than human, who lived lives parallel to humans, but had magic and were made of fire. Often when they died it was in a fiery blaze. Or so the stories I read had stated.

They also took over the lives of humans, pretending to be human, though I wasn't sure if that meant they could shapeshift to be someone who already existed, or had a form that could blend in with humanity. Either way it was a confusing and terrifying prospect.

I had often thought of those stories I'd overheard and the thing I'd seen in the desert, wondering if they were one and the same. Therapy and doctors told me that entertaining the thought meant I was nuts. No such thing, they said. But this wriggling mass of shadow and power sure looked like something. All in my head? Maybe. If that was the case then why was I so afraid?

"Why?" I asked it, seeing it move in the darkness as some sort of giant, and feeling bold. Would answers help ease my guilt? "Why did you kill them?" Why my unit? Why kill them at all? I thought about Micah's words about the battle between mankind and angels. Maybe it wasn't a jin but some sort of angel dropped down to seek vengeance for God having created humans. It all seemed such a pointless waste of time, as much of religion did, hate for a species, skin color, orientation or whatever.

I watched again as the men who'd served with me answered the siren call and died. An explosion of humanity, blood and gore no less gruesome than the first time or the thousand nightmares since. Despite the clarity in the thing's form, I still couldn't see how he/it/they did it. Will? A thought? Magic? Or did it move so fast I couldn't see? Not that it mattered as this was all in the past, and what had Micah said about the past? Ghosts were memories of the past, right? Isn't that what this was? A ghost of a memory? Did that mean it couldn't hurt me? Perhaps it meant more that fear was nothing but a useless emotion like so many therapists had claimed in the past?

I got up and walked toward it, leaving the safety of the tent.

There was a brief flicker of roiling terror filling my gut that it would suck me up and rip me apart too, only that time had passed. I had survived. Escaped. This was a dream. I swallowed it back and kept moving, not willing to let it control me anymore.

As I approached, the wailing wind went from deafening to silent, like it was waiting for me. That gaping face twisted and writhed until it turned in my direction. It seemed to blast me with terror and the emotion rolled over me, ingraining itself into every pore and making my skin crawl until I wanted to rip it off. I paused a moment to process, breathing in the emotion, the tightening of my lungs, and overwhelming need to run and recognized it as not mine. Fake. Like those few seconds when you fall asleep and suddenly dream of falling and jerk awake, the world disjointed and clarified all at once. I shook off the weight of it and continued forward.

"Not real. This is the past," I reminded myself out loud. A dream couldn't hurt me. Even if it was a dream from the past. "I need Micah back," I told the creature. "If you can't help me, then you're worthless to me. Powerless." I pushed down the terror, walking toward that mass like it was nothing more than a puppy in need of cuddling. "You haunt me, but you're powerless. Only a memory."

The face snarled at me, a dark limb of swirling dirt reached for me, but passed right through me. Harmless.

"Worthless," I restated. "If you can't help me find Micah then you're worthless. The memory, the fear, and the worry, all of it is worthless." The fear slaked away as if it had been some sort of coating. Micah had faced his fear and come out angry with himself that he'd lost time. I wasn't willing to lose more time either. Not to fear or anger. And not the time I planned to spend learning how to adore him.

"Bring him back to me or leave me be," I demanded. I

reached the feet of the swirling darkness and stared up into the monster of heat, sand, and power. In many ways I could see more of it, almost give it a defined shape, and in others there was nothing I could have recalled specifically about the creature, even if there was a creature at all. A trick of my mind?

"Worthless," I muttered again. Memories like this. Distorted lies of the past. "You're not even real." A ghost of a past memory from a fucked-up brain like mine. "Stupid worthless nightmares."

I turned my back on it then, no longer afraid or even caring if there was a creature. He couldn't help me and so had no power over me anymore.

When I turned the tent was gone. In its place was the dark looming shapes of tombs, St. Louis Number One. I frowned seeing a shimmer in the distance, heard voices. A child appeared before me. Small, undefined, and black-eyed, vaguely familiar. From Micah's garden perhaps? But hadn't that been a dream? A trickle of fear inched through my stomach and it smiled. Fire seemed to burn beneath its skin digging channels of orange magma through its veins. The thing from the desert, not whatever Micah's monster from the garden is. I scowled.

"Worthless," I told it again. More dreams to play on my fears. At least now I knew it was my monster and not Micah's.

It held out a hand, offering me something that glowed.

"What is it?" I demanded.

Your choice. The words whispered on the wind around me. The child's lips did not move.

I snarled at it. "Choice of what? Will it bring Micah back to me?"

Micah, the wind called his name a dozen times fading into the distance and I wanted to scream. *Choose.*

I reached for it, not caring in that moment if it was a trap or a way to drag me off to some other place. It was like the glowing object in a video game, something I knew I needed, though didn't know why. I took it, feeling something solid beneath my fingers but unable to see it.

Touching the child set me on fire. There was no other way to describe the feeling. Burning from within, like my insides were liquefying and pooling in my core, but unable to escape the shell of my body. I gasped at the pain, the intensity beyond anything I'd ever experienced in a dream before. Was it real?

I fought for breath, choking back the fire and trying to catch air. Flashes of a million things rolled through my brain as if I'd been there and they were my memories. An older woman as a child looking at another woman in period clothing. Her lifetime flashed before me. Multiple marriages, children born and lost, family ties severed with injustice, rage, and pettiness. She had been a bitter thing in the end. Stirring up discord for the few moments of power it made her feel. I had never met her, but knew her every motive. Couldn't recall her name, but could retell her life if someone asked. The trails of shadowy ooze stained the memories of her life, making some areas too dark to see, and even eating away at the edges of her psyche.

The vision shifted away from the woman and to Micah standing on a path in the woods staring at something as undefined as this child before me. My breath caught as I waited for something to happen or to feel what he did. Only Micah's eyes were blank in that moment, nothing more than a doll staring lifeless into the void. The memory didn't continue, though I tried to mentally grasp at it to keep him in my thoughts.

Again the vision changed, this time to a ceremony in the darkness in which two people nearly died over greed and a girl went missing. These two were tainted by the slime of shadowy darkness as well, parts of their lives captured in the waves of memory much like bugs in amber. Suspended in motion, beautiful, yet lifeless, and powerless. They were another battery added to the charge of energy in a city full of restless *others* uncontrolled by the simplicity of humanity.

Power arched outward, emanating from the city like some sort of nuclear reactor. It was a constant pool of movement, life, energy, and memories to fuel something I couldn't quite understand. The thing before me used it to survive, that much I knew. In fact, most of the unexplained in the city used that well of endlessly swirled static charge to exist. Somehow, I was now plugged into them, viewing the other side while still not really part of it. The power seeped from the child before me, leaving burned trails in the ground beneath its feet and ropes of color, like a giant spider web, spanned outward, fading into the distance, feeding on life from things I couldn't see.

The most terrifying part of the child-thing, was the sparkling cord of energy that bound it to me. The second I saw it, I began to tug and try to rip it free, only it wasn't a physical thing I could touch. The more I struggled the hotter I burned. The fire scorched so hot through my mind I thought I'd die. Each vision like a brand, etching the memories into my brain though they weren't mine. A thousand lifetimes, a million scenarios. It was too much, the weight endless and suffocating. I sank to my knees under the pressure, unable to let go of the child even if I wanted to.

Worthless? That wind voice asked.

"If all you can give me is fear, then yes," I said, not caring if it killed me. "Worthless. Memories are worthless. Ghosts of the past. Nothing but memories. Useless. Give me back Micah. Without him my life is meaningless." I was being overly dramatic, but it didn't seem to matter in that moment because the child was confused by the intensity of my need for Micah, and angry that I defied it. Fear it understood, even anger, but not my defiance or the desire to hold Micah in my arms and protect him.

The child snarled, and the weight of something physical transferred between us, from whatever their non-corporeal hand was to mine, an item.

You owe me, it said, and *I will collect.* Then it vanished, leaving me kneeling, not in the desert or even Micah's yard, but in the cemetery, something dark in my grasp.

The fire vanished so abruptly that I sucked in too much air and choked, coughing and gasping for breath through lungs burning with the weight of too much air. I tried to focus on whatever it was in my hand, the weight of it feeling like lead. My palms smoldered from the fire, skin blackened and charred. I thought it should hurt more, but it only mildly ached. The thing looked like some sort of ring. Not a wedding ring or anything so mundane, no this thing was a snarled mass of multiple metals, gnarled and discolored rocks, and negative pulses of energy. Instinct alone kept me from casting the nasty thing into the darkness to be done with it.

The world around me swirled and moved like a wet, acrylic painting instead of reality. The edges of reality smearing as I blinked, almost like my vision was covered in water. My breathing calmed enough that I could sort of focus on the rolling waves of the landscape. I was pretty sure I was in the cemetery. Real or a dream? I wasn't sure of either in that moment.

A distant sound of voices forced me to struggle to get to my feet. I closed my fist around the distorted ring-like thing. The child had given it to me for a reason. I had to hope it was a chance to get Micah back. I stalked forward in the shifting wet landscape, feeling like my limbs were stuck in sludge. There were glimmers of things, shapes that moved around me, almost like people, only they were smeared shadows, and odd, stunted movement, as though they were on another plane than I was. I couldn't touch them, even when I reached in their direction. It was like watching a movie soaked in water, colors and life leaking through scene to scene, but not really meshing.

I followed the sound of voices, feeling like my body weighed a thousand pounds. The trek slow and painful. But I found the open grave, and in this place, it was truly open. Not covered or even lined with police tape. It was a doorway, gaping into darkness much like the LaLaurie house had appeared at night, a lifeless, soul-sucking void. The edges of it scorched and even scored, like something with claws had grabbed on to the edge and tried to keep itself from being dragged inside, only to fail in the end as the gouges vanished into the darkness.

Near the grave stood two figures, more defined than the shadows and almost completely solid. I blinked a few times wondering if what I was seeing was real, and my heart lurched at one of them.

Micah!

"Fuck!" I cried, though my voice seemed lost in the wind and swirl. They must have heard me because they turned, Micah and a very tired looking Sarah. I tried to run, only again wading through the distance dragged my pace to a crawl like walking through a tanker spill of molasses. Was this a dream? Because if it was, it was the best and worst ever.

When I finally reached Micah, I took his mouth with mine, kissing him fiercely and feeling my heart race with joy. He returned my kiss, whispered things to me that didn't make sense, not words, but mixed sounds. He felt real, warm, alive, and solid beneath my touch. I wanted to wrap myself around him, like that would somehow save him. I pulled away to look at him and Sarah, and while they looked like themselves, real, whole, and physical rather than shadows, the edges of Sarah's form seemed to be fading.

Micah said something. I saw his lips move, heard scattered bits of sound, only I couldn't make out any words. He held Sarah's hand with one of his and touched my face with the other, trying to tell me something, though what I didn't know. The odd world distorted everything, including the sound and the movement of his lips.

"I can't understand you," I told him. Was it only me who was lost in miscommunication?

Micah frowned and glanced at Sarah. They didn't speak to each other. But he stroked my face and looked sad. No. I didn't like that look directed at me. Sad acceptance, like we were all lost now.

My brain was a little slow most days, and today seemed no different as things started to slowly fall into place. Sarah and Micah were here in this distorted world, probably looking for a way out too. My first thought was that this was all an elaborate dream, only it felt too real. Despite the odd misshapen landscape and endless shadows, something churned in my gut, reminding me of little things, the air on my skin, the burning in my hand where the boy had touched me, the feel of Micah's lips on mine. And while it was great to see him, it meant I was likely stuck as well. Wherever we were, world between worlds, dream dimension, whatever. Was there a way out?

I frowned and looked around, world shifting and bleeding color at the edges. We stood at the open grave, it being the most defined thing in the cemetery. Figures, almost shadows, moved around us, untouchable.

Maybe we were even standing on the other side, whatever it meant after death? This was too much for my already overworked brain.

Micah reached for my hand, gripping it and reminding me

of his presence as I seemed to be drawn into watching the shadows move. He spoke again, but I shook my head, as I couldn't understand him. He frowned, an expression I didn't like seeing on his face.

I wanted to reach for him and soothe away the irritation, but found I still had one hand clamped on that gnarled evil ring, and that hand was still burning. I held it up, feeling the heat, though no pain, and frowned at it myself.

Micah reached for it and I pulled my hand away, afraid I'd burn him. But he caught my wrist and held it up. Did he see the glow like I did? The fire? The memories? The rage? It wasn't even a positive thing, not pretty like I might envision a quest object in a video game, more like water and oil creating grease rainbows of pulsing power.

I opened my hand so he could see the ring, though wouldn't let him touch it. He didn't need that stain leeching onto him like it had to me. He frowned over the ring then glanced at the tomb. He moved my wrist toward the grave, pointing at the gaping hole which looked almost like a mouth in that moment. Fear roiled through my gut. It made sense to give it back to the darkness. I tried to throw the thing into the hole. It was only a few feet and shouldn't have been an issue, but it clung to my hand, attached as though it had been superglued.

"Fuck," I cursed, though I knew they probably couldn't make out what I said.

Micah let go and pointed me toward the grave. I got the idea. Put the ring in the giant gaping hole. Sure. Stick my hand in there, 'cause that wasn't a nightmare we'd all had once or twice in our lives. Childish fears, I reminded myself. This was all a dream after all, right? Only if it was a dream, I didn't want it to end and awake to find Micah gone again.

I looked at him, trying to convey with my expression every-thing I wanted to say but knew he wouldn't understand in this disjointed world. He squeezed my hand and gave me a tiny reassuring smile. Message received. I sighed and leaned forward to kiss him lightly, which he accepted.

I was crazy about him. A few days and I knew that we were far beyond a training situation, at least on my side. I wanted to know everything about him, wake up to his adorable smile, listen to him laugh over my stupid jokes, and make cookies for him while he crafted to sort out his head. He nodded, kissed me once more, and I pulled away to head toward the tomb.

I approached the grave, Micah's hand in my empty one, his grip firm and leaving me to hope that this would all be over soon. I remembered what Jared had said about putting the ring back in the grave and he would get Sarah back. Maybe it was a metaphor, maybe it was real. The child had given me a ring—was it the right ring?—, and I could give it back to the grave. Would it somehow break the hold of this odd other world and let us all go?

The gaping hole seemed to extend and grow into something large enough to walk through as I got closer. Twice I tried to shake off the ring toward the grave, only nothing happened as the glowing thing clung to me. Not really a ring, I realized briefly, but a mark of some sort of magic, if that was at all a real thing. Whatever deals or contracts the woman and her family had made in life, clung to me in a bond that needed life to continue. Since I was the nearest *life* it stuck to me, only I wanted no part of it.

The open doorway into darkness looked like a void. I could feel it dragging in tiny particles of that distant energy. A slow-moving vacuum of life, and like it was feeding, I could see the bits of life it stole from Micah and more from Sarah who had been stuck there longer. I had to close the portal, if that was what it was. Would returning the ring do that? Fuck, I was like a teenager given the job of brain surgery and told to wing it with several lives hanging in the balance. And while I hoped it was all some elaborately detailed dream, I suspected it was a reality stranger than anything my exhausted brain could conjure up.

Standing at the foot of that doorway into an abyss of darkness, I hesitated. Would it be so simple? Leave the ring and close the portal to shut off that constant drain? Would it leave us stuck? Could I even let go of the ring as it was bonded to my hand?

Micah and Sarah stood behind me, both clinging to each other, and Micah's hand tightening on mine. They were counting on me to not be a coward.

The memory of crying like a baby and clinging to another soldier while others died around us in the desert flashed through my head. Odd for a dream to have that flash of memory in the middle. But it made my gut hurt when the feeling of being a fucking coward, again filled my head. Not this time, I thought and lifted my hand toward the grave.

I thrust my fist and the smoldering ring into the darkness, expecting to drop whatever and pull back. Only the darkness wasn't simply a lack of light, it was like jelly, thick and viscous, enclosing my hand and sucking me inward. In panic I tried to rip my arm backward as the mass dragged me forward. It swallowed my arm up to the shoulder as I glanced back at Micah, fear and horror on his face and Sarah's beyond him. They both grabbed my remaining free hand and pulled, like they could somehow free me from the shadow. But their strength was nothing compared to that void. The two of them were dragged forward with me, feet scraping at the dirt, and I fought harder, trying to keep my boots planted and outside the grave, even if it took my fucking arm off. A thousand horrific ideas filled my head of what might happen if I were pulled into that grave.

The fire in my grip cooled to ice, burning in a different way, spreading a numbness through my limbs as the shadowy ooze sucked me inward. And I floundered as the darkness drew me into its embrace. It took only seconds for it to begin covering my legs and torso. Micah and Sarah still pulled, and I gasped for breath as it poured across my face, feeling like slime against my skin. With the last large gulp of air, I shoved off their hands so they wouldn't be pulled under with me, and prayed that my sacrifice would free them from whatever this other world was. My own life to free them was all I had left to offer. If that was what it took, so be it.

The cold numbness spread over my limbs. My vision faded beneath the ooze as my lungs burned with lack of air. Life was leeched away from me like a thousand pinpricks siphoning away blood instead of my soul. The black, inky, void devoured everything.

The heaviness suffocating me in that ooze as I stared up at a hole gaping through the darkness. It was so far above there was no way I'd reach it, but light glowed from beyond it. I blinked a few times unable to keep focused and clear under the onslaught of pressure.

Things fed at me. Tiny moving shadows eating away at my body like insects in the darkness. They writhed like maggots, burrowing into my soul. The pain was excruciating, but I was paralyzed and helpless. I prayed Micah had gotten away.

It was rage that made me struggle to look again, finding the opening far above through a blurred gaze. Rage and fire. Not mine, but something that felt familiar enough that the separation of the emotion was difficult. Fire leapt through the opening above, a burning mass of bright energy and anger. If I had the strength to be afraid, I would have been. Only suffocating in the darkness, being eaten alive, I couldn't move. It reached for me, a terrifying form of twisting flames, crackling and snapping in the darkness. It wrapped arms around me.

Mine, it said as I screamed, the fire engulfing me. Ice seared away, awakening my nerves and lighting me in a web of agony as I burned. The ring and the maggots melted away as the fiery being engulfed me in a devouring embrace. The final darkness that overtook me then was blissful with its all-consuming loss of awareness.

CHAPTER 26

I woke feeling like I'd been underwater too long. My lungs ached from the sudden onset of too much air and my limbs felt heavy. There were machines attached to me. Beeping and alarms filled the tiny beige room with noise and color as I blinked at a white, tiled ceiling and dimmed fluorescent lights.

Nurses filled the room, the uniforms unmistakable despite the molasses movement of my brain. There were pops of color, sound, and motion that wavered in and out of focus. I think I dozed a few times, dreamless losses of consciousness that lasted only a few minutes, I think, because the scene around me didn't change. Doctors, nurses, voices, machines, and the same tiny room.

Several times they spoke to me. The sound of their voices meshed, watery, and muted. Once or twice I thought I made out the question, "What is your name?"

"Alexis Caine," I replied, not sure if my lips were actually moving or not. But then I slept again, body too heavy to fight through the exhaustion.

When next I woke, I actually felt somewhat normal. And I had to pee like a motherfucker. Holy shit. I blinked, tried to orient myself and took in that I was in a hospital, the only thing attached was an IV line giving me fluids. I could feel my body well enough to know that if I didn't get up, I'd piss the bed and there was no catheter.

It took a bit of effort to get myself to the edge of the bed, and ready to get vertical. My legs and arms felt weak, like they had been overused and abused. A male nurse appeared in the doorway with a clipboard. He did a tiny lurch at seeing me up and set the clipboard on the rolling table before he was by my side, steadying me.

"Need to pee," I told him.

"Okay," he agreed and helped me up, moving the IV stand to roll with me. We waddled to the bathroom. He helped me to the giant area beside the toilet and pointed to the bar beside it. "Hold on to that so you don't fall over."

"Planning on it," I promised, reaching for the handle. Thankfully he let me pee in peace. I was able to wash my hands and open the door before he was back to help me into the bed. How had I gotten to the hospital? Had the fall given me a concussion I hadn't noticed? "Can you tell me why I'm here?" I asked the nurse.

"I think we all have a lot of questions about that," the nurse said. "But your brother is on his way. So hopefully we'll have some answers soon."

I frowned. "But I don't remember coming to the hospital at all." Why would Lukas be on the way? Wouldn't he have been notified the second I'd been admitted? I knew from the vague memory of waking up the first time that I'd obviously been in the hospital at least a day, since there had been so much in and out of consciousness. "Did I have a concussion?"

"You're severely dehydrated and malnourished, but no concussion," the nurse said. "Do you remember hitting your head?"

I thought about when I'd passed out and smashed my face on the sidewalk after Micah disappeared—Micah, was he still missing?—, though my face didn't hurt anymore. "I fell, but I don't think I fell hard enough to break anything."

"That's good. If you're feeling okay, I can get some food ordered for you."

"Food would be good," I said, suddenly feeling like I hadn't eaten in forever. I'd even eat those stupid sugar pillows people called beignets if I had to.

"Let me get some food for you then." Once he'd helped me back into the bed, he grabbed up his clipboard and left.

I frowned at the room, not recognizing it from the hospital I'd been at in New Orleans. But there were multiple hospitals in New Orleans. Perhaps I hadn't been to this one before? At least it didn't look like a psych ward. I'd seen enough of those in my life to recognize just about any of them. And since they weren't limiting my access to the bathroom or facial tissues, I didn't think I was on any sort of suicide watch.

Dehydrated and malnourished? How did that happen? I'd been eating fine, at least two meals a day plus snacks. Maybe I'd been out a few days? That could explain the dehydration but not being malnourished, that took longer than a few days to develop. I frowned at the questions popping up in my head. Overthinking was a skill I had on a good day, today it was out of control.

Had it all been a dream? The cemetery, seeing Micah and Sarah? The excruciating pain of being eaten by the shadows and then rescued by fire. Too many questions. I prayed it was all an elaborate dream. Anything else was terrifying.

I laid back and dozed a bit more, jolting awake every few minutes when I felt some sort of electricity run through my limbs. I imagined the feeling equated a bit to being hit by lightning. Little shocks of muscle spasms would make a body part tremble for a minute or two before passing on to another part of me. It was a bit unnerving, but didn't hurt as much as it was uncomfortable.

The food came, and while it was a bland plate of chicken breast, mashed potatoes and gravy, and a white roll, it tasted divine. I ate every bite, and wondered if I could request more. Why was I so damn hungry? Why did I want bananas? It was an almost visceral need as my gut twisted with desire. Like instead of water I needed a fucking banana. Maybe I really was going nuts.

"Mr. Caine?" The nurse was back, popping his head around the open doorframe.

"Yes?" I asked, pushing away the finished tray.

"Your brother is here. Along with a Micah Richards, are you okay with seeing them?"

Micah was here? Micah was found? Holy fuck! I nearly leapt out of bed, but a muscle spasm heaved through my left calf, in a horrible charley horse, making me curl up over it until it passed.

"Just a second," I groaned, rubbing at the pain, and trying to breathe through it.

"You don't have to see them if you don't want to," the nurse said after a minute.

"No, please. I do want to see them. Sorry my muscles are acting odd," I replied when the pain finally passed.

"It's part of the malnutrition. That's why we still have the bag on you. You'll probably need a potassium drip soon too. I've already got a note in to the doctor about it. We're waiting on some of your blood tests and when we pulled your records you have a long list of allergies. So we kept your care basic."

"Appreciate it," I said. "Drugs and me don't mix well. Can I see them now? Lukas and Micah? Please?" Was this real? Were they here? I had so many questions.

"Sure. Give me a moment to bring them down." He vanished and I tried to keep myself calm waiting by singing to myself, "Ninety-nine bottles of beer on the wall."

I feared falling asleep again and awakening to find they weren't here, wherever here was, or that Micah was still missing, or that I was still lost in some sort of unknown grave being eaten alive by evil shadow maggots. I could have used a craft in that moment, sort of like Micah did when he needed to clear his head, crochet or even coloring, like was big when I'd been in the psych ward. It would have been something to focus on as it felt like forever before footsteps and voices approached the door. I was in the fifties of remaining bottles when they finally arrived.

Lukas was the first through. He flew at me, wrapping his arms around me and holding tight enough to hurt. I blinked at him, and then Micah who reached for me as well. I held out an arm so I could wrap them both in a hug.

It was Micah. He felt real, solid, and whole in my arms. Lukas was a bit more confusing as he looked more like me than I'd ever recalled him looking. His face was covered in scruff and hair a mess like he'd missed a trim or two, and that made no sense.

"I'm so happy to see you guys," I told them.

Lukas took my face into his hands. "Is it really you? Fuck."

"It's okay," Micah whispered. He stroked Lukas's back and leaned forward to kiss my forehead. "You're okay, right?"

I blinked at him, a thousand questions in my head. "I think so. Some weird muscle cramping. What happened? Where did you go in the cemetery?" I asked him.

Micah shook his head, his expression guarded. He flicked his eyes toward Lukas. "Let's focus on you for a minute, okay?"

Lukas still held on like he was terrified I'd be yanked away from him at any moment. I rubbed his back and shoulders and met Micah's gaze, feeling something unspoken transfer between us. Something had happened.

A sick realization sank into my gut as I looked at Lukas's disheveled appearance and Micah's blank mask. I'd lost time. That was what Micah was trying to tell me without making my brother lose his shit. Not a few days like I originally suspected. How long? Weeks? Months?

Had the cemetery dream been real? Micah had watched me dragged down into the abyss, unable to help. Was he traumatized by the memory? Did he remember at all?

Micah turned to the nurse. "Is there a doctor we can talk to? Get an update from? We'd like to take him home as soon as possible."

The nurse nodded. "I'll send word to have him come down. I know the police wanted to talk to Mr. Caine before he left as well."

"Is he in trouble?" Micah asked.

"I don't think so. More they were worried about how he got into the state he was in."

Micah nodded, like he understood and waved the nurse off. "If we could start with the doctor that would be great."

"Okay," the nurse agreed and left.

I stroked Lukas's hair. "Hey, buddy. You're a bit of a mess, yeah?" I told him.

He pulled away enough to look at me. "You need food. You were already so thin... Fuck. Have you eaten?"

I pointed to the tray. "Just did." Though I was still hungry. "Bland hospital food, yay, right?" I settled back against the pillows and let the tension ease a little. My muscles still twitched and spasmed. It was lessening, but still annoying.

Lukas jumped up like he had a spring in his feet. "There's a good size cafeteria." He looked around the room, confusion on his face for a minute. "We passed it on the way up. Let me get you some food. What do you want?"

"Um, anything other than bland chicken and potatoes? I'm craving bananas like crazy. I could eat a dozen at least. Maybe some turkey too." That sounded divine, and weird. "Not like together on one sandwich, but like maybe a banana and a turkey sandwich?"

Lukas looked at Micah.

"I'll stay here with him. It will probably be a while before the doctor shows," Micah said.

Lukas held on to my hand, grip almost painful. He stared at me like he thought I'd vanish any second.

"I'm fine," I told him. "Starving, but fine."

Micah moved around him to sit on the edge of the bed beside me. Lukas stared another moment and then finally nodded, before letting me go. "Don't either of you leave this room until I get back," he commanded.

We both nodded like bobblehead dolls. Lukas looked back a dozen times before he left. Micah deflated a little once he was gone. He curled up beside me, resting his head on the pillow beside mine, and I stared at him, loving those pale blue eyes and the dance of freckles across his nose.

"I really hope this is real," I said. The nightmares, if that's what they were, needed to be done. No more darkness, shadows, or fire.

"How are you really feeling?" he asked.

"Starving," I said because it was the truth. "And more than a little confused. I lost time, yeah? More than a couple of days?"

He nodded. "A month."

That took a minute to process. I'd been missing a month? It felt only like seconds. "Gone like you were gone?" I asked. Vanished, untraceable, presumed dead, which explained why Lukas looked so broken.

"Maybe?"

Wow, did I have questions. "You and Sarah okay?"

"Yes," he agreed.

"The cemetery?"

He was silent for a minute or two. "I sort of have a vague memory of a dream of you and me and Sarah in the cemetery." A mix of emotions rolled across his face as he fought to keep his mask in place. He looked away, his lips tightening as though he were trying to fight back tears.

Not a dream, I thought. He remembered more than he wanted to. "I dreamed of you being pulled into the grave. We tried to hold on, but you pushed us away."

"Hmm," I said. Not willing to add to his anxiety with the truth of what I remembered. How much of it was reality? We couldn't share dreams, right? So there would be no reason that his dream would match mine, unless neither were dreams.

"Sounds terrifying," I offered without confirming or denying anything.

He gripped my hair and turned my face toward him, anger clear in his eyes. "Stop trying to save me. Especially at your expense."

"I can't control what you dream," I told him. He knew, or at least suspected that what he remembered wasn't a dream, even while I wished it were. But I also wasn't going to stop trying to keep him out of harm's way. "You're pretty hot when you're mad."

He let out a frustrated sigh and let go to lie back down beside me. "The police found us, me and Sarah, both unconscious near the open grave."

"The same night you went missing?"

"Yes," he said. "Well it was almost morning. They'd already gone by the grave a bunch of times. Two dozen cops in the cemetery that night and we appeared out of nowhere, with no one able to explain how it happened."

"You were right behind me. Where did you go?"

"I thought I heard Lukas say he'd found Sarah. Thought you would have heard him too and would follow. Next thing was the dream... and then waking up at the grave."

I thought about that for a moment. Had he been grabbed by the curse of the grave that had taken Sarah? Why hadn't it taken me? Instead I'd gone all the way back to his house and encountered something else. The demon from the desert? I still had too many questions to make sense of it all. "I went to sleep in your garden." That much I was positive of.

"I know. We have you on camera," Micah said.

That was an interesting revelation. "Just me?" I wondered. Were the black-eyed child and moving gnomes real? I wasn't sure Micah would ever sleep again if he saw those things in his garden.

"The camera glitched around three a.m. and you vanished before it came back on. Out for like thirty seconds and you were gone." Something in his voice changed, a hitch of fear, I realized.

"It wasn't your monster," I promised him. "It was mine."

He looked at me with a confused frown. "What do you mean?"

I shrugged. Saying it out loud would make me feel crazy, and sitting in a hospital, I didn't want to chance someone listening and have them commit me. "Maybe it can wait until we're home?" I glanced around. "What hospital is this anyway?"

"Piedmont Atlanta Hospital."

Atlanta? "Georgia?"

He nodded. "We got the call late yesterday that you were here. Couldn't find a flight right away so we drove. Sorry it took so long. Lukas started off at the wheel but couldn't keep under the speed limit. And it's been a while since I've driven, but I had to take over. I'm a bit more of a cautious driver."

"How the fuck did I get to Atlanta, Georgia?" It was all more than a little overwhelming. The dream, losing a month of my life to who knew what, finding myself in another state with no memory of how I got there, and the strain the month had obviously taken on my body. I thought about the fire thing. Jin or whatever it was, who claimed I belonged to it. While it had burned away the shadows, it seemed to have done something to me as well. Taken over, perhaps? Or maybe the loss of time and memory was from the shadows? Could I have survived a month unconscious in the ether somewhere? I had so many questions I wasn't sure where to begin.

Micah reached up and stroked my face, turning it a bit so I could stare into his beautiful face. I really hoped this was real. "Don't dwell, okay? I let the time I lost eat me up for months, the questions, the fear, the uncertainty, and it did nothing for me. Let's focus on getting you well and home, yeah?"

The memory of those shadows eating me flashed through my brain again. The pain, the fear, the certainty that they were death of the soul. Had Micah experienced the same before? Either way, those memories didn't need to be shared. Though I wasn't sure I could brush them aside. I nodded. "Okay."

He leaned forward a bit to kiss me, then laughed a little. "Need to trim this beard else I can't find your lips."

I smiled back, feeling a little lighter as he wrapped his arms around me and snuggled in beside me on the small bed. "Whatever you need," I promised.

CHAPTER 27

I t took almost seven hours to gain my release from the
hospital. They wanted to keep me another night but I
refused, needing away from the hospital and to wrap myself in
my little family for a bit. Lukas watched me eat, then dozed in
the chair beside my bed while we waited for the doctor to
appear. He jolted awake every few minutes or so like he was
afraid he'd open his eyes and I'd be gone. Micah stayed curled
up beside me on the bed, fingers stroking my arm, head resting
on the pillow beside mine. The nurse didn't protest.

I had to suffer through a potassium drip which made me feel
like my arm was on fire. The doctor appeared with a handful of
test results, a frown about my malnourishment, and a list of
vitamin deficiencies. I'd lost weight again. Weight I didn't have
to lose. He didn't want to release me, but I didn't think making
me eat was a reason to add to big hospital bills, and I knew the
VA wouldn't pay for an extended stay.

Apparently I'd been in the hospital four days after walking
into the ER on my own and collapsing. Unconscious for two
days before I'd given them my name so they could try to find out
who I was and where I belonged as there had been no ID on me.

I didn't ask where my ID or phone went because the comments from the doctor about my unknown identity and rough shape made Lukas's expression tense. They had contacted the police, who did a missing persons search, finding my profile, and Lukas's contact information.

The police even stopped by to ask a handful of questions I couldn't answer. How did I get there? Where had I been? How did I get in such bad shape? Had someone been holding me captive? I felt like a broken record with a playlist of "I don't know," and "I don't remember," on repeat.

By the time I was allowed out of the hospital it was after eight at night and I think we were all exhausted. We stumbled to Lukas's car and Micah got behind the wheel. Lukas curled up in the backseat next to me, wrapping himself half around me like we often did as kids when we'd been hurt or sad. I sighed softly at having him close. Not many understood our connection as twins, but it had always been that way, a comfort thing. Growing up we were never alone and that bugged me. Once I'd enlisted, I realized that loneliness could have different meanings. Having Lukas back with me now, made me feel safe. That was all that mattered right at that moment.

"I'm taking us to a hotel for the night," Micah said as he steered us out of the hospital parking garage. "We'll head home in the morning once we've all had some rest."

Lukas grunted.

"Any chance we can stop at a drug store for basic stuff?" I asked. "Like clean underwear and something to shave with?" They'd given me basic scrubs in the hospital, but I wanted to feel like me and not some escaped psych patient.

"I brought stuff," Micah said. "It's in the trunk. Would have brought it up to your room, but..." He hadn't wanted to leave me to go get it, I deduced from what he left out. I thought about that as we drove and the city passed us by. He wasn't taking us to the nearest hotel. In fact, he took us out of downtown and to the edge of the city. Lukas fell asleep, only to jerk awake twice more before Micah pulled us into the lot of a tiny Quality Inn. He turned back and looked us over. "I need to go in and get us a room."

"Okay," I agreed.

"Don't leave the car."

"Hadn't planned to," I promised. Was he afraid I'd disappear again? I had plenty of healthy fears about that happening to him too. "I'm not going anywhere."

Our eyes met and he nodded, then got out to make his way to the front desk. At least I could see him through the big glass entry door. I ran my hands through Lukas's hair. He was a mess. Thinner than I'd last seen him, scruffy, and unkempt. I'd have to call Mom and Dad too. Would it be the circus Micah's disappearance had been? I hoped no one treated Micah or Lukas as badly as they'd treated Tim.

I sighed and closed my eyes, half falling asleep because the opening of the trunk woke me. I glanced back to find Micah pulling bags out of the back. He rolled them around the side of the car and tugged my door open. "Can you get him to come inside? We're around the corner from the desk."

"Sure," I said, and dragged Lukas, half-conscious out of the car and into the hotel. I was barely upright myself, though having eaten a couple times I didn't feel quite so dizzy. At least the room was close. We leaned on each other and while he didn't open his eyes, he moved along with me.

The room was uninspiring. Two giant beds, a good-sized bathroom, and the standard dresser/tv set up. We were on the first floor, and the large window overlooked the outdoor pool, but Micah shut the drapes and closed out the night sky and pool lights. I helped Lukas to the bed furthest from the window, yanked off his shoes and pulled the blanket over him.

"Don't go anywhere," he grumbled at me.

"I'm not," I promised him. "Gonna shower, I think."

He glared at me a moment, like he was searching for a lie. Finally he nodded and closed his eyes. He was out in seconds.

Micah locked the door, then dug through one of the bags to hand me a small dragon-shaped bag.

"This is cool," I said. "Did you make this?"

"Of course."

When I unzipped it, I found my toothbrush, paste, my electric razor set, a comb, and a small tube of the hair stuff Micah had given me.

"Are you hungry?" Micah asked. "I can order food while you shower."

A shower sounded like heaven right that minute. And pizza. I was pretty sure I could eat a whole damn pizza. "Starving. Any chance a pizza place is close?" I remembered then that he couldn't eat cheese. "Or maybe something you can eat too?"

"Pizza is fine," Micah said. "What do you want on it?"

"Pepperoni and pineapple. Yes, I know I'm a heathen, but sweet and salty does it for me."

Micah's lips curved up into a smile and he opened his phone to order pizza. I found my way into the bathroom to clean up. It was the first time I had really looked at myself. I looked like a homeless man. Grizzled, emaciated with bags under my eyes, and so much gnarled, dark hair that I didn't know how Lukas or Micah had recognized me at all.

Trimming the beard came first because it itched and added weight to my face that I wasn't used to. The initial cut wasn't very neat and I left a huge ball of hair in the trash. The razor took care of the rest, trimming it to a respectable length. I even clipped on the extra side bits to remove some of the overgrowth on my sideburns. A barber could clean it up better, but at least I looked half like me. I couldn't do much about the ratted mess of my hair. So I stepped into the shower.

The spray of the water hurt, even turning down the pressure or changing the temperature made my skin ache. Too much sensation, I think, like I hadn't been a real living, breathing person for a while and I'd forgotten how to feel. I had to turn the water off to scrub my hair because it was too much to stand under the spray. After three full lathers and rinses, my hair finally washed clean. I hoped there were no bugs or anything.

Fuck. And now that was in my head. I washed it again.

After a while the door opened a crack and Micah poked his head in. "Pizza is here."

"Okay," I said. There was a towel wrapped around my waist, and I leaned over the counter trying to see my scalp and make sure I wasn't infested with lice or some shit. It was one of my few phobias after an elementary school incident had shut down the entire school for a week.

"What's wrong?" he asked.

I sucked in a deep breath, wondering if it was worth sharing this fear and making myself sound crazy. "I have a phobia," I admitted. "Of lice." I swallowed as uttering the word made me feel like squirming. "I don't know where I've been…"

He blinked at me a moment before stepping into the bathroom and closing the door. He shut the lid on the toilet and motioned for me to sit. I felt heat burn my cheeks with embarrassment. What if he found something? I'd be a thousand times more horrified, even though I couldn't remember where I had been for the last month. Those couple of months I'd lived on the streets I'd worked hard to remain bug free, using homeless shelters as much as I could and staying away from others.

Instead of searching my head, he combed my hair, and even used my beard trimming scissors to cut away some of the length. He massaged some of the hair stuff into my scalp, taking his time to run over every inch of it without the fear or hesitation I had.

"Nothing," he said.

"You're sure?" I gripped the towel, heart racing.

"Yes. Your hair and scalp is pretty dry, but I have a good hair mask that can help. It's at home." Instead of leaving my hair down to dry, he tugged on it, combing it away from my face, and wove it into a French braid, leaving the tiny tail of it on my neck. "This should keep it from tangling too much."

"Thank you," I said. "Sorry..."

"It's okay," he said. "We all have something."

"Part of the training, right?" I asked feeling like the question put out there a thousand others. Was I still worth training? Was he still interested? Had my time away changed us enough that it wasn't even worth the effort?

"Yes. Part of the training."

"What's your something?" I asked as he pulled a little bottle of moisturizer out of his own little toiletry bag and began applying it to my face.

"Birds," Micah said.

"Birds?"

"I hate birds. They have dark eyes that seem to stare right through you. When I was a kid and we lived in this little town in China while my parents taught, they had billions of pigeons. Or maybe it wasn't that many, but it felt like that many. Everywhere you went there was a sea of them. They'd do that funny noise and even peck at us for food." He shivered. "I hate birds." He applied something to my lips three times, each time I felt like my skin sucked it up. Finally he leaned forward and kissed me lightly. "Let's eat, then get some sleep."

The pizza tasted odd, almost unfamiliar though it was a national brand. I ate half of it while Micah ate a salad, then I got up to brush my teeth again. I'd already done it a half dozen times and still felt like my mouth was unclean, or even numb, though it looked fine when I glared at it in the mirror.

Micah made me drink another bottle of water, insisting my taste buds were off due to dehydration. I was willing to take that as an explanation over any of the thousand other scenarios that filled my head.

Finally I pushed everything aside, leaving nothing on but a pair of boxers which hung off my hips, and I crawled into bed beside Lukas. Micah didn't bother with the other bed, he curled on the other side of me, sandwiching me between the two of them and wrapping himself around me. That was all I needed to drift off to sleep.

CHAPTER 28

I woke slowly the next morning, from a deep and thankfully dreamless sleep. Micah was still curled up in my arms, but Lukas was no longer behind me. Fear churned in my gut for a moment until he emerged from the bathroom looking freshly showered.

"You should use my shave kit," I whispered, not wanting to wake Micah. "Make yourself look human."

He narrowed his eyes at me, but vanished back into the bathroom. The box of pizza was open and the other half gone. Lukas always did like cold pizza for breakfast. I had never been a fan of congealed cheese.

I snuggled back down into the blanket with Micah, breathing in his scent and enjoying the warmth of his body against mine. Still no morning wood. I guess he couldn't fix everything and make me normal. The thought almost made me laugh. Me, normal. Those words didn't belong in the same sentence together. I saw ghosts, fire demons, and shadow monsters. Nothing about me was normal. In his arms, that was okay.

Micah sighed and shifted, stretching a little.

"Morning," I said as he absently reached up to stroke my jaw, fingers tracing my beard and the edge of my lips.

"Hmm," he grumbled. "Not a morning person."

"Yeah, me neither." But I was once again starving and Lukas had eaten all the leftover pizza. Did this hotel have one of those breakfast things? "I need to find some food. Are you hungry?"

He opened his eyes and stared at me, blue gaze soft and sleepy. "I could eat. But coffee..."

And with that suggestion I needed a cup so bad. "Fuck, you had to remind me?"

He gave me a tiny grin. "There should be food in the lobby right around the corner."

"No one goes anywhere alone," Lukas said, re-emerging from the bathroom looking a little more cleaned up, but still not scruff-free. I debated getting up and dragging us all out to get coffee, then reached over and grabbed the phone instead, ordering breakfast brought to the room.

"Must not be busy," I told them. "They said it would only be twenty minutes or so." Micah was back to his sleepy position, tucked under my chin, eyes closed, arm around my waist. I relaxed against him and watched Lukas move around the room like he had energy to spare. From getting enough rest maybe? Though I knew agitation when I saw it, especially in my brother.

"Lukas," I called. He continued to pack, like we had somehow unpacked everything when we'd come in last night, though I knew we hadn't. "Lukas," I said again.

He looked up, glaring at me. "What?"

"I'm okay," I told him.

His glare intensified.

"I am."

"You are not fucking okay. You vanished for a month and show up in another state looking like someone took your skin for a joy ride and left you at the hospital on death's door. And you are somehow *okay?*"

I flinched, his words stirring something familiar in my gut, the vague edge of a memory or something. I shoved it down. Not wanting to dwell on the new idea he put in my head. "How about I'm going to be okay? *We're* going to be okay."

"And if it fucking takes you again?" He demanded.

"You don't believe in that stuff," I reminded him.

"Until you fucking vanished on camera."

"Micah said the camera glitched."

"Yeah, and you were out cold on the bench when it went out, and when it came back on you were gone. You wanna convince me that somehow you woke out of a deep sleep and raced off into the night in less than thirty seconds?"

"I can't tell you what I don't know. I don't remember what happened or where I've been."

"Seems to be a lot of that going around. The 'I don't remember' plague." His gaze fell to Micah who was wrapped up in my arms. There was anger there. Undeserved.

"It wasn't his fault," I said.

"I should never have introduced the two of you. I thought you'd help each other heal. Not... Not this."

"What happened in the garden was all about me, not him. Not his monster, mine," I said. Let him think I was crazy. That was fine so long as he didn't blame Micah for something none of us had any control over.

"I thought you don't remember?" Lukas threw back at me.

"Where I was for the past month? No. What happened that night, yes. Do I understand it? No. But you said I don't need to." The expressions that crossed his face then was a play of confusion and then understanding. "I fell asleep in the garden and dreamed of the thing from the desert. In the dream it led me to Micah and Sarah." Of course there had been more to it than that, but Lukas didn't need that in his head. "That's what I remember. My demon, not Micah's."

Lukas stopped moving, frozen in place for a minute, silent, thinking, perhaps even brooding. I felt Micah awake and tense against me. His face buried against my collarbone like he could hide from the angry words. How many times had he been in the middle of them? I hated that he had to be there while Lukas raged and threw angry eyes his way.

"How do you know they aren't one and the same?" Lukas finally asked.

I processed that for a moment. First that Lukas was acknowledging that he believed. Not in our stories and the broken mindset of two men who had survived trauma, but that something was really lurking beyond what he could see. And second, how did I know they weren't one and the same? The noises, the time lost, the stalking in the garden? Instinct really. The familiarity of the thing from the desert was something I couldn't describe to anyone. It was like meeting an old lover you'd thought you'd forgotten, but seeing them reignited that visceral memory of your time together.

The thing that had awoken us at Micah's place felt... different. More playful perhaps? Not as defined. Maybe that was only because I had yet to actually meet it. My demon, if that was what it was, specialized in terror, almost seemed to feed on it. The horror and terror of that day in the desert, the bone chilling black-eyed child in Micah's garden, all to assert its power over me. *Mine* it had said before saving me from the shadows, or death curse, or whatever it was. A scary thought that it considered me its property. And the idea that I couldn't remember the past month because something else might have been at the helm... not that giving him that explanation was going to ease his worry. Hell, it made mine worse.

Which was better? To be lost in an unknown world, or to

have something else take over your body and live your life? I wasn't sure.

"I know it wasn't. It felt different," I gave him lamely. "I'm not sure how to explain it to you—" without terrifying everyone in the room.

"Great. So there are two somethings out there. Shadows or whatever. Stalking you both. Ready to rip either of you out of this world at any time?" Of course he would put together the gist of it without my help. There were probably more than two. The fact that Micah and I both seemed to have some *other* being following us around was more coincidence than by design, I thought. Sarah had been taken too. Jared had seen something. Part of the curse of whatever had been on that ring? Or another shadow thing? I wasn't sure we would ever know.

"If we run will it follow?" he asked.

I wasn't sure what *it* was. "Run where? I first met it in the desert of Afghanistan, now it's here, do you think it can't find me anywhere?"

"We could go home to Mom and Dad."

"No." Those were memories I didn't need to return to. A life that was no longer mine. And he was suggesting he leave his job? His apartment? Sky? And for me, Micah? "No."

"Running never helped me," Micah whispered.

"And you haven't vanished again," I pointed out. "Maybe it was a one-time thing. Besides, you guys don't know I didn't have a concussion and spent the past month not knowing who I was."

Lukas gave me a droll stare. "And you happen to forget the past month when you remember the rest of your life? Oh and never mind that they did a CT scan on you when you collapsed in the ER and found no trace of head trauma."

I sighed, too tired to fight, too happy nestled in Micah's arms to even think about arguing with Lukas. "I'm not sure what you want me to do."

He growled and paced. "I'm not sure what to do. I can't protect you."

"I don't need you to."

I got another glare for that remark.

"Seriously. I love you, Lukas. I didn't realize how lonely I was when I served until I came home. Not for a relationship, but for my best friend, which is you, you moody jackass. So how about you sit the fuck down and wait for breakfast with us, then we'll head home? Solve the world's problems another day?"

We had a bit of a glaring contest then, him angry, me determined. That too was familiar and made me smile remembering stuff we'd done as kids. He'd always been the overprotective big brother, didn't matter that we were the same age and had mostly the same build growing up. His sense of responsibility was a huge part of his personality. "Food and then home, yeah?" I prodded.

"Fine," he agreed, begrudgingly throwing himself onto the unused bed and picking up the TV remote.

"Do us a favor and answer the door when food comes, okay?" I asked him.

He turned his head my way, giving me the 'are you kidding me?' look that I'd seen enough times in my life to have memorized. It made me laugh.

"Please," I said. "I'm sort of warm and snuggly and don't want to get up until there's coffee to be had."

"Mmm," Micah mumbled against my skin, his breath warm and waking up parts of me I thought should still be sleeping. "Coffee."

"Drug of choice," I agreed.

Lukas gave us an irritated huff as he began flipping through channels. "Fine. Assholes."

The drive home was uneventful. After they'd fed me enough to nourish an army, Micah and Lukas took turns driving, not letting me behind the wheel. We even stopped at a grocery store on the way out of Atlanta, picked up a small cooler, and filled it with cold cuts, fresh fruit and veggies, and lots of water.

The entire seven-hour car ride had been a careful dance of not speaking about anything important. No questions about where I had been, or why Lukas looked like crap, or what had happened. Was all this because I'd disappeared? He'd lived without me for years while I'd been in the service, not hearing from me for months at a time. I wasn't sure if it was the idea that some paranormal thing took me, or something else he left unsaid.

Instead I'd filled the tense silence on the drive home with my horrible singing voice as I danced along to the radio. Lukas tried to be annoyed with me, but it never lasted.

When Lukas pulled up in front of his apartment, I wondered a few things. "Who's looking after Jet?" I asked Micah.

"Sky," he answered as we got out of the car and started unloading bags. There wasn't really all that much. Lukas hadn't brought more than a backpack, but Micah had a small suitcase which had both his and my stuff, which was a good thing because there was no way Lukas's clothes were going to fit me now. My own clothes hung on me, loose and oversized. "She's been staying at my place." So Micah wasn't alone. I understood that. However, with the way Lukas's shoulders tightened at the mention of her name, I wondered what I'd missed.

When we entered his apartment, I knew. Apparently my brother had come apart at the seams. The place was a mess. Books everywhere, dirty dishes in the sink, bed unmade. And there was a bit of a smell. When was the last time he'd emptied the trash? Everything needed to be cleaned. I frowned and glanced at Micah who shared my expression of concern. Obviously he hadn't been in here either since I'd vanished.

Lukas brushed by us, heading into his room with his bag and moving around the apartment like he was suddenly embarrassed that we were seeing it this way. "Give me a few minutes to clean up," he said.

Micah held up his phone, flashing me the screen and a text to Sky. I nodded, understanding. Something had happened.

Standing in the mess that was his home, I thought maybe there was more that had happened and wondered if I should have pushed harder.

"Maybe Micah and I should go to his place?" I suggested.

"No," Lukas said hotly, like the discussion was closed.

I shared a glance with Micah, then went to the kitchen to begin cleaning. He began in the living room, stacking up books, stripping the cover off the couch, and throwing away fast food containers. I filled the dishwasher, wiped down the counters, and swept the floor. Micah took many trips to the bedroom to put away books. Apparently Lukas had spent the entire time I was gone reading everything he could get his hands on about the paranormal. I didn't know if that should worry me or not.

"Was he not working?" I whispered to Micah as Lukas stuffed what looked like every piece of clothing he owned in his washer.

"On leave," Micah said. "He was too much of a mess once we saw the video of you in the garden. I tried to call and stop by, but he would never answer the phone or the door."

That wasn't good. Idle Lukas was an unhappy one. "And him and Sky?"

He shook his head. "No idea. I know they have barely spoken in the last month. Sky has been putting in full-time hours at the shop to help out, and Lukas hasn't come in once. Even when I ask him a business-related thing. He refers me to his accountant."

I frowned and took out the trash, thinking we'd need half a dozen air fresheners to ease the stink of the apartment. By the time I stepped back inside, Lukas was in a tizzy, yelling at Micah about letting me go outside.

"Stop," I demanded, pushing Micah behind me and getting in Lukas's face. "I took out your fucking trash, since you couldn't see fit to do it. I've gone outside by myself a million times in my life. Even served my country halfway across the world. I'm fine."

He glared at me, then glanced at Micah. "I think you should go home."

Micah blinked and then nodded, gathering up his stuff.

"Wait," I begged him. "Fuck." I grabbed Lukas's shirt and made him look at me. "I'm fine. I'm here. I'm safe and alive. Can't you be happy for that?"

"Thrilled," he said hotly.

I flinched as if slapped by the sarcasm in his tone, and let him go. "Wow. I'm sorry to be such a burden on you." I glanced around at Micah's bag and the few things I knew were mine. "I think maybe I should go."

"You're not going anywhere. Hell, if I could ship you home to Mom and Dad right this minute I would. Maybe I should have left you in the psych ward."

"Fuck you! You don't get to say what I do and don't do," I threw back at Lukas. Why was he being such a jerk? "I'm not five. What's wrong with you? I was gone so you become an asshole? How is that an excuse to treat your friends like shit when they are trying to help you?"

Lukas grabbed me by the shirt and shook me. Micah

reached for him, but I put a hand up to stop him. Lukas wouldn't actually hurt me.

"I thought you were dead. Everyone told me you'd jumped into the river and we hadn't found you yet. Do you have any idea how many times they told me I should have left you in the mental hospital where you were *safe*? How many nights I spent unable to sleep, walking the river shore, looking for any sign of your body. It made no sense that you would get up and leave Micah's garden to go off and kill yourself, but neither does some unseen boogeyman taking you. Easier for everyone to believe you offed yourself. And do you understand how fucking hard that was for me? I spent years worrying about you. Wondering when someone in uniform would show up at my door to tell me you were gone, only for you to come home and die on my watch? Could you stop fucking chasing death for a while?"

I blinked at him, letting the words sink in. Of course they'd treated him like shit, giving him worst case scenarios so he'd expect it when they found my body. Only he'd been down this road before. Maybe it was more intense when it was your brother instead of a guy you barely knew, but he had seen how everyone treated Tim. I'd only heard and read about it.

"I thought you believed in me," I said absorbing his anger and pain and letting it pass. "You knew I wouldn't do that to you."

"Do I? Micah had vanished. I pushed you together. Didn't think you'd get attached that fast, but when he was gone from the cemetery you fell apart. You offed yourself before we could tell you he'd been found. That's what everyone told me. And I tried to rationalize that it wasn't my fault for steering you into that relationship, but if that's why you were gone, it *was* my fault."

"I'm not so fragile that I'm going to jump off a bridge over a little heartbreak." Okay so I had entertained the idea, but only for a minute or two. Lukas didn't need to know that.

He let go, hands gripping the air for a minute before he reached for me and wrapped me in a huge hug, his face buried in my neck. I felt tears, hot and warm on my collar bone. "I *knew*. But everyone kept telling me otherwise. How many times do you have to hear it from everyone until you believe? It was endless. Even Mom and Dad were prepared for the worst."

I hugged him back and met Micah's concerned eyes. He shook his head. This was a familiar road for him. His phone chirped with a text and a moment later he went to the door, quietly opening it to let Sky in. I rocked Lukas in my arms and let him cry. There was nothing else I could do to reassure him I was back and going nowhere again willingly. I didn't have the answers he wanted, or even the words to say to help him understand.

Stroking his hair and his back I gave Sky a look that I hoped conveyed a lot. Lukas wanted me to have someone to focus on, to give me a purpose, but I think he needed that more than I did. Would I always be here? Who knew? What was important was that Lukas wasn't alone even if I wasn't.

While I didn't know all the details about what had happened with Sky previously, I knew he was super protective of her. The idea that he'd pushed her away to maintain some fantasy that he was somehow responsible for my death made me so pissed at everyone. Couldn't anyone give him some fucking hope?

Sky approached cautiously, and I turned Lukas a little so he could see her. He flinched and shook his head.

"It's okay," she said, reaching for him.

"It's not. I can't even protect my brother. How am I supposed to protect you?" He demanded.

She put her hands on his face, using her thumbs to wipe

away his tears, then cupped his cheeks until she could stretch up to brush a kiss across his lips. "He's home and safe. I'm here and safe."

"Not because of anything I did," he said sounding heartbroken.

"That's okay," Sky assured him. "We don't expect you to be Superman. You need to be here for us. Can't that be enough?"

I let Lukas go, giving him a little nudge toward Sky. He turned completely and enfolded her in his arms. She accepted his embrace and almost seemed to melt into it.

She kept murmuring, "We're safe. It's okay."

It was one of those moments that I realized as put together as Lukas was, it was all a façade. He'd lived so long under the mask of control, that when something didn't go right, he didn't know how to deal with it. Chaos was sort of my brand rather than his.

Focus, he'd said he wanted for me. Something more than the past. It was what he needed too. I patted Lukas on the back. "How about you go and take a nap. I know you haven't been sleeping well."

He looked at me, exhausted, full of fear and loneliness, afraid we would all vanish from his life, I think. "I don't know..."

"I'm going to order a grocery delivery for you," I told him.

"I want you to stay here," he begged.

"I can't hide forever." I glanced at Micah thinking there was more in life I wanted than to lock myself away. "We can't waste our lives waiting for something bad to happen. I want a chance to live it, without constantly looking over my shoulder."

"But we don't know what happened..."

"No," I agreed. "And as you told me before, we don't need to. We can still move forward and try to find something new to focus on. You have someone who needs you." I motioned at Sky. "I'd like to try too. Yeah?"

He frowned but stared at me with a mix of emotions plain on his face. Fear, worry, anger, and sadness, but also understanding. "Text me the minute you get to his house. I'll be watching on the cameras."

"Creepy, but okay." I glanced at Sky. "Can you handle the groceries that I order?"

"I can put my own damn groceries away," Lukas grumbled.

"I want you to relax."

Sky nodded. "We're good."

I looked at Micah. Was he still okay with me coming home with him? I really wanted to curl up in his space and watch him craft if that was what he needed, or even mindlessly watch a show with him. I was too emotionally exhausted to do much more, but the idea of sitting in his presence and enjoying the calm acceptance he gave me, was enough.

"I've already ordered an Uber for us," Micah said. He looked at Lukas. "We won't be walking home. And I'll make sure we both text once we're home. It will be from my phone since we have to get Alex a new one, but we can call if that's better for you. So you can hear his voice?"

It took a moment, but Lukas finally nodded. He pulled Sky close, dragging her with him to the couch where they both collapsed curled around each other. I used Micah's phone to order groceries for delivery and hoped there were easier days ahead. Lukas needed back to his normal routine which I had interrupted by showing up in his life. I felt kind of bad about that, but couldn't keep punishing myself for not being like everyone else. Maybe this was the chance I needed to really be me. Even if that me was messed up and a little nuts.

CHAPTER 29

M icah's place was different inside. He'd reorganized the entire layout; the lower floor had been changed to a craft space instead of having it all hidden away. The futon was pushed off to the side, looking mostly unused and Micah's sewing machine had a prominent place toward the back of the room. A new wall of cubes had appeared and little colored boxes filled it. I recalled he had a smaller one upstairs originally, and this was like that only four times as large.

That worried me since he tended to go crazy with crafts when his head got too loud. Was the closet so full he'd have to expand outward? Had he slept at all while I was gone? He looked okay. No bags under his eyes, or weight loss. Not like Lukas. That didn't mean he'd been taking care of himself properly. It could mean he was better at moisturizing his face than my brother was.

"Do you have groceries?" I asked once we'd gotten off the phone with Lukas.

"Yes. Sky always makes sure there's food here. Are you hungry?"

"Not at the moment. I wanted to make sure the pantry was

full before we settled in for a bit." I heard the familiar thump of Jet jumping down from something, and a moment later he appeared from the loft. He let out a little "erp" sound from the top of the stairs and raced my way. A moment later he wove around my legs giving me happy little mews.

"Hey, buddy," I said. "Missed you too."

I bent down to pet him and scratch his head. "You been taking care of daddy? Giving him lots of snuggles while I was gone?"

"He has been very clingy," Micah said.

"Protective," I corrected and gave the cat a kiss on the head. "Good boy." I stood and looked at Micah. "Sarah is really okay?"

"Yeah, she and Jared went home. She was a little dehydrated, but physically okay."

"Does she remember anything?"

"Not really?" It was more a question than a statement.

"Like you don't really remember anything?"

He shrugged. "It's bits and pieces that I'm not sure if they are a dream or not. She and I are keeping in touch. I sent her a text that you were back."

I reached out to touch his face, thinking again that he was so beautiful. Delicate bone structure, but nerves of steel. "How about you? Are you okay?"

"Maybe? Happy that you're here, safe."

Remembering how he explained his previous return I wondered if that had changed something between us as well. We'd barely begun to know each other, then I was gone. Would we fit anymore? "It feels like only a few days for me," I confessed. I didn't feel any different. "Do we fit?"

Micah studied me for a minute. "When I got back..." he paused as if debating whether or not that was the right phrasing, but continued, "Tim was bitter. I was confused, a little lost, and disoriented. He sort of went on the attack... like Lukas."

"Protective, yet blaming." That made sense. Normal human emotions, even if they weren't always rational. "Is that why you didn't fit anymore?"

"I didn't feel exactly the same," Micah said. He bent down to pet Jet, who seemed thrilled with the attention. "I mean I felt like me, only more aware? I'm not sure how to explain it. For a few days I tried to ignore the little things. Small signs that we didn't fit anymore. His irritation, backhanded comments, and short tone. At first it was Tim, then it was everyone. They were placating, looking at me like I was broken. Eventually, I decided it was me who had changed and not everyone else. Now I'm not so sure."

"Are you bitter? Angry that I was gone?"

"No. That would be silly. I don't think you had any more control over what happened than I did."

"Even if people told you I'd killed myself."

"They told everyone in my family that too. That I'd done something and they hadn't found the body. Or got lost and died of exposure. It's how we as humans rationalize the unknown."

"What do you think happened?" I asked, wondering if his suspicions ran in the same terrifying directions mine did.

"I think it doesn't matter now that you're back."

"So we move forward like nothing happened?" I wasn't sure I could do that. My brain was already working through a dozen scenarios, and none of them friendly.

"Will dwelling on it help either of us?"

I sighed. He was so fucking good at truth bombs. "No," I agreed.

He nodded. "Then let's find a new normal. What is normal for us at least."

"Weird as we may be?"

He gave me a tiny smile. "Yes."

"Sounds like a plan. How much crafting did you do while I

was away?" I headed to the closet to look at what Micah's anxiety might have wrought, but when I opened it, I was surprised to find it very organized. The wall of fabric was gone, likely in the bins that had been placed along the back wall. And the sections of closet rods were sorted into specific things with paper signs on each section: *WIP, Done, with errors, Ready for Sale*, and *Micah's collection*.

"A little," he acknowledged.

"Were the signs your doing, or Sky's?"

"I sorted them. Sky put the signs. I think it was because I kept telling her I needed this or that put in a particular place and she couldn't remember."

The section that was Micah's looked mostly new, but since the prior mess was gone, it was hard to tell. Some of them looked to be his size, but the coat I'd tried on before was there, along with a few others that looked more my size than his. The area for the shop was mostly clear, just a few bags, and a small throw. The error section was actually pretty small too, surprising me. Micah was a bit of a perfectionist, so I'd assumed he'd find lots of little errors with things.

"I cleared out stuff. Brought old projects to the shop and priced them to move to make room for new stuff."

I smiled at him. "A good thing, yeah? Not staring at all the stuff you thought didn't turn out right?"

He shrugged. "I guess. I didn't realize before how much having that stuff in there got me down, my wall of messed up projects. I had Sky help me go through them. We donated the stuff that wasn't saleable to the college textile department, and took the rest to the shop. Most of it has already sold. And the college was grateful for the fabric even if they had to cut stuff up."

"What's up in the loft now?" I asked.

"I rearranged it to the sleeping area. I needed the table for the sewing machine and a real chair." His cheeks pinked. "My back started to hurt from being hunched over so much. I'm not as young as I used to be."

I had to laugh at that, and leaned forward to give him a kiss, which he accepted. "Still my boy toy?"

He groaned. "Sometimes you're so weird."

"Yeah but my weird works with your weird... old man," I teased.

"Jerk. If I'm an old man, then you must be a dinosaur."

I put my hand over my heart. "Well I never..."

We both broke out laughing. I pulled him into a hug and kissed the top of his head before letting him go to study the new downstairs craft layout. The sewing machine sat on a full-sized table and was inset into it. A chair which looked more like an office chair with a huge back and webbed lumbar support sat on a clear mat tucked into the table. The set up looked pretty sweet actually. Like he could roll from the wall of cubes to the sewing table to a corner table which looked to be set up for cutting.

"It looks a lot more comfortable of a set up than the one upstairs was," I said, then narrowed my eyes at him. "Have you been sleeping at all?"

He sighed and looked at me. "A little. Sometimes I'd dream of you."

"What about the noises from outside?"

"Only happened once while you were gone."

Well that was good news. Could whatever heightened activity he'd been experiencing be caused by my presence? No. He said it had started before I arrived. So maybe it was something the other tour guides had done? I hated not having all the answers. The sad part was, that not having all the answers was life, and even before vanishing, if that was what had happened to me, I had decided I would live life and stop hiding from it.

"When days went by, after you disappeared, and I didn't hear it, I thought it took you, and that's why it was silent."

Fuck. I frowned at him. "It was not your fault."

He hugged himself. "The night the noise showed up again I went out into the garden and demanded it bring you back." He looked away. "Nothing happened."

I couldn't help but smile. "That's great."

"Not great," he said, glaring at me now. "I wanted you back."

"Not that part," I agreed, waving my hands. "But that nothing happened again. It's a noise. As annoying as it is."

He sighed. "It hasn't happened again. But I also moved up into the loft and sometimes sleep with earplugs in. So maybe I'm not hearing it?"

"Either one of those work for me," I assured him. I headed up to the loft to look at the space. That too, had changed a lot. Jet's little bed was still there, but most of the storage was gone. A fan had been set up into a small area of the pony wall to circulate air. And the space felt cool and clean, dust free.

There was a large mattress looking thing pressed up against the wall in the corner, and made up to look like a bed. It wasn't huge, maybe a queen at most. And it wasn't thick enough to be an actual mattress. One of the storage chests sat at the foot of the mat, the one that normally contained the extra pillows and blankets. And there was a small cube shelf next to the bed that had an alarm clock, a small lamp, and a stack of books as well as an e-reader.

The area would have been a perfect little bedroom if he'd put up curtains or something to block out the light from the rest of the space. I wondered if we could get some shades or something.

Micah had followed me up. "It's still pretty cramped, but I

sleep better curled up by the wall since I'm alone and all. I think I'm used to small spaces."

"I like it," I told him. "Thinking maybe we could put some curtains or something at the edge there. Sort of privacy and room darkening all at once?" I pointed to the area in question.

He examined it. "Sure. I could make some Roman shades. That's easy enough."

For him, easy. For me, I'd have to buy something and hope it fit. I wasn't even sure I knew what a Roman shade was, but I smiled, agreeing with his idea. "Sounds great. Do you have some fabric that will work for it?"

He nodded. "I have a section of home décor fabric that will work, and some room darkening liner. It's downstairs in the green bins."

"Color coordinated bins?"

He shrugged. "Helps me find stuff fast. The quilt cottons are a little more complicated because I have them broken up by pattern instead of color, but still in bins with a certain design on them." He went to the chest at the end of the bed and opened it. A second later he pulled out a new quilt. This one was green, with leaves and tiny dragons. It was part the roll of strips he'd had me choose, and the little dragons. He must have gone back for more of the fabric. Micah handed me the quilt and I opened it, marveling at the pattern and the size. It was huge. I wrapped it around myself, loving it instantly. This was better than any of those cheap Walmart comforters I'd had.

"You fucking rock."

A smile curved the edge of his lips. I grinned at that little break in his mask. How long would it take to tear it down again? A few hours? Days? Weeks? "You thought I'd be back?" I asked him.

"I hoped," he admitted. "Your disappearance didn't fit the others."

"Because I didn't vanish in a state park? I'm sure people vanish in the middle of big cities all the time."

He nodded and looked somber for a moment. "A lot of those are due to drugs or sex trafficking. You don't fit either of those profiles."

That was true.

"I thought maybe you got lost in that other place. The one that sucked you down." He glanced away. "I kept dreaming that I couldn't save you."

I pushed the blanket back, letting it fall onto the bed, and wrapped him in my arms, reminding him of what we'd told Lukas earlier. "I don't need you to save me. I need you around, yeah?"

"Yeah," he agreed, accepting my embrace.

I glanced at the bed. While I was tired, I wasn't tired enough to sleep and it was only four in the afternoon. Did he need a nap? "Are you tired?"

"A little, but not enough to sleep?" He said, more a question than an answer, like did I understand? And I did. He had stuff in his head he needed to sort out.

"Do you want me to go?" Maybe I should have stayed with Lukas. Though I kind of thought he needed time with Sky to finally sort out what was in his head.

"No. I like having you here." He seemed to think for a minute. "Not because it assures me you are really back, but you help slow my thoughts, calm the everyday anxiety? Like my brain knows that if something happens, whatever it is, you'll know what to do."

"Even if that something is run away screaming," I agreed.

He laughed. I loved that sound. "You're so damn snarky."

"Are you complaining?"

"No." He rubbed my arms, like he was reassuring himself

that I was real. "Let me set up a bath for you. A twenty-minute soak and your skin should feel better."

"Yeah? That easy?"

"You'll probably have to repeat it over the next few days, but it will help."

"Okay," I said. "What will you do while I bathe?"

"Watch you. Maybe crochet?"

"Sounds like a plan." I followed him down to the bathroom and watched him fill the giant tub and add a bunch of things to it. Whatever they were smelled heavenly, and the heat wafting in little steam trails off the water looked deliciously inviting. I stripped without thinking about it, and slipped into the tub, sinking down until the water reached my chin.

Micah brought some new crochet project in and sat down beside the tub, working his magic while I half dozed in the heat. It was amazing. My body awakening slowly to the sensation like every muscle had been cramped up to avoid pain or something. By the time the water began to cool and I was pruney, every inch of me felt softer, smoother, and more awake than when I'd found myself in that Georgia hospital. We barely spoke the entire time and that was okay as the silence had been comforting.

"Do you want me to shave off the rest of the beard?" I asked him after he handed me some shampoo that was supposed to help moisturize my scalp.

"No. I like it. I'm a bit of a texture freak if you haven't noticed. I think that's why fiber arts are so appealing to me."

And I could see that. Even at the shop he had the tendency to touch things. "I guess I'm pretty good texture right now, all scaly and dried out. Well, I'm pruney now," I said holding up a hand. And I had to admit my skin felt so much better, not as tight, and more flexible.

He gave me a small smile. "Make sure you keep drinking

more water too. Our skin is our largest organ and needs lots of fluids inside and out."

"Maybe *your* largest organ," I teased.

He laughed. "You're so weird." Micah brought me fresh clothes. A pair of boxers he'd obviously made as they had giant fire-breathing dragons on them, shorts, and a Simply Crafty T-shirt. While I was sleepy enough to nap, Micah didn't appear to be. So I suggested something else to keep him busy.

"Maybe you can work on those shade things and I can help? Give us both something to focus on?"

"Sure," he agreed and led me back to the cubes and the section he had set aside of decorator fabric. "You choose the fabric." He went to a particular section and opened it, pulling out stacks of designs, some neutral, some wild. I chose a neutral one because I didn't think we'd be changing them all that often. Micah took the stack to the cutting table. Then dug out a measuring tape and disappeared into the loft for a minute, coming back with a piece of paper, and notes written on it. Measurements, I thought.

"Tell me what to do to help," I said.

He glanced at the futon. "Can you hang out while I work?"

I thought about it. "Is that what you need?"

"Your presence while I sort things out in my head, yes," he agreed.

I smiled and went up to the loft to retrieve my new quilt. That thing was going with me everywhere from now on. I brought it down to the futon, wrapped myself up in the quilt, and curled up on the futon to watch him.

"Craft away," I said. "Let me know when you need help to hang them."

He nodded and began to work.

I watched him for a while. After about an hour of watching him cut and sew, I got up and made us food. Throwing together some wonton chicken tacos and rice. He ate absently while he worked on some cord that wrapped the pieces for movement. Whatever this pattern was made little sense to me. But I cleaned up and he finished the batch of them, then dug through a drawer in the kitchen until he pulled out some small plant hooks.

"I'm ready to hang them if you're still willing," he said.

"On it," I agreed. I took the hooks and helped him carry up the shades. Hanging them was easier than I thought. Since it wasn't a full standing loft, reaching the top area where the hooks went was easy. Micah measured and marked a spot, I screwed in the hook. The curtains went up. He showed me how they pulled open and how each small section of cord could be tucked away to keep Jet from playing with them. The guy was brilliant.

"You're amazing, you know that?"

"Hmm," he said, noncommittal. Humble and more than a little self-conscious as well, I thought.

"Do you still have those dreamcatchers I bought?" I asked him, remembering the shop I'd gotten them from and the original plan I'd had for them.

"Yes." He headed downstairs for a moment and when he returned it was with the bag of stuff as if he'd never unpacked it. I didn't comment on that, leaving him with whatever motive that was. The dreamcatchers went up beside the shades, centered on each, some on the inside of the loft, some on the outside. The largest one I'd bought, over two feet in diameter, I hung over the head of the bed.

"This should be some protection against bad dreams, right?" I prodded him.

He gave me a humoring smile. "Sure."

"You're such a skeptic for all you've seen," I said.

He shrugged, then grabbed my shirt and pulled me close for a kiss. I sighed into his lips. "This okay?" he asked.

"Yes," I promised, the thought of having him wrapped around me, instantly making me hard. "Well, hey, that still works."

"Yeah?"

"Yeah," I agreed.

"Good." He tugged at my shirt. "Get naked, I wanna sex you up."

And fuck did I need that, but now *I* was the one feeling a little self-conscious. "I'm pretty skinny."

"So?"

"And I have no idea where I've been."

"I have condoms. I'm on PrEP." He reached back to one of the drawers in the cube to retrieve a pack of condoms and a bottle of lube. He dropped them on the bed beside the pillows. "The hospital ran a bunch of tests."

Always prepared. "I doubt STDs were on the top of their list."

He gave me a little smile. "What are you afraid of?"

"Honestly?"

He nodded.

"Hurting you. Not being enough. Waking up to find this is all a dream. I'm afraid of a lot actually."

He yanked me down until my lips met his in a fierce kiss, and sweet baby Jesus was that amazing. The strength of his hands in my hair, his force on my lips, he left no doubt of his motives. I sank into his mouth, exploring every crevasse of it with my tongue, and teasing his in return. Fine. If he wasn't going to chicken out, I could do this thing, right? And oh fuck did I want to. I stripped out of my shirt, kicked off my shorts, socks, and boxers while watching him strip too. He was beautiful, though I'd been wrong. He'd lost a little weight, mostly through the hips and tummy, easily hidden by his clothing. But wow.

"Wow," I said looking at him. He was still everything that turned me on. Those amazing blue eyes, the freckles dotting his tiny nose, and the sweep of pale brown hair falling across his cheekbones. The sleek musculature of his body made me think very naughty things. Like how bendy was he? His thighs and butt were a soft flow of skin, looking almost feminine, but not quite. I longed to run my hands over that flesh, trace the curve of his ass, and kiss the base of his spine.

He gave me a sweet smile. Mask not fully gone, but little cracks in the exterior. He stepped into my personal space, grabbed me, and dragged me down onto the bed. In charge, and that was more than okay. Skin against skin, I sighed, marveling at the heat.

"Fuck me," he said.

I put my hands on his face, kissing his lips, then the tip of his nose and examining his eyes. "You're here with me?"

"Yes," he sighed. "And you're here with me." His lips found mine, and we dueled for a while. The warmth and flavor of him alive and vaguely familiar on my tongue. That at least was the same. Dehydration or something more sinister, at least Micah was Micah in my arms.

I rocked my hips against his, pressing my cock into his. He groaned. "Fuck."

"Yes," I agreed. His precome leaked against my thigh, and I ran my hands over his pale chest to find his dusky nipples and play with them, still kissing him like he was the air I needed. "Can I explore? Touch you? I want to memorize every bit of your skin," I whispered.

"Sure," he agreed, almost seeming confused. I remembered back to the videos I'd watched of him, and how it was never foreplay for him. It was him getting fucked or sucking off someone. He'd always been silent, small noises muffled by the mask he'd worn to hide his identity. I wondered a lot about that. Did that mean he didn't enjoy the foreplay, or was it not necessary for the camera?

"Do you not like being touched?" I had to know if it bothered him.

"I don't need much," he said.

"But that doesn't mean you don't like a little foreplay, yeah?"

"Yeah," he agreed.

"Good. Think of me as a texture freak too. I want to memorize the texture of your skin, the lines of your muscles and the feeling of your thighs." I kissed his lips again, dueled his tongue with my own and breathed a sigh of happiness at his body pressed against mine, but I wanted more. I rolled him beneath me and ran my hands over his chest and stomach, studying the smoothness of his skin. Soft, with a hint of definition, his body was sleek and sexy. His nipples a duskier pale brown than pink, and when I brushed my thumbs over them, they pebbled. I bent to taste one, sucking it into my mouth and swirling my tongue around it. He rewarded me with a soft sigh. That was a start at least.

"Don't hold back your cries with me, okay?" I begged. "Be real, so I can know what I'm doing right." I licked at the nipple again, biting it gently then blowing warm breath across his wet flesh.

He shivered. "You're doing fine."

"Fine..." I narrowed my eyes at him over the word and turned to the other nipple while playing with the already abused one by rolling it between my fingers. He pressed his hips into my thigh, seeking friction. The wetness of his cock sliding along my skin. But I was nowhere near done.

I found a slow dance of exploration, tasting his skin as I slid my mouth in a soft trail of kisses down his body. His belly button and hip bones were as sensitive as his nipples, making him tremble beneath me. He gave me little sighs and wrapped a hand in my hair, but didn't try to force me in any particular direction, though his cock was hard and dripping.

While I longed to wrap my mouth around his length, there was more I needed to explore first. My own cock ached with the weight of need, begging for touch, friction, and heat. Not yet, not until I knew every inch of his skin.

There were freckles on his right hip, even a few on his pale thighs. I lifted his right leg to study those marks, adding small kisses to each and lapping at the trail from hip down over his thigh and toward his round little ass.

"Fuck," I grumbled at him, kissing the bottom of his butt cheek. "You're so fucking beautiful." I wanted to taste his legs, and even trace the arches of his feet, but the view... legs open, cock hard, a hint of his hole beneath his heavy sack... it was almost too much. It was a concentrated effort to not come right then and there at the sight of him.

I kissed the bottom of each ass cheek, separating them with my hands to study the dusky clench of him. Would it be weird for him if I did what I'd longed to do every time I saw a video of his fine ass? This wasn't porn, real life was messier, sometimes clumsy, and sometimes amazing. I didn't mind all three. Would he?

"Can I?" I asked, not sure if I could voice the words. Instead I leaned in to taste his balls. Those weren't as familiar. He'd often hidden them, trapped them in girly underwear to give the illusion of things that didn't really matter to me. They were good size, the skin soft and delicate beneath my tongue as I sucked them into my mouth. This time he gave me a full moan. That... again I had to fight back coming.

His cock, in general, dissipated the illusion of femininity since he was a decent size and girth, enough to fit firmly in the palm of my hand. That part of him wasn't slim and delicate.

Sad, that he'd hidden it away, though I was more than a little pleased to be one of the few who had been given uninhibited access to it.

When I let his balls go it was to lick a trail up the underside of his cock and tease at his glans, and he writhed beneath me, hips thrusting toward my mouth. But I wasn't ready for that yet. Instead I lapped at his precome, savoring the salty edge of sweetness on my tongue. I couldn't remember anyone tasting this good, but most often I'd only given head on a guy wearing a condom. Even the flavored ones couldn't really mask the underlying chemical of the sheath.

I traced the line of his cock, down around his balls, to that dark taint beneath, and the clenching hole. At first, I hesitated a little, never having tasted this end of the passion. I traced the rim of him with my fingertips, breezing over the surface, studying the crinkled edges and delicate texture of the muscle. Then I bent forward to taste it. The edge of worry in the back of my brain, but there was just his skin and soft, salty flavor beneath my tongue.

He shuddered. "Fuck!"

I lapped at the ridge, enjoying the different feel of this skin against my tongue, then licked up to the taint again and nipped at that little flesh, knowing what was beneath.

"In me," Micah demanded. "Fuck, you are such a tease," he complained.

"Tease?" I wanted to know. "I'm exploring..."

He reached down and gripped my hair in an almost painful handful, forcing me to look at him. "Fuck me."

"I should stretch you."

Micah put a firm hand in my hair and yanked me up until we were face to face, then rolled us over so he was on top. He shoved a condom and the bottle of lube my way. "I don't need it, but I do need your cock in my ass right now."

"Demanding much?" I teased, taking out a condom, then sliding it on. I was pretty liberal with the lube but still worried. He growled impatiently at me. "Is this what they mean when they say bossy bottoms?" I asked him.

He gave me narrowed eyes then shoved me flat onto the bed and grabbed my cock. "I'll show you a bossy bottom." He lined us up, using a hand to guide the head of my cock to his hole, but kneeling above me enough that I could almost see the way his dusky hole sucked me in. This was vaguely familiar, the warm heat, a tight clench of muscles around the length of me, swallowing me. I fumbled for breath, trying to hold back an orgasm to give him what he needed.

Micah seated himself fully, his ass parted and resting on my hips, with my cock nestled deep within him. He closed his eyes, wiggling his hips a little as if to find the perfect angle. His hands rested on my chest, firm, and in control. Which was actually a huge fucking turn on. Micah, small, beautiful, and a ball busting power bottom.

"Fuck," I grumbled at him. "You're going to make me come."

He opened his eyes and gave me a sexy little smile. "Isn't that the point? Pretty sure that's the point." He wiggled again, then moved his hips up, gliding the length of me, until he reached the tip and then sliding back down. "Hard to get the right rhythm this way," he said.

"Yeah?" I reached out to grab his hips and hold them so I could thrust into him. His sigh was immediate, his dick leaking precome over his stomach and dripping down the length of him. He added a little twist to his hips each time I pressed into him deep, but I could tell, while it was good, it wasn't enough. He was searching for something, an angle or a speed, I wasn't sure, only that this position wasn't quite doing it.

I lifted him off, and turned him, muffling his protest with a kiss, before pressing him chest down onto the bed and sliding back inside him. I lifted one of his legs, pressing the thigh upward to give me a better angle, and felt myself slide a tiny bit further into him.

His moan was deep. I tested the position, moving my hips around, pressing hard into him, drawing sexy noises from him, even as I had my arms wrapped around him like a cage, while I pulled back to thrust back in. He reached back to grip my hair, turning his head until our lips met. This. Yes, this was the perfect spot.

Micah met my thrusts, let his hips move against mine, finding a delicious rhythm of speed, force, and depth while I held him tight. Our mouths fed at each other, his hand wrapped in my hair almost hard enough to hurt, but he guided us together. Fuck, it was so good, deep inside him, swallowed by his heat, intensity, and passion.

I could hear the rising heights of his pleasure, feel his body gripping me with each shove into his warmth, until we were both dancing on the edge of pleasure. A cacophony of sounds better than any porno could ever pretend to portray. The slap of our bodies together, a slight sting of pain with the delicious rising wave of bliss. The need to fill him, coat his insides with my come, while I devoured his lips had me seeing stars.

Micah's hand tightened in my hair, enough that I suddenly couldn't move, and was left only with the swing of his hips and clenching body around my encased cock. That was the end of it. A fiery kiss, with his tongue jabbing into my mouth like my cock was driving into his body. The heat, friction, and need poured from me like fire down my spine. I half screamed into his lips, filling the condom but still thrusting as his body followed mine into orgasm, his body tightening around me, as though milking me for every last bit of pleasure.

"Holy fuck..." I whispered into his lips as we both rode the wave slowly downward as we both trembled. His spend covered the sheet and his stomach, and I couldn't help but wish it had branded me instead. "Next time," I said.

"Hmm?" Micah asked.

"Thinking how I want your come all over me."

He rewarded me with a tiny smile. "Next time," he agreed.

"And who knew I had so many kinks," I said. "Bossy bottoms."

"Not many let me be in control," he admitted.

"Well I'm all on board." So on board my body gave another little twitch at the thought of him bossing me around again. "All in..." I promised.

CHAPTER 30

This time we did nap. Both of us wrapped in my new quilt, curled up into the corner. I didn't realize it wasn't a nap, but actual sleep until the sound of something jerked me awake. I glanced at the clock. Three a.m. It was the only light source in the loft now that we had the curtain up.

Micah appeared to still be asleep. His back to the wall, and chest to me, using me as a shield. And that was okay. Jet was curled up in his bed, seeming undisturbed by whatever had woken me.

I laid there listening. My brain immediately latching onto the time and the possibilities for what may have woken me. Micah hadn't heard much of the thing in his garden. Was that intentional maybe?

I closed my eyes and began to doze when I heard it again. Something I couldn't quite identify. An unnatural, animal-like sound. Not from inside. That was at least reassuring.

Carefully I reached for Micah's phone and unlocked it to check the camera feeds. Nothing. All was still. How frustrating. I put the phone aside and curled myself protectively around Micah. It was okay if he didn't hear it and I did. I hadn't spent the last few years haunted by it. He could use the break. It took several minutes and lots of singing to myself about bottles of beer before I fell back to sleep.

The morning started off normal enough. We had sex, showered together, and I made breakfast. We checked in with Lukas, to make sure he and Sky were okay, and made plans to head to the store to get me a new phone before much else happened.

We were a little slow moving though. Micah really didn't do mornings. Even after a full pot of coffee, he wanted to cuddle with me on the futon, but it was Wednesday and he had to work the shop today and host an evening ghost tour.

"What about the cemetery tour?" I asked him.

"It's daytime only now. Once per week per tour guide. I'm the only one certified right now, though there are a few others who have applied. So that tour is always full." He touched my face, running his fingers along my cheeks, which he'd been doing a lot in the past twenty-four hours. "I looked for you every time I went in there."

"Don't dwell on it," I said. "Weren't you the one who said that?"

He sighed and stretched. "I don't want to start the day."

"Maybe you should call in. Tell the boss he needs to get his ass up and open the shop," I joked, wondering if Lukas even knew how to open the shop.

Micah smiled. "More likely it would be Sky."

There was a knock on the door that made us both frown. I untangled myself from Micah and made my way to the door, a bit surprised to find Detective McKnight standing there.

"Mr. Caine," He greeted me. "Your brother told me you were back."

"And I already talked to the police in Atlanta at length," I said. "I don't know anything about what happened to Sarah or the other tour guides."

"I'm not here about that." He held up his phone and tapped the screen. It was a video. It looked like me, a scruffy, hobo-looking me, wandering around an airport. "I have questions about where you were for the past month."

"Me too," I said. "Because I have no fucking clue."

"Do you know where this video was taken?" He asked.

"I'm assuming Atlanta since that was where I was found. But I also had no ID on me, so I'm not sure how I would have gotten on a plane."

"LaGuardia," Detective McKnight corrected.

I blinked at him. "New York?" How had I gotten to New York and then Atlanta? "When is the video from?"

"A little over a week ago."

"But how..." I was so confused.

"That's also what I'd like to know," Detective McKnight said. "There's no record of you ever taking a flight. And the cameras seem to glitch a lot at LaGuardia since this is the only video there of you that we can make out."

"I'm not sure what to tell you," I said. "I don't remember the past month."

"I'd like you to come down to the station, answer some questions, and review some other footage we have of you."

That sounded ominous. "Am I under arrest for something?"

He gave me that fake cop smile. "We would appreciate your cooperation."

"But I'm not under arrest," I clarified.

"No," he agreed.

I glanced back at Micah who now stood behind me. "Can we meet you at the station?" Micah asked.

Detective McKnight frowned. "I'd prefer he come with me now."

"I'd prefer to show up with Lukas at my side," I said. "Since he knows the law better than I do." And maybe an attorney because something was giving me bad vibes.

"Fine. I expect you in one hour." The tone implied that if I didn't comply, he'd set an APB or some other cop shit on me.

"One hour," I agreed. Micah was already dialing Lukas. I shut the door wondering at that moment how I could so thoroughly forget an entire month of time, that I would need videos to tell me where I was. Had I truly forgotten? Or maybe it was that I wasn't the one at the wheel. The latter idea scared me because it was beginning to feel like a real possibility.

LETTER FROM LISSA

Dear Reader,

Thank you so much for reading *Stalked by Shadows!* This is the first mystery in the Simply Crafty Paranormal Mystery series. There will be more books coming soon.

Be sure to join my Facebook group for fun daily polls, writing snippets, and updates on new releases to this series and others. For a sneak peek at my work before it's published join my Patreon group. Patrons receive three new chapters a week and many other perks. For monthly updates on what's coming out and character shorts subscribe to my Newsletter. Also check out my website at LissaKasey.com for new information, visiting authors, and novel shorts.

If you enjoyed the book, please take a moment to leave a review! Reviews not only help readers determine if a book is for them, but also help a book show up in searches.

Thank you so much for being a reader!

Lissa

ABOUT THE AUTHOR

Lissa Kasey (Sam Kadence) is more than just romance. She specializes in in-depth characters, detailed world building, and twisting plots to keep you clinging to the page. All stories have a side of romance, emotionally messed up protagonists and feature LGBTQA spectrum characters facing real world problems no matter how fictional the story.

ALSO BY LISSA KASEY

Also, if you like Lissa Kasey's writing, check out her other works:

Hidden Gem Series:

Hidden Gem (Hidden Gem 1)

Cardinal Sins (Hidden Gem 2)

Candy Land (Hidden Gem 3)

Survivors Find Love:

Painting with Fire

An Arresting Ride

Range of Emotion

Kitsune Chronicles:

Witchblood

Inheritance Series:

Inheritance (Dominion 1)

Reclamation (Dominion 2)

Conviction (Dominion 3)

Ascendance (Dominion 4)

Absolution (Dominion 5)

Haven Investigations Series:

Model Citizen (Haven Investigations 1)

Model Bodyguard (Haven Investigations 2)

Model Investigator (Haven Investigations 3)

Model Exposure (Haven Investigations 4)

Evolution Series:

Evolution

Evolution: Genesis

Boy Next Door Series:

On the Right Track (1)

Unicorns and Rainbow Sprinkles (2)

Simply Crafty Paranormal Mystery Series:

Stalked by Shadows